I0674173

While waiting on the book to go to press, my sixteen-year-old son, Charlie, was diagnosed with osteosarcoma bone cancer. While all of my children and my wife have contributed significantly to this endeavor, I would like to dedicate this story about a battle fought amongst the stars to Charlie as he fights his battle against this horrible disease. His strength and determination in the face of this battle make him my hero.

I would also like to thank our WKA family and his teammates for their love and support—Go Knights! Finally, thank you to Charlie's doctors, and especially to his incredible nurses, who truly are heroes.

Acknowledgments

I never realized how many people contribute to the creation of a manuscript. To all of them, I am truly grateful.

Foremost, I want to thank the joy of my life, my wife Sallie, without whose help and support I would have never made enough coherent sentences to convey the story I'd wished to tell.

To Mindy Kuhn and the entire Warren Publishing team for allowing me the opportunity to make this book possible.

To Sara Kelly for her continuous words of encouragement after every edit.

To Monika Dziamka for her great suggestions and for challenging my viewpoints and perspectives.

To Amy Ashby for always encouraging me and pointing me in the right direction.

Personally, to Fair Cousins for the hours of editing and advising, my college roommate Chris Rakestraw for his direction, my kids for continuously suggesting new songs for inspiration, and of course my wife Sallie, who occasionally gave up and just rewrote parts of the book for me.

I NEED A HERO

A NOVEL

RON CLAMP

ISBN: 978-1-957723-83-9 (hard cover)
       978-1-957723-84-6 (soft cover)

Warren publishing

Published by Warren Publishing
Charlotte, NC
www.warrenpublishing.net
Printed in the United States

Prologue

Thirty Years Ago, on the Planet Wilhelmina,
in the Wilhelm Galaxy

P atty pulled her sandy brown hair back into a ponytail and slid the small elastic band tight against her head. The grit and grime smeared into the sweat on her body from earlier in the day made her itch, and she couldn't stop thinking about how lovely a hot shower would feel. She could just imagine the feeling of jets of warm water rippling from her hair and running down her body.

Patty studied her fingernails for a moment and bit into the hangnail on her right index finger. The nail caught on the inside liner of her pocket every time she reached for something. Patty wasn't sure how she had split the nail. She bit into the nail and pulled, spitting the remnant from her mouth, almost relishing the pain because it reminded her she was alive, then studied how close to her cuticle the split had traveled.

Patty removed her tablet from her backpack, updated her daily log, and notated her observations from the day. Her scientific mind could not deviate from her usual habit of study, contemplation, and fascination with her subject of choice: the legends of old. Given her present circumstances, they'd been eclipsed only by thoughts of survival.

Saying one has a scientific mind while studying and trying to make sense of centuries of mythology seemed to most to be counterintuitive. Few could fathom there being any correlation between the two. Patty passionately believed that all mythology had to have some basis in reality. This expedition had accomplished much to confirm many of her hypotheses, but with the turn of events, she would not be able to return to Earth with any proof. *If a return to Earth will even be possible*, she thought.

After stowing her tablet, Patty mused that the reddish-orange star around which Wilhelmina orbited was so different from the sun back home. Raised in the North Georgia Mountains, Patty used to love to watch the sunset from the top of Blood Mountain, north of Cleveland. With the multitude of colored sunrays peering through the clouds in crisp autumn skies, dusk had always been her favorite time of day. From the top of Blood Mountain on a clear day, Patty could just make out the distant skyline of Atlanta on the western fringe of the horizon a hundred miles away. The summer weather forecast in the southern states of the United States was always the same during the summer months: hot and muggy, followed by scattered thunderstorms, followed by hot and muggy.

Here on Wilhelmina, from the top of the planet's highest jagged peaks, the warmth of the enormous red orb, Ilios, felt pleasant. However, Patty was already bracing herself for the falling temperature, which would happen as soon as the sun went down. On Earth, temperature swings were much less dramatic.

Off in the distance, to the south, she saw high cumulonimbus clouds. She realized that once they developed, she should expect strong winds and heavy rain. Here in the mid-latitudes of the planet, the warm, moist air from the tropical regions to the south collided with the cooler air from the mountainous region to the north. It had rained torrents every evening since she had marooned herself and the crew of the *Prometheus* on this Godforsaken planet.

Half of Ilios had already disappeared below the western horizon, and the sizeable purplish-pink moon, Selene, was high in the sky, working its way westward across the firmament. The moon gave off an eerie Mountbatten-pink glow unlike any planet or moon Patty had ever seen or read about. Patty saw huge craters on the surface of the moon even without the use of binoculars or a telescope, its strong gravitational pull having been the savior of Wilhelmina from multiple catastrophic asteroid strikes over the millennia.

The mission to Wilhelmina signified the happiest time of Patty's life. It was the culmination of years of research, an opportunity to legitimize the theories and hypotheses that had swirled inside her head and imagination since she was a little girl. To crown her victory, Lt. Chuck Grimball had asked her to marry him, and she had accepted. Their life had been full of happiness, love, and hope. They planned to marry as soon as they returned to Earth. He had asked her to marry him only two weeks before the *Prometheus* departed on its career-making mission.

Not only had many of the discoveries substantiated her belief that people inside the Milky Way had descended from the Obsidians, but her initial observations also implied much more. The Obsidians and their cousins on Earth might have a common ancestry; indeed, they may have even descended from the fabled Titans. If only she could have landed near the capital city she had spotted from outside the asteroid belt, the vastness of the universe may have shrunk in the mind of all of humanity.

Patty wiped a tear on her shoulder, her cheek grazing the top of her recently acquired lieutenant's bars. She had received her promotion a few weeks before, immediately after discovering the passageway. She had felt like she had really accomplished something. She was on top of the world. Then, with the *Prometheus* on the cusp of accomplishing her mission, everything fell apart. After weeks of hard work, Patty discovered a route that led to the heart of the ancient capital. The archeological treasures she had already discovered through her scope exceeded all hopes. Morgan, the team leader back on Earth, who was also the brother of Lt. Cotterill, the *Prometheus*'s first officer, sent her a personal letter to congratulate her on her discoveries.

With a path forward found, Lt. Cotterill ordered LTJG Chuck Grimball to take the ship's barge and verify the safety of the passage. After Lt. Grimball and his unit left the ship, trouble began. First, all communications systems failed, as though the signal were being jammed. Patty resorted to flashing Morse code, employing the lights on *Prometheus*'s bow to warn Chuck that a large vessel had appeared on the situation board and he should return to the ship.

The *Prometheus*'s captain was in Engineering when the large vessel first appeared on the screen. The second he came back to the bridge and saw the size of the ship, he gave the command for the crew to go to battle stations and ordered the helmsman to follow the barge through the labyrinth of asteroids.

The bridge officers, Patty included, had been concentrating so hard on the vessel approaching on their six, they never saw the speedy torpedo boat turn into their path and discharge a hail of torpedoes. *Prometheus* suffered two hits on the starboard bow in quick succession. Most of the officers and the captain died instantly. The impact had been so severe, Patty's helmet cracked when she slammed into her control panel headfirst. The barge took a torpedo amidships and exploded, killing everybody on board.

With Lt. Cotterill mysteriously missing and presumed dead, Patty became the senior officer in charge of the *Prometheus*. She had to roll the dead helmsman out of his chair onto the floor to gun the engines. In retrospect, Patty realized she was lucky she hadn't flung the *Prometheus* headlong into a tumbling asteroid. She made it through the asteroid field and was confident she faced no immediate threat from the mammoth ship on her six. Positive the vessel could not follow, Patty concentrated on locating the torpedo boat lurking somewhere off her starboard bow.

Due to the severity of the damage to the starboard bow, she had been forced to evacuate the crew and seal off that entire quarter of the ship. The torpedo boat, sensing victory, charged from amongst the asteroids at the *Prometheus* and released its one remaining torpedo. Patty responded the only way she could. She spun the *Prometheus* into the path of the oncoming missile.

The closure rate between the torpedo and *Prometheus* was short enough that the missile never had time to arm itself. It slammed into the damaged bow of the ship without exploding, causing minimal additional damage. Patty, in a rage, pushed the throttle to maximum and ran the small boat over, breaking the back of the vehicle, which promptly disintegrated.

On the situation board, Patty discovered the vessel outside the passageway was not giving up the chase. It was using its massive guns to thrust asteroids out of the way, plowing through the narrow but densely packed asteroid field. With the massive vessel still pursuing them, Patty had no alternative. She turned the *Prometheus* and fled.

Patty feigned circling the fringe of the planet to convince the ship she planned to exit through the field on the other side. As soon as she was behind the planet, she launched and detonated every weapon she had into the field. The exploded munitions created a facsimile of the remnants of a destroyed spacecraft. Patty released anything and everything in the ship not fastened down into the floating refuse to enhance the impression. She then turned the *Prometheus* and landed deep inside the wilderness on the dark side of the planet Wilhelmina.

Once the *Prometheus* landed, Lt. Cotterill appeared on deck as if the remaining crew members had not just cheated death. Stepping over the bodies of their dead shipmates, he assumed command. Rumor amongst the crew was he had inexplicably strapped himself into an escape pod moments before the ambush by the torpedo boat. Cotterill ordered the crew to disembark and scatter, retreating into the mountainous jungle to hide. Over the next few days, Patty had made her way to the highest peak she could find. With her soul empty and her whole world in shambles, she watched and waited, scanning the sky for any sign of the behemoth ship presumably still out there searching for them.

Patty still couldn't believe Chuck was gone. The bond they shared made Patty feel as though a piece of her heart had escaped from her chest, leaving her empty and alone, only a shell of the woman she had been.

With tears flowing down her cheeks, she lowered her hand to rub her stomach. Chuck hadn't even known he would be a father.

Chapter One

Thirty-Six Years Later
Present Day, Near the Martian Moon Deimos,
Earth's Solar System

Admiral Mitchell fumbled with the controls on the old-fashioned ham radio. Frustrated, he yelled at his executive officer, "Git yer butt in 'ere 'n mak' this thing transmit!"

He tossed the microphone in disgust. The spring from the spiral extension cord, which connected the handset to the radio, stretched, and the mic bounced back at the admiral, then fell to the floor, swinging just above the floor of the bridge.

Commander Cousins shook her head. She knew all too well that when the admiral's colorful and passionate nature was excited to either a feverish pitch or by utter frustration, his accent became undecipherable to anyone whose descendants lacked a fanatical enthusiasm for the Jacobite cause during the Forty-five Rebellion. Still, she had the greatest respect for the man. She had no doubt that had *he* been in charge at the Battle of Culloden in Scotland on 16 April, 1746, her home country's monarchy would have descended from the Stuart clan. Instead, the sixteenth of April commemorated a Scottish massacre.

Once Admiral Mitchell reached that point with his mood, there would be little she could do to calm his high-spirited nature.

"The radio's settings are correct, sir. You are transmitting at 275 gigahertz per Admiral Halsey's orders. Why can't we just use the ship-to-ship radio, sir?"

"We hae bin thro' this," the admiral exhaled, recognizing that the commander was having difficulty understanding his Scottish accent. "We do not waant Central Command tae know what we ur up tae. Now juist do lik' I ask 'n mak' this dang thing work."

He grumbled, struggling to keep his irritation in check.

Cousins shook her head again and muttered under her breath, *Och aye the noo*. Oh, yes! Just now!"

Not choosing to spend the night tied to any figurative ship's capstan, she kept her thoughts to herself, but she said aloud, "You have to hold the red button when you speak, sir, and release the button to hear."

"Forget it. You just tell Halsey th' marauders ur where we suspected 'n that he hud better git stairted if he is gonna go thro' wi' this. We wull not be able tae distract Space Command for long."

The commander was not happy. She was positive once Space Command figured out what they were up to, it would be she whom High Command would execute. While only a commander, her post as the ship's executive officer meant she was in charge of running all the ship's day-to-day operations, subservient only to the captain of the ship. Not wanting to place the careers of the ships' captains in jeopardy, admirals Halsey and Mitchell had relieved them and were serving both as captains and admirals of the respective fleets. Reluctantly, she grabbed the mic and relayed Admiral Mitchell's message.

"This is Commander Cousins of the *Tyche*. Admiral Mitchell asked me to convey to you that the marauders are where the two of you suspected, and you had better attack now if you are going to. He warns we cannot distract Space Command for long."

Admiral Halsey's voice crackled over the speaker. "Ten-four, Commander. Tell the old geezer to take care of my boys if we don't return. Halsey out."

Cousins expected a coarse retort from Admiral Mitchell to Admiral Halsey in exchange for calling him an old geezer. To her surprise, he showed no emotion. He reached for the mic, pressed it, and in an uncharacteristically calm voice, said, "Best o' luck, ye old mukker. Mitchell out."

His usual agitated expression returned, and he gave new orders to Cousins.

"Commander, prepare to tak' th' *Tyche* to full throttle 'n flood th' airwaves wi' reports tae Space Command that th' Fifth 'n Seventh Fleets ur under attack. Jam every frequency so they believe we caused thaim tae lose command and control of th' *Fortuna* and th' Fifth."

The commander rushed from the captain's quarters, setting the admiral's charade in motion. She pressed the mic on the side of her helmet, and with a firm, authoritative voice she repeated the admiral's order to the crew: "Take the *Tyche* to full throttle and prepare to flood the airwaves with reports to Space Command that the Fifth and Seventh are under attack, on my command."

Cousins paused. "Now!"

The *Tyche* leaped forward. The ship's communication officers began broadcasting news of their ambush to Space Command. They flooded every frequency to try to deny SC enough bandwidth with which to communicate or reconnect to the Centralized Bilateral Control units belonging to the ships of the Seventh or Fifth Fleets. The Centralized Bilateral Control allowed Space Command to manage every aspect of command and control of any ship, including weapons and navigation. Halsey and Mitchell did not want SC to interfere, or worse, to thwart the mission.

●●●

On the *Fortuna*, the cloud of anxiousness that had been troubling Halsey lifted, replaced with worry for his sailors should his plan fail. The constant gloom of defeat, after three years of futile fighting, had infected the mental fiber of the whole fleet. Halsey was unwilling to live with it any further.

"It is now or never," he whispered to himself.

His resolute words were spoken with authority as he issued his command. "Order the Fifth Fleet to turn off their CBC units. Begin the attack, now!"

From the Martian moon Deimos sprang a half dozen SC destroyers from the Fifth Fleet. Four destroyers emerged from the shadows of the crater Swift, while the other two exploded into open space from deep inside the crater Voltaire. The destroyers' afterburners were glowing red-hot as they pushed the ships across the space between the amoeba-shaped moon and the Obsidian flotilla. For the first time since the start of the war, the Obsidian ships seemed unaware of the incoming threat.

As the destroyers sailed between the Obsidian two-man watchdog craft, their rotary cannons vaporized the boats. Four of the SC destroyers diverted and screamed toward their primary targets, the umbrella of destroyers protecting the battle space surrounding the two Obsidian battle cruisers and one mammoth Obsidian spacecraft carrier, the *Atramentous Sow*. Inverting and then diving, the other two destroyers started their torpedo runs on the Obsidian battle cruisers.

With the sun behind her, the battleship *Fortuna* was screaming toward Halsey's objective: the carrier vessel. The Obsidian destroyers' sensitive sound-detection equipment picked up the sound waves from the SC battleship and turned to intercept her, exposing their vulnerable sterns to the Fifth's destroyers, when the inconceivable happened. All the fleet's CBC units came back online. Despite the crew's best attempts to override the CBC, the *Fortuna* went vertical and turned away from the flotilla of Obsidian vessels, but the four SC destroyers continued their path of travel. Just before they could release their deadly weapons at the Obsidian destroyer screen, all of their weapons went offline. At maximum velocity, they sailed past the Obsidian destroyers and continued in the wake of the now retreating *Fortuna*.

The two SC destroyers making their torpedo run on the Obsidian battle cruisers were not so lucky. Inexplicably, their torpedoes armed themselves while still inside the launch tubes. From the rear-facing monitor on the *Fortuna*, Admiral Halsey watched as his ships exploded and then disintegrated.

The look of fury on the admiral's face said it all. "We had them!" he roared. "We took the Obsidians completely by surprise!"

He took a long, deep breath and thought, *If only I could get my hands on who is responsible for thwarting our attack.* He sat down hard into his seat, trying to reconcile the deaths of his destroyer crews. The thought of the letters he would have to write to each of the families was painful. These were sailors he knew and had fought alongside for years. The men and women of his fleet had entrusted their lives to his care, and now they were dead.

Mentally he began preparing himself for the probable court-martial he knew was coming. *If not a court-martial,* Halsey reflected, *then at least a strong rebuke from the admiral of the fleet, Admiral Cotterill, and possibly dismissal from the service.* At present, he could not decide which scenario he found the most distasteful.

With his right hand, he pressed his commlink for his executive officer. "XO, get Lt. Paschal from Engineering up here, on the double. I have new orders for him."

Two Weeks Later, Present Day, Tucson, Arizona, Davis-Monthan Air/Space Force Base, Earth

The hot Arizona sun caused sweat to glisten on the brows of Commander Charlie Jackson and Lt. Paschal as the commander ducked under the fuselage of the Altima engine for the hundredth time. The engine had been hard to find, hidden between the other ships scattered about the graveyard of craft. Since Paschal's arrival a week earlier, the pace set by the commander of the *Perseus* had been nonstop. Paschal had not even had a chance to unload his duffel bag into his small berth, let alone learn his way around the ship. But, given her small size compared to the *Fortuna*, he was sure figuring out the ship wouldn't take too long.

Third in command of the *Perseus*, Lt. Jacob Jackson sat on top of the motor twenty feet overhead, watching Charlie talk to the new lieutenant. He wished his brother would quit gabbing and install the cam so he could finish connecting the wiring harness. Despite the overwhelming brightness of the sunshine reflecting off the sand surrounding them and the metallic fuselages of the ship, Jacob couldn't shake the feeling of a dark shadow looming over him. The shadow had been his companion for years, ever since his girlfriend, Hope, had died in a car accident. He had long since accepted that the feeling of gloom was a permanent aspect of his life.

Jacob watched as Charlie stopped to inspect a tear in his uniform. Charlie had snagged the shoulder of his flight suit earlier, tearing the wildcat patch sewn on his left sleeve just below his commander's insignia designating him as skipper of the *Perseus*. Tired of nursing the jacket, he pulled it off and tossed it on top of the box of rigging Paschal had just delivered.

Charlie slid the cam closer to him and looked up into the hole where it needed to be mounted. Without removing his gaze, Charlie asked, "So, Paschal, how much of your story did you tell Space Command after they transferred you from the *Fortuna*?"

Sweating from the heat, Paschal turned his Power Air Purifying Respirators control to maximum to increase the amount of cool air being pumped into his helmet before answering. The Space Command issued Power Air Purifying Respirators to provide head protection, oxygen supply, communications, and climate control. The PAPR was required to be on a sailor's person at all times. The unit's power supply was built into the sailor's uniform and would automatically connect when placed on the head.

"I doubt Space Command even realizes I was on the *Fortuna* at the time of the incident. Admiral Halsey had me transferred to a tramp freighter headed to Space Station Victory before we were

I NEED A HERO 13

even back within sight of Earth. When I arrived, the Fifth was still at anchor around the base, and SC had already sent Admiral Mitchell and the Seventh back out on patrol."

"Trust me, Space Command knows you were on the *Fortuna*. There is little that they don't keep track of. Thanks to the CBC, Beijing can tell you how many cans of tuna were on board at the time of the attack."

Paschal squirmed. "Yes, maybe so. But the records on the *Fortuna* might not be all that Space Command wants."

From the corner of his eye, Charlie saw the hesitant look in the lieutenant's eyes through the face shield, which he had lowered to keep cool air trapped inside the headgear. Charlie wondered what the LT was trying to hide.

Charlie bent down and turned the part, aligning it with the hole so all he had to do was lift, insert it, and twist it into place. Paschal slid under the equipment to help. Charlie had to give him credit. He wasn't afraid of work. Rather than yell up to where Jacob sat, Charlie clicked the mic on the side of his earpiece.

"Be ready to bump the motor to help lock the cam in place. You set?"

Jacob didn't reply. He simply toggled his mic two short clicks to let his brother know he was ready. Paschal popped his visor up, put his hands under the cam, and looked the commander in the eye.

Charlie smiled and said, "Jacob and I count a little different from most. We will lift on three."

Paschal nodded that he understood. Charlie dropped his chin and grunted, "Three!"

Keying on Charlie's body language and not his words, Paschal timed his heave perfectly with Charlie's. The round shaft of the cam hit the hole exactly and hammered home just as the motor twirled. The new part was sucked upward the rest of the way into the hole, and both Charlie and Paschal smiled a look of relief as they heard the threads lock into place.

Still grinning, Paschal laughed. "If I am ever on the bridge and you give the order to fire, at least I will understand the count."

Breathing heavily, Charlie placed his hand on Paschal's shoulder. "Don't worry. If we are ever in a position to fire on the enemy, I won't be counting to three."

From above them, Jacob dropped to the ground. Kneeling to look under the machine, he grinned.

"That went better than expected," he said, nodding at his brother. Then he asked Paschal, "Did he tell you to heave on the count of three?"

"Yes, but my dad used to do the same to me, so I wasn't surprised." Listening to the motor, Paschal added, "The generator sounds good. I would have never believed the crew could rebuild it so quickly."

Charlie dusted himself off after regaining his feet. "The crew of the *Perseus* might not get to see much action, but making something from nothing is our forte."

Paschal looked around at the massive graveyard of planes. "This place couldn't have had an additional plane or spacecraft added to the inventory in over forty years. Still, the enormous amount of hardware here is unfathomable."

"Yeah," Jacob replied, dragging a set of cables from the rigging box. "We have spent a lot of time here. Not to mention a half dozen other places just like it. You could build a whole armada using just the junk left to rot."

Jacob glanced up at the sky and then down at all the parts scattered about. "I hope the wind doesn't pick up until the drones are finished loading the equipment. That will make it hard to work around all these obstacles."

The three men looked up just in time to see a drone from the *Perseus* pass by overhead. Studying the wisp of a cloud above the drone, Paschal said, "If there is nothing else I can do here, then I had better get to the loading bay and prepare to accept our cargo. I am not looking forward to loading the drones back up in that tight overhead bay. It would seem the *Perseus* was only designed to work in space, not on the hard deck."

Charlie glanced over at his ship. The pronounced nose of the craft was facing the opposite direction, but he could just make out the four teenagers standing on her bow, waiting their turn to carry their load with one of the ship's four drones. He could see inside the hold all the way to the deepest recess of the cargo bay. The ship seemed much bigger on the ground than she did when she was in space. Not that she spent much time there. The *Perseus* rarely found an excuse to achieve much more than a low orbit, and Space Station Victory was a place they rarely visited. He turned back to Paschal.

"The *Perseus* was originally a type of hybrid corvette or a brigantine. She was built to fight, but Space Command chose to modify her to serve as a repair ship."

Studying how awkward the equipment was going to be to rig, Charlie added, "Take your time, lieutenant. It will take us a little while to rig all four pieces of hardware. Not to mention all the crates."

Despite being given permission to catch his breath, Paschal turned and started jogging back to the ship. Yelling over his shoulder, he observed, "I bet she could scoot if she still had those outboard engines."

Charlie started to respond, but it was too late. Paschal was out of earshot. He turned and grabbed the rail running around the perimeter and across the top of the equipment and heaved. When he reached the top of the engine block, he lay flat and pulled the large frame of his shoulders under the jamming emitter.

Jacob watched with interest to see how Charlie was going to extend his arm through the hole. "You are never going to reach the strap. You won't be able to see."

Charlie grunted and shoved himself farther into the hole. Right now, he worried more about how he was going to get back out if he got wedged into place, instead of worrying about catching the strap, which was supposed to keep the rigging from slipping out from under the ends of the equipment. He studied the large bolts holding the jammer in place. There wasn't a wrench anywhere on the *Perseus* large enough to remove the bolts if the engine head had to be removed so he could get back out.

"Just make sure I don't have to stretch when you toss it up. It is a little tight up here."

Jacob snorted. "I don't think the problem has anything to do with how tight the access point is. The problem is that you need to lay off Sonefeld's cooking. Seconds are one thing, but fourth and fifth helpings smack of gluttony."

Charlie was quick to offer a retort. "Now if that isn't the pot calling the kettle black. I could cut the budget for the pantry in half if I didn't have to feed you."

"Well, at least I put in my full three-mile run every day. Maddie is not going to be pleased when she sees you have an extra two inches around the middle."

Charlie glanced down at his waistline. "Let's just get this rigged so we can get out of here."

•••

Andrew Rushing, a volunteer working for the Eighty-first Readiness and Reclamation Division (an army unit based out of Camp Victory on loan to Space Command), was ready to get out of the heat. He had been watching his brother and cousins lifting equipment from the salvage yard and setting the machinery onto the rear deck of the *Perseus*. There, sweaty crew members lugged the heavy loads into the ship's bay. The drones the others were flying were much more maneuverable than his, making Andrew angry they wouldn't attempt to deposit the equipment directly into the tight quarters of the ship. He glanced down from his vantage point high on top of the *Perseus* and felt the sunburn on his usually ruddy arms burning. He had applied plenty of sunblock, but now he wished he had taken the commander's advice and put on a flight suit. He saw the commander and LT scrutinizing the rigging below, so Andrew knew it wouldn't be long now.

The first to land his craft, his brother, Roland, had already headed in to get water under the pretense he was coming right back. Andrew knew as soon as he heard him say it that Roland was done for the day. He and Roland, along with their three Oglesby cousins, had been working on the *Perseus* with her crew for the last seven months. Jake and Richard were above average at flying the drones. Olivia, the youngest Oglesby, always seemed to master anything she tried, but when flying she was too cautious, in Andrew's opinion. Besides, she preferred working down in the lab or with the engineering teams. As he watched the preparations below, Andrew realized he was sad this would be their last job with the team. The whole crew was great. Besides, finding another job with a cook as good as Dan Sonefeld would never happen. The brothers and their three cousins had all put on weight since being hired by Commander Jackson.

The commander slid his helmet back on his head and keyed his microphone. "We are ready for you, Andrew. Take it slow. There isn't much room to maneuver."

Andrew didn't bother to reply. He clicked his mic twice to acknowledge the commander and applied power to his drone. Taking his time, Andrew circled his craft in a long, smooth arc around the outside perimeter of the salvage yard. He had been hovering his craft out of his line of sight at about fifteen hundred feet, using the drone's online cameras and the miniature map monitor on his controller to keep track of his position. With his thumb, Andrew lowered the four cables the commander and LT would need to secure the load to his drone. As the machine came into sight, Andrew saw the clevis hooks trailing through the air behind the fuselage. As it got closer, he made out the distinct whine of the four turbofans that kept the drone airborne, even over the sound of the *Perseus*.

Andrew gently lifted the nose of his machine, and the cables swung forward under the centerline of his craft. Roland and his cousins always positioned their drones above their loads and then lowered the cables, concentrating on the position and attitude of their unit instead of the location of the ball holding the rigging. Not properly visualizing the task caused problems and resulted in wasted time, in Andrew's opinion. Andrew watched as the wires swung forward and began to counter the other way. He tilted the nose, first forward and then back with each swing of the steel cables to make them stop swinging. He backed off the throttle, lowering the drone, and moved the first hook close enough to the LT for him to grab it and fasten it to the spreader bar attached to the apparatus the commander needed to retrieve.

After the commander and LT secured all four of the clevis hooks to the load, Andrew took the slack out of the cables. The commander and LT scrambled, checking every connection, making sure the rigging was secure.

Next, Andrew rotated the camera on his drone to survey the entry to the shipping bay on the *Perseus* to determine if the crew was ready for him. None of the others would attempt to park their drones in the hangars above the payload area. He saw Thompson and Curry, both from Engineering, sweating hard, having secured Jake's drone into place. Lt. Paschal fought with the anchor straps Havard and Woodward couldn't get to lock so the drone wouldn't move. Thanks to the exceptional vision Andrew had inherited from his father, Andrew made out a small tear in the lieutenant's flight suit. His elbow was stained with blood from a cut Paschal must have gotten fighting to secure the weight of the drone. Each of the four machines weighed as much as a full-size pickup truck.

Andrew had turned sixteen the day before. He could still almost taste the cake Sonefeld would have baked for him if the laid-back chef had only known. The five cousins had a pact never to have birthdays. Once they turned twenty-one, international law required them to report for their one year of compulsory military service. Prior to the war, most reported at age eighteen.

The oldest of the cousins at nineteen, Roland's license showed he was seventeen, but soon he would have their cousin Jake issue him a DD214, which would show he served for three years in the army. That would be the end of him ever having to worry about being drafted into military service. Their cousin Jake would ensure none of them would ever have to serve because Jake could hack into anything. He routinely infiltrated the international registry to update their ages. For a small fee, he had even penetrated the Department of Veterans Affairs database and created complete service records for other individuals wishing to embellish or fabricate their faux military service records.

Andrew remembered playing with Jake when they were little, but both Richard and Olivia lived with their mother in upstate New York when they were young. It was not until after Richard's and Olivia's mother reunited with Jake's father that Andrew was ever around them. Andrew had taken to Olivia right away. She always doted on him, treating him like it was her responsibility to take care of him, even though she was only two years older.

Richard was kind-hearted and protective; the teens had nothing to fear when he was around. Fast and nimble, built like a linebacker, and with a gaze that could give you a chill, Richard could make even the largest man shy away from him. He especially considered it his duty to intimidate anyone who showed an interest in Olivia.

The five were a tight-knit group—a family.

Wistfully, Andrew thought back to when his and Roland's only concerns were avoiding the children who made snide remarks to them about their deceased mother and making sure they got good grades in school. Man, that seemed like a long time ago ... a different lifetime. Andrew was only ten when he and Roland had moved with their father to the space base in Alabama after their father transferred to serve on the UCSC *Constrictor*. He had assured them that moving to Alabama would give them all a chance to start over and put the family's past behind them. His father was proud he would be at the helm of the most powerful ship ever built—a behemoth that could level an entire city in one pass but maneuver almost better than an air force fighter.

He bought both Andrew and Roland scale models of the gigantic ship and spent every evening helping them assemble the kits. Roland loved toying with the engines and moving parts of the model, particularly the armament. Roland had a comprehensive understanding of every weapon on the vessel and capabilities of each. He could open the model and explain how every weapon system on board functioned.

The death of their mother had affected Roland much more than Andrew. Roland was old enough that he could remember every detail of her passing, but he never talked about it. Every now and then Andrew would see Roland's eyes glaze over, and he knew that Roland was remembering what it was like when their mother was still with them.

Andrew was less interested in how the weaponry worked. His passion was piloting the ship itself. His father had lain in bed with him every night, making the model roll and turn, explaining how, from the helm of the bridge, he made the ship perform ballerina-type moves. Andrew could feel the bed roll with each maneuver and imagine the g-force pushing him back into his pillow as his father painted an image down to the finest detail. He explained the importance of breathing to maintain focus. Inhale deep, exhale slow. Remain aware of the whole battlefield while focusing on the target.

When Andrew couldn't visualize how his father made the ship perform a move, he would stop him and question him. With a faraway look in his eye, his father would explain, then theorize maneuvers he dreamed of but had not yet mastered.

Andrew dreamed of what it would be like to fly such a magnificent vessel. When their father was away on duty, he and Roland were always playing video games, pitting their skills against each other. Despite being younger, Andrew routinely won.

Jarred from his daydream as the six-foot-tall speakers on the side of the *Perseus* started thumping, Andrew rolled his eyes. That meant Commander Jackson was in the mood for some oldies. When people say they like the oldies, they usually meant some solid gold Tommy Thomas Band or something along those lines. But no Thomas for the commander. His idea of oldies was ancient. Andrew liked to tease that the commander's songs were fashionable back when Lincoln sailed the seven seas. When Jefferson wrote the *Iliad*. *Old* stuff. Andrew loved to joke with the commander about his music, but actually he found that the more he listened to it, the more the music grew on him.

The commander clasped his hands, signaling Andrew to tension the cables anchored to the load and hold tight. Then the song "Something Just Like This" by The Chainsmokers and Coldplay rattled the ship. The words from the retired classic—recollections of mythological gods and superheroes—danced amongst the fuselages of retired craft.

•••

The lyrics held special meaning to Commander Jackson and his brother, given their mother's love of the legends of old. For Charlie, the symbolism embraced his personal desire to have his wife's respect, provide for her, and for her to know he would always protect her. In essence, Charlie hoped Maddie would always trust him implicitly and know that if needed, he would be there to be her hero.

Due to Maddie's independent nature and self-sufficiency, this was a marital challenge. On their way to get married Maddie had made it clear to Charlie. *I do not need a man. It would be nice to have one, but I can take care of myself.*

•••

Andrew had both hands on the controller, trying to steady the drone, while the commander and LT inspected their rigging one final time. *I wish the commander would hurry up!* Andrew's nose was itching, and he needed to wipe sweat out of his eyes.

Despite the itching nose and sweat, Andrew found he had been patting his foot to the beat coming out of the immense woofers built into the side of the *Perseus* directly below him. Engrossed in the music, he missed the signal from the commander to raise the load. *Uh-oh, he looks agitated,* Andrew thought to himself and added power to his controller. The weight rose, but it snagged under the edge of another plane. The commander, frustrated, signaled for Andrew to put the load back down to start over, but Andrew ignored him. This was when Andrew wished he didn't always get stuck with the most gutless of the four drones. It would also be nice if the commander didn't always assign him the most difficult lifts. He backed off a second and rotated the load, then eased the joystick forward and gunned the throttle. Effortlessly, the package eased up through the opening. The commander signaled Andrew to load it up, choosing to ignore how Andrew had disregarded his earlier signal.

Andrew banked the drone, making a large winding loop around the *Perseus* while coiling the four large cables back onto the winches under the drone. With the load secured directly underneath and tight against the fuselage of the drone, Andrew flew the piece of salvaged equipment directly into the cargo bay. With barely any room above or on either side of the hovering craft, he gently set the load down. Without even backing out of the cargo area, Andrew released the clevis hooks, rotated the machine, and eased his drone straight up into its dock. The crew usually loaded the machines by easing into the docking bay from the front. Loading from below, the machine only had two millimeters of space on either side.

Still crouched on top of Jake's drone, Lt. Paschal shook his head in disbelief at the young kid's skill.

With a grin on his face, Commander Jackson's steward, CPO Lapillus, held out his hand, waiting on Thompson and Curry to pay up. Neither believed the kid would attempt flying the drone into the crowded bay, let alone do it successfully. Neither seemed to mind losing their bet, though, considering how much work the kid saved them.

Curry swore. "Unreal. If given ayy shot, ay bet da youngun could park da *Perseus* in ayy space dok without 'ur scratch."

"He was lucky, if you ask me," mumbled Thompson.

Andrew's assignment complete, he loaded his controller back into the case to deliver it to Lt. Paschal down in the loading bay. The case closed. Andrew looked around the top of the ship to make sure he hadn't forgotten anything. Satisfied, he reached and grabbed the two handles on the case and heaved. When he did, the lid slung open and the drone controller tumbled out, beginning to slide toward the edge of the *Perseus*. Andrew pictured the huge drop down to the ground and started to dive after it when someone grabbed him from behind.

Ensign Megan Marie, or M&M as everyone called her, tried as best as she could to prevent Andrew from sliding over the edge and dropping ninety-five feet to the ground. But Andrew, being tall and lanky, pulled her with him. They skidded across the deck, the soles of M&M's boots grinding against the metal. Close to the roof's edge, Andrew saw old man Ballentine pluck the controller from the air just as it started to sail airborne over the side.

Andrew's forward momentum was too much. M&M was yanked off her feet, and the two of them slid down the slope of the ship, neither one able to get any purchase against the sleek sides. She was lying facedown, refusing to release the shoulder straps to Andrew's harness while he kicked his feet wildly as he skidded on his back. Andrew heard M&M swear at him, "*Boka choda,*" in her native Bengali.

Andrew desperately searched for any seam he might dig his fingernails into. He knew he was about to dive feet first to his death. As his boots cleared the edge of the steep drop-off, he came to a sudden, screeching halt. The nylon strap to his safety harness between his legs stretched as it dug into his groin area, and he heard M&M grunt. His weight almost yanked his shoulder straps from her hands. Andrew looked up over his shoulders into M&M's face and marveled. He could not imagine how, at only five foot two, she had managed to hold on to him.

No longer sliding, he glanced behind M&M to see Petty Officer Carney and SPC Kyra Blaney sprawled facedown on the roof of the ship. Each had one of M&M's legs, and they were straining to keep her from sliding farther, saving them both from tumbling over the side.

At the loading bay door, Curry gasped, and Thompson shook his head. All the color drained from Lapillus's face. Thompson slapped Lapillus on the back.

"That was close," Thompson said. "I won't wager against him operating anything with a set of controls again. Nevertheless, the boy is gangly and a danger to himself doing anything normal. You know, like walking. He's only a teenager. He hasn't grown into his boots yet."

It took a moment for Andrew's heartbeat to return to normal and for him to remember to breathe again. Carney and Blaney fought to pull him and Ensign Megan Marie back onto the roof of the ship. Once everyone was on their feet again, Andrew noticed M&M had two burn marks on her elbows, scrapes on the chin guard to her helmet, and a tear on the front of her flight suit, revealing the armored ceramic plate inside. As she removed her helmet, Andrew noticed her flushed face despite her olive skin, and her usually neat short black hair was in disarray and matted with sweat from her exertion.

He smiled sheepishly and muttered, "Thanks."

From the look on Ensign Marie's face, Andrew knew the next duty roster she issued would have him scrubbing toilets down in Engineering. M&M ran daily ship operations and did not accept foolishness lightly. Embarrassed, he disappeared below deck as soon as he was certain he hadn't hurt anyone else.

As soon as he stepped into the mess hall, Roland admonished him. "You trying to get yourself killed, dipstick?"

Olivia rushed over to Andrew. "Leave him alone, moron. It could happen to any of us."

Roland noticed that Olivia's face was pale. Obviously, Andrew's cheating death had affected Olivia more than she wanted to admit. Roland, his nose wrinkled and a scowl on his face, said, "True. But Andrew seems exceptionally gifted at almost dying."

He turned from Olivia and slapped Andrew on the back. "You okay, goofball?"

"Sure. I'm fine. But Ensign Marie scratched her arms up. I heard her fussing at the commander over the commlink for allowing me up there unattended."

Olivia's heart had been beating wildly inside her chest ever since she had known of the accident. She had been fond of M&M ever since they had first met, but now the ensign's abilities and status had taken on mythological proportions in Olivia's mind.

Olivia swooned. "M&M is the best. You should be glad she likes you. She wouldn't have risked her life otherwise."

Ensign Marie was sweet, but there wasn't anyone on the ship brave enough to cross her when she was angry.

What Olivia hadn't shared with her family was that somehow she had witnessed the entire experience through M&M's eyes, as though she had been right there with her. Olivia was not willing to admit what she had just experienced because she did not want them to think she was crazy. Especially in light of the stories they had all heard about her aunt, Andrew and Roland's mother. They had all read the news articles describing her death, and none of them wanted to admit the fact that those same genes flowed through all of their own bodies.

With "Something Just Like This" still echoing inside his mind, Andrew thought to himself how ludicrous it was to sing about wanting to be a hero. Heroes fought, bled, and died—like his father. Andrew had no interest in being a dead hero. Then again, he had to confess, right now in his eyes, M&M was his hero. He was just glad she wasn't dead.

Six Years Earlier, Montgomery, Alabama, Earth

Long before the people from the base came to tell them the Obsidians destroyed the *Constrictor* and their father had made the ultimate sacrifice, Roland had already shown Andrew, who was ten, the news reports. Roland, three years Andrew's senior, warned him that soon Social Services would separate them and place them in foster homes. Social Services would force them to live with some stranger who just wanted to earn a check for keeping them. Together, they agreed they would allow no one to separate them.

Two hours later, from the window of their father's car where they were hiding, they saw the white military sedan with two sailors in their best dress-white uniforms. The soldiers passed them en route to their home, coming to tell them they were now orphans. In the van behind the sailors was the counselor from the base's human services department.

Roland whispered, "That's the one who will send us away."

As soon as the cars passed, the two of them headed west toward Texas until the car no longer had a charge. After that, they walked and caught rides when possible. They ate when they found food and struggled on until they caught up with their cousins, Olivia, Richard, and Jake Oglesby in Tyler, Texas. Once the cousins were reunited, the five became inseparable. They all shared three common goals: to never go hungry, to stay together, and to make sure none of them had to fight in the same military that stole Andrew and Roland's father.

Present Day, Tucson, Arizona, Davis-Monthan
Air/Space Force Base, Earth

The only member of the crew of the Perseus who seemed uncomfortable with the ship's leadership was the ship's XO, Lieutenant Dillon Myers. Serving a commander who did not religiously follow orders was not a good fit for an officer who desired the opportunity for advancement. Moreover, serving aboard a reclamation/repair ship offered little promise of a chance to prove oneself by engaging with the enemy. He believed combat was his only chance to earn his step in rank to Commander. Myers was positive at least one if not both brothers were only one step from being thrown into the brig and court-martialed. He lost sleep at night, worrying they might flush his career down the drain by association.

To date, the brothers' salvation from such misfortune was because of their close relationship with Admiral Halsey, the second-highest-ranking American in Space Command. Never had he requested any piece of equipment or sent them on any mission where the Jackson brothers had not delivered, usually in a timely manner. That is how the crew of the *Perseus* found themselves in the hot stifling desert heat outside Tucson, working eighteen-hour days. Recently assigned to the *Perseus*, LTJG Paschal reported for duty to fill a vacancy in the Engineering department. In his possession, he had sealed orders direct from Admiral Halsey to Commander Jackson requiring the *Perseus* to secure the equipment presently residing in the hold.

Admiral Halsey, in no way kin to the famous American naval admiral of World War II, could have played the part of the war hero in a movie. The only thing missing was the tobacco smoke wafting about his person. The other difference, which no one mentioned in his presence, was his total lack of success against the enemy in recent memory. Of course, today's world was quite different from Earth in the 1940s.

The admiral may have lacked success on the battlefield, but he had discovered things more important to him. He felt he had fulfilled his purpose in life through those things even if he had fallen short of his career goals. The pride he had for Charlie Jackson and Jacob Jackson was immeasurable. Both boys exceeded his every expectation. His confidence in Charlie knew no bounds, and his concern for Jacob kept him up more nights than any misgivings he had about the invading Obsidian armada. He worried about what happened on the night of Jacob's girlfriend's death, his gut telling him Jacob bore no responsibility in Hope's tragic passing. It broke his heart Jacob could not bring himself to talk about it. More than once, Halsey considered suggesting Jacob go speak to a counselor, someone who might help him vocalize the feelings that had such a profound effect on him. However, in the current environment, that would have spelled doom for any chance Jacob had with Space Command.

Halsey had been in love with the boys' mother, even though to her, he was some lowly second lieutenant when they served together on the *Prometheus* during the ship's final voyage to the Wilhelm

Galaxy. His biggest regret in life had been not sharing his feelings with her prior to her going missing. He hoped she was looking down from heaven and understood why he had taken the boys under his wing.

Halsey had once met Charlie's father and knew Jacob's father by reputation prior to his disappearance. After they lost their mother, the boys were all alone.

In the beginning, his unspoken love for Patty motivated him to take the boys in. In hindsight, her gift of the boys had resulted in his most significant life achievement. She left him two young men whom he loved as though they were his own sons.

Present Day, RMS Centaur, *Somewhere in*
Space Over Earth's Western Hemisphere

On any warship, space for a private conversation was hard to find, but on the RMS Centaur, it was even worse. For every sailor, there seemed to be three Royal Marines. Admiral Halsey and Commander Windsor stepped aside for the fifth time as they were passed by a unit of bootnecks. Each marine jumped to touch the Royal Navy slogan *"Si vis pacem, para bellum,"* Latin for "If you wish for peace, prepare for war," emblazed over the door leading to the mess hall. The marines were using the hallways to get in their daily five-mile runs.

Halsey wondered if the captain of the *Centaur* carried so many marines to better fight the enemy or to keep the British Guardsmen sailing the ship from rebelling. Nowhere on the planet was the sentiment for withdrawal from the international collective stronger than in Britain.

With Captain Ryan away on personal leave, Commander Windsor had been left temporarily in charge. Otherwise, this meeting would have been much more difficult to arrange given Ryan's rabid support of the leadership in Beijing.

Finding an empty turret, Windsor ushered Halsey inside and closed the hatch. To make more room, Windsor rotated the controls to the rotary cannon and slid the seat forward.

In little more than a whisper, Halsey exclaimed, "I am telling you, Eddie. There is not another unit out there who more closely matches the description given in the prophecy than the *Perseus*."

"I agree, but what I question is how much of that is due to your influence, sir. Does the Eighty-first match the description because you comprised the unit to fit the prophecy?" questioned the commander.

Windsor did not ask in an accusing manner. He had the greatest respect for Admiral Halsey. The commander only wondered how much influence the prophecy had in what he was seeing. "Don't you think the *Perseus* is undermanned?"

"If I had meddled, I would have made sure the *Perseus* had a full compliment. The *Perseus* only has sixty-two men and women. Like all of us, she is shorthanded. Other than members of the senior staff who were assigned by Space Command, the entire crew of the *Perseus* has been handpicked by Commander Jackson. The only crew member I placed on her is Lt. Paschal. You remember Paschal?"

Sensing Windsor was not convinced, Halsey continued. "More importantly, Commander Jackson's reputation as a fair but competent officer means most of the men and women requested transfers to serve under him. There is no greater compliment than people requesting to serve under you."

After a moment, he added, "Another perk is no member of the crew has any family to speak of. Nothing dissuading them from a long cruise."

"Isn't that a step down for Paschal?" inquired Windsor. "If I recall, he is rumored as a potential replacement for Commander Cousins, to serve under Admiral Mitchell on the *Tyche*."

"No. Paschal is only a Lieutenant Junior Grade, but he would make a fine replacement. If Admiral Mitchell and I had our way, we would reassign Commander Cousins to the *Perseus*. But we cannot ask her to take such a demotion. Besides, SC would never allow it. Despite being shorthanded, the Eighty-first has undoubtedly repatriated more old equipment for the war effort than any other unit in SC, despite the best efforts of Space Corps Central Command to thwart their every move. Part of what makes the group so successful is the unique blend of high-tech skill sets the team members have."

"Studying their manifest, it appears the *Perseus* has unlisted personnel. What about them? And the age of the crew? Are you worried that might pose a problem?" asked Windsor.

Semi-attached to the unit was a small group of teenage volunteers. Although the commander paid them a small stipend, they were there mostly for the food. Talented with video controllers, they flew the drones the unit used to lift and carry cumbersome pieces of equipment.

The crew of the *Perseus*, having served together for so many years, most even before Commander Jackson was in charge, were ten to fifteen years older than the average SC sailor. With a crew very much set in their ways, the *Perseus*, from the outside, appeared old-fashioned. Still, Halsey knew Charlie would not trade his team members for any other unit and was proud of the fact they had more combined experience than even a typical ship of the line.

Halsey also knew the real secret to the success of the Eighty-first was the leadership of the commander and First Lieutenant Jackson. Commander Charlie Jackson had spent a year teaching history to cadets at the Space Academy and served a few short tours of duty on a couple of the massive SC battleships. Much of his career, though, Charlie served on the ship he now commanded: the *Perseus*.

Meanwhile, Lieutenant Jacob Jackson had spent little of his time shipboard. Instead, he had spent most of his brief stint before the war as a member of a Space Corp think tank. An outstanding mechanical engineer, he had a brilliant career ahead of him. However, Jacob inexplicably had requested a transfer to serve under his brother when Charlie took command of the *Perseus*. Halsey had a sneaking suspicion he knew exactly why Jacob had chosen to transfer.

He'd always had a fondness for the Jackson boys. Over the years, he'd tried to use his influence, what little he had, to promote the boys' advancement in the service. He had also taken great pains to keep them out of harm's way. That was how Charlie wound up commanding a repair ship instead of a ship of the line, which, with his intellect and sound judgment, was where he really belonged. Jacob had been even more difficult to keep out of harm's way. His talents had been harder to hide from SC and from greedy admirals who would have loved to have him on the bridge of their flagships.

Over time, Halsey had observed that Jacob was more intellectual while Charlie was more of an intuitive thinker; he had a strong tendency to trust his gut. Jacob, on the other hand, was methodical. He preferred to gather facts and follow them to their logical conclusion. Still, the brothers did have similarities. Both had unlimited energy and an intense work ethic. They also possessed the detrimental habit of not letting orders stand in the way of achieving results.

By military standards, some might consider the boys' leadership style lax, informal, and unconventional. The crew admired Jacob for his creative ability and his reputation for thinking outside the box. The consensus was that Commander Jackson didn't even know there was a box. Most of the crew had now been serving together since the war began. The members of the crew had the highest regard for both brothers.

Halsey placed his hand on Windsor's shoulder. "Just come meet the commander and his brother and judge for yourself."

Present Day, Tucson, Arizona, Davis-Monthan
Air/Space Force Base, Earth

The Eighty-first, having found the equipment their orders required them to produce, was wrapping up operations and loading their equipment into the *Perseus*. Paschal decided to take advantage of the time to move his gear down to his new quarters in the goat locker. Lapillus, seeing him struggle with bags, grabbed the lieutenant's stuffed duffle to help, leaving Paschal to only have to carry his briefcase and dress uniform.

Paschal asked, "What is the deal with the speakers mounted on the outside of the ship?"

Lapillus laughed. "We spend a lot of time salvaging equipment from places just like this. The commander loves to listen to music. More than one admiral has dressed him down for blaring music while in port. I think he enjoys playing the rebel."

Paschal shook his head in disbelief. "I have heard rumors about such a ship. I didn't realize it was the *Perseus*. The ship has old gun and motor mounts? Is it true she was once a corvette?"

Lapillus looked at the size of Paschal's bag, then at the pneumatic transport tube, the PTT. Realizing the bags would never fit, he shook his head and pointed Paschal toward the seldom-used stairs.

"From what I have heard the captain say, the *Perseus* is an older third-generation repair ship initially used by the now-defunct US Space Force. No one knows for sure how old she is because the US Space Force captured her and converted her for use from Altima decades ago. She was later mothballed, but Space Command recommissioned her several years before the start of the war when tensions were beginning to mount and added her to the Unified Central Space Command."

Knowing all UCSC vessels received their orders directly from Space Command and that they were all equipped with a system called a CBC (Centralized Bilateral Control), which enabled the entire UCSC to act in concert, Paschal asked, "I saw the CBC down in the hold. The commander hasn't been written up for not installing it?"

Lapillus laughed. "We are just an old repair ship. I doubt SC even knows we exist, especially since the *Perseus* is technically on loan to the army. You know the old saying: Out of sight, out of mind."

He wrinkled his brow disapprovingly and added, "I have heard rumors other ship captains are complaining because it robs them of the ability to take advantage of any unexpected opportunity that might present itself."

Paschal thought to himself, *You don't know the half of it.* Not sure of the steward's politics and in no mood to argue, Paschal said, "High command defends the system, stating in the fast-paced, technical universe of today, no captain can make decisions and be alert to strategic goals comprehensively enough to effectively fight the enemy alone."

"Yes, sir. I have heard SC's arguments for how they run things. I don't trust anything that comes out of SC in Beijing. This is not the same space force I enlisted in during the last war."

During the last war, Earth defeated a much larger force while defending Mars from invasion. In Operation Sledgehammer, the CBC enabled two fleets of UCSC craft to destroy five fleets of Obsidian invaders with only one loss. The lost ship was the UCSC *Constrictor*, Space Command's answer to the Obsidian B Class battleship. The B Class ships were the largest, most deadly warships in the universe.

With a much clearer understanding of Lapillus, Paschal replied, "No. It really isn't."

Silently, he wondered, *Just how many of the crew feels the same as the commander's steward?*

Chapter Two

Present Day, Tucson, Arizona,
Davis-Monthan Air/Space Force Base, Earth

T he entire ship was abuzz with activity as Commander Jackson walked up the gangplank onto the *Perseus* and stepped into the pneumatic transport. Effortlessly, the tube propelled him up two floors, and he reemerged onto the bridge. Immediately, "Commander on deck!" rang out.

The crew knew the commander had a propensity to leave the second the ship's cargo was secure. Far below, generators were buzzing, warming the engines in preparation. Without bothering to look up from his console, the XO, Lt. Myers, said, "You have a personal post from your wife and a flash directive came from SC."

"Thank you, Dillon," Charlie replied, as he examined the flash traffic.

"Holy crap!" he shouted. "Why am I just now getting this? Sound to quarters!".

"Good grief! What has he done now?" chuckled the helmsman, Chief Petty Officer Stuyck, to himself, then added with a grin, "If Maddie is coming all the way to this Godforsaken place, then he must have royally screwed up."

Charlie overheard the chief and glared at him.

"It's the flipping admiral, you moron! That dang fool will be here any minute!" Charlie yelled.

Behind Charlie, the sentry yelled, "Admiral on deck!"

Charlie turned around, red-faced. He found himself nose to nose with Admiral Halsey.

"Dang fool, huh?" growled the admiral.

Behind the admiral stood two sweaty, grease-covered sentries. Both were doing their best to stand erect and look straight ahead. They did not want to catch the eye of their commander. Both were confident he was about to cop it big time. Unless the admiral threw the commander into the brig or relieved him of command, they both understood their next visit with their commanding officer would not be pleasant.

"Commander Jackson! I have two questions for you, and for your own good, I hope you can answer the first question with the answer I want to hear!" roared the admiral.

"Yes, sir!" answered the mortified commander.

"Yes, sir? Maybe you should allow me to ask my question before you reply!" retorted the admiral.

The commander stood smartly at attention and stared straight ahead, sweat dripping from the tip of his nose.

Halsey took a step back. "Jackson, have you located the equipment I instructed you to find and deliver?"

At that exact unfortunate moment, the pneumatic transport propelled Jacob headlong into the admiral. Jacob looked in horror as grease and sweat stains from his body and hands smeared all over the admiral's khaki pants and shirt from where they made contact.

"Ah! Dang, it! You got grease all over my uniform!" roared the admiral as he gave Jacob a murderous stare. "So, Lt. Jackson, I am so glad you decided to show up. I believe I will have both of you tied to the capstan and flayed alive!" growled Halsey.

Jacob recovered his balance, stepped back, and snapped to attention. His eyes were as big as saucers. "My apologies, Admiral."

The red-faced admiral turned his angry stare away from Jacob and back to Charlie. "I find I must repeat myself! Jackson, have you or have you not found the equipment I requested?"

Simultaneously, both brothers responded, "Yes, sir!"

Charlie looked at Jacob, who quickly realized his error and shut up.

Charlie answered again. "Yes, sir. We secured the last of the cargo into the hold so we can deliver it to you, sir."

Halsey lowered his bushy eyebrows and asked, "So how long is it going to take you and this group of misfits you call a crew to make it operational?"

By this time, Charlie had regained his composure. "We have rebuilt the equipment, and it is operational now, sir. We only need your orders for where you want us to deliver it."

Charlie's answer took the admiral by surprise. He expected it to take another week. He knew the *Perseus* was good, but Charlie's crew exceeded even his wildest expectation.

"Son, that answer is the only reason I am not going to bust you in rank down to airman and throw you in the brig."

"Thank you, sir," replied Charlie.

"Now, for my second question, Commander. Is this the *Perseus*'s idea of an appropriate greeting for an admiral? Is there a single member of your crew, other than your XO"—the admiral eyed Lt. Myers suspiciously—"not covered in grease and God knows what?" He sniffed the air. "Does anyone on this ship not smell to high heaven?"

"I highly doubt it, sir," replied Charlie.

The admiral seemed tired, and Charlie noticed for the first time the admiral had aged since the last time he had seen him.

The admiral ignored Charlie's reply and continued, "It is now my unfortunate duty to discipline the person responsible for allowing an admiral to arrive onto the bridge of the *Perseus* undetected."

Charlie hesitated for a moment and then replied, "The person responsible is me, sir. I gave strict orders not to be interrupted unless by enemy fire or if God himself appeared."

The admiral chuckled to himself, loud enough for only Charlie to hear. "Most commanders consider an admiral on their bridge to be both."

Charlie, with his most serious face, replied, "An enemy—never, sir! As for God? I am not allowed by the articles of military conduct to question the race, creed, or religion of any member of my crew, sir. But if you see fit to leave me in command of the *Perseus*, I can assure you every man and woman on board my ship will understand how closely related you are to the Supreme Being, sir."

Admiral Halsey was a strong advocate of extreme ownership. While most people in positions of authority within SC passed the blame for failure on to their subordinates, Halsey expected those under him to accept responsibility for the people under their command. Instead of passing blame down the chain, Charlie was taking the burden on his own shoulders.

What Charlie didn't know was that Halsey knew where the blame belonged. The reason he made it aboard the *Perseus* undetected was that he had arrived via the same support ship, the *Adrestia*, they had been working with for the last three weeks. The *Adrestia*, attached to the 309th Aerospace Maintenance and Regeneration Group, received direct orders from him not to provide the *Perseus* with any warning of his presence. He had warned the crew that if they permitted word of his approach to reach the *Perseus*, they would not escape his revenge.

Charlie, growing uncomfortable with the admiral's long silence, cleared his throat and continued. "I am sure if we examine the ship's log, we can ..."

Meanwhile, Lt. Meyers was visibly startled upon hearing the admiral's comments. Still, performing his job, he immediately spotted three ships on an intercept course for the *Perseus* the second they hit the atmosphere. Without hesitation, he sounded the alarm for the *Perseus* to go to battle stations. On the bridge and all over the ship, all hell broke loose.

Men and women scattered in every direction toward their battle stations despite a full admiral standing in the middle of their bridge.

The grease smudges on his uniform increased exponentially as they squeezed by to get to their stations. Charlie turned and leaped over the back of his seat, buckling his harness.

The admiral appeared impressed by the crew. Despite his presence and the crew being covered in sweat, grease, and grime, the team on the *Perseus* had shown they had the discipline and training required to fight.

The admiral laid his hand on Charlie's shoulder and said, "Please ask your crew not to shoot down my ride, Commander. They would have known in advance to expect those ships had you installed your CBC as directed. Then again, the *Perseus*,"—the admiral studied the bridge—"might struggle with too much interference from SC."

Sure enough, as the admiral was still speaking, Myers had identified the new arrivals, and the situation board had already updated to show the ships were friendlies.

"Sorry, sir," Charlie said sheepishly.

"Now, Commander, we must discuss business. I observed the *Perseus* only has two masts to support your antenna. You have your third antenna mounted directly to the hull. Get a third mast erected back there and have that antenna mounted correctly," ordered the admiral.

"Yes, sir, Admiral. Lt. Jackson, you heard the admiral's orders. Add a six-inch mast directly behind the conn and remount that antenna."

Charlie turned back to face the admiral and lowered his voice. "Does this mean I am being relieved of command, sir? With a third mast, the *Perseus* will no longer be a sloop. She will technically upgrade in status to a ship. A commander is not qualified to command a ship, sir."

The admiral grinned. "Unbelievable. Here I am an admiral of a fleet and to overlook such an egregious detail. Since that is the case, Commander, let me be the first to congratulate you on being promoted to captain."

As he spoke, he took Charlie's hand and shook it. The admiral released Charlie's hand and patted the different pockets of his coat.

"Somewhere in here, I have orders for you to that effect. I hope they are still legible with all the grease on them."

Receiving the promotion directly from the hand of the man who Charlie had spent most of his life trying to emulate made the promotion even more special. The promotion startled Charlie. He and Maddie had long since come to terms with the possibility he would never become a captain. During his last leave, they discussed his retirement from the service. He was close to having served the required fifteen years. Still, as excited as Maddie was by the prospect of him retiring, he could not help but feel unfulfilled by his career so far. Charlie always had high expectations of himself and felt as though he had failed to fulfill some sort of destiny. He was confident the admiral's recent arrival signaled the end of his career.

The admiral, having congratulated Charlie, signaled he was ready to get back to business.

"Now, Captain, you and I need to find somewhere a little more private to discuss the punishment for allowing an admiral to board your ship unnoticed. If you have anyone on board you trust with the responsibility of overseeing this ship, I need to see you and Lt. Jackson aboard my skiff."

With that, the admiral stepped into the pneumatic transport and disappeared.

Chapter Three

Present Day, Tucson, Arizona,
Davis-Monthan Air/Space Force Base, Earth

The first thing the Jackson brothers noticed as they entered Admiral Halsey's skiff was his staff's absence. The second thing they noticed was the crew had disabled every electronic device on the craft. The didn't just turn things off; they had dismantled anything that might be used as a listening device.

The brothers came to attention and saluted the admiral as he rose from his desk. The admiral halfheartedly acknowledged their salute and indicated for the boys to stand at ease.

"Boys, I requested you both come speak with me because I have two sets of orders for the *Perseus*. The orders from SC are straightforward. They are here in this packet, addressed to Captain Charlie Jackson."

The admiral leaned back and got comfortable in his chair. "I did not ask the two of you here to discuss the orders from SC. My orders are totally off the books, so you can accept or decline. I asked both of you here because I believe neither of you can accomplish my proposed mission without the help of the other."

Admiral Halsey pointed at the chairs, indicating he wanted the brothers to have a seat. Charlie and Jacob sat as directed, both sitting on the edge of their seat, leaning toward the admiral, their eyes locked on his.

"Only with the help of God can we possibly hold off the Obsidians for more than another ten to twelve months as things stand now. If people will get their heads out of their tails and think strategically, I believe we can turn this thing around.

"It is common knowledge the Obsidians know every move our fleets make. They outnumber us in ships, and their ships have proven more powerful, faster, and it seems their captains are omnipotent. They know our plans before we do.

"I, along with many of my peers, believe their newest strategy is to convince the people on Earth that the Obsidians are invincible. So far, they have been convincing. We have yet to destroy a single ship of theirs of any significance. Our theory is if they can destroy our confidence, then the people of Earth might rise and overthrow the planetary government. The people would then install a new government willing to discuss terms. We believe that is why they are not bothering to attack any of our moon bases or colonies on Mars. Why destroy infrastructure if they can convince us to capitulate?"

The admiral rubbed his forehead. He struggled to believe the war against the Obsidian Empire was now in its third year. The fight to establish a beachhead on Earth was fierce. Despite the Obsidian advantage of being able to land troops at any unopposed location on the planet, the fierce counterattacks by Earth's land, air, and sea forces overwhelmingly defeated the Obsidians' every overture.

The war to control space, by the admiral's own admission, had been a miserable failure. Pundits claimed the only reason Earth still had colonies on Mars and military space stations on the moon was that the Obsidians did not consider them to pose any credible threat. The warships in port on the moon and Martian bases were virtual prisoners because of the almost impenetrable Obsidian blockades that denied them access to space. Obsidian ships, on the other hand, were free to travel unmolested anywhere they went.

Halsey reached behind him and pulled out a sizeable antique map, the type they used to print on paper. Carefully, he rolled it out on the desk in front of him. "Now, we have convinced SC to allow us to conduct a modest operation. As you will learn from your orders, we plan to deploy the *Perseus*, *Shelter*, and *Nicodemus* here along the Strivo asteroid belt. This corridor is the only natural choke point between the Milky Way and Obsidian galaxies. Every ship of war and all of their supplies have to either come through here or jump into our galaxy through the Taverius Space Bubble."

Over the last three years of fighting, Space Command had lost every significant engagement with the enemy. The common perception was that Halsey's Fifth Fleet was only one engagement away from no longer existing as a fleet. Already, rumors had spread that Beijing had considered combining the Fifth and Seventh into one squadron.

Jacob spoke up. "Admiral, permission to speak?"

Halsey nodded his head. "Speak now. In a week *Perseus* and her crew will be in the Strivo Corridor."

Jacob pointed out the obvious. "Sir, the *Perseus* is not capable of subspace travel. It will take the *Perseus* twenty years to travel there."

Halsey nodded. "We have secured an obsolete space ring that will fit the *Perseus*, with a few minor alterations. It can easily make the jump. Now, how we get you back is a different question. We will figure that one out when the time comes."

Neither of the brothers said anything and remained stoic, so Halsey continued. "None of the ships we are sending are strong enough to take on an actual warship alone. Capital warships travel back and forth through the bubble. Hopefully, you can avoid any contact of that nature. Obsidian supply ships, on the other hand, cannot make the journey through the bubble. Older ships must get through the corridor and then jump subspace. Your mission is simple. Destroy commerce and cut their supply lines."

Charlie interjected, "Sir, why the *Perseus*? Space Command did not design the *Perseus* to destroy commerce. We only have one gun, unless you count the two-rotary cannon."

"Even the rotary cannon might prove unpleasant to a cargo vessel," Halsey replied. "I convinced SC to include the *Perseus* because you are experts at making something out of nothing. We plan to outfit the *Perseus* with two six-man SWAL teams. The *Shelter* and *Nicodemus* should be able to handle the occasional destroyer the Obsidians might send to protect their cargo vessels. The goal is for the *Perseus* to enable all three ships to be self-sustainable at the expense of the enemy because, I must warn you, SC has no capability of offering any resupply. Do you understand?"

Both men nodded they understood. Charlie wondered to himself, *What on earth did getting two SWAL teams cost the admiral? The specialized Space, Water, Air, and Land Assault Teams are in short supply. Space Command cannot afford to give every battleship one, much less two.*

"Now, that is the official explanation I gave SC for including you on this mission. No one at SC seems too concerned about the loss of any of you," he added rather bluntly.

Inwardly, Halsey questioned the wisdom of what he was about to do. Fear of losing either of the boys, trying to keep them out of harm's way, had so influenced his decisions in the past. Now he was about to send them on a mission that had little chance of success, based on a superstitious belief in destiny. His only consolation was his confidence that their mother would approve of what he was about to propose.

"We need to discuss the real reason I want to include the *Perseus* and the two of you."

Halsey stood up and turned to open the door behind him, then nodded for someone to join them. A young man slipped into the room. He wore the distinctive uniform of a British Space Guard Unit.

"Gentlemen, I would like to introduce you to Commander Windsor. Most people know Commander Windsor as Prince Edward."

Halsey turned to the prince. "Eddie, these are the two we discussed. This is Captain Jackson and Lt. Jackson of the *Perseus*."

The prince studied the brothers with a dubious expression on his face. Neither brother had had time to shower to remove the grease all over their hands and faces. They were still in the same dirty fatigues they had been wearing earlier.

The brothers couldn't blame the prince for seeming unimpressed. The strongest impression they could make on the prince right now was how bad they smelled.

Finally, the prince offered his hand.

"It is nice to meet you," both Jackson brothers murmured.

The prince remained silent, wondering if the admiral had lost his marbles. It had to be difficult for him to imagine that these were the two the prophecy spoke of.

Halsey pressed on. "Eddie, I need you to share the legend of the jewel."

Prince Edward still seemed somewhat taken aback. He looked at the admiral and studied the two brothers again before he spoke. "My family has a jewel. It is not part of the crown jewels, but our family has protected this jewel with even more ferocity than any other we possess. I cannot tell you how we came to possess the jewel or even where the legend originated. Not because the information is secret. But because no one in our family knows."

Both brothers seemed confused. Charlie asked, "What type of legend are we talking about?"

Hearing his voice and seeing the confident way Charlie held himself when he spoke, the prince recognized something about the captain that spoke of greatness. He couldn't place what. Something about his posture or maybe the deep-set, insightful-looking eyes, maybe? The prince's confidence increased. If there was any truth to the old wives' tale his parents had taught him since his youth, then the man standing before him was the man who would fulfill the prophecy. He reached inside his coat and pulled out a silk pouch.

"Inside this bag is a rare star sapphire. When my grandfather gave me the stone, he called it the 'Stone of Destiny.' They say the crossbars represent Faith, Hope, and Destiny. My grandmother claimed the stone's real name is Asteria. The legend contains a prophecy that claims that during Earth's darkest hour, this stone will travel to the farthest reaches of the universe. When it returns, it will bring with it salvation for our kingdom. I have taken a few liberties. By kingdom, I assume that to mean our planet."

"How is this jewel supposed to be our salvation?" Charlie asked, his expression doubtful.

"No one knows," interjected the admiral.

The prince shifted his weight from one foot to the other. When he did, Charlie fixed his gaze on his left leg, noticing that it had been replaced with an artificial limb.

"I have included a data chip in the bag. On the chip is everything I know about the jewel and legend. There is also a rather lengthy digital copy of a book. If nothing else, it will make for interesting reading. I only ask you to protect the jewel and chip. You must not let it fall into any other person's possession, friend or foe."

"So, am I to understand you are entrusting us with a priceless jewel? Are you aware we are going on a mission from which we might not return?" Charlie asked Commander Windsor.

Prince Edward lifted himself up straight and pulled back his shoulders. "I am aware that everything about you and your mission runs parallel to the legend as I know it. I am not a superstitious man, but I understand duty. If there is any possibility that the legend behind this stone might be true, then I must insist you take it."

The prince felt a great sense of relief, as if a huge weight had been lifted from his shoulders. There was no longer any doubt in his mind he had given the jewel to the man who would someday be Earth's salvation.

Perplexed, Jacob asked, "What are we supposed to do with the jewel?"

Prince Edward lowered his gaze somberly. "That question I cannot answer. The legend says you will know when the time comes."

He handed the silk pouch to Charlie and turned to the admiral. "By-your-leave, sir. If I may be dismissed? My ship is expecting me. I need to be underway before someone notices I am missing."

The admiral gave him a crisp salute, which Windsor smartly returned.

As the prince exited, he turned. "Good luck, chaps. I do not expect to see the jewel again, but I look forward to meeting you again under more favorable circumstances." He looked at Halsey and nodded his head. "Admiral." Then he closed the door behind him.

The admiral turned back to the brothers. "Captain Jackson, you leave for the Strivo in less than one hundred and twenty hours. I suspect you will need time to prepare the *Perseus* and get her connected to the space ring. In the interim, I expect you to deliver my hardware to the *Fortuna*."

"Yes, sir, Admiral!" Charlie replied with a crisp salute.

Halsey returned the salute and stepped forward to give each of the men a hug. "One last order. I expect you to spend time with your wife before you leave, Charlie."

He glanced over at Jacob. "I expect you to stay out of trouble!" he said good-naturedly. "Good luck to both of you."

"Thank you, sir," both brothers replied.

Chapter Four

Present Day, Space Station Yuma, Earth

The admiral had said that they had less than one hundred and twenty hours before they departed. But leaving so soon would be extremely difficult since the supply depot had not yet found them a dock to berth to receive supplies. And they hadn't had any additional briefings from SC or any planning sessions with the other captains.

Once SC took over, it seemed to Charlie and Jacob like time itself slowed down. With the *Perseus* floating just outside of the ordnance docks, waiting, all Charlie had to occupy his time with was to fumble with the jewel in his pocket and wonder what it might mean. What was its purpose? Each time his fingers touched it, he felt as though it was emitting an impatient energy that matched his own.

Charlie worried that, like many SC missions, after multiple delays the mission would change or be canceled altogether. The only thing the *Perseus* had accomplished in a timely manner so far was to deliver the parts the admiral had requested. The crew loaded the whole contraption into the admiral's barge.

As they parted company with the admiral, Charlie and Jacob laughed loud enough for the crew to hear.

"By the time the admiral makes it back to his flagship with all his equipment, he will decide the crew on the *Perseus* was clean enough to pass inspection after all," quipped Jacob.

Charlie laughed and replied, "The admiral is one tough bird. He didn't even flinch when I suggested loading it into his barge. I wonder what he wants with all that old electronic jamming equipment, anyway. It was advanced equipment in its day, but it could never hide the signature of his flagship. Even the CBC seems useless at jamming the enemy."

Jacob looked thoughtful. "Maybe that is the point. The admiral isn't trying to jam the enemy. He is trying to thwart the CBC! If strategically placed on board the admiral's ship, that old equipment could definitely accomplish that much."

"But if he plans to place it on his own ship, why did it have to have an independent power supply?" Charlie asked. "Why not plug it into the power source on the ship?"

Jacob didn't even hesitate to reply. "Because the CBC can do a lot more than allow SC to take the helm, navigation, and weapons controls. Space Command has access to every electronic device on the ship. If they lost control for any significant amount of time, SC would run diagnostics. It wouldn't take them long to figure out how they lost communication and who was responsible."

Charlie looked as though he were pondering the significance of Jacob's assessment, especially in light of the story Lt. Paschal had shared with him.

"Jacob, I want you to drag your feet installing our CBC unit on the *Perseus*. For the present, only connect the *Perseus* into the space ring's CBC. With a little creativity, SC will be none the wiser."

Jacob laughed. "We have served on this bucket three years. I haven't even taken it out of its crate. How much slower can I get?"

"The *Perseus* has seldom left low orbit since I have been in command," Charlie replied. "I doubt SC even knows we exist. Even most of the *Perseus*'s reclaim missions, though successful, have been pretty much off the books. Now, I fear all that will change."

"I agree," Jacob replied. "How did you talk the computer geeks into staying aboard? Are they actually old enough to enlist?"

Charlie chuckled. "Oh, yes. At least none of them are too young. Those kids are a lot smarter than we give them credit for. They are not your run-of-the-mill kids who have spent too much time playing video games. A couple have a serious penchant for hacking. It turns out some have now celebrated their sixteenth birthday several times."

"Are you suggesting they changed their birthdates in the international registry? That's impossible!"

"It seems it is more possible than either of us might have believed." Charlie replied. "It turns out they are all cousins. None of them were fond of having to serve their required time in the military. I promised if the group of them enlisted, I would see to it the time they have worked with us will apply against their time served. I suggested in the long run that time served aboard a low-orbit repair ship is about as safe a place to serve as they will ever find."

After a moment, Charlie added, "Every one of them signed on immediately except the youngest. His name is Andrew, Roland's younger brother. He said he is only seventeen, so SC required him to obtain a guardian's signature. The following morning, he came back with all the appropriate papers, signed and notarized. I am happy to see him return because, of the five, Andrew is the most talented. Even though the older boys give him the worst of the drones, he still flies circles around them."

"But we are departing on a mission to the opposite side of the universe. Without a plan to get back!" Jacob stuttered. "They still signed up?"

Charlie laughed. "Well, I may have failed to mention that. The truth is, we need those kids. They are an integral part of our team. Not only that, I did a little research. I didn't mention it, but it turns out I knew the Rushing boys' father. Ian Rushing served as my helmsman on the *Constrictor*. The most talented pilot ever to serve in Space Command. The younger boy looks like his father."

•••

Charlie had welcomed the delay on many fronts. While Charlie couldn't take leave to go home, he could have Maddie meet him at the supply depot, SS Yuma, then travel on the *Perseus* back to their point of departure, Space Station Victory. Easy enough for any officer's wife thanks to Space Command Officer Partner Enterprise, or SCOPE. Captains joked that the officers' partner organization facilitated more travel miles for their significant others than SC required of their captains.

The officers' spouses were also a better source of information even than the intelligence services. There was no better disseminator of what was really happening within Space Command than the gatherings of ships' officers' spouses from all over the Milky Way. Since their marriage, Maddie had been very involved with SCOPE.

Charlie thought to himself, *I should mention to Maddie our inability to find a berth. She could probably have some wife grease the wheels and find us a dock faster than the base commander.*

The elevators from the old Yuma Proving Grounds were much less efficient than the new elevators outside Columbia. The technology used to build SS Yuma was already outdated even before the base was complete. Charlie wondered why the facility was still such a major supply hub.

The *Perseus* had not yet been assigned a dock, so it took longer for Maddie to find a conveyance from the space station to the ship than it did for the ride up the elevator. Maddie's eyes sparkled as she greeted Charlie, gave him a hug, then leaned back so she could caress the new shiny epaulettes signifying his new rank as captain, one resting on each shoulder.

Charlie smiled and said, "I finally earned a raise."

It wasn't that they needed the money; Maddie had assured him her parents had left her with enough resources after they passed away, so the two of them could afford a decent lifestyle once he hung up his flight suit for good. Still, Charlie wanted to be the one who provided for his family. He did not want to live off his wife's inheritance.

As Charlie predicted, she was proud he had made Captain, but it displeased her when he told her he had accepted a mission that would send him to the other side of the universe. Maddie had served her time in the military, so she understood the reason you served was to go where they sent you.

With venom in her voice, she said, "But they can't ship you to the other side of the universe three months before you are ready to retire! We knew your days on *Perseus* were almost over but ... a desk job ... You earned the right to run out the clock behind a desk. They cannot make you accept the orders."

"I know, but Halsey—"

"Don't use the admiral as an excuse for accepting these orders. You and I both know SC will let you step aside."

"Maddie, I can't let the crew down!"

"Oh. You can't let the crew down? What about me?" Maddie said with tears appearing in the corners of her eyes. "Three years. For three years I have been stuck at home alone, and now this?" She pushed Charlie away and turned to face the wall, sniffling.

Charlie tried to reason with Maddie. "You haven't been stuck at home alone. Besides, what about SCOPE? You said yourself you can't step away from your duties now. One last mission and I promise I will retire if that is what you want."

At the mention of SCOPE, Maddie grew silent, crossing her arms tightly as though embracing herself. She wondered if Charlie was insinuating anything with the comment. Surely he had to have a clue. The one thing she had learned from the spouses of Space Command's officers: *There are no secrets.*

After a long moment of silence, she said, "You were going to come home so we could start a family. Ever since we fell in love, all I've wanted was you and to have a child or even children together. The one thing I have never had is a family."

Charlie stuttered, "We will still have children someday. You and I are already a family."

She turned, paused as though to say something more, hesitated, then picked up her bag and left, her eyes never once glancing at her husband.

Charlie had planned for Maddie to stay until the departure date, but the manner of her exit left Charlie not knowing what to think. She boarded the very next plane home and left without even saying goodbye.

Chapter Five

Present Day, Space Station Yuma, Earth

A t 516 feet long, one might think the *Perseus* would be roomy. In reality, the ship being only fifty-two feet wide, the most significant personal space on the entire ship was the captain's small quarters. The ship's layout allowed everyone else on the ship a cubicle, ninety-six inches by forty-eight inches by thirty-six inches. They had drawers on the back side of their cubicle, a small cabinet where they hung a few clothes, and some shallow shelves behind their pillows.

One half of the ship housed the engines, the bridge (which doubled as the fire control center), all the workspace, and fuel. The rest of the vessel consisted of one large cargo bay.

No one understood how little space *Perseus* had better than Quartermaster Stidham. Her responsibility included finding a suitable place for, and to keep up with, every item on board the *Perseus*. That cargo, much to her chagrin, included crew members. SC had passed word down to her that besides having to provide a space to house the teenagers, she was also responsible for finding an appropriate place to house two six-man SWAL teams and all their associated assault gear.

Her solution was simple. Her manifest listed dozens of prehistoric cargo containers at the supply depot waiting to load into the cargo bay of the *Perseus*. She got busy and found two extra shipping containers. She had one container divided into sections to house the kids and the two SWAL teams. The other container she designated for the teams' equipment and a simulator training facility. She also set aside some personal space for miscellaneous items she thought might make her a small fortune once the standard rations gave out. Alcohol was the most common commodity smuggled on board, but Stidham had long since learned, on a long voyage, chocolate was worth more than its weight in gold.

It didn't take a rocket scientist to figure out something was up, and the *Perseus* was full of rocket scientists. Stidham already caught the kids attempting to go AWOL once they learned the *Perseus*'s destination. "Desertion" was an ugly word, and she hated the thought of having to watch the captain line the kids up in front of a firing squad or, worse, receive orders to pull the trigger herself.

Everyone aboard seemed apprehensive, and tensions were running high. It was one thing to be stuck on a ship during a mission, but it was altogether different to be stranded on a ship waiting in port. It felt like the wheels were spinning, but no one was getting anywhere. Everyone was getting on one another's nerves. Stidham talked to Sergeant at Arms Wells and Assistant Sergeant at Arms Goldsmith. Together, the three of them created a plan to watch all the crew, especially the kids.

Charlie, realizing the crew needed a purpose, began a fresh new regimen of simulated drills. He focused on emergency procedures. The crew became adept at performing under all types of adverse conditions. Crew members cross-trained in other people's positions and also learned to fight without being able to hear over the white noise Jacob pumped through the sound system and with zero light. Many of the drills began with no alarm. Only the small warning lights located in every corner of the ship alerted them to their duty. The crew was always trained to use the warning panels to remain aware of the ship's status.

The only kid Stidham didn't worry about going AWOL was the youngest, Andrew. He had to be torn from the simulator every time the ship sounded to general quarters to perform drills. Andrew seemed to be fascinated with the flight simulator. Stidham studied his scores and was shocked to learn that he routinely scored higher than Stuyck, who had been piloting the *Perseus* longer than she had been a member of the crew.

To her surprise, the captain was also aware of the situation and was paying attention to young Rushing's progress. He even assigned Andrew the unused operations seat directly behind the captain's chair on the bridge as his official duty station. The chair hadn't functioned properly in years. Paschal from Engineering tore it apart and completely rebuilt it from the floor up.

As if Stidham didn't already have her hands full, the ship's medical officer, Dr. Laird, protested her use of the containers as living quarters. The architects redesigned the cargo hold on the *Perseus* without gravity plates. That made it easier to load and unload the heavy cargo they built the *Perseus* to repair. The doctor kept complaining to the captain and anyone who would listen that the SWAL teams and kids would lose muscle mass and their bones would experience atrophy without gravity plates. Laird also insisted the hallways must remain clear so the SWAL teams and any crew members concerned about their bodies wasting away could get in their recommended daily exercise. Finally, he threatened if Stidham did not address these issues immediately, he would be forced to jeopardize the mission by filing an official complaint to SC.

Stidham addressed the problem with the captain. Charlie suggested she consult with Lt. Jackson and find a solution. Together, she and Lt. Jackson assured the captain they had found an answer, so Charlie promptly dismissed it from his plate of worries. Charlie did not give the issue another thought until he heard rumors that the destroyer, which had been sitting in the dry dock next to the *Perseus*, was missing one of its gravity plates. He thought about addressing the rumors with both Jacob and Stidham but decided it was better he not know.

Even though Charlie didn't want to hear anything else about gravity plates, the next morning the issue reappeared on his plate, needing his attention. It turned out the newly acquired gravity plate's lowest g-Force setting was about 10 percent greater than it should be. The SWAL team leaders loved it so much they barraged the captain with requests to increase the g-force ship-wide. The kids, on the other hand, rebelled to the point Sergeant at Arms Wells had to post a guard in front of the control panel to prevent either group from messing with it.

Finally, Charlie worked out a compromise with the SWAL team leaders, which allowed them to increase the g-force during their morning runs. After having time to think about the advantages, Charlie decided the idea had merit, and he increased the g-force anytime he drilled the crew in simulated battle.

They ultimately received their orders to depart thirty-one days and six hours after their scheduled departure time.

Charlie reflected on the fact that "Top Secret" was stamped on all his orders. Despite this, everyone on board the *Perseus*, the *Shelter*, the *Nicodemus*, the Supply Depot, and anywhere he ventured in town seemed to know where they were going and what their orders were once they got there. Even worse, it appeared to be general knowledge the *Perseus* was leaving without a return ticket home. Charlie worried. *If SC can't keep a secret from the general population, then shouldn't we be worried that the enemy might also know of our intentions?*

Charlie discussed his concern with his fellow captains. SC declared Captain George of the *Nicodemus* the commodore of the small fleet, him having seniority. With his hard-to-follow Swabian German accent, he dismissed Charlie's concern. "Cahptain Jahckson, I hahve ze utmost confidence in Spahce Commahnd. Ze CBC will ahllow SC to mahke any necessary ahdjustments to ensuah owa sahfety ahnd ze success of owa mission."

Charlie protested, "But having contingencies in place would still be a good idea. If for no other reason than to prepare our crews in case SC uploads a new plan of action. Our crews must know how to respond."

Present Day, Space Station Victory, Earth

Right before they jumped into subspace, the first good news of the war for Space Command broadcast live on the BBC. Admiral Halsey's Fifth Fleet lost contact with their CBC. They overshot their landing zone by twenty klicks and entered from subspace astern a fleet of six Obsidian destroyers. The news report said Admiral Halsey was unable to get the CBC back online in time to react, so the Fifth had to improvise and act on their own accord. The Fifth annihilated three of the destroyers before the Obsidians made their escape back into subspace. An official from SC lamented the fact the CBC had failed. He expressed confidence that had the fleet been able to get it back online in time, SC would have destroyed all six destroyers.

Charlie shook his head in disbelief. He failed to fathom people's complacent response to the charade. Growing disgusted after having perused all the opinions of the different journalists, none of whom had obviously ever served on a man-of-war, Charlie turned off his bunk light, inserted the disk given to him by the prince into his tablet, and started reading the manuscript, *The Destiny Scrolls*.

Physical books were a relic from a bygone era, but Charlie still loved the feel of pages bound together by thread bindings, and the beautiful covers. True, the contents of *The Destiny Scrolls* were inside the file given to him, but the words seemed to lose some of their timelessness. More to the point, it was hard to get any sense of scale to how large the document might be. The file opened to where Charlie had last left off, and he resumed reading.

Chapter Six

The Destiny Scrolls
Over Ten Millennia Ago in the Milky Way,
Garden of Eden, Mars

Eden was a beautiful place. It had endless underground aquifers and a mild climate. Every square inch of the planet was lush, and vast fields of every type of produce imaginable were abundant. Orchards grew the sweetest, most beautiful fruit known to all humanity. Grains, flax, and vegetables grew in abundance. The planet was literally the Garden of Eden.

People coveted her vineyards and distilleries throughout the universe. Thanks to the legal trade of this commodity, Eden's coffers overflowed. Besides the planet's four main spaceports, there were hundreds of smaller ports. These small ports were havens for the less savory ships that supplied the universe with Eden's intoxicating beverages. Many kingdoms had strict prohibitions of the liquors. Despite this, trade thrived. To King Hephaestus and Queen Aphrodite's reprobation, most of the business was duty-free.

Despite some seedier degenerates who soiled the kingdom's reputation, many outsiders referred to the planet simply as the "Garden." Eden's enemies also referred to her by many other names. Her most bitter enemies referred to her as "Mars." The despised name originated from the surname of the captain of her fiercest warship, the Ares. Rumor was, her Captain, Mars, was the queen's true love. The two had known each other since their youth. The king had given Mars command of the warship Ares, hoping Mars might die in battle.

Mars was known for his lust for blood, his chaotic nature, and his thoughtless aggression. Whereas his enemies loathed him, his loyal crew adored him, both as a leader and a man. The crew of the Ares referred to him as "The Ram." Every time the Ares won a victory, his popularity amongst the general population of Eden increased, much to the chagrin of the king. The people called the Ares the "God of War."

Between the disdain the king had for him and some of his more self-destructive habits, Mars had as many enemies within the kingdom as he did outside. Despite his popularity with the general population, the only person in the universe who seemed to have any influence on Mars was the queen.

The Edenite kingdom spanned the entire Milky Way. Eden deposited small colonies in every corner of the universe. The king was generous, and the queen sincerely loved her people. Most considered their rule benevolent.

Throughout the kingdom, treason, however, was not tolerated and was met with lethal force. Law and order, though maintained with a firm hand, was just and not overly repressive. Capital punishment was rare, short of treason. The usual penalty for even the more serious crime was merely exile. The king established a penal colony on the closest habitable planet called Terra, today known as Earth.

Terra was a frightening place with enormous reptiles that dwarfed the men and women exiled there. Given no tools or weapons with which to defend themselves, people were forced to live beneath the ground in caves. They only ventured out sparingly to find food. Many of the more skilled prisoners traded their services as craftsmen, tradesmen, or indentured servants for more favorable living conditions. The overseers employed them to build large cities, pyramids, and temples. In the beginning, they built cities mostly to support the administrators appointed to oversee the prisoners. With little supervision from Eden, sparse fiefdoms sprang up all over.

When the kingdom fell, none of the mighty warships of the time—Zeus, Poseidon, Demeter, Apollo, Hercules, Artemis, Hermes, nor any of the rest—ever fired a shot in defense of the kingdom. The might of the Empire all ended with the stroke of the queen's pen.

Queen Aphrodite negotiated a peace alliance with the Edenites' most powerful nemesis, the Obsidians. Across the universe, the deal became known as "The Poisonous Fruit."

Chapter Seven

Present Day, Space Station Yuma, Earth

The captain's meeting had gone much worse than Charlie had feared. With little leadership being offered by the commodore, Captain George, Charlie had tried to take the lead by pointing out what he considered obvious. Plopping down onto his bunk, Charlie tried to review the facts as he had presented them and understand why he had failed.

A subspace jump would not carry a ship as far or as fast as a hyperjump, but ship captains preferred it for many reasons. One advantage was a craft could change course in mid-flight if they required a last-minute change in destination or saw danger in the reentry area. The ability to change course allowed captains to redirect their ships away from danger.

The second reason captains preferred a subspace jump was it took less than ten to fifteen seconds for the ship's guns to come back online. After a hyperspace jump, it took hours to bring them back online because all the firing mechanisms were removed prior to the jump and then reinstalled. With an enemy ship pouring fire into your hull, fifteen seconds felt like an eternity. An hour was an automatic death sentence. The smallest destroyer could eliminate any ship if given enough time. The only exception might be a

B Class Battleship, as long as its shield emitter was operational. It was doubtful even a battleship could destroy one.

The advantages of jumping subspace using a space ring provided the captain with many more benefits. The ship's captain had much more ability to maneuver. A vessel equipped with subspace travel ability had to dedicate all its command/control and engine power to maintain the jump. Space rings were independent operating systems. The crew could fly a pre-programmed flight path or control the space ring from the bridge of the ship. They were very advanced technology when first introduced. Unfortunately, they were not reusable.

During the captain's meeting, Charlie emphasized all the advantages of the space ring. Instead of asking for the enviable position of jumping last, he argued the *Perseus* should lead the way, even though the *Perseus* only had one gun. If an unsuspecting target of opportunity were in her path, that one gun would be almost impossible to defend against—at least for the first shot.

Charlie's second argument seemed to be even clearer to him. If the *Perseus* made contact, the other two ships might alter course. Together the three ships could surround the enemy and coordinate an attack, or if they encountered a superior force, then the *Nicodemus* and *Venture* could redirect together or separately, depending on the situation.

Neither Captain George nor Captain Josiah of the *Venture* would entertain the suggestions. They also adamantly opposed running the idea up the chain of command. Charlie was baffled by their complacency and willingness to depend on SC for the safety of their ships and crews. They seemed to have complete trust in SC's plan for the mission and ability to control and adjust if needed.

Charlie even heard through the rumor mill that neither captain put their crews through any drills nor practiced contingency plans. Charlie could not understand the complete blind faith in SC. Maybe that was what happened when captains were promoted without truly overseeing anything or having to make decisions for themselves, their ships, or their crews.

Despite the views of the other captains, Charlie continued to deliberate the possibilities and formed a simple plan of his own. Since he could not override the CBC, Charlie decided if he saw trouble anywhere in the drop zone, he would drop out of the space ring. That would make the reentry rough, but it would allow Charlie much more control of where they reentered from subspace.

Charlie hoped all his worry was for naught. Still, he felt the other captains were being negligent by not having a plan in case the worse happened. Having reached no conclusion as to why the other two captains would not entertain his suggestions, Charlie grabbed his tablet, scanned his email, then returned to where he left off in *The Destiny Scrolls*.

The Destiny Scrolls
The Ares
Over Ten Millennia Ago in the Milky Way

The Ares *may have had scars, but every shell an enemy sent sailing into her hull seemingly only strengthened her. On the horns of the colossal ram head sculpted into her bow were thousands of brilliantly cut topaz gemstones, each representing an enemy ship, either destroyed by her powerful guns or captured by the men that made up her crew.*

The gemstones on the horns and eyes of the ram were deep blue and light blue topaz. Near the base of the horn, it filtered into a densely packed array of sky-blue topaz. The blue topaz of the horns evoked images of the wind, sky, and water, until nearing the sharp tips of the horn. Topaz jewels on the pointed ends transitioned from blue to a spattering of opaque gems, culminating in reddish-orange topaz gems that had a luminescent, blood-like glow.

Covering the actual head of the ram were wine-colored topaz accented by brilliant diamond chips. The head burst through an oblique-shaped shield of twenty-four-karat white and yellow gold. In the upper left corner, slightly behind the shield, was a twenty-four-karat palladium-peaked warrior's helmet of the Corinthian style, the dark recesses of the mouth, nose, and eyes comprised of nephrite jade. The jade's calcium, magnesium, and iron-rich amphibole mineral, tremolite, gave the foreboding impression of a dark knight seeking to release the soul from the confines of a victim's body. On the side of the helmet was a platinum image of a dragon with its tail thrashing angrily. The horse plume on the apex of the helmet covered the crown from the temple of the forehead to the back of the helmet, adorned with the darkest rubies imaginable.

To the upper right of the steely shield were a spear and sword, which crossed over a pale-yellow topaz scabbard. The jewels that comprised the sword were too brilliant to identify other than the tip, which was a barbarous composition of blood-colored reddish-orange gemstones accented with a sprinkle of rubies.

The vestibule, containing the crest, was shaped like a cuirasse esthétique, *otherwise known as a heroic cuirass. A musculature of a male torso idealized and embellished the titanium relief. In the dark recessed voids of the body armor was a hauberk. The individual chain links of the shirt of mail armor were embellished with solid black jade.*

Ancient cultures believed icy blue shades of topaz gemstones fought off chaos and negative emotions. They thought the gems promoted learning, understanding, and peaceful communication. The effect never seemed to influence the behavior or attitude of the ship, her captain, or her crew.

Now, on perhaps her final mission, to negotiate a universal peace, and hailed by some as the most important of her entire career, the fate of the whole kingdom of Eden might well be decided. Her reputation was one of death and destruction, more so than an emissary to end centuries of bitter conflict, so the Ares *seemed ill-suited for the mission.*

The captain of the ship tried to stand as Queen Aphrodite stepped onto the bridge. Too many years of constant preparedness for the unexpected found him strapped into place, the latches to his harness locked. His battle gear was secured tightly to his seat.

The queen glared at him as he clumsily released the harness and jumped to his feet.

Unamused, the queen said, "You are on the most important peace mission in the history of mankind, and you arrive wearing all of your battle gear with every gun poised to open fire!"

Captain Mars, although slightly embarrassed, did not smile or show the least bit of humility. "Your Highness, those guns are the only reason the Obsidians are here suing for peace. Power is the only thing their race understands or respects."

The queen's expression softened, her fondness for the captain allowing him much leeway. She held out her hand and said, "Captain, the jewel."

For the first time ever, the captain seemed shaken, his hands visibly trembling, and sweat beaded on his brow. He had understood this moment was coming, and he had consoled himself by telling himself he was prepared for it, but the captain found he no longer possessed control of his hands or his feet. He never considered how much the jewel meant to him or to his ship. Could the spiritual connection between him and the Ares really be broken merely by relinquishing a jocale? Did the word itself not imply that the ruby, the symbol of their close interpersonal relationship, was only a plaything?

The queen firmly repeated herself. "Captain, the jewel, or else you will spend the rest of your days living in a cave on that miserable planet, Terra."

All the battle-hardened sailors on the bridge turned white when they saw a tear roll down the captain's left cheek. Nothing prepared the crew for the drama that was transpiring. The most fearless and brave man they had ever known was crying.

The captain lowered his head and whispered, "As you wish, my dearest Queen."

He turned and stepped to the center piedistallo, located directly beneath the sizeable main monitor, and caressed the niche containing the jewel. Then he stepped back and held out his hand. At first, nothing happened. Whether the captain was struggling to give the silent order or the ship was having trouble obeying, no one could decide. Finally, with no fanfare, a massive ruby appeared in the captain's palm.

The huge motors on the Ares never missed a beat. The lights on the bridge continued to shine, and the gravity plates continued to secure the crew and Ares's passengers to the floor, yet somehow, every man on the vessel immediately recognized a change. It was as if the very soul of the ship had left her, leaving a void in her heart.

It unnerved Queen Aphrodite to witness the captain of the Ares shedding a tear. For a moment, it overwhelmed her. What if the Obsidians couldn't be trusted to honor their promise?

Part of the terms of the treaty with the Obsidians required she must surrender herself to become a permanent resident of the royal Obsidian household, or, in other words, a hostage. She and the Obsidian queen agreed that to ensure the peace between their two kingdoms, they would both ransom their persons.

Surely, Queen Jezebel's tears had been real when she talked about her children. She convincingly pleaded her case that no more innocent blood needed to be shed in this most unholy war. After all, the universe was large. If their two races could live together peaceably, then who else was there to fight? No other kingdom could possibly threaten their existence. And if an enemy did rise, their combined forces would be indomitable.

Queen Aphrodite asked her servants for a private moment to pray. Just as importantly, she needed the time to compose herself. She could never allow an Obsidian to see her lack of resolve. After all, the Obsidian queen seemed almost gleeful when she delivered herself to the palace on Eden. If she had that much inner fortitude, then Aphrodite knew she, too, must be equally brave and strong.

The Queen, certain she had recomposed herself, gave the crew the private signal. The royal barge backed out of the bay doors and left the safety of the Ares one last time.

•••

As soon as the royal barge docked with the Obsidian flagship, the queen knew something was amiss. She saw armed guards lining every wall in the docking bay. The soldiers were not in dress uniform. They were in full combat gear. As she stepped off the barge, she expected to be greeted by a member of the Obsidian royal family. Instead, she was greeted by a lowly security officer.

The queen stood there in the middle of the platform, and not a soul spoke to her. She also remained mute, watching as every member of her crew and the royal guard were systematically searched from head to toe. They then marched the crew and her guards out of the bay.

"Why are you doing this?" she hissed. "My personnel are to return to the Ares."

The security officer in charge refused to even look at her. "Those are not my orders," he said. "Guards! The captain requires the queen's presence on the bridge."

Then he unceremoniously turned his back to the queen and followed his men through the side door of the bay where her staff and crew had disappeared.

Six heavily armed soldiers faced the queen. All Obsidians had extremely large ears, but the man in front of her had exceptionally large ears, even by Obsidian standards. Another trait Obsidians were known for was their head full of long flowing black hair. The only place this Obsidian grew hair was his ears and nose. Crustaceans hung down from his nose, far enough she was confident he could reach them with his tongue.

He leaned in and gave the queen a toothy smile. "Your Highness should follow me."

The queen felt a fleeting moment of sheer repulsion. Besides the nasty broken teeth, the man's breath was atrocious. The queen stepped forward to follow the man, and the guards fell in around her, two men positioned on each side of her and one bringing up the rear.

Like every citizen of Eden, the queen had served her mandatory year of service in the military during her youth. During her initiation training, she had fallen in love with a handsome young ensign. Even though her father had pledged her to marry the future king, she contemplated running off with Mars. Regretfully, Mars was more committed to the military than to love. Heartbroken, she served her time and married the future King of Eden.

One thing she remembered from her military training was the proper transport of weapons. From the corner of her eye, she saw that the guards' weapons were not only fully loaded but also had their safeties off.

Despite having married the future king, she and Mars had remained close. After being given command of the Ares, *he discovered his strong connection to the ship allowed him special abilities. One of those was the ability to visit and communicate with Aphrodite in her dreams. Since that discovery, they shared all their special moments with one another. Through this time spent in clandestine dream rendezvous, they knew each other better than anyone else.*

That was until she met Jezebel. The stronger she became in her convictions that the two queens could bring this awful war to a conclusion, the further she and Mars drifted apart. Nevertheless, anxiety was now sweeping her away. She didn't know why, but her plan was falling apart. She longed to escape all of this, all her responsibilities, and drift off to sleep so Mars could rescue her from all her miseries one more time and hold her in his arms.

The queen stepped onto the bridge of the Obsidian ship and looked around. No one seemed to notice her presence. The Obsidian Captain, Gunter, was studying his main monitor, memorizing every line of the Ares.

Vastly superior to his own, the design of the ship was brilliant. The bow had the legendary adornment, which so famously sent fear into the hearts of his men. He heard that when angry, the ship looked like a beast about to engorge itself on the blood of its enemy. The luminescent electrical shields that deflected incoming fire caused the ship to glow like it was on fire. While beautiful, it didn't seem all that frightening now.

Gunter observed that, like all Poseidon-class ships, the Ares was divided into five sections. Ares, being a member of the Zeus/Hera class, was longer than a true Poseidon-class ship at 887 feet, as opposed to 729 feet. Other than the difference in scale, she corresponded with descriptions of any of the famous ships of the line. The basic shape of the vessel was like an asymmetrical airfoil. Except for the nose cone, the first section of the ship was sleek and aerodynamic. The captain could tell this ship would slip through any atmosphere with delicate handling and little drag. The center section of the vessel was square and stocky, each side made in a way that the crew could add accessories: additional guns, engines, cargo. No one knew how many configurations existed. They could also use the center section of the ship to allow smaller ships to dock. The tail section curved slightly downwards like the tail of a whale about to dive. Out of the smooth, rolling surface protruded four massive engines. They located large directional thrusters on the sides of the ship, which explained why all the vessels of the class were so highly maneuverable.

The two sections forward and aft of the center docking area housed the guns—all except for the rail guns and the six small rotary cannons on the corners of the fuselage. The captain knew the heavy caliber and speed of her weapons were deadly. No one knew for sure the exact number or caliber of the weapons because they were recessed into the ship. The gun ports on the Ares were too numerous to count from where he was standing. The captain only knew they were ferocious. Once they were set into motion, the fire they could lay down was devastating. Having never seen it, he could only trust the few eyewitness accounts who survived to tell the tale. They said the two sections revolved around the core of the ship. Sailors claimed the angrier the ship became, the faster they spun.

"Someday soon, I will command one of your sisters," Gunter said to himself.

He stood up, after satisfying his curiosity for the moment, and turned to address the queen.

"Your Highness, welcome aboard our humble ship, the Dark Night.*" Casually, the captain walked around the battle station until face-to-face with the queen. "I trust our hospitality has been adequate?"*

The queen did not say a word. She held her head high and continued to look the man in the eye.

Captain Gunter continued, staring straight into the depths of her soul, "My Lord has asked you to accept his apology for not meeting you in person."

Aphrodite replied frostily, "Captain, I am not here on a social visit. I am here to honor my word and deliver the final stone to your king."

"Yes, Your Highness. My Lord advised me you would honor your word. With heartfelt generosity, King Fromm has decided he only wants the jewel. You may return home."

Since infancy, the queen was taught never to let her emotions betray her, but the captain momentarily surprised her. Tears formed on the edges of her eyes, and her hands trembled.

"Return home?"

"Yes, Your Highness. My Lord petitions for one small thing in return."

Having regained her composure, the queen looked the man in the eye. "What small thing might that be?"

Utterly devoid of expression, but with a gleam in his eye, the captain replied, "The Ares.*"*

The queen felt anger rising within her. She realized the mistake she had made. The Obsidians based their entire culture on honor. If she fulfilled her promise, the Obsidians would have to keep their word. But until she personally placed the last jewel into the king's hand, the treaty was void.

Now she was trapped. With no way to fulfill her promise, the Obsidians would attack her kingdom at will. History would show it was her fault if Eden fell. She studied the problem and thought, As long as I possess the gem …

She knew the Ares *would never surrender under any circumstance. Mars respected her command to turn over the gem, but nothing she said would ever convince him to surrender. However, without the stone, the* Ares *would be powerless to defend herself.*

Not if, but when the Ares *was provoked, the Obsidians would have justification to destroy the captain and the ship they despised more than any other: Eden's "God of War." Now she understood why they explicitly requested the* Ares *be the vessel that delivered the final stone.*

The queen understood what she must do. If only she had the strength and inner fortitude to forge the connection between her and Mars.

She had already written the destiny of the men on the Ares *and the mighty ship in stone because of her carelessness.* I should allow them to choose how they fulfill that destiny, *she thought.*

Aphrodite reached into her pocket, closed her eyes, and squeezed the jewel. She tried to slow her breathing and repeated over and over to herself, "Speak less, listen more. Speak less, listen more. Speak less, listen more."

At first, nothing happened. The Obsidian captain, seeing tears streaming down her face, laughed unmercifully.

It was the first officer who noticed it first. "Captain?"

But the captain, reveling in the distress of the queen, ignored him.

"Captain!" the first officer screamed in terror. "The *Ares*!"

The captain pivoted to look at the screen, and the queen opened her eyes. There, in all its glory, radiated the *Ares*, shining as bright as a star.

Every engine on the mighty ship roared its fury, and the *Ares* leaped forward. With every gun firing and fire spewing from her bow, the *Ares* threw herself right through the Obsidian ship!

Chapter Eight

Present Day, Space Station Victory, Earth

Charlie was ill-tempered on many levels and in a cavalier mood. With no apparent consideration for any other vessel, he thumbed through his music playlist and turned on *Perseus*'s exterior speakers.

The journey to the Strivo had begun ominously for the crew as they departed Space Station Victory. The low-end drive on the space ring would not engage so that Stuyck could navigate into the launch zone.

Charlie ordered Stuyck, "Ignite the main thrusters and get *Perseus* moving toward our designated launch point."

Stuyck hesitated. "Sir, the *Perseus* is still in the no-wake zone."

"We will address the repercussions when we return. If we delay, the war might be over before SC gets around to issuing new orders."

As the *Perseus* rumbled past Admiral Mitchell's flagship, the cup of coffee the admiral was nursing flew all over him. Mitchell yelled in his thick Scottish accent, "XO! Ye git Jakeson back 'ere richt noo! Hurry, afore thay mak' thair jump tae subspace!"

Megan Marie alerted Charlie, "Captain, Admiral Mitchell's flagship, the *Tyche*, is hailing the *Perseus*."

Charlie clicked his mic twice to acknowledge M&M. He reached over with his right hand and severed the connection.

Charlie and Maddie had parted company with tension between them. Maddie was furious with Charlie for going, and Charlie was just mad. They had not spoken again after Maddie had left without saying goodbye. As the *Perseus* prepared for the jump to subspace, the refrain from the Foreigner song "Cold as Ice" blared through the loudspeakers.

●●●

Back at Charlie and Maddie's home in South Carolina, the neighbors complained to each other about the archaic music being played loud enough for the whole neighborhood to hear.

Maddie was no longer furious with Charlie. She only felt grief. For once, Maddie had felt content. Only a few more months of loneliness before she would have Charlie to provide a shoulder to lean on and a soul to share her thoughts with—someone who cared enough to listen to her talk. Now, instead of coming back to be with her, Charlie had chosen his career over her. Just like every other person she ever thought had loved her.

Maddie had cried all the way from Arizona. The tears in her eyes as she drove home from the airport flowed like an underground spring. Now, her heart broken, she had no more tears to shed.

●●●

On the outside looking in, Charlie and Maddie seemed like the perfect couple, and only Jacob knew how stormy their relationship could sometimes be. But what could one really expect of a relationship that began at gunpoint?

Chapter Nine

Three Years Ago, Space Command's
Central Intelligence Headquarters, Earth

Jacob studied the stairs leading into Space Command's Central Intelligence Headquarters. An assignment in Intelligence was the last place he expected his orders to send him after graduating from the Space Academy. He had hoped to receive an assignment to a ship of the line, preferably a battleship. If not, then at least a destroyer. Even a reclamation unit like the one Charlie served on during his first three years seemed preferable to this assignment. Jacob liked to keep to himself and wasn't much of an extrovert. He could only imagine what it would be like to serve with a bunch of self-confident, arrogant spies.

Jacob was disappointed his brother Charlie could not make his graduation ceremony, but Captain Halsey refused to allow anything to keep him away. Halsey had been a perfect father to him ever since he was in elementary school. Or at least as good a father as a man could be, considering he also commanded Space Command's oldest battleship, the UCSC *Fortuna*. Even after the incident during his freshman year at the academy, the captain moved heaven and earth to protect both him and Charlie. There was never a day that Jacob hadn't thought about the accident, which he felt certain caused Charlie's career to lumber along at such a slow pace. Jacob had never understood whether it was some implication of wrongdoing or the fact Charlie was missing from his post on the *Constrictor*'s fateful final voyage that had done so much irreparable harm.

Though the images and sounds of that day were permanently seared into his psyche, he still couldn't bring himself to discuss it with anyone, not even Charlie, with whom he shared everything. Had it not been for the incident, Jacob consoled himself, Charlie, at the time the recently appointed first officer on the *Constrictor*, would have died on board the battleship along with all his friends and shipmates. Right before Space Command ordered the *Constrictor* to the Tavarius Space Bubble to intercept an Obsidian fleet, Charlie had to request emergency leave to rush home to Jacob's aid the night Hope died. He drove all night, over two hundred miles, to come home.

Charlie had served most of his career on the small reclamation/repair ship, the *Perseus*. His promotion to the *Constrictor* was his career's big break. After the loss of the *Constrictor*, and hostilities ending between Earth and the Obsidians, he spent the next year teaching history at the Space Academy before being assigned to the *Atlantis*. Jacob had actually taken his required history class under his brother. That class was the closest he ever came to earning a score of less than an A. Charlie wanted to make sure Jacob deserved his grade. Charlie's assignment to teach history at the Space Academy was why Captain Halsey bought the house where they all currently lived on the outskirts of Washington, DC.

Jacob ran up the last fifteen steps, breathed in deeply, and walked through the doors to the building. The lobby looked nothing like the sterile, unambiguous halls and classrooms back at the academy. The floors of the lobby were a white marble tile, the luster of the stone so shiny he looked down between his feet and saw his reflection. Large tapestries covered the walls, depicting images from famous battles throughout the history of Space Command. On the back wall, between the two lines leading to the metal detectors, hung a picture of the *Constrictor*, the most significant, fastest, and powerful battleship Earth had ever built. In the distant background was the fleet, rushing to her aid before the two B Class Obsidian battleships, the *Suidae* and the *Sus Scrofa*, destroyed her in yardarm-to-yardarm gun battle, killing all 749 of her crew. The *Constrictor* tragedy had proven that no lone Space Command ship could stand toe-to-toe with an Obsidian B Class. The cataclysmic battle that followed ended the seven-year-long war between Earth and the Obsidians, thanks to the newly developed CBC units. They allowed Space Command's much smaller fleet to destroy the Obsidian flotilla, which had reigned terror over Earth's forces.

Inlaid into the floor in the center of the room was a large Space Intelligence Seal. Images of water jetting from the outer band of the seal glistened in the light, fabricated from blue pearl granite. The massive star on the seal had sixteen black basalt rays emanating from the center, each representing an individual division of the intelligence community. Dead center, a giant owl sat perched on a limb with its back facing out. The carnivorous bird's head looked back over its shoulder, representing the all-encompassing eye of the service. It gave the eerie impression that its eyes followed you no matter where you walked in the room. The whole purpose of the intelligence service was to know every detail of the threats facing Space Command—threats that might potentially harm Earth, her colonies on Mars, or the military space stations on the moon. Space Intelligence's directive was to thwart those dangers or if not, to at least give SC advanced warning.

Jacob was not sure how he had earned this post, but he had a sneaking suspicion Captain Halsey was behind it. Why the captain would want to entrust him with the secrets of the galaxy was beyond him, since the captain seemed confident Jacob was usually only one step away from bringing trouble into their household. Charlie, though, had always enjoyed the captain's unbridled confidence. Even though Charlie refused to let Jacob take blame, it seemed the captain knew the truth about where the fault lay. After Charlie returned home and took responsibility for the accident to protect his younger brother, never once did the captain question Charlie's innocence.

Jacob stepped into the nearest queue, fidgeting, wondering how long it would take the three giddy girls ahead of him to have their papers processed so he might have his turn. He looked down at the scars on his knuckles. Even now they were a constant reminder of the accident. He hooked his thumbs around the straps holding his backpack so he would not have to look at them.

Behind him, he heard a group entering the building, laughing, and Jacob turned to see who was causing all the commotion. A young woman, doing her best to avoid the advances of one captain and two young commanders, walked across the middle of the lobby. With total confidence, she walked right across the large seal in the floor, stepped around the barrier defining the line leading to the counter, and slid into place directly in front of Jacob. The captain and commander followed her, still battling to keep her attention from the other side of the pylons. Jacob wanted to mention the line began behind him but decided it wasn't worth causing a fuss.

The young lady reached around to remove the barrette holding her hair in a bun while still talking to the officers. It shocked Jacob to see how much hair she had when it tumbled down past her shoulders. The highlights from her hair in the bun had given him the impression she was a blond. As her hair fell over her shoulder, he realized her hair was surprisingly a light brown, the highlights making it warm and shiny looking. Her brown eyes sparkled from the light coming in through the atrium covering the lobby, and he noticed she had a small, obscure beauty mark on the right side of her nose.

Not good at guessing age, Jacob decided she must be three or four years older than he was—for sure, not any older than Charlie. She stood about four or five inches shorter than Jacob, which would make her somewhere around five foot six, her petite frame deceptively obscuring the fact she sported solid muscle-toned arms. Jacob studied her, realizing she could pass for a sister to Hope.

Three girls at the counter, their paperwork now complete, headed for the door. The young woman said goodbye to her admirers and stepped up to the counter.

Behind the counter, the clerk recognized her immediately. Jacob noticed a hesitation on her part upon seeing the young woman, but she greeted her warmly. "Ms. Everett, I am happy to see you again. How may I help you?"

"Please, call me Addison, Joan. I am here to see Admiral Cotterill. He is expecting me," she answered, while over her shoulder discreetly studying the faces of everyone else in the building.

In a complete breach of protocol, she had used the main entrance to the building, there being safety in large public crowds. Usually, she would have slipped into the building without being seen arriving or leaving.

The clerk looked at her computer screen and asked, "I assume you know how to get to his office?"

Addison answered, "I do. Thank you, Joan."

Jacob watched Ms. Everett as she walked toward the entryway, past security, and into the main building. Jacob noticed Ms. Everett look over her shoulder one more time to study the crowd in the lobby. The two guards waved her through without even checking her credentials. Before she stepped through the metal detector, Jacob noticed she pulled a weapon from her ankle and handed it to security. She promptly retrieved it as soon as she made it past the metal detector and then vanished.

From behind the counter, the clerk, Joan, cleared her throat for the second time. "Next," she said, all the niceties she'd had for Ms. Everett gone.

Eyeing Jacob with an air of suspicion, she added, "Might want to shoot a little lower, hotshot. She is way out of your league."

Jacob, returning his attention to the purpose at hand, turned and gave the clerk a grin. The clerk, seeing Jacob's dimpled smile, blushed.

"Welcome to Intelligence," she said.

After studying the papers Jacob had handed her, she added, "Mr. Jackson, I see you are being transferred to SC Evelin, Advanced Technologies from—" Joan looked incredulously at Jacob "You are being transferred here straight from the academy?"

"Yes, ma'am. It was a letdown. I was hoping for a better placement," replied Jacob. The dimpled smile that Joan had seemed to find so attractive was gone. "I graduated with honors, but obviously, I didn't impress the right people."

"Mr. Jackson, being sent to SC Evelin straight out of the academy is nothing to sneeze at. As a matter of fact, it is unheard of. You obviously impressed all the right people. Some people spend their entire careers trying to make it there. Positions in any of the Advanced Technologies departments are amongst the most coveted posts. SC Evelin is the cream of the crop."

Joan continued to study Jacob's documents.

"People with your security clearance shouldn't use the main entrance." She reached into a file cabinet and pulled out a sealed envelope. "In this portfolio are instructions that direct you to your recommended point of entry and the prescribed security protocols. I scheduled you for two weeks of orientation after you start on the fifth."

Now Jacob blushed, wondering if he'd missed the memo that was supposed to teach him all of this. "Thank you. I will study the packet, and I will not mess up again."

Joan smiled. "You didn't mess up. But if you buy me dinner, I will help bring you up to speed."

The offer of a date took Jacob by surprise. He wasn't sure who blushed more, he or Joan.

"Dinner sounds great, but someone has advised me I need to shoot lower. *You* are definitely out of my league," said Jacob. With a half grin, he added, "I am not familiar with the inner DC area. Where do you suggest we eat?"

Joan fluffed her hair and gave Jacob an even bigger smile, her eyelashes fluttering. In beautiful cursive, she wrote her contact information and a note on Jacob's orientation package. "I get off at five. You have plans for tonight?"

Jacob studied the note Joan wrote on the envelope. "I do now. Dinner at your place. You're on. What do I need to bring?"

Joan studied Jacob as though he were a morsel of candy. "Buy a bottle of wine, and I will do the rest."

Jacob turned, bumping into the person in line behind him, and mumbled apologies. As he left, Joan studied his backside, ignoring her next customer. As he exited the building, Jacob turned and looked back at Joan. She gave him a smile and a wink.

Chapter Ten

Three Years Earlier, Space Command's
Central Intelligence Headquarters, Earth

Secretary of Intelligence Admiral Cotterill seemed shocked when Addison walked into his office and closed the door. He fumbled with some papers on his desk and stammered before he coolly greeted her. He did not seem pleased with Addison, but she wasn't sure why.

In her opinion, he should have considered her mission a resounding success. She had infiltrated the Obsidian weapons-smuggling operation and set the Obsidian's guerrilla forces on the South American continent back months, possibly for good. The numbers of executions amongst the guerrillas within their own inner circle had decimated their leadership and caused thousands of fighters to flee back to their homes in fear.

Addison's handler had been explicit in her instructions. She was not to mention to anyone the millions in funds she diverted while in Colombia. Her handler did not even want Addison to share with her what she did with the money. The fortune, now resting in banks in several offshore accounts, comprised enough funds to equip, arm, and feed an entire army for ten to twelve months. Addison would sleep better once she understood what SC expected her to do with the funds. She assumed she would learn more from Admiral

Cotterill, but he never once mentioned it. He only seemed highly agitated she had deviated from her assignment of observing instead of taking it upon herself to destroy the entire clandestine operation.

Silently, she reflected on what few options had been available to her. The men in charge of the funds had unfortunately discovered her while she was uploading their entire computer database. If she hadn't acted when she did, they would have distributed the funds, and she would have been dead. She didn't see an upside to either scenario. While she reflected, Admiral Cotterill, now red in the face and sweating profusely, continued berating her, suggesting she retire and consider another form of employment outside of the service. Throughout her career, Addison had met with the admiral dozens of times. She had never seen him so angry, barely in control of his emotions. Addison thought to herself how much she would love to remove her revolver from her ankle holster and place it in the admiral's big mouth.

Addison, keeping her cool, apologized for not understanding the full scope of her assignment and promised she would not let it happen again. Dispirited and confused, she left as soon as the admiral dismissed her.

Addison made her way down the hall, headed in the general direction of the main exit of the building. Purposefully ensuring the cameras guarding the building would clearly see her leaving, she ambled until she saw several men headed in the opposite direction. She slipped into the middle of the group and carefully made her way back into the heart of the facility.

Addison avoided any of the main hallways where she knew cameras routinely perused, watching for anything out of the ordinary. She found the small office she was looking for at the farthest end of the hall where her handler worked. She slid into the restroom immediately adjacent to it. The temperature in the bathroom was freezing, apparently to keep people from getting too comfortable. The tiled floors and walls amplified the sound of Addison's feet as she entered the last stall.

From the rim of the toilet in the booth next to the wall, she used her lipstick applicator to tap out a coded message against the cover of the air conditioning duct. As Addison tapped out the message, the sound echoed from every corner of the room, and she waited, hoping her handler would find a way to answer her questions. Several times she heard people enter the restroom and leave. After each visit, she again tapped out her silent plea for help.

Addison was in the middle of repeating her message for the fifteenth time when she heard someone enter the restroom. Quietly, she lowered herself back onto the toilet and listened as the person opened the door to the stall next to her. Just as Addison heard the door latch, someone else entered the restroom to wash their hands.

After an extended visit in the first stall, finally, the hydraulic door hinge to the restroom pulled the door shut after the person left, and the woman in the booth next to her sneezed. Addison responded to the sneeze by saying, "Bless you."

From the neighboring stall, her handler's sweet but gravelly voice said, "Where I am from, people say *gesundheit*."

Addison wanted to laugh. "Where I am from, we don't talk to people while they are using the toilet."

The gravelly voice didn't laugh. "What happened?" The tone of her handler alerted Addison that things were worse than she feared.

In a soft whisper, Addison said, "I got caught accessing their database. I uploaded a complete copy of the data onto the secure server so we can review it. I was busted red-handed. I didn't know what else to do. I eliminated the opposition and transferred all their financial resources to a group of offshore accounts. I downloaded enough counterintelligence onto their computers to implicate key members of their leadership of espionage and framed the security chief for the murder of the two men I had to eliminate. They were torturing him for information while I made my escape."

Addison almost had sympathy for the man, knowing the torture the revolutionaries would subject him to. There was no doubt her plan to frame him succeeded because she could still hear in vivid detail his screams and cries in her dreams. Her sympathy only went so far, though. She also still remembered the numbers of people he had tortured to death for his own amusement.

"Okay. You did the only thing possible. I am glad you made it out alive. Someone within SC is not happy with our success, but I do not believe they know about the missing money," replied the woman in the next stall. "I can't figure out who isn't happy or why. I believe we have a mole here who must have been benefiting from the South American operation. Either that or they sympathize with the Obsidians and would like to see us renew the conflict. I know for sure you are in grave danger."

"So what now? What do I do with the money? It is an incredibly large amount. And where should I go to lie low?" asked Addison.

"Keep the money and consider it an inheritance. You will need it. I am only sure of one thing: you are no longer safe. This has gotten too dangerous. It is time to do what you do best and disappear. You need to reinvent yourself."

The inheritance remark pained Addison. She knew her handler understood she was an orphan. Not having a mother defined how Addison had perceived herself her entire life. A small girl whose own mother was not willing to fight to keep her. Addison knew that was the reason SC had recruited her for many of the missions they assigned her. She had absolutely no ties. No one would notice if she went missing, and no one existed who might ask questions.

"I will protect the money until you find a better way to use it," Addison said.

The gravelly voice became firm and authoritative. "Agent Everett. I gave you an order on how to use that money. Those orders are final. Do you understand?"

Addison conceded, realizing her handler must truly fear for her safety to hand down such an order. "Yes, ma'am. I understand."

"Good." Addison's handler sounded much more pleasant. A small backpack slid under the divider to the stall. "I have prepared a new identity for you. All the details are in the information packet, and I have uploaded your new persona into the international registry."

Addison opened the bag and glanced at her new passport. Maddie. Her new name was Maddie, with an "ie." She liked the name spelled that way.

The handler continued, "Memorize the file and destroy it immediately. For your safety, you must disappear until we uncover what is going on. I worry soon we will be back at war with the Obsidians. Be prepared for the possibility that this is most likely our final goodbye."

A chill ran down Maddie's spine. Her handler wasn't offering her an escape plan or a place to lie low. She was ordering her to adopt a new identity and to disappear for good. Maddie knew she had no choice but to accept her handler's advice and vanish. She had made personal enemies of some of the most powerful people in the universe, and she understood that, eventually, she would end up paying for it with her life. But as bad as things sounded, Maddie might need extrication to escape the city.

Maddie picked the bag up off the floor just as another person entered the restroom. Neither Maddie nor the woman in the stall next to her made a sound, her handler's tension reverberating through the metal wall between them. Maddie was positive she heard the door to the restroom open and close while the person in the first stall flushed. Then she listened to the booth open, water run at the sink, and the door to the restroom open and close one last time. Maddie knew her handler had left. Quietly, she pulled out the outfit in the backpack the handler had given her, put the data disk in her bra, and pulled a blond wig down on her head. With confidence and purpose, she walked back through the main lobby and straight out the front doors of the building the same way she had entered it.

Chapter Eleven

Three Years Earlier, Space Command's Central Intelligence Headquarters, Earth

Outside the building, Jacob had grabbed a four-piece chicken strip basket for lunch and was now doing his best to flag down a cab. As the yellow taxi with the checkerboard rooftop pulled alongside the sidewalk and the vacancy light turned off for Jacob to get in, the woman who had cut in line in front of him earlier slid past him into the back seat. She looked different—wrong hair color, new dress—but Jacob was positive she was the same woman. Jacob was an easygoing person and willing to overlook almost any slight once, but under no circumstance would he tolerate it twice. He used his knee to prevent her from slamming the door closed and jumped in beside her.

He stared at her and said, "Evidently, we are traveling in the same direction."

Maddie looked back at the young second lieutenant with a look of disbelief and said, "I don't see you having very much success with that as a pickup line."

Jacob smiled at Maddie. "Seems to be working so far."

The cab driver sat, impatiently looking over his shoulder, waiting to hear where they wanted to go, assuming they were engrossed in a lover's spat. "Where to?" he asked.

Maddie sneered, "Go to the zoo so I can return this animal back to where he originated."

Jacob, not to be outdone, said, "First, you don't think my pickup line will work, and now you want to take me home to meet your mother?"

Having been reminded one too many times today she did not have parents or anyone else to care about her, Maddie lost her composure. With tears welling up in the corners of her eyes, she unloaded on Jacob.

"You prick. It so happens I don't have a mother. I don't have a father, either. You don't understand what it's like to live knowing you have no one in your life to call when things aren't going well. Why don't you take your stupid cab and go home to your mama!"

Maddie reached for the door handle to get out, but Jacob grabbed her by the arm. "Stop. I'm sorry. I never knew my father, and I lost my mother when I was eight, so I can empathize."

Maddie didn't remove her hand from the door handle; she only stared at Jacob. After a long pause, she said, "I'm sorry."

Noticing the tears forming in her eyes, Jacob smiled a goofy smile at her.

"Yeah, life can be hard sometimes," he said, then hesitated, waiting to see what she would do. "Rough day?"

Maddie's face brightened a little. "Let's say it hasn't been a good one."

"Well, it can only get better. Where you headed?" asked Jacob.

Maddie had to think for a minute. She had just gotten off a plane earlier that morning from Panama City. Everything she owned was back home in Charlotte. She studied Jacob a minute and decided for once in her life she just wanted to tell someone the truth.

"I don't know yet. I returned from an overseas assignment and had to leave in a hurry. All my baggage is in a tent in the middle of a jungle, and now I have orders from my handler to disappear. You?"

Maddie somehow felt relieved, having vocalized her dilemma.

"I have a few days before I report for duty, so I am headed home. My ..." Jacob thought for a moment how best to explain. "My family lives south of the city, in Arlington. I plan to crash there until time to report for duty."

Jacob paused again. "If SC stranded you in DC for a few days, my family has a guest house out back no one is using. You are welcome to crash there if you like."

Maddie chewed her lip. She didn't need to get involved with some green-behind-the-ears second lieutenant. Besides, what right did she have to include him in her troubles? For all she knew, someone was stalking her this very moment, hoping to kill her. Or worse.

Jacob, sensing her hesitation, clarified: "I am not asking you out. You are on your own this evening. I have a date."

As the smile appeared on his face, Jacob sensed Maddie relax.

Maddie thought about the options she had available. "Okay. Are you sure your family won't mind?"

Jacob laughed. "My brother isn't due home for at least another week. He serves as the first officer on the *Atlantis*. The captain who raised us left to return to his ship. He commands the UCSC *Fortuna*. That's the sister ship to the *Constrictor*, who the Obsidians destroyed during the war. Only Space Command knows when the captain might return."

"Wow, a whole household of space jocks. As long as it is no trouble, I will take you up on your offer," Maddie said, a smile spreading across her face. In her head, she offered a prayer of thanks. Just when she didn't know where to go next, an opportunity for a place to lie low fell in her lap.

The house Jacob took Maddie to was a pleasant surprise. But first, she made Jacob wait in the taxi while she ran into a store to buy some clothes and personal items. Jacob yelled out the door behind her, "Grab a swimsuit. You can swim in the pool."

The main house was very spartan, each room filled with the barest minimum in furniture. The living room contained three love seats, two of which reclined with cup holders in the middle for a drink. In the room's center sat a large coffee table. Maddie assumed they primarily used the room to watch sports because the coffee table was full of sports magazines. Each stack of magazines was in neatly organized piles. She also noticed someone was a Braves fan.

The kitchen was the one exception. The kitchen was obviously well used. Pots and pans hung above the stove within easy reach. In the center of the room sat a large, solid-hardwood cutting block, the center filled with divots from regular use. Maddie, following Jacob out the back door, found herself on a raised patio with two grills pushed into the corner, both with covers draped over them, and a kamado grill by the door. A bag of wood chip charcoal leaned half open against the stand that supported the egg-shaped grill.

Maddie took two steps down off the patio onto the apron of a kidney-shaped swimming pool. The faint smell of chlorine hung in the air. Jacob was leading her to an apartment that looked like a small bathhouse. The back of the bathhouse backed up to a thick hedge shaded by a stand of hardwoods that seemed to drop down into a small valley. The double glass doors were the only entrance or exit Maddie could see at first. Jacob entered a four-digit code into the lock on the door and slid it to the side for Maddie to enter. While she looked around, Jacob went to the far wall and lowered the temperature on the air conditioner.

On the opposite wall, Maddie noticed a metal door exiting out the back of the building. Glancing through the window, she could see there was a small utility shed behind the apartment, surrounded by the stand of hardwoods she had already spotted. She considered the layout ideal: a good view of any threats approaching from the front, and plenty of cover if she needed to escape out the rear.

"Sorry it's hot in here. We don't use it often, so we rarely bump the AC any lower than eighty. It will cool off pretty quickly," apologized Jacob.

"Trust me, this feels fine. I lived in a jungle for the last month. There were mosquitos larger than hummingbirds there," Maddie said, laughing.

Jacob stepped into the small bathroom, digging under the counter to replace the almost-empty roll of toilet paper.

"What were you doing in the jungle?"

The sound seemed to echo off the slate floors where Jacob was working.

Maddie started to spin a tale to explain, then remembered how nice it felt to tell the truth. Besides, he would never believe the truth anyway.

"Nothing much. Overthrew a counterinsurgency, stole a substantial fortune, killed people who asked too many questions. You know, the usual stuff."

Jacob moved on to replacing the towels with clean ones, throwing the used ones in a basket to take back to the house and wash.

"So, were you in Colombia or Venezuela? I understand the Obsidians have a small standing army down there itching to make our lives miserable."

Maddie almost panicked. She could not imagine any plausible reason Jacob would know such things unless Space Command had sent him to find her. She half expected him to turn around with a gun in his hand.

"How are you so knowledgeable about the situation in South America?" Maddie asked, trying to hide the suspicion in her voice. She bent as though tying her shoe, releasing the clasp that held her backup weapon to her ankle.

Jacob slid the dirty laundry basket out the door and stuck his head around the corner. With a big smile, he said, "I start every day by reading the headline news. It's in every paper. Fighting has broken out amongst the small army factions. They are killing each other faster than Unified Command ever could. You timed your departure well."

A wave of relief washed over Maddie. Carefully, she slipped her pants leg back down over her ankle holster.

"Wow, sure sounds like it."

Maddie had a strong urge to grab a tablet to read the latest news, curious what the media was reporting.

Jacob stepped out of the bathroom and picked up the laundry basket. "Okay, it's all yours. I am having dinner with the girl from the counter at the agency at seven, but there is plenty of food in the fridge. Help yourself to anything you want."

Maddie frowned. "Do you mean Joan Resciniti?"

Jacob smiled and looked thoughtful. "Well, I didn't get her last name. But Joan is her first. I heard her speak to you when you checked in."

Maddie grinned. Jacob might think he was going for dinner, but if she knew Joan Resciniti, Jacob wouldn't be home until after breakfast tomorrow morning at the earliest.

"This your first date with Joan? Surely you go to the trouble of learning both the first and last names of girls you date." Maddie couldn't help but laugh.

Confused, Jacob asked, "What's so funny? She an ax murderer or something?"

Still laughing, she shook her head. Maddie said, "No, you will have fun. The only danger you can expect tonight is an assault on your chastity."

Jacob tried to force a jovial expression, but Maddie noticed a glum look spread across his face.

•••

Jacob and Maddie lay out by the pool the rest of the afternoon talking. While Jacob wasn't oblivious to the fact Maddie was a beautiful woman, he wasn't physically attracted to her. Instead, her easy disposition and warm personality made him think of what a great sister she would make. He considered the term "mother" but couldn't imagine a woman with a body like Maddie's as a mama. Her muscle-toned legs were every bit as firm as her arms. Even with the modest one-piece bathing suit, he noticed she didn't just have a slim waistline; she had abs.

Jacob knew there was something up with Maddie, with the way she had rushed out of Central Intelligence earlier wearing different clothes and a wig. But he couldn't help but feel like there was something very real about her. Jacob was surprised to find himself relaxed in the pool chair, eyes closed, quietly talking about things he had not thought about in ages.

Maddie had a way of disarming people, allowing them to speak freely. She listened intensely, never appearing to judge, and always seemed to know when to gently interject just enough to encourage the continuing dialog. Maddie seemed to be genuinely interested without making it feel like she was fishing for information. Jacob told Maddie about his mother going missing in the Wilhelm Galaxy and the captain coming to stay with them, finally deciding he couldn't entrust them to anyone other than himself to raise.

Jacob hesitated, wondering what it was about this woman he had just met. He had never discussed or shared the thoughts going through his mind presently. The emotions Maddie evoked with her questions sent a whirlwind in him to which he couldn't articulate an appropriate answer.

"None of us really discussed my mom. Charlie was always there. So was the admiral. But we never discussed how her vanishing made us feel. We just banded together, determined to survive."

"What would you have talked about?"

"Men are supposed to be strong. Charlie and the admiral both have the depth of character required to handle adversity. I always felt weak seeing them shoulder the pain without complaint."

"Maybe you, the admiral, and your brother are more similar than you think. Maybe they lack the ability to express their feelings also?"

"Doubtful. Neither lack decisiveness. Obviously, neither lost Mom with unfinished business. I cheated myself. There were things I failed to enjoy while I had the opportunity. When the admiral informed us that Mom was gone, I realized I'd wasted my chance."

"None of us are privy to the length of our mortality. I plan on making every moment of my life count. I always tell Joan: I will sleep after I die!"

Jacob laughed but thought to himself how much he would love to sleep an entire night without being awakened by a horrific nightmare.

"I didn't have time to address Mom's disappearance. I was scrawny when I was young, so I had enough to worry about, preventing other kids from bludgeoning me. Charlie tried to intercede, but by the time I made it to high school, Charlie wasn't around."

"Well, you obviously grew out of the scrawny stage," she said with a mischievous grin.

"It was the admiral who helped. He enrolled me in boxing with Charlie. We spent most of our time pumping iron, but we did learn to defend ourselves."

"I enjoy a regular workout regimen. It allows me time to think."

"The admiral said the best thing for teaching you to think is learning to play chess. Charlie played, but he preferred to spend his time with the admiral, learning to fence."

As easy as Maddie was to talk to, he couldn't bring himself to tell her about the accident. Despite wanting to discuss his girlfriend's death, Jacob couldn't. The tragedy of losing Hope still hurt too much for him to even say her name aloud, even though the accident had occurred over six years ago. Jacob acknowledged to himself he must address the issue. But not now. He was not ready.

Maybe part of the reason Maddie was so easy to talk to was because Jacob knew she had secrets, and yet he knew she had been vulnerable with him, even if it only consisted of unloading on him in the cab. He had the distinct impression she did not often lose control.

Jacob did tell Maddie about dating a few girls while in the academy after Hope passed away. The relationships always ended the same. They wanted to take it further than Jacob was willing to or capable of. They usually decided there was something wrong with him. Chastity was not a word many people nowadays understood. The more times someone discarded him, the more convinced he became that a sexual relationship was too important to be entered casually.

The only person Jacob pictured ever talking to about the accident was Charlie. They had gone through so much together. He could not imagine being all alone in the world, isolated like Maddie with no support system. At least with Charlie, he had a brother he knew would always have his back. He also had the captain, who, despite allowing little leeway, Jacob knew was always there for him if he ever needed him.

Maddie also found it amazingly easy to talk to Jacob. She had never really opened up to anyone. Her world consisted of falsehoods and made-up realities. Sometimes she wondered who she really was. It had felt so good to actually tell someone the truth about her life for once.

Maddie automatically started with her usual fabricated childhood story, but she remembered she had already told him she didn't have parents. She shared with Jacob the trauma of her mother leaving her at the door of a Methodist children's home, promising to come back for her and never doing so. Abandoned only two weeks prior to her seventh birthday, Maddie was confident her mother would return, just like she did when she was dropped off at school. Maddie hadn't panicked until the day of her birthday.

Dozens of parents would visit the home and fall in love with Maddie, bringing her presents and showering her with praise. Then they would vanish, never to visit again. It wasn't until after she reached adulthood that she learned they lost interest when they found out her mother could not be bothered to sign a TPR. How simple would it have been for her mother to sign a Terminate Parental Rights form? It wasn't like she ever had any intention of returning to take her home. The experience reinforced in Maddie's mind she was not worthy of love.

She envied Jacob's relationship with his brother and the admiral.

Life at the orphanage was a conundrum of constant change and complete rigidity and predictability. Maddie quickly learned people left and were never seen again. Her mother, friends, the caretakers at the orphanage—no one important in Maddie's life was ever permanent. The only constant at the group home was the regulated schedule. Maddie had understood that with so many orphans residing in the group home and so few caregivers, things had to happen on a rigid schedule.

The only advantage to growing up in an orphanage was that Maddie had learned to be successful. She had learned to be self-sufficient, superficially charming, and sneaky. Most importantly, life at the home made her strong. Maddie learned at an early age she could only depend on herself.

The most painful part for Maddie was the fact that she knew her biological mother had married one of the wealthiest people on the planet, Wade Adams, and had had three more children. Not once had Maddie's mother made contact with her, not even a birthday card. Maddie explained how the first time anyone had told her they loved her was after she started dating. It didn't take her long to figure out the guys she dated were in love, but not with her. Just her her—just her body. Maddie explained she had written relationships off. Never again did she intend to be taken advantage of. She didn't need a man or a lover; she needed no one. She didn't need a man to be her hero. Maddie could take care of Maddie.

Maddie concluded her story with, "I may be more like a man than I care to admit. Sharing feelings doesn't come naturally to me. You are easy to talk to, Jacob."

It wasn't until Jacob's stomach growled that he realized he would be late making it to Joan's place if he didn't leave immediately.

Chapter Twelve

Three Years Earlier, Charlie and Jacob's Home, Arlington, Virginia, Earth

Desperate to keep abreast of what was happening in Central America, Maddie was sitting in the kitchen reading the news when she heard someone pressing the buttons on the keypad to the front door. She looked at the clock, surprised to see it was only 9:30 p.m. Jacob wasn't kidding when he shared his opinion about sex outside of marriage. Maddie had to admit his convictions impressed her.

The beeps on the door lock grew more persistent. Maddie considered opening the door for him. Still, ingrained habits die hard, and something did not feel right. Quietly, she reached over and slid her hand under the towel she had left lying on the table after she came in from the pool. With her thumb, she gingerly released the safety on her small Smith & Wesson .32 Bodyguard.

Jacob was either having trouble with the keypad or he didn't remember the code because it was taking him a long time to get the door open. Then she realized whoever was out there trying to enter the house didn't know the code. That might mean someone tracked her to Jacob's home and was now coming for her. Still, her pragmatism dismissed the possibility. Anyone contracted to eliminate her would be a professional, and she would have never heard a professional's approach.

Now, more curious than scared, she slipped off the stool and eased over closer to the door. If the person ever got the door open, she would greet them looking straight up the barrel of her .32. A .32 might not have the knockdown power of the .40 caliber she usually carried, but a shot right between the eyes at point-blank range would not end well for anyone on the receiving end.

Standing to the side of the doorway, she listened. Finally, whoever was at the door entered the correct code and the lock clicked. The second the person turned the handle, she grabbed the handle on her side and yanked the door open, placing the revolver right between the blue eyes of a stranger. The man's eyes grew wide, but Maddie noticed they did not show fear. With surprising speed, the stranger grabbed the handgun, his hand around the chamber so the mechanism would not fire, and twisted it out of her hand. In one fluid motion, he rolled the grip of the gun into the palm of his hand, pointing it at Maddie.

He said, "Lucky your finger wasn't in the trigger guard or it would be broken." Carefully aiming the revolver between Maddie's eyes, he stepped back. "You are too young for the captain, and Jacob brings no one to the house, so maybe you can tell me who you are and why you are aiming a revolver at me in my own house?"

Despite the obvious differences, Maddie knew instantly this was Jacob's brother. Slowly, with her hands up, she stepped back into the light of the foyer.

"I am a friend of Jacob's. Sorry. You startled me. Jacob said you wouldn't be back for at least another week."

Maddie felt her heart flutter because the man standing in the door took her breath away. He was not as broad in the chest as Jacob, but he was about two inches taller and had piercing blue eyes. However, at this moment, they looked extremely dangerous. As he stepped sideways through the door, placing his back to the wall, she noticed the way he carried himself. He moved with confidence and spoke with authority. He knew he was in control of the present situation.

Charlie surveyed the room. "So where is Jacob?"

Charlie's eyes continued to wander until they stopped on Maddie's. He wavered when he looked into them. They were a beautiful soft brown with hints of hazel around the edges. Her healthy-looking skin had a beautiful tan, giving her arms and face a golden glow, except her cheeks, which had a touch of pink. Charlie wondered if her dermatologist had ever warned her about the dangers of UV rays.

Maddie shrugged her shoulders, really wishing Jacob was there to explain her presence to his brother.

"Jacob had a date at seven. Considering who he is dining with, he might not return before sunrise," Maddie answered, in as soft and innocent a voice as she could muster.

Charlie admired how well toned the young lady was. Perfect. Slightly muscled yet very feminine. Charlie studied her face one more time. "Any true friend of Jacob's would know better."

From behind Charlie, Jacob cleared his throat. "Know better than what?"

Charlie wheeled around. He was relieved to see Jacob but still leery of the woman who had pointed the gun between his eyes. Jacob leaned against the front door frame.

"I see you have already met Maddie. She got stranded in town for a few days, so I offered her the pool house. Please don't kill our guest, Charlie. That would be impolite."

Charlie studied Jacob for a second and looked back at Maddie. First making sure the safety was on, he spun the gun around in his palm and handed it back to Maddie, grip first. After she accepted it, Charlie extended his hand, offering to shake hers.

"Hello, Maddie. I am Jacob's brother, Charlie."

Maddie studied Charlie's hand for a moment, then extended hers to accept his handshake. Her eyes locked on his.

"It is very nice to meet you, Charlie. I am Maddie, with an 'ie.' Everyone always insists on spelling it with a 'y,'" Maddie said in a very uncharacteristically chatty way.

They stood there staring at each other, neither offering to be the one to look away first.

●●●

Jacob wondered what he was witnessing. Both Charlie and his guest were acting strange. "You two need to move because I'm starving. Anyone want something from the grill?"

Maddie's eyes broke away from Charlie's, slightly embarrassed and feeling a little flustered but not sure why. She asked Jacob, "I thought Joan cooked dinner?"

Jacob, walking toward the kitchen, answered over his shoulder without stopping or turning around. "I'm not sure she planned dinner to be the main event tonight. I must have given the wrong impression when Joan and I met."

●●●

Jacob, Charlie, and Maddie sat around the patio table eating kabobs and talking until after midnight.

Jacob asked, "So how long will you be home before you have to report back for duty?"

"The *Atlantis* returned home early, was paid off, and the crew sent home," Charlie answered. He worried about what that meant. He feared SC might furlough and leave him Earthbound, the cuts amongst the officers high because of the number of ships being deactivated. Charlie added, lamenting, "When my time to reenlist comes around, they might release me from the service for good."

It was getting late. Charlie called it a night. Jacob and Maddie soon followed.

Within an hour of falling asleep, Jacob woke up tossing and turning, drenched in sweat. He couldn't remember all the details, but he knew he had been dreaming. Not that he needed to remember—all his nightmares revolved around the same theme.

Even in the dark, Jacob could sense the dark cloud swirling around the room. Ever since Hope's death, Jacob could sense the cloud swirling anytime he was stressed or depressed.

Jacob tried to shake the feeling of despair and the cobwebs from his mind so that he could drift back to sleep. He lay staring at the ceiling, knowing it was a useless exercise. He compared it to an ant walking around the rim of a funnel. Once the ant slipped over the edge, it could only spiral farther down into the abyss. His dreams comprised gurgling screams beneath dark cloudy water. He knew he needed to act, to do something, but he was paralyzed, unable to do anything but listen to the screams over and over. They would stop only when he woke with a start, lathered in sweat. The nightmares had been a nightly ritual since the accident. It seemed the more tired he became, the worse the dream.

As soon as the sun rose the following morning, Jacob raced down the stairs, relieved to be free of the nightmares that plagued his sleep. He started cooking breakfast, the scent of bacon pulling Charlie out from under his covers and down the stairs before Jacob finished scrambling the eggs.

Chapter Thirteen

Three Years Earlier, Charlie and Jacob's Home,
Arlington, Virginia, Earth

The following morning, Charlie slid out of bed as soon as he heard Jacob leave for work, intending to slip out to the pool house to invite Maddie to breakfast. Maddie had been staying in the pool house for a few days now. The three of them had spent most of their time sitting around the pool during the day and enjoying meals cooked on the grill in the evenings.

Jacob and Maddie seemed to have such an easygoing relationship. They joked and laughed together as if they had been friends for years.

Charlie never remembered Jacob mentioning her name before, so he assumed they were just friends. He couldn't help but wonder how long they had been friends and why he had never talked about her.

Charlie found Maddie mostly pleasant but somewhat disarming. Every time he looked at her, it was as if she was smiling with her eyes. Her lips matched the smile in her eyes, but it seemed like she had a secret that she wasn't telling. It must have been a happy secret because her eyes seemed to dance.

When he got to the pool house door, he saw Maddie was already up and had set Jacob's computer on the small kitchen table. They had never used the table to the best of Charlie's knowledge. It had been shoved into the corner of the pool house and someone, probably Captain Halsey, had stored stacks of boxes full of old papers on it. Charlie assumed they contained receipts. Maddie must have cleaned it off to make room for the computer.

Charlie, curious, peered through the window in time to see Jacob's sign-in page appear on the screen. After a few brief online adjustments by Jacob, he watched as Maddie ran his laptop from the guest house. Charlie, feeling like a stalker, went back to the house and started breakfast. When Maddie showed up, she claimed she had overslept.

Charlie was not sure what he had witnessed, but he was certain Maddie was more than a second lieutenant who had retired from SC. His best guess was she was connected to the intelligence service. She did not deem him "authorized to know." That disappointed Charlie, considering the time they had spent together over the past few days. Charlie was intrigued by her and wanted to know everything about her.

The two of them enjoyed an extended breakfast together. Charlie announced he needed to hit the shower and run errands. Maddie, not sure what she intended to do with herself all day, continued to sip on her coffee.

Charlie asked, "Got any plans today?"

Maddie paused, seeming to think for a moment. "It seems my social calendar is empty right now. I guess I might lie around the pool some."

Charlie had a straightforward dating rule. If you took a woman out you didn't know, only invite her to lunch. Charlie had served onboard spacecraft for so long, he could eat lunch in fifteen minutes. Quicker, he reasoned, if the company wasn't pleasant.

"I have a few errands to run, but if you don't mind tagging along, would you want to catch a quick lunch? The errands won't take long."

Maddie studied Charlie. She must have been calculating whether he was simply being friendly or if he had just invited her on a lunch date. Then she answered, "Okay. Like I said, my social calendar seems to be open right now."

When he asked Maddie to lunch, he was thinking something fast and light. But the two of them enjoyed talking so much while running his errands, Charlie decided instead to take her to the small restaurant where he had taken the girl he used to date, a beautiful Obsidian girl who had immigrated to Earth with her father just after the war. As they were walking to the restaurant, Charlie stepped back to slip around her and keep himself on the side of the walkway closest to the road. He reached around her once more when they made it to the entrance to open the door for her. She looked approvingly at these gestures, and he didn't yet realize that she had never been out with anyone who understood the nuances of proper manners.

The quick lunch turned into more than an hour of laughing and talking. They had arrived early to beat the lunch crowds. Their waitress, seeing large crowds gathering outside the doors, wanted to speed the couple along, but there was something sweet about how the two of them hung on each other's every word. Charlie, realizing they had monopolized the booth way too long but not wanting his and Maddie's time together to end, asked, "What do you say to ice cream?"

Maddie seemed to be enjoying herself too. Besides, what else did she have to do? "Depends. Do you eat chocolate or vanilla?"

"It doesn't matter. I always get so much chocolate syrup on whichever I order that no one can tell the difference either way." Charlie laughed. "You?"

"No one has ever accused me of being vanilla," Maddie said playfully as Charlie led her across the plaza to the ice cream shop.

Over there, Maddie had to taste every flavor the store offered. Charlie, generally not the patient type, savored every moment as Maddie discussed the pros and cons of each flavor. Charlie listened to Maddie's vivid descriptions of each. Moving down the aisle while also conversing with the young girl behind the counter, she finally made it to the multitude of chocolate variations. She described each as she debated, starting with the plain chocolate. As Maddie got to the mint chocolate flavors, her description of them made Charlie imagine a sinful mixture in his mouth, both rich and minty all at the same time. After so many great descriptions, Maddie unceremoniously ordered a vanilla cone dipped into hot chocolate fudge.

Maddie and Charlie, eating their cones, walked across the parking lot to an old-fashioned bookstore. Some titles on the store's shelves had been out of print for decades. On a dusty bottom shelf, Charlie found a complete volume of books by his favorite writer, Patrick O'Brian. Charlie exuberantly summarized the tale of Captain Jack Aubrey and his close friend, Stephen Maturin, to Maddie.

Maddie watched and listened as he studied the binding on each cover. As she listened to Charlie tell the tale, she could feel the roll of the ocean under the keel of the HMS *Surprise* as it prowled the sea searching for her prey. When they left the store, Maddie slid the owner's business card into her purse, thinking what a wonderful present the books would make.

Still not wanting to call it a day, Charlie suggested a movie. He explained he had not been to a theater to see a film since he and Jacob last went with their mother. In other words, years. Maddie listened to Charlie describe the moments he shared with his mother, her heart yearning for even one memory of her own with a parent who loved her. Halfway through the movie, Maddie laid her hand on Charlie's, his hand turning over, palm up, and their fingers interlocking.

By the time they finished the movie, Charlie's stomach was growling again. Never having adjusted to the more fashionably late hours people ate at nowadays, he suggested dinner. Maddie, as much as she wanted the day to continue, reminded Charlie that Jacob had suggested grilling together.

The tail end of a passing summer thunderstorm greeted them at the door as they left the theater. Under the portico, waiting on the last drops of rain to stop, they nestled into the corner of the building. Charlie and Maddie, still clutching each other's hands, leaned into each other and softly kissed.

Chapter Fourteen

Three Years Earlier, Charlie and Jacob's Home, Arlington, Virginia, Earth

The next few weeks were a blur for Jacob. Maddie had taken his invitation to crash at their place for a few days seriously. She and Charlie would both show up in time for the breakfast Jacob cooked every morning and served on the table next to the pool. Jacob would then leave and head to town for another boring day of orientation while Charlie and Maddie hung out by the pool. Maddie already had a sensational tan, but by the third day even Charlie, who had not had a tan since he was in college, was turning as brown as a nut.

After a long, mind-numbing week, Jacob opened the door to the house to find Charlie and Maddie lying together, sleeping on the couch. Charlie was lying flat on his back with his head resting on the soft armrest, his right arm dangling off the sofa and his knuckles barely touching the floor. Jacob had his arms full of groceries and a brown paper bag containing two bottles of wine.

Jacob used his chin to keep the wine he bought from falling off the grocery bag onto the hardwood floors leading from the foyer into the kitchen. He experienced a tinge of jealousy at how comfortable the two of them looked lying there together. Maddie had her head resting on Charlie's left shoulder, her mouth and nose almost buried in the crook of Charlie's neck.

Her left arm was slung across his chest, her hand inside Charlie's half-unbuttoned shirt. Maddie's fingers embraced his left shoulder in a way that seemed more intimate than if Jacob had walked in and found them in bed together having sex. Jacob couldn't help but admire Maddie's firm, muscled arms and her long, well-toned leg draped across Charlie's legs. He turned his gaze away when he noticed the shorts she wore did *not* cover the nice round shape of her bottom. He saw Maddie had nothing on under her shorts, the tan line from the bikini he had seen her wearing earlier visible.

As he turned to go back to the kitchen, he saw Maddie's bikini top thrown across the room, caught on the corner of the couch. As he turned the corner into the kitchen, Jacob's elbow knocked one bottle of wine over as he set it down, causing it to roll off the counter. Jacob narrowly missed grabbing it before it plunged toward the floor. The sound of the bottle shattering caused a flurry of activity in the den as first Maddie, then Charlie, scrambled to their feet, hurriedly repositioning their clothing.

Charlie yelled out, "Jacob? Is that you? You okay?"

Jacob, on his knees trying to sop up the wine all over the floor, yelled back, "Yes, sorry. I knocked over a bottle of wine."

Charlie and Maddie scurried around the corner, wide-eyed. Jacob couldn't help but notice Maddie also had nothing on under the thin camisole she was wearing.

"Wine? Are we celebrating something?" Charlie asked with surprise.

Still mopping up the wine, Jacob replied, "Nothing special. I told Joan that Maddie was staying here, and I invited her to come grill steaks with us tonight."

Jacob stood up and went to the sink to wring out his dish towel. "I hope that is okay with you two."

Charlie bent down to help pick up pieces of the wine bottle, but Maddie, still standing in the door, struggled to hide the shock on her face.

•••

Maddie couldn't believe Jacob had told someone at SC Intelligence where she was staying. Her first reaction was that she needed to run, both for her safety and for Charlie's and Jacob's, but when she looked at Charlie, she knew she couldn't. She only hoped she wasn't placing him in danger by staying. She wished she could take him into her arms and tell him everything. How she could feel so strongly about someone she had only known for a few weeks was beyond her. As dangerous as staying was, she couldn't leave without knowing whether this thing between them was or wasn't real.

The one thing she believed was that if she ever had to come clean with Charlie and tell him the truth about her life, then, like everyone else, he would push her away.

A few hours later, with their dinner guest on the way, Charlie volunteered to man the grill. Maddie asked Jacob if he would run her down to the local strip mall. She did not want Joan to be the prettiest girl at the dinner table tonight. Not finding what she was looking for, she took much longer than usual to pick out the perfect dress. Unlike most women she knew, when Maddie went shopping, she went to the store knowing what she was looking for, bought it, and left. Today, though, much to Jacob's chagrin, she couldn't find what she wanted. After going through every dress in the store, she finally found the perfect one hanging on the return rack outside the door to the dressing room. She took the black spaghetti-strap dress into the dressing room. She loved the way the short flared skirt showed off her legs.

When she got to the register, she realized she didn't have enough cash to pay for her selections. Discreetly, she slipped her fingers into the secret compartment of her wallet and pulled out the new debit card her handler had given her. She went blank for a minute and realized she had failed to memorize her new PIN number. Jacob, who must have sensed her hesitation and assumed she was short on cash, stepped forward and slid his card to pay for her purchases. Out of the corner of her eye, she saw Jacob notice the sexy new nightgown she had also picked out. His expression didn't give away any form of judgment.

As they drove, Maddie pondered what she knew about Jacob. On one hand, he projected confidence. In other ways she sensed his insecurity. Jacob reached over and started another of the oldies he seemed so infatuated with. Jacob's music certainly differed from what she listened to. The songs always seemed to tell a story or set a mood when either Charlie or Jacob chose them. The words to the song made Maddie realize that she and Jacob were a lot alike. They both hurt deep inside.

Some group named Imagine Dragons was singing. The beat of the drums was vibrating the floorboards in the car. The words resonated with Maddie. She wondered what happened in Jacob's life that made him so withdrawn. The words to the song were engaging. One line really was haunting. How could Jacob seem to relate with being a "zero"?

Yes, Jacob seemed withdrawn and was not forthcoming about something, but he didn't have low self-esteem or lack confidence. Surely there was more to Jacob's withdrawn tendencies than only the loss of his mother when he was very young.

They almost made it back home before Jacob said anything.

"I don't know the exact nature of what you do at the agency, but I hope you will carefully consider how you handle whatever this is going on between you and Charlie. He doesn't deserve to get the wrong idea and then have you vanish on him. If you have secrets, then you need to be as open as you can with him so he knows what he is getting into."

Maddie didn't reply or speak to Jacob the rest of the way home. She wondered, *What would Charlie Jackson's reaction be if he knew my past?*

•••

Jacob and Maddie had not been home long before the doorbell rang. Jacob opened the door to find Joan standing under the small overhang of the portico. Slung over her left shoulder was a leather bag that could have been either a purse or an overnight bag, Jacob wasn't sure which. The strap crossed over her shoulder and clung close to her body between her breasts.

Jacob gave her a small hug and welcomed her inside, trying not to stare at her long, slender legs, which were barely covered by the short skirt she wore. The knit skirt fit snugly with different color stripes that wrapped around Joan's shapely hips. Most of the thin lines were shades of pink, broken up by the occasional aqua, gold, or white stripe. Joan wore a snug-fitting black tank top tucked into the skirt. The top accentuated the gentle curve of her hips and slim waistline. The front fit tightly across her chest and was cut low enough to reveal enough cleavage that Jacob had a hard time concentrating on looking Joan in her eyes. Jacob admired how she looked in her high heels, and the sweet scent of her perfume invaded Jacob's nostrils, the smell enhancing the pheromones she was putting off, drawing him in closer and closer.

Jacob was glad they were eating with Charlie and Maddie tonight and thankful she hadn't looked or smelled this good the night of their first date when he went to eat at her place. He doubted he would have had the inner fortitude to resist her obvious sexual advances given the effect she was having on him at this moment. Joan seemed to sense she had awoken a primordial animal desire in Jacob and was well pleased with herself.

Charlie stepped around the corner, holding out his hand to greet her, ushering her past the kitchen directly from the foyer into the living room. Jacob slid back into the kitchen, making sure the food he had in the oven wasn't being overcooked. Friends might say two things about Jacob: he was an excellent cook, and he loved to eat. Jacob was almost always hungry. The sides he was preparing in the kitchen smelled even better than the steaks Charlie had on the grill.

Charlie, having welcomed Joan, stepped back out onto the patio to flip the thick ribeye steaks he was cooking, giving Joan an opportunity to step into the kitchen to speak to Jacob in private.

In almost a whisper, she said, "Jacob, I need to speak to Addison—" Joan hesitated, embarrassed by her slip of the tongue.

"I mean Maddie, in private for a moment. People from the agency came to my home and questioned me, searching for her."

Jacob looked at Joan inquisitively. "Searching as in need to contact her? Or looking for her as in ...?"

Carefully, looking back over her shoulder, she whispered, "Looking for her as in she is in serious danger. Two men who I highly doubt are from the agency came to my house looking for her, posing as agents. They had a photograph of the message I wrote on your orientation package, which had to come from the agency security cameras. I also suspect they know we are eating dinner together tonight. They showed me pictures of a woman they believed to be Maddie leaving the agency with you in a taxi. They asked your name and where they might find you."

Jacob considered what being in trouble at the intelligence agency might mean. "Do you think Maddie has done something illegal? If they are looking for me, why haven't they come to speak with me?"

"I can answer that one. I looked up your agency records. Your address on file is an apartment on campus at the Space Academy, but I doubt it will take them long to put the pieces together and come here to question you," replied Joan. "Maddie and I know each other from our time together serving on the *Enterprise*. I know Maddie might bend a rule here and there, but I would bet my life she would do nothing illegal. Besides, the guys asking questions looked more the mercenary type."

Jacob peered out the kitchen window that faced the driveway. "Is there any chance they may have followed you here?"

"I saw two guys trailing my car before I left on my way here. I will wager they are almost to Philadelphia by now," Joan said, a grin on her face. "I asked my former roommate to swap cars for the weekend. She is going home to see her parents. I saw the two goons pull out of the alley down the street in a decrepit Toyota a few minutes behind her. I think they placed a tracking device on my BMW."

"What do you think will happen when they figure out it's your roommate driving your car, not you?" asked Jacob, genuinely concerned for Joan's former roommate.

He saw the hesitation in Joan's eyes.

"I think we need to go speak to Maddie."

Jacob walked over to the counter and picked up the bottle of chilled red wine. He raised the bottle over the sink and struck it against the rim, causing it to explode.

Thunderstruck, Joan asked in an exasperated voice, "Why did you do that?"

Jacob shook his head. "Dang, that was our last bottle of wine." He peered across the living room out the two sliding glass doors and saw Charlie flip the last steak onto the platter.

"I guess I will have to ask Charlie to run to town real quick and get more," Jacob said, giving Joan a quick wink.

•••

Joan and Jacob intercepted Maddie inside the door to the pool house. Joan eyed Jacob, then looked at Maddie. Maddie told her she could speak freely, as she trusted Jacob implicitly. Maddie didn't say a word as Joan retold her whole story, adding key points she had failed to mention to Jacob in the kitchen—like the fact Joan was aware Maddie had just returned from a mission in South America where she'd had to flee under duress. Also, Maddie was in extreme danger, and her handler had ordered her to disappear.

Joan said, "Your handler approached me after I sent her word people were looking for you. She has instructed me to provide proof Addison Everett is dead."

After she finished listening to what Joan had to say, Jacob half expected Maddie to pack her few belongings and run.

Instead, with a tear in her eye, she told Joan, "I have met the man I think I am meant to be with forever. I can't run away. Help me."

Chapter Fifteen

Three Years Earlier, Charlie and Jacob's Home,
Arlington, Virginia, Earth

Jacob always considered patience to be his greatest virtue. The first few weeks of serving at his new position at Space Command's Intelligence Service in the technology division had been a real test for even his patience. His immediate supervisor, Jules Gustafson, was an absolute tyrant to work under. She always nosed around, studying what people were working on. Jacob had already heard the rumors that she reputedly waited until someone was on the cusp of something big, then swooped in to take credit for the work. Jacob didn't care if she took credit for everything he did, but her standing behind him, breathing over his shoulder, got on his nerves.

Meanwhile, Maddie had been living with Charlie and Jacob for so long, she no longer seemed like a visitor. Out of respect for the admiral, Jacob knew Charlie would not allow her to move into the house with him, but Jacob suspected Charlie was sleeping in the guest house more nights than he did in his own bed. Jacob had anticipated someone cornering him to ask where they might find Maddie, but evidently Joan had done a good job of throwing the men off her trail, and they had moved on to search elsewhere.

Maddie and Joan were not convinced the men were really gone. They decided Maddie needed to make some alterations to her new identity. Maddie and Joan asked Jacob to do the unfathomable: they asked him to open a remote link from work and allow Maddie to use his security clearance to contact her handler and make the necessary changes to her identity. Joan offered to help Maddie but quickly acknowledged her security clearance was nowhere near high enough to do Maddie any good.

Jacob initially refused to even consider the request. He told them he was too young to spend the rest of his days in Leavenworth or Colchester. Finally, after arguing their case until the wee hours of the night, Jacob agreed, on the condition he must watch and know everything Maddie did on his computer.

Jacob and Maddie agreed to start first thing in the morning, hoping Ms. Gustafson would be less attentive than usual. It still took a while to get Maddie logged in through his laptop at the pool house, thanks to Ms. Gustafson lurking outside Jacob's cubical inside SC Evelin. Once Jacob had gotten Maddie in, she was astonished to learn how high Jacob's security clearance really was. The file on her mission to South America was much bigger than she remembered. As she studied it, Maddie realized the reason she hadn't seen most of the data in the file was that it was so high above her own security clearance. She was not able to retrieve the directory to most of the files using her own login. She quickly created a back door into the databank so she could peruse it later.

That part of her plan complete, she shot off a secure message to her handler. While she waited for a reply, she opened her personnel file. Jacob read as fast as possible, learning much about the mysterious woman his brother seemed so infatuated with. What he read confirmed most of what she had told him. The parts of the story she left out were unbelievable. If half of what he read was accurate, then in her short career, Maddie had made enemies across half the universe.

As Jacob read, an instant message popped up on his screen. "Why are you contacting me?"

Maddie replied, "I was informed I need to die?"

"Correct."

"Then supply a body," Maddie replied.

Jacob sat and watched the instant message window, wondering what that directive really meant.

Finally, the mystery person Maddie was speaking to replied, "Do not contact me again."

Then a long series of computer code appeared in the window. Thinking quickly, Jacob hit Ctrl-Print Screen. Jacob was not confident he got the whole code because as he released his finger from the button, the entire message disappeared.

Maddie spent a few more minutes fiddling with her personnel record. The most notable thing Jacob noticed was the image of Addison Everett changed to a woman whom Jacob did not recognize. Silently, Jacob watched as Maddie made other changes. Blood type, new fingerprints, and retina image were all edited, and then Addison Everett disappeared.

Jacob opened a notepad and hit Ctrl-Paste. In the window, the computer code Jacob saw on his screen earlier appeared—at least most of it. Jacob wasn't sure, but he still wondered if he missed the last few characters.

A couple of moments after he closed the screen, he sensed the presence of someone looking over his shoulder. He glanced at his supervisor's desk and saw her half-eaten sandwich still sitting in front of her, along with her purse and security card. She seemed to always leave the card lying under the edge of her monitor. Jacob looked up and smelled her stale breath filtering down on him.

She stared at his blank screen and said, "You will never amount to much around here if it takes you this long to get started every day. You should at least open a file and pretend to be studying it."

Chapter Sixteen

Present Day, En route to the Strivo Corridor, Intergalactic Space

While neither Charlie nor Maddie was happy, the fact was the journey had begun, and everyone's focus was back on the mission. Charlie and Jacob had already worn the crew out running battle simulations, and Charlie's dark mood was not making things any easier. Neither Charlie nor Jacob allowed any rest for the weary.

The *Perseus* remained under the control of the CBC for the entire hop. Once they locked their hull into the space ring, SC had taken complete control of the ship. Jacob questioned why they even bothered having a crew. Now, with reentry less than fifteen minutes away, every man and woman on the *Perseus* locked themselves into their battle stations.

The crew of the *Perseus* had been training nonstop ever since they entered subspace. Over the course of seven weeks, they simulated every scenario Charlie or Jacob dreamed up. Both brothers felt assured by the exercises that the crew was as prepared as possible.

The one scenario neither brother ever considered as a possibility unfolded. The CBC controlling the three ships dropped all three into the landing zone simultaneously. Before anyone could react, the *Nicodemus* and the *Shelter* burst into flames and dissolved, no debris anywhere. They vanished.

The flaxen horn on the *Perseus* wailed, and every collision light lit up. Diligently trained to watch their warning lights, every crew member braced for impact. On the screen, Charlie saw three incoming missiles. Jacob, ever vigilant, hit the release button for the ship to disconnect from the space ring, and the *Perseus* banked hard to starboard.

The *Perseus* barely cleared the space ring before the missiles struck right where the ship was, moments before, locked in. Immediately, the ring broke into three distinct pieces and continued to travel through space, tumbling aimlessly end over end.

The extreme g-forces on the hull of the *Perseus* caused a container in the hold to break loose, and the shifting load caused the ship to go into a flat spin. On the primary monitor, the image was moving so fast that neither the helmsman, Chief Stuyck, nor Charlie could make out any point of reference to use to guide the ship and recover control.

Between labored breaths, Charlie called out, "Stuyck, reduce the power to idle and neutralize the stick and rudder!"

Panting, Stuyck replied, "I am trying, Captain, but I cannot bleed off enough speed. I need some point of reference to orient the ship!"

Jacob leaned far to his left, fighting against the lateral g-forces, to reach the controls to the monitor. Jacob, always quick to see solutions to a problem, even under immense pressure—or in this case, the proverbial fog of war—turned several knobs, which changed the refresh rate on the screen. The *Perseus* was still careening wildly in a flat spin, but the monitor now showed the path of travel in slow motion. Stuyck used the tumbling pieces of the space ring as a reference point. By concentrating on that point, he was able to bring the *Perseus* back under control.

Charlie saw the faint blur of an Obsidian destroyer and two corvettes to the port side of their direction of travel. To the starboard side, he made out the vague blur of the asteroid belt.

As soon as Chief Stuyck regained control, Charlie shouted, "Bank hard to port toward the waiting warships."

The gun crew opened fire, and Charlie yelled, "Stuyck, turn the *Perseus* hard to starboard!"

The poor *Perseus* made its best attempt at a barrel roll and took off at full throttle toward the asteroid belt.

As soon as the bow entered the leading edge of the asteroids, Charlie ordered full reverse on the engines to bleed off speed. Once satisfied, he ordered all ahead one-third.

At first, Stuyck performed exceptionally well, guiding the ship through the tumbling metallic masses of iron, nickel, iridium, palladium, platinum, gold, magnesium, and other metals, but it rapidly became apparent the asteroids were too densely packed. With each brush against the floating masses, the *Perseus* shuddered, and the crew could hear ominous creaks and groans as the shields, which prevented the asteroids from puncturing the vessel, pushed against the metal superstructure. Stuyck grazed one asteroid after another, so Charlie had no choice but to call for the *Perseus* to come to a full stop.

The situation map showed the problem to be compounding faster than Charlie feared. Instead of three ships, Charlie watched as a fourth ship entered the zone and came to a stop. Charlie assumed it must be a support ship, perhaps a small fuel tanker. Simultaneously, the first three ships opened fire. Projectiles slammed into the asteroids all around the *Perseus*.

Charlie keyed his intercom, and over the deafening sound of cannon fire, he shouted, "Lt. Jackson! Get Andrew up here stat!"

To Charlie's dismay, Myers had taken the liberty of moving Andrew's duty station from the bridge where Charlie had assigned him and placed him back with his brother and cousins two floors down.

He looked at Stuyck. "Slide over and make room for the kid."

Again, Charlie keyed his intercom. "Jacob? How do those warships keep missing? We are sitting ducks! Can't they see us?"

Jacob replied, "I think they can see us fine. I think their guns are homing in on the steady drone of our engines. All these asteroids are causing us to echo from every direction!"

At that moment, the pneumatic transport ejected Andrew onto the bridge. Charlie pointed. "Set your butt right there and strap in!"

Jacob shouted, "Charlie, if you don't get this tin can moving, eventually one of those pricks will get lucky and lob a shell right up our six!"

Charlie released his rigging and leaned over Andrew. "That joystick is only a video controller. Consider this ship nothing more than one large video game. I have seen you in the simulator. Now, I need you to lose those warships by flying us through all this mess. You got it?"

Andrew didn't say a word. He imagined his father sitting at the helm on the *Constrictor*. In his mind, Andrew heard his father admonishing him to breathe in deeply and exhale slowly. His father always told him to first try to understand what you must overcome. To accomplish that, your brain needs fresh oxygen. He tuned out the sound of the shells hammering away all around them. Carefully, Andrew studied the controller and then the screen. He took the controller, using his thumb to adjust the settings, and the view on the main screen zoomed out until he could see all the way around the *Perseus*. Then he wiggled the joystick, and the *Perseus* moved sideways a little and started forward.

Charlie strapped back in and keyed the mic to talk to Jacob privately over the noise of the ship.

"I have an idea," he said. "Get down to Engineering and prepare two small probes with external speakers. Engineer a way to deposit them in our wake. I will also have a present sent to you. Hopefully, there will be an opportunity for us to throw it out the back of the bus too."

Jacob turned and vanished into a pneumatic transport. Andrew had already moved the *Perseus* deep into the asteroids without a scratch.

Charlie paged his quartermaster. "Stidham. Those thermal bombs you have been complaining about? I need you to have them delivered aft to Lt. Jackson. If all goes well, I intend to get rid of them for you."

Andrew was adding distance between the *Perseus* and the warships, but they were still lobbing shells all around her. Moving deeper into the belt, the echoes of the engines ricocheting from the asteroids seemed even more random. Finally, the three ships gave chase. Despite their much narrower superstructure, they seemed to have much more difficulty maneuvering than the *Perseus*. Soon, they were taking damage with every turn of their rudder.

Charlie studied the warships' every move. The crew could not tell from his lack of expression what he was contemplating, but they had all served under Captain Jackson long enough to understand a plan was forming. Finally, the ships ceased firing and it became obvious they had given up pursuing the *Perseus*. They had all worked themselves into the abyss. None could figure out how to exit the quagmire. Every time they dared to maneuver, they took even more damage. All three ships had damaged guns, antenna, and sections of their hull sliced open.

On the *Perseus*, the crew watched as one corvette attempted to send out a repair crew to cut away some wreckage. The repair team cut a long cable attached to a sonar mast, which caused the ship's bow to drift to the port side, causing the corvette to ram into random asteroids. The corvette was making so much leeway it looked like an automobile dog tracking.

More crew members watched with interest to see what might happen. The repair team eventually cut the last cable holding the mast. About that time, the corvette glanced another asteroid, and the tumbling mass bounced into a gun turret, crushing it. The asteroid swept down the side of the ship, dragging both the sonar mast and the repair crew out to space. Soon after, the corvette started breaking up.

Charlie keyed the mic. "Jacob, our friends seem lost and can't find their way out. Launch a probe into the middle of the group and play the sound of our engines in a continuous loop. Maybe that will help mask our sound while we try to move to a more advantageous position. It would be nice if they inched closer together."

The entire ship felt a little thump. At first, Charlie thought Andrew had brushed against an asteroid. He glanced at Andrew, who shrugged. Then, he realized what caused the sound. Jacob had taken the deck-to-deck pneumatic transport located near the exterior bay doors and modified it to use as a launch tube.

On the situation monitor, Charlie tracked the small satellite Jacob launched as it weaved its way through the minefield of asteroids. At first, it surprised Charlie that anyone on the bridge could maneuver the probe so well. Then it dawned on him what Jacob must have done. Concluding what Charlie was up to, he must have retrieved another of the young teenage hackers and given them a flight controller. Once the probe got close to the destroyer and corvette, Jacob turned on the P.A. system. Both the destroyer and corvette quickly repositioned their guns and fired in the general direction of the probe with everything they had.

None of the shells came close to their target. Instead, with every shot, the labyrinth of asteroids multiplied exponentially as they shattered into smaller pieces, making it even more arduous for the Obsidian ships to move.

Charlie ordered Andrew to fly the *Perseus* in a large loop, shying away from the Obsidians, and maneuver out of the minefield. This took several hours, but the *Perseus* eventually made it into the open space of the corridor. The stranded Obsidian ships had long since quit firing, although the distinct sound of the *Perseus*'s engines was still heard humming amongst the rocks.

Ensign Marie hailed Lt. Jackson. "Sir, I am picking up lots of clicks, whistles, and pulsed calls. I believe the Obsidians are trying to talk to each other. I believe we can deny them communications if that probe can generate more background noise."

Charlie inquired, "Lt. Jackson, M&M, what do we know about how they interface?"

M&M responded, "No one knows for sure, sir. At the academy, they told us they do not utilize radio waves. That much we know."

Jacob added, "Our fleet has had no one survive an engagement long enough with an Obsidian warship to report back any new observations. From what we have seen so far, I am venturing to guess they use sound waves for both communication and targeting, conceivably more. There is an acoustic theory I heard about when I worked at SC Evelin, which suggests they understand how to detect steady monotone sound waves from afar. Theoretically they could pinpoint a steady cosmic vibration faster than the actual sound wave could reach a receiver. That would be a determining factor for them to use acoustics over the distances needed in space. If that is the case, they might be able to detect vibrations faster than the speed of light."

"Jacob," Charlie ordered, "have Engineering prepare to launch the second probe with an oscillating speaker. Connect the sound system to my personal music library. I would like to test that theory. I think you might be on to something."

It only took Engineering a few minutes to make the necessary modifications. It took longer to locate Charlie's music library. The technicians, Curry and Carney, glanced through the Captain's music library and joked about his taste while they worked. There were classics ... and then there were *classics*.

"Wonder if he listens to anything from this century," whispered Petty Officer Carney. "If we must listen to classics, I wish he would choose some old-school Jimi Hendrix. He summed it up best— 'When the power of love overcomes the love of power, the world will know peace.'"

Curry shook his head. "Carney, you are a crazy ol' coot with yo pot belly and bald head. Hendrix isn't worth an ounce of salt. Besides, if peace broke out, where would we be? Back on Earth gazing at the stars? What the Captain needs to play is some good ol' ELO, or better yet, Queen. Nothin' tops Electric Light Orchestra! And Queen? Queen was the bomb!"

Carney grimaced, making a mental note to never discuss music with Curry again, and he let Lt. Jackson know they were ready.

Charlie immediately recognized the thump of the improvised launch tube. The situation board started tracking the second probe directly.

"Lt. Jackson, if we can deny the Obsidians' communication and sonar, I want Andrew to maneuver the *Perseus* in close enough to deploy those thermals." Charlie said. "We will assemble an IED."

Jacob replied to Charlie, "I see where you are going with this. We can use the asteroids as shrapnel. We can hit them with rubble from one side, and the shock wave might thrust them into the asteroids on the other."

Jacob began calculating angles on the situation map and placing pins where he decided the explosives might produce the desired effect. Andrew, weaving between obstacles, directed the *Perseus* toward the designated drop-off points. In the meantime, Charlie thumbed through his playlist. When he found what he was looking for, he hit "play."

The music was so loud that even the crew on the *Perseus* heard the deep bass through their helmets. The lead guitar strummed, and the words to the timeless classic—which no one professes to like, but somehow still knows—"Hotel California" played. The rat-a-tat-tat of the drums reverberated through the hull. Charlie hoped the Eagles song was appropriate because while the Obsidians were free to check out any time they liked, he had no intention of allowing them to ever leave.

Charlie placed the song on a loop. It played over and over unabatingly. The crew of the *Perseus* wasn't sure if Charlie was trying to cover the sound of the *Perseus* or trying to drive the Obsidians insane. They worried they might be the ones to succumb to the torture first.

After placing the charges the way Jacob had instructed, Andrew slogged the *Perseus* back to the safety of the wide-open corridor. Occasionally, one of the Obsidian ships would fire an indiscriminate shot. Whether they thought they had located the *Perseus* or were trying to extinguish the sound of the music provided lively debate amongst the crew. The Obsidians seemed to accept the fact they were hopelessly hemmed within the asteroids. Neither of the remaining vessels dared try to maneuver to escape.

Charlie studied the trajectory Jacob assigned each warhead. He and Jacob argued about the pros and cons of the way Jacob had placed them, and the argument seemed to grow rather heated, especially considering Charlie was the captain and Jacob only a lieutenant. Most captains encouraged opinions, but only when requested. There didn't seem to be any observance of the chain of command between the brothers over this issue. "The textbook insists we must have the bombs detonate close enough to breach their shields," argued Charlie.

Jacob shook his head in disbelief. "Forget the textbook. You are wrong! We must use the asteroids as shrapnel to achieve the best effect."

The crew listened in awe at the exchange. Jacob won the debate. Devoid of any expression, Charlie ordered the detonation of the warheads.

The shock wave from the bombs shoved the Obsidian ships backward, savagely slamming their hulls into the surrounding asteroids. The vessels broke apart as remnants of asteroids crashed into them from every direction. Charlie saw the destroyer snap in two when a small asteroid passed through it amidships.

On board, the crew watched. No one dared to say a word. The shock wave passed underneath the *Perseus*, lifting her by the bow, then gently put her back down.

After several minutes of reverential silence, Charlie cleared his throat. As though he and the crew had not just watched hundreds of Obsidian sailors die and the loss of their own ships, Charlie ordered, "I want damage reports on my desk. Stuyck, return to the helm and set a course to intercept the fourth vessel."

Chapter Seventeen

Present Day, the Strivo Corridor

Charlie and Jacob wore identical perplexed expressions. What they presumed was a supply ship turned out to be a total enigma. The ship never offered to flee. It just sat there as if waiting for them.

Once the *Perseus* approached close enough to bring the unidentified ship into focus on their screens, they were even more perplexed. The ship was unlike anything they had ever seen. It bristled with weapons along the walls on the round sections of its fuselage. Charlie had confidence he also saw the rifled bore of at least one, maybe two, rail guns protruding out the prominent nose of the craft.

Charlie's immediate reaction was to direct the *Perseus* to disappear back into the asteroid field. After a moment's uncertainty, however, he ordered the *Perseus* to come to a full stop at her present position. The ship in the distance seemed lifeless.

For once, Charlie wished he could ask SC for counsel, but that option was not available. Regular radio simulcast would take two weeks to travel to Space Command and the same length of time for the *Perseus* to receive SC's reply. Another option was to install the CBC stored away in the hold of the *Perseus*. The crew also retrieved the unit from the space ring on their return trip back to intercept the mystery ship. Jacob announced he could salvage it and have it operational within two or three days.

Unfortunately, Charlie had no faith in the CBC. It seemed to him the CBC posed a greater danger than the enemy. He possessed questions he couldn't answer. Was the CBC the problem? Were the Obsidians able to compromise the system, or did the problem stem from SC itself? These were frightening questions. Might SC have a traitor or mole feeding the Obsidians information?

The one thing Charlie and Jacob agreed on was that the ship they discovered was not Obsidian. Charlie began to doubt whether the Obsidian warships that attacked them even knew of the vessel's presence. He studied the footage of the attack. The newcomer didn't appear on his situation board until late into the timeline. That only proved the *Perseus* might not have picked it up on the situation board immediately. It might have been on the scene the entire time and they had missed it.

"How could we have missed it?" Charlie mused almost to himself.

"Where could it have come from?" Jacob wondered aloud.

Charlie ordered his crew to stay on high alert. He left standing orders that if the mystery ship made the least movement, whoever the watch officer was at the time should direct the *Perseus* to retreat into the asteroid belt.

Charlie wanted options. He assigned his teenage hackers the task of charting escape routes within the belt. *Perseus* launched several small probes into the belt, and Charlie had the kids working around the clock mapping out navigable routes. Charlie noted how well every one of them had flown the small probes with never a mishap.

Eventually, he limited the mapping project to the Oglesby kids and started cross-training the Rushing brothers to serve at the helm of the *Perseus*. He increased the difficulty of the drills until soon they both outperformed Chief Stuyck, who watched, imagining himself being reassigned to a much less desirable position onboard ship.

Once Jacob pronounced all the repairs to the ship acceptable and the hold secured, Charlie had all nonessential personnel stand down. He wanted his crew rested before investigating the mystery ship closer. Charlie wasn't sure what to expect. In his experience, he found the unexpected always happened when men and women were tired or hungry.

•••

Charlie invited Jacob to dinner in his personal quarters. While the crew devoured their meager rations in the mess hall two decks down, Charlie wanted to be able to meet with Jacob and talk with a degree of privacy.

No warship allowed much personal space for their crews. The *Perseus* was no exception. Each crew member on the *Perseus* had their own small cubicle. They divided most of the enlisted personnel into six common areas with nine berths in each area. The berths lined the walls down both sides of the long slender hallways. The cubicles were large enough for an average-sized man to sleep. There was one closet area on each side of the hall where everyone had enough space to hang their dress uniform, and SC issued each crew member a footlocker to store the rest of their possessions.

The *Perseus* allocated the officers a little more space. The two areas for the officers, affectionally known as the "goat locker," had four cubicles, each with a common area intended for all eight officers to share. *Perseus* was three officers short of her full complement, so they used the three extra bunks as an additional storage area. Berths for the officers on the *Perseus* were the same size as the berths for the enlisted men, but each officer had a small closet to store dress uniforms. Lt. Myers and Lt. Jackson each had a private room. This allowed them additional storage space and a small but functional desk. The one redeeming grace on the lower deck was that, usually, at least a third of the crew members were at their stations or working elsewhere on the ship at any given time.

The only cabin with any comfortable space was Captain Jackson's. Jacob envied the fact Charlie had enough room to entertain. The

Captain's quarters on the *Perseus* were not considerable, but it had a very comfortable foldaway bed. The large table occupied most of the cabin. It served as a dinner table, the Captain's desk, and often as a worktable. If no one wore combat gear, the table sat six people. That only left Thomas Lappilus enough room to serve the captain and his guests.

At this table, Charlie and Jacob pondered what the *Perseus* should do next. Jacob took a bite of his sandwich. With his mouth still full, he asked, "Have you read any of the files on the disk the Windsor guy gave us?"

Carefully placing his napkin back in his lap, Charlie replied, "Yes, I have read every file on the disk. They seem to be bits and pieces of a disjointed book of mythology. Not sure why he insisted we read them."

"My thoughts exactly. Do you remember when the captain of the *Ares* nose-planted his ship into that Obsidian battleship?"

Charlie laughed. "When the queen delivered the jewel?"

"Yes. Now try imagining the ship the Obsidian captain describes in the book."

Charlie closed his eyes, wanting to dream up some great wisecrack in response.

"Holy crap!" Charlie exclaimed suddenly, jumping out of his seat so quickly that he slammed his head into his bunk located directly overhead.

Charlie landed back in his seat with a thud and massaged his head with his hand to see if he was bleeding. "But that is a fairy tale that happened … what, nine or ten millennia ago?"

"That story might be a fairy tale, but can you give a better description of the ship less than eight klicks off our starboard bow?"

Charlie looked doubtful. "What are you suggesting?"

Jacob shrugged his shoulders. "We aren't accomplishing anything sitting here looking at it. I say we try to board her. Why feed and carry two SWAL teams if we aren't going to utilize them?"

Charlie laughed. "I sure hope there isn't a ghost crew over there waiting for us. Speaking of SWAL teams, do you feel tired all the time?"

"Not tired. I am just sore all the time."

"Me, too. I asked Doc Laird to examine me, curious what was happening. Those dang SWALs have been playing with the gravity plates again. If you go hit the scales, it will shock you to learn you have gained twenty pounds since we left port."

Jacob grinned. "With Dan cooking, I have probably gained more than that. That man knows how to cook!"

"It would not surprise me to learn everyone on board is in the best shape of their lives."

"They claim it is theoretically possible for a human to adapt to a gravitational environment between two and three times that of Earth. I would think that constitutes a serious exercise regimen," Jacob stated.

"If I want to exercise, I will go use the exercise equipment," Charlie replied wryly. He stood up and rubbed his head. He looked up, making sure he latched his berth, and said, "I think it is time to go to work. We have a ghost ship to capture!"

Chapter Eighteen

Present Day, the Strivo Corridor

"**W**hat the heck is the captain thinking? Hypothetically, if we approach without being blown to oblivion, what then?" asked Bedenbaugh. Medium height with chiseled features, this was the young Aussie's first assignment since graduating from commando training.

"Why don't you focus on your job? If the captain says we can take her, then we can. Besides, look at her. Not a gun, antenna, or light has changed since we found her here," huffed Benson.

Although the youngest of the SWALs, Benson had more combined combat experience than any other team member outside the two team leaders, Shealy and Peck. With his easygoing but dominant personality, he easily commanded as much respect as either.

"You have never read that story about the Trojan horse, have you?" growled Bedenbaugh. "Mark my words. I refuse to emplane that thing first!"

Confidently, Benson slammed his magazine back into the breach of his weapon, twisted the bayonet on the end, and exclaimed, "Don't worry. I will go first. You just make sure you are right behind me, covering my six!"

•••

Despite sitting in a universal shipping lane with an unidentified pocket battleship sitting off his port bow, Charlie did not appear to be in much of a hurry. For the next thirty-six hours, he drilled his crew. Charlie wanted them to practice every scenario imaginable. Unfortunately, he did not have the foggiest idea of what to expect. There were advantages to having two gung-ho SWAL team leaders at his disposal. Charlie passed all the infiltration planning over to the team leaders, Shealy and Peck, so he might concentrate on other things.

After making a few suggestions, Charlie didn't dare offer Jacob any more advice concerning how to best lock on to or enter the craft. Jacob was a professional and much better versed than anyone else. That left Charlie with overseeing the maneuvering to position the *Perseus* directly behind the stern of the warship.

Jacob divulged no secrets from his time at Space Intelligence's think tank, but Charlie had observed enough to know Jacob's ability to plan and execute a mission was unparallel to anyone he had ever served with. It was Jacob who first raised suspicions that installing the CBC might compromise the *Perseus*. He never would say why he believed the apparatus was dangerous, but he certainly took no initiative to install it either, even with Lt. Myers complaining that not installing it constituted a major violation of orders. Charlie, at one point, half expected Dillon to send an official letter of protest to SC, but they had been serving together for years now and no one at SC seemed to be the wiser.

•••

With so much idle time, Charlie decided to exercise the teenagers some more. He had them simulate maneuvering at high speed within the asteroid belt using their newest maps. His goal was for them to become experts at allowing the *Perseus* to disappear somewhere only the foolish would dare follow. Or to use Charlie's favorite Alexander Pope quotation, "Fools rush in where angels fear to tread." Unfortunately, the next line in the poem read, "Foolish people are often reckless, attempting feats that the wise avoid." By preparing, Charlie wanted to ensure that the *Perseus* wasn't the fool in question. The small probes had been mapping the field nonstop since *Perseus* launched them. It surprised Charlie how much data the boys and Olivia had already accumulated.

"Sorry, sir," young Andrew whimpered. He had hit the same asteroid three times in a row, trying to make a high-speed turn around it on the simulator. "Are you sure the computer can accurately predict the *Perseus*'s capabilities? I am certain if the simulator will allow me a little more power in the turn, I can make it around Jaws."

"Jaws?" questioned Charlie.

"Yes, sir. The guys and I have given some of the more interesting 'roids names."

"So why did you name that one Jaws?"

"Because when we were young, my mother used to take Roland and me to the beach every summer right before we went back to school. Every year, the week before we went, she would make us watch this old movie called *Jaws*. The film had a shark in it that scared the crap out of me. You know, like the thought of having to make *Perseus* circle that 'roid!"

Charlie laughed and patted him on the shoulder. "If the simulator says *Perseus* can't make it, then she probably can't. But there is one factor the simulator cannot account for."

Andrew perked up. "What factor is that?"

"The ingenuity and determination of her crew. Keep trying, because if someday our lives depend on being able to make it around Jaws, I want to know you are ready."

Charlie hung out with Andrew and practiced with him, making a couple more attempts at slingshotting around Jaws. After the second disastrous conclusion, Charlie patted him on the shoulder again and left.

Andrew rebooted the program and set about hitting "start" again when he had an epiphany. The way Captain Jackson spoke reminded Andrew of his father. That sounded like something he would say. Lost in thought, Andrew grabbed his backpack, removed his tablet, then laid it on the table and stuffed everything back into the storage compartment. Grabbing his tablet, Andrew began thumbing through his pictures, trying to find what he was looking for. He stopped on a photo of the crew of the *Constrictor*. In the picture, to the left of center in the front row stood his father. Andrew zoomed in close to study the man next to the captain of the ship.

Andrew almost dropped his device. He couldn't believe what he saw. The Executive Officer in the photograph was Captain Jackson.

Andrew thumbed through more of his father's pictures. In every photo of his father posing with his friends, Captain Jackson was always close by. In the final photo, Captain Jackson had his arm draped over his father's shoulder. They were both laughing. Andrew knew his father hadn't been overly fond of the captain of the *Constrictor*, but he had always bragged that his ship had the best team ever assembled to fly and fight her. He had claimed they were undefeatable.

Andrew was confused, though. If Captain Jackson was the *Constrictor*'s first officer, then how was he here today? Andrew turned off his tablet and tossed it back into his knapsack. More determined than ever, he hit the start button on the simulator to take another crack at Jaws.

•••

Charlie stood outside the door to the simulator, reflecting on the impossible mission the *Perseus* had been assigned, wondering why the admiral had really sent them. His plan must comprise more than only disrupting commerce. If not, then a destroyer instead of the *Perseus* and two obsolete frigates would have made more sense. The *Perseus* wasn't equipped for this. The one thing he knew was the admiral did everything for a reason. He was the smartest man Charlie had ever met. *What did the admiral know that he hadn't shared?*

If the mission's primary purpose really was to disrupt commerce, then without the frigates, severing the head from the Obsidian monster would be as impossible a task as the monumental task given to the mythological Perseus of removing the head of Medusa. It would not be accomplished through mad fighting skills. It would require quick, clever thinking. Charlie knew for the admiral to convince Space Command to even allow the mission had been a feat. There was no telling who he had to blackmail to get permission.

Still, Charlie was optimistic. The addition of the SWAL teams was a stroke of genius, giving the *Perseus* the perfect means to accomplish her task. In the mythological story of Perseus, Perseus acquired a curved sword and sickle. The patches the SWALs proudly wore on their shoulders were comprised of a curved sword and sickle, perfectly portraying their lethal nature.

Discovering that white noise blinded their enemy was every bit as effective as Hades's cap, which made Perseus invisible in the myth. Now, as he studied Andrew practicing in the simulator, Charlie realized he had the final piece. Andrew was the winged sandals. The *Perseus* was evolving into an effective fighting machine.

•••

Charlie and Andrew's training session in the simulator was challenging both mentally and physically. After leaving Andrew in the simulator, Charlie pulled his helmet off and slipped an earbud into his ear. He wiped the sweat from his brow and ran his hand through his hair, noticing it was getting long. It had been a while since he had paid a visit to SPC Rakestraw or Lappilus for a haircut.

Charlie slipped the knapsack, which every crew member wore everywhere they went, off his back and clipped his helmet to the carabiner on the side. The first lesson they taught every crew member was to never to go anywhere without his or her helmet. SC also required them to always wear their compression suits, even when they slept. Built into the flight suits were inflatable tubes that added pressure to the extremities to keep their blood flow normal, and fiber optic lines that monitored the rest of their vitals.

Between the outer liner and compression suit were pockets designed to hold hardened plastic plates, which served as supplemental armor to the Kevlar material from which they made the flight suit. Charlie didn't mind wearing the plate, but Jacob had advised him that several crew members recently had failed daily inspection for having removed theirs. Charlie made a mental note to emphasize the necessity of maintaining personal battle readiness.

The helmets offered more than protection of the skull's exterior from an impact. They contained probes that prevented the brain from sloshing around inside the head. During an impact or rapid deceleration, the helmets' sensors controlled the brain from moving inside the skull, to prevent concussions or worse.

Slipping his knapsack back on, Charlie headed back to the bridge to familiarize himself with Jacob's infiltration plan and make his final preparations.

Chapter Nineteen

Present Day, the Strivo Corridor

There is an old military axiom that states, "No plan survives past the first shot fired." On the *Perseus*, it should have said, "No plan survives past the first time Charlie opens his mouth."

The *Perseus* was moving into position to lock on to the hull of the mystery vessel when Charlie, on the fly, ordered the crew to invert and attach to the bottom of the battleship. Something convinced Charlie he spotted hatches there. If so, the SWALs might board the ship without having to breach the battleship's hull.

Sure enough, the hatches were where Charlie had predicted, and they opened. Charlie heard Peck yelling, "Okay, Benson! You first! Go, go, go!"

Benson slid onto the floor of the ship and scanned the hall with his gunsight. He then gestured to the men below him. "All clear!"

Deck by deck they searched the ship. Charlie and his team caught up to the SWAL team by the time they were ready to breach the doors to the bridge.

Like the rest of the ship, the bridge was empty. Charlie noticed everything had a thin layer of dust. He heard the low hum of the engines, and even though he still had his face shield and air-producing PAPR on, he could tell the ship's life-support systems were functioning.

Charlie keyed his commlink. "All of you keep your hoods on until we can get a bio team up here to do an environmental study."

He changed the frequency and spoke again, "Jacob. Status report?"

Jacob sounded a little muffled: "The outer decks lack any gravity control. The layout of the ship compartmentalizes the gun decks. It is as if the outer hull of the ship encapsulates the center structural mass."

"Okay," Charlie replied, "until we have a report from the environmental study, decontaminate everyone. Have the crew withdraw. Leave only a small guard detail."

Most of the crew members filed out, and Jacob posted a few sentries throughout the ship.

"Jacob, I need you to meet me on the bridge before you go back to the *Perseus*."

"Aye aye, Captain."

●●●

Charlie and Jacob sat side by side in Charlie's cabin, finishing the last two steaks on the entire ship. Rather than have Dan prepare their meal, Jacob decided he wanted to cook the steaks himself. The meat had been marinating all day long in paprika, crushed black pepper, kosher salt, granulated onion and garlic, cilantro, and red pepper flakes. Even before Jacob placed the steaks in the oven to broil them, the smell of the seasonings had crew members sticking their heads in to see what was cooking.

Both Charlie and Jacob preferred their meat with a touch of pink, but not knowing how old the meat was, Jacob erred on the side of caution and cooked it till the last of the color disappeared.

"Big day," Charlie stated as he cut into his steak. "What is your take on the bridge's layout?"

Jacob, as always, did not wait to swallow his food before replying. "That ship has some amazing features on board, not to mention some serious firepower. I can't figure out how to operate it. The control panels look ancient."

Charlie swallowed. "I don't have a clue how command and control operate, but if it had serviceable controls, I believe she would be a serious contender against almost anything."

"The crew is working hard at getting her cleaned up," Jacob added. "Once complete, she will be a beautiful ship. Her lines are more elegant compared to anything I have ever seen before."

He took another bite of steak, chewing noisily.

"I am looking forward to the final results of the diagnostics on her engines. The initial survey implies more power than anyone would know how to use, but several of the motors amidships I cannot even get to turn over."

"Let's get her moved out of the passageway, and maybe you and Engineering can make her operational," Charlie replied. "Speaking of operational, what should we do about the CBC?"

Jacob rolled his eyes. "I have been following your advice and have packed the logbook full of entries so we can show we have been under duress. Maybe they will buy the argument we haven't been able to spare the resources to get it operational before now. I have also misplaced a few key parts to slow down the installation. But we are a 'reclaim unit.' Nobody will believe we couldn't pull off a few simple repairs. In reality, we could have built one from scratch by now!"

Charlie agreed. "But that doesn't answer my question. What are we going to do?"

Jacob's fist bumped Charlie on the arm. "The answer to that is above my pay grade. I am going to defer to you."

"Gee, thanks," said Charlie, deep in thought. A look of worry appeared briefly on his face. "The decon of the ship will be complete within the hour. Let's play with her and see if we can even make her move. She can't sit here in the middle of the passageway. After that, I assume our only option is to connect the CBC. How much trouble did you have retrieving the CBC off the space ring?"

"Not much. The mounting hardware is toast, but the antenna, transmitter, and CBC unit are fine."

Charlie frowned. "I wish we had better luck finding more of the *Shelter* and *Nicodemus*. The Obsidians had to hit them dead on the nose as they entered from subspace. It is impossible a destroyer could have inflicted that much damage otherwise."

"And there is no way that could have transpired unless they knew we were coming," added Jacob.

"That," Charlie said, "leaves only three possibilities, (*a*) they have some very advanced tracking systems, which I think we can testify they do not; (*b*) they have extremely high-placed spies inside SC—I mean, it is true everybody and their brother knew where we were going, but it would have taken someone in Central Command calling the shots for them to hit us dead on the nose like that—or (*c*) someone has connected the Obsidians directly into our CBCs."

Jacob's eyes lit up. "That is genius! Why can't we use the CBC from the space ring to find out?"

"What do you have in mind?"

Perplexed, Jacob replied, "I haven't got that far yet. Maybe we can send out an invitation somehow and see who answers."

"I think we have already sent the invitation, and we probably don't have long to wait to garner a reply. Those two corvettes and destroyer have not phoned home. It's hard to believe someone hasn't noticed they are missing—someone is bound to come looking for them."

"Lovely."

"I have just about convinced myself our Obsidian friends didn't know about our prize ship. It might be best they didn't. Early results from the environmental study indicate the dust we saw on board is human remains. Laird can't seem to get a correct reading on the dates of death. His results keep saying fifteen millennia." Charlie laughed. "It concerns him there may be a biological danger."

Jacob chuckled. "That ship's old. But she isn't that old."

"Have you found a name or any indication as to whom she might belong? How old is she?"

Jacob shook his head. "That ship has scars, maybe, but not a square inch of metal fatigue. The fluids look like someone has recently changed them. All the energy banks read full. Other than all the strange symbols and amazing sculpted figurehead on the bow, she looks new. I have never seen anything like her. She reminds me of the old sixteenth-century sailing ships that had snakes or a sea serpent motif on their bow. I found a picture that looks like the sculpture."

Jacob opened his tablet to show a picture of the image. "The head of Medusa and everything. They called the carving an aegis. It is the shield that *Zeus* and sometimes Athena carried into battle. The sapphires alone would make her more expensive than any ship ever built by SC."

"Often, on the figurehead, crews carved a female figure exposing one or both breasts, alluding to the belief that naked female breasts calm the elements, unlike women aboard a vessel, which the crews used to consider a sign of bad luck. I am not sure our female personnel would appreciate that either," Charlie added.

"I have known a few that might." Jacob laughed. "But something has been puzzling me. The day we boarded her, my team and I used a plasma torch to breach several bulkheads. I took a crew down there to repair the damage, but it was already repaired! I asked around, but no one took credit for having fixed it."

"A lot has been going on. Somebody will remember it, or you will find someone mentions repairing it in his or her report. What floor did you remove a bulkhead on?"

"The bulkhead that leads into the forward gun deck. It scared me to death when we broke through and saw all those high explosives. I banned the use of the torch after that."

Jacob pushed his empty plate away just as Charlie's commlink chimed.

"That's our cue," Jacob said. "Decontamination is complete. Let's see if those engines are gutless wonders or if they are as lean and mean as they look."

Chapter Twenty

Present Day, the Strivo Corridor

The Obsidian convoy scrambled the few defenses they had. Something was coming up on their six in a hurry. The sound was reminiscent of Obsidian destroyers, but what could be so important anyone would risk cruising at full throttle so close to an asteroid field? Since the campaign began in the Milky Way, random asteroids drifting into the central passageway had already damaged three vessels.

The destroyers rattled dust off the ceilings of the lead cargo ship as they sped past. Captain Fernandez, in the lead Obsidian merchant ship, swore under his breath to his first officer. "That destroyer and two corvettes will never know what hit them in this asteroid belt. There is no way they can hear what lies in their path of travel making that much noise! Signal the convoy to reduce speed until those sound waves dissipate." By the time he relayed his orders to the other ships of the convoy, the three warships had disappeared. Captain Fernandez knew his convoy was now sailing blind. It would take hours before they could safely proceed at their usual speed.

Charlie and the crew of the *Perseus* observed from the safety of the asteroid belt as the convoy slowed down right in front of them. Had the destroyer and corvettes appeared ten minutes later, they would have caught the *Perseus* red-handed and destroyed her before she made it back to the safety of the asteroids.

Jacob murmured to Charlie, "That Obsidian destroyer and two corvettes won't find what they are looking for. I am pretty sure they are responding to our calling card. Thank God we got our new toy tucked away safe and sound before they showed up."

Charlie did not respond. He was too busy studying the ships in the convoy straight in front of him. Finally, he replied, "The little surprise we left for them should keep them preoccupied for a while. Why do you think those cargo ships are slowing down?"

Jacob turned his scope back toward the convoy. "If our theory is correct, then I venture to guess our friends out there have just been temporarily blinded."

"Maybe," Charlie replied. "All the same, let's stick to the battle plan. Hopefully, we can also deny them the ability to communicate."

He paged Megan Marie. "M&M, analyze those clicks, whistles, and pulsed calls and see if we can figure out what they are saying to each other."

Charlie eased back into his chair. "Lt. Myers, feed the crew and then we will sound to quarters. A person fights better on a full stomach. Besides, there is no telling when we might eat again."

Oblivious to the fact he had just assigned Megan Marie a task, he turned. "M&M, get the two SWAL team leaders up here on the double."

After making a few modifications to his plan with SWAL team leaders Shealy and Peck, Charlie then ignored all the preparations being made around him and studied his potential foes. With everything in place, an eerie calm followed the hurried frenzy aboard the *Perseus*. The mechanical sounds of the equipment and the humming of electrical current powering different stations on the bridge seemed to echo from the metal walls inside the *Perseus*. Jacob felt as though he was hearing the plethora of sounds made by the working of the ship for the first time.

Once, Roland started to ask the captain a question, but M&M quickly hushed him. The chain of command was structured to allow a captain privacy to think without distractions. Roland was ushered back to his post, and the crew on the bridge sat back and waited.

Time passed slowly now that Charlie no longer seemed to have any sense of urgency. The loudest sound heard on the bridge was the crisp crunch of the apple in Charlie's hand each time he took a bite. At last, the stillness on board the *Perseus* had grown unbearable. The last Obsidian ship had long since cleared the point, but Charlie had still not given the order to start the attack. He leaned against the pedestal on the bridge, eating his apple and watching the screen as if watching a movie in which he had little interest.

The pedestal resembled a support on which a museum curator might mount a statue. The lower terminus of the face trim was thicker and wider than the trim on the augmented top. It stood alone in the center of the bridge directly under the large monitor that hung from the wall like a large window, usually showing where the ship was headed. Charlie was definitely interested, though. He was learning much, watching how the various captains handled their ships. He also developed a strong impression of the small fleet's commodore. Charlie surmised that the commodore was a cautious leader who trusted little to chance.

Meanwhile, Captain Fernandez, on the lead Obsidian ship, took this opportunity to reorganize his convoy. The lead ship almost came to a complete stop while he waited on the other ships to catch up and form a nice straight line. Once the line formed, the captain directed all the ships to sail past him and tack in succession until their order had been reversed.

Jacob reported to Charlie the only vessel with any weapon of significance was the lead ship. The best Jacob could determine, the forward-mounted gun was a Mark VI projectile weapon—the same armament the *Perseus* carried.

Charlie studied each ship. They were pretty much what he expected. The Obsidian sailors understood how to sail their ships. They might be slow in maneuvers compared to a warship, but they were efficient all the same. Each tacked in the precise spot as the ship before them. Charlie also formed the opinion that every vessel was undermanned. He could not put his finger on what convinced him of this. It was something he believed every good captain should be able to tell after having been in space for a significant portion of their adult lives. Charlie didn't realize how much stronger his intuition was than the average officer.

Charlie, tired of watching, threw his apple core into the trash. "Lt. Myers, if we carry that lead ship, then I believe the lot of them are ours. Sound to quarters!"

The familiar wail trumpeted throughout the ship. The red luminescent lights had been shining for some time, and M&M dimmed the white day lights. None of the halls reverberated with the sound of running feet. Aware of what Charlie was planning, the crew had been sitting in their battle positions with the straps pulled loosely over their shoulders ever since Sonefeld served out the meals. When the horn finally sounded the crew to quarters, they only needed to reach up and pull their harnesses tight.

Charlie sat back into his command chair and latched each strap, making sure all were snug but comfortable. He then reached over to his console, opened his music player, and hit play.

The exterior of the *Perseus*'s hull vibrated as the sound reverberated at almost uncomfortable levels, but for the Obsidians, the volume was deafening. The numerous small satellite loudspeakers surrounding the fleet of cargo vessels had taken *Perseus*'s crew hours to place in Jacob's prescribed locations.

On the Obsidian ships, the sound drowned out the commands they were trying to send between them. The lead ship, commanded by Fernandez, having initiated a maneuver that would place her back to the forefront of the convoy, took a severe turn. Instead of a smooth, sweeping arch around the ship in front of her, the crew panicked at the deafening sound and missed stays. The cacophony caused the helmsman to misjudge the distance between him and the ship to which he was directly astern. He buried the bow of the lead ship into the stern of the vessel they were trailing.

Perseus responded like a panther dropping from a tree onto its prey, convincingly predatory despite the true nature of the ship's design. For a brief second, *Perseus* drowned out the music by the sound from her afterburners and leaped forward as though a giant hand had given her a shove. Chief Stuyck guided the *Perseus* forward in a broad, sweeping arch, positioning the ship directly on the six of the commodore's vessel. *Perseus*'s engines reversed, and the crew fired grappling hooks through the thin skin on the large cargo vessel. The *Perseus* and the commodore's vessel slammed together when the crew of the *Perseus* reeled the cables to the hooks back in.

Momentum from the *Perseus* shoved the already-struggling commodore's ship even deeper into the back end of the other craft. The forward momentum must have damaged the electrical system because the forward ship immediately went dark.

Now with the *Perseus* grappled to the commodore's ship, the SWAL teams went to work commandeering the vessel. They used explosive charges to launch the round attack cylinders known as insertion balls deep into the hull of the Obsidian ship. The doors on the ball flew open, and the SWAL team in Ball One found themselves on target. With lethal efficiency, they subdued the crew manning the bridge.

SWAL Team Leader Peck signaled the bridge was secure, so sailors from the *Perseus* swiftly boarded and assumed command and control of the ship while it disengaged. The *Perseus* surged to the head of the line, using her guns to make sure none of the other vessels fled. The crew on Commodore Fernandez's ship struggled to control the craft since the nose of the ship refused to budge from the stern of the ship ahead of them. Excess weight on the port side was causing the two ships to list to starboard, threatening to place both crafts into an out-of-control roll.

Fernandez's crew, who had been relieved of their positions, watched as team members from the *Perseus* fought viciously to regain control of the ship. Captain Fernandez, recognizing the perilous position they were in, ordered his crew to help.

Once control of the Obsidian ship was restored, the *Perseus*'s team members secured Captain Fernandez and his crew in the ship's mess hall. Peck, meanwhile, led his team to secure the small disabled Obsidian freighter. The Obsidian crew of the damaged vessel, operating only on auxiliary power, seemed relieved to have help once they realized the SWAL team did not intend to exterminate them.

Meanwhile, near the stern of the lead ship, the second SWAL team had missed their target altogether. The team's planned insertion point was the engine room. When the doors to their insertion ball opened, a wall of water slammed them backward into the walls of the cylinder. They had inserted directly into the Obsidian ship's wastewater tanks. Even with their self-contained air supply systems, the stench was overwhelming.

Eventually, the entire Obsidian fleet surrendered, and the *Perseus* escorted the ships into the asteroid field. The crew of the *Perseus* hid the ships out of sight, deep within the confines of the tumbling masses of metal and rock. Charlie consolidated the Obsidian crews onto the largest of the vessels and posted Shealy's SWAL team to prevent them from attempting to do anything foolish like conspiring to regain control of their ships.

The crew of *Perseus*, positive they were well camouflaged amongst the asteroids, waited patiently for two days before the destroyer and two corvettes reappeared, then headed back toward Obsidian space. They traveled much slower on their return trip, apparently confused by the absence of the convoy they had passed earlier. Jacob pointed out damage on the destroyer and one of the corvettes. The present the *Perseus* had left for them inflicted serious bruises but apparently did not deliver the knock-out blow Charlie and Jacob wished for. Charlie was comfortable in the knowledge that neither ship would forget their surprise anytime soon.

Chapter Twenty-One

Present Day, the Strivo Corridor

odern-day warships were void of windows, but the *Perseus* was a third-generation ship built in a different era. Though she was a space-worthy vessel, no one would have referred to her as modern. One of the unique features of the *Perseus* was the captain's quarters. Charlie's cabin had beautifully sweeping windows that followed the oval shape of the hull. Usually, they were kept closed with thick titanium shutters on the exterior of the ship. When they were open, the cabin more closely resembled a prehistoric sailing ship from the early 1800s than a starship. While the cabin was not near the stern of the ship, the windows looked out over the back of the ship's superstructure and offered terrific views of the space through which *Perseus* sailed.

Over the next several weeks, the *Perseus* executed several successful attacks on Obsidian convoys and a couple of other minor skirmishes. Things had been going so well, Charlie celebrated by having the shutters opened to view their prizes. Charlie invited Jacob, Chief Stuyck, and three of the teenagers to dine with him. Since being granted command of the *Perseus*, he made a habit of inviting different members of the crew, not just the officers, to eat with him as often as the requirements of the service would allow. Not just the officers. He had given every member of the *Perseus* an opportunity to enjoy the private stores of food for which only a captain could find room.

Usually, the crew members enjoyed the food and only spoke when spoken to. Charlie had always found this disconcerting. It was hard to make small talk when everything you said as captain of the ship was accepted as gospel. Many of Charlie's friends, upon making command rank, had found the isolation unbearable. Despite violating SC rules, many of them would invite a friend or a lover to travel with them on long missions for the company.

The teenagers, on the other hand, had not yet learned the unspoken rules of the service about the Godlike stature of a captain. That was part of the reason Charlie enjoyed their company. He also enjoyed watching the ferocity with which they ate. The quality of Charlie's food did not adequately explain their insatiable appetites, especially early enough in the cruise to still have ample stores and with the coffers overflowing with fresh meat and fruits from their captured prizes. In addition to the plethora of explosives, the Obsidian ships seemed to contain almost anything a sailor might desire.

The open shutters prompted Andrew to ask, "How long can we survive this far out in space on a ship as old and obsolete as the *Perseus*?"

The question took Charlie aback. Like all captains, Charlie was fond of his ship. Despite knowing all her problems and shortcomings, he was much more likely to emphasize her strengths.

It mortified Chief Stuyck the little punk would dare ask such an impertinent question. He started to give him a stern rebuke, but Charlie stopped Stuyck with a raised hand.

Charlie leaned close to Andrew.

"I have known this ship most of my adult life, but I have not always been her captain. At one point or another, I have served almost every function there is to perform on her." Charlie leaned closer and looked Andrew in the eye. "Would you consider me old and obsolete?"

A horrified look appeared on Andrew's face, having realized the blunder he had made with his comment.

Charlie reached up and lovingly caressed the bulkhead. "No, the *Perseus* is not old. She may not be the ideal ship for our present mission, but for what she was designed to do, she is in her prime."

•••

After Stuyck and the boys retired for the evening, Jacob remained in Charlie's quarters. He and Charlie stood looking out the windows at all the ships they had captured and stowed away amongst the asteroids. They admired the pocket battleship with all her guns.

Charlie spoke first. "I sent all of our logs and reports back to SC via simulcast. Our encounter with the destroyer and corvettes on reentry from subspace. Our capturing the seven merchantmen. I reported our three most recent prizes and the two we had to destroy. Sixty-three ships captured and five ships destroyed, three of them ships of war."

Jacob replied, "I hope you also sent the cam footage. Otherwise, they will dismiss your reports as fantasy."

Charlie nodded. "Yes, I sent the footage. I also sent word I refuse to install the CBC. They should have received my message by now, and arrangements for my court-martial have most likely already started."

With satisfaction in his voice, Jacob replied, "I am glad you told them. I would rather be court-martialed for insubordination and dismissed from the service than die a fool's death. Then again, they may hang us. At least we will all hang together."

"No. I decided not to install the CBC. I bear the responsibility." Charlie sighed. "There is one detail I left out of the reports."

Charlie looked at Jacob and nodded at the old battleship. "I did not report her."

The brothers continued looking out the windows.

Finally, Jacob spoke. "I have been spending a lot of time on that ship, working. Yesterday, I went back to look at the bulkheads we cut with the plasma. I know this will sound crazy, but I don't think anyone on the crew made those repairs. I believe she healed herself."

Charlie appeared undaunted. "I can't explain why, but I believe you. Since the first time I stepped onto her bridge, it felt like she was alive."

Jacob laughed. "Great. They will not shoot us for insubordination. They will lock us away in the looney bin."

Jacob hesitated for a second before he continued. "I am glad you didn't include her in your report."

Charlie patted Jacob on his shoulder.

Jacob cleared his throat. "How do you expect SC will respond?"

"I guess a lot depends on how the war is going. They can't order us home. Without a space ring, the return trip will take *Perseus* twenty years. If they can afford it, they may send a ship to retrieve me for a court-martial hearing."

Jacob shook his head. "From the radio waves we have picked up, that probably will not happen. The signals are a few weeks old, but according to the news, it sounds like they barely have enough ships left to prevent an invasion. We are hopefully the least of their worries."

Charlie grinned. "Let's hope for *modus vivendi*."

Jacob toasted Charlie. "Amen. To an agreement to peaceful coexistence between us and the powers that be."

Chapter Twenty-Two

Three Years Ago, Space Command's
Central Intelligence Headquarters, Earth

J acob lost count of the number of hours he put in during his first three months with the research team at SC Evelin. It hadn't taken him long to understand why most of the team members found apartments within walking distance of the research facility. Jacob, on nights he was too tired to make the drive home, just crashed with his head on his desk.

Except for Gustafson, Jacob really liked all his fellow team members. Gustafson, he sensed, spied on everything he did. More than one team member secretly complained she somehow pilfered their work and submitted it as her own. Jacob could not imagine any other way Gustafson contributed as much work as she took credit for, considering how few hours she worked.

He pushed back from his chair and headed down to the lunchroom to get something to eat before it closed for the night. Jacob could live awhile without sleep, but he really liked to eat. As he passed Gustafson's workstation, he noticed her security card still lying under her monitor where she always left it. He wondered how she got past security and moved around the building without it. Much to his surprise, he noticed she had also forgotten to log out of her computer.

Curious what she was working on, he glanced at her screen. He was shocked to see the monitor was a mirror image of his own. Jacob glanced back at his screen to compare the two. He walked back over and leaned over his keyboard. He opened his favorite sports channel. Casually, he walked back to compare his monitor to Gustafson's. As he suspected, the sports channel was now open on her monitor.

Angry, to say the least, he started to turn her computer off, but then had an idea. Jacob glanced around to make sure he was alone. Everyone else had left for the night. He casually strolled over to where one security camera was monitoring the office. Once he was directly under the monitor, out of view of the lens, he pulled out his phone and filmed a short video of the office. Once Jacob had a few minutes of footage, he inserted a data chip into the phone's port and copied the file. Standing on a chair, he carefully placed the chip into the back of the monitor and pressed play. The monitor flashed red twice and then started to play the recording on a continuous loop.

Confident no one could see him, Jacob quickly walked back over to Gustafson's monitor. Jacob searched her browser for any access file or program that might allow her to infiltrate his computer. He didn't find a program, but what he did see shocked him. There were thousands of file folders marked with such high-security clearances he didn't even know what many of them meant. Jacob saw she had two restricted folders that received internal flash traffic. In the first folder, she set her settings to burn any incoming message immediately after reading. All the flash traffic in the other folder showed Gustafson sent large data files to somewhere in South America. In the last file, there were records of large amounts of currency being transferred, many of the transactions in gold bullion.

Quickly, he inserted his data strip into Gustafson's computer and uploaded a quick file he used to allow him to access his work computer from home, making only minor changes. Not wanting to leave any trail that might be traced back to him, he changed the settings to upload Gustafson's video stream and data files to an anonymous cloud drive. He placed the data strip back in his pocket, walked back underneath the security camera, and erased the loop.

Before he shut his computer down, Jacob changed his password, then picked up his phone. Joan answered on the first ring. "Hey, good-looking," Joan said, pleased he had called her. "You still at work?"

"Just leaving. You up to grabbing a bite to eat?" asked Jacob.

"Awesome!" Joan said, thrilled. "What do you have in mind?"

"It is late. Would you mind if I grab Chinese and we eat at your place?" Jacob asked.

Jacob called the order in and picked it up on his way. Joan, surprised at how swiftly he made it to her apartment, still had her lipstick tube in her hand when she opened the door.

Jacob whistled. "Wow, you look great. Maybe I should have made reservations instead?"

Joan, tired of how Jacob never seemed to reciprocate her advances, stepped outside the door and wrapped her arms around his neck, kissing him hard on the mouth.

"Not tonight. Tonight, you are not making it out of my place until I have taken advantage of you," she said jokingly.

The taste of her lips still on his, Jacob questioned the wisdom of being alone with Joan tonight. He wasn't sure she would take no for an answer again. Worse, she was slowly wearing him down, and the last few times they had gone out, he had found it increasingly difficult to resist her.

Once they were inside her apartment, she led him by the hand to her couch. On the coffee table in front of them, she laid out two of her best plates and a bottle of wine. A candle was flickering between the crystal wine glasses. Carefully, Jacob served their food from the white cardboard boxes onto the plates and poured them both a glass of wine. The meal served, he raised his glass and clinked it against Joan's.

As they ate, Jacob told Joan what he had discovered. Joan, having a hard time focusing on anything other than Jacob, at first had difficulty concentrating on his story. At least until he opened his tablet and showed her Gustafson's database, which he had uploaded to his cloud drive. Joan whistled softly.

"The files Gustafson has hidden away are highly classified files. Whatever her security clearance, there is no way she warrants this type of access," she said, taking another sip as she studied the files. "What do you think this means?"

Jacob shrugged. "The only explanation I can think of is she is selling top-secret data. Can you imagine any other plausible explanation?"

"Not really. Do you have a plan? What are you going to do?"

Jacob, wondering how best to proceed, said, "Not sure. Obviously, I need to turn her in, but to whom? The best I can make out, she is receiving the files from someone else in SC with an even higher security clearance than hers. It might prove dangerous to report her to the wrong person."

Joan thought to herself. She took another bite of food, then answered, "You are right. You need to give this to someone you trust. I think you should ask Addison how to proceed."

"Who?" Jacob asked, trying to remember where he had heard the name.

"Oh, I'm sorry. Maddie," replied Joan.

Maddie had been spending all her time with Charlie at the house and had not requested any other favors from him since the night she asked him to help her log into the computer. Charlie told him he had asked her to marry him and that she had accepted. Jacob didn't want to second-guess Charlie, but it all seemed too fast to Jacob. Besides, Charlie wasn't even sure how much longer he would have a job. Marriage seemed premature right now.

Hesitant, Jacob asked, "Why Maddie?"

"I am working the front desk because I screwed up and uncovered things that were not supposed to be known. Maddie and I shared the same handler. I know she was working in South America right until everything went crazy down there. If anyone knows anything, it will be her. Besides, there is no one in SC I would trust more than Maddie."

Jacob thought hard, trying to come up with a better idea, but he drew a blank. He pulled out his phone and dialed Charlie.

Pouting, Joan said, "I didn't mean you should go talk to her tonight."

Jacob winked at Joan. "You threatened to take advantage of me! I thought I should find an escape plan."

He placed the phone against his ear, waiting on Charlie to answer, and leaned closer to Joan. "You are welcome to come with me."

Still pouting, Joan teasingly pushed him away. "Who is taking advantage of whom? Jacob, are you straight?"

Jacob laughed. "Well, I am not gay if that's what you are asking."

On the phone, Jacob heard Charlie reply, "Well, I have often wondered. I am glad you called to clear that up."

Jacob laughed out loud. "Sorry, I was talking to Joan. You have often wondered?"

It was Charlie's turn to laugh. "Just kidding. You coming home, or are you and Joan getting into trouble together?"

"That depends. Can I speak to Maddie?" asked Jacob.

Charlie put Maddie on the phone. Jacob began explaining to Maddie what was going on, but Joan stopped him.

"You should only discuss this in person," she whispered to him and took the phone. "Hey girl. I am having trouble with my tablet. Any chance I can run by and have you look at it for me?"

"Sure. I will come to you. Does that work?"

The tone in her voice conveyed that she recognized the code immediately.

Joan answered with a simple, "Yes," and handed the phone back to Jacob. Jacob put the phone back up to his ear, but the line was dead.

"What was that all about?"

Joan studied Jacob for a moment. It frustrated her she had such a handsome man sitting in her apartment who seemed to have no interest in her.

"Maddie does not want Charlie to know about her past," she replied.

"Why?"

"I don't know everything about Maddie, but I know she has made some serious enemies. She fears if Charlie learns about her past, he won't want her anymore."

"That is stupid. Why?" asked Jacob.

"You don't know what it's like to have secrets you can't talk about. I will tell you one thing. Life has never been kind to Maddie. Now, she has found someone who is kind to her, who really cares for her, and she fears doing anything that might jeopardize that."

Silently, Jacob reflected how well he understood. He scooted closer to Joan and put his arms around her. Jacob was so tempted to pick Joan up and carry her off to bed. He knew that would make her happy, but he had promised himself: *Never again. The next time will be with the one I will keep forever.*

Jacob held Joan tight and whispered in her ear, "You asked if I am straight. I am. It isn't that I am not attracted to you. You tempt me all the time with your beautiful eyes and sweet smile. You are gorgeous. I just want to wait until I am sure I have found the one person I am meant to be with forever."

Joan wanted to cry. She had initially been mostly interested in Jacob because of his wit and remarkable good looks. Over the past few months, she had begun to realize there was a lot more to Jacob and that she really liked him. Maybe even enough to quit seeing any other guys. Sometimes, the most crucial part of any message was the part that isn't said. She understood the wanting to wait on the person you would be with forever. She also understood that this person, for Jacob, was not her.

Chapter Twenty-Three

Three Years Earlier, Charlie and Jacob's Home,
Arlington, Virginia, Earth

etween the three of them laboriously researching, Maddie,
Jacob, and Joan had managed to piece together enough
information to feel confident there was a mastermind inside
Space Intelligence who was not only helping the Obsidian-supported
rebels in South America but was also calling all the shots. Jacob
and Joan became convinced someone had fabricated the Obsidian
connection to throw people off the real perpetrator's trail.

Maddie was not so confident. Maddie wasn't sure of the truth,
but she was positive she had learned as much as could be gleaned
virtually. She believed the only way she would ever get any closer to
finding out the truth was by accessing the sealed South American
files right at their source. Since that was impossible given their
limited security clearances, the next obvious step in her mind
was to gain access to someone's computer who had the necessary
permission.

Jacob had only been joking when he suggested she march into
Admiral Cotterill's office and log on to his computer, since the
admiral was the one person in the entire agency who would most
likely have unfettered access to anything imaginable. The fact he
oversaw the whole intelligence agency didn't faze Maddie in the

least. Maddie seemed to think the best approach was to walk right in through the front door of the admiral's office. Jacob believed a more subtle approach might be in order and proposed a better plan to get Maddie into the Intelligence building.

Jacob knew the *Penetrator*, the prototype destroyer used by SC Evelin, was scheduled to arrive in two days. The next day at work, Jacob volunteered to stay late the following evening to retrieve the onboard processor from the *Penetrator* and replace it with an updated one. Jacob would return the old processor from the CBC to SC Evelin for further analysis and upgrades.

On the evening the *Penetrator* was scheduled to arrive, Jacob stayed at SC Evelin until everyone else had left for the day. On his way out the door, Jacob veered by Gustafson's workstation and discreetly grabbed her security card from its usual resting place.

Jacob drove by his home to retrieve Maddie, and they headed to Andrews Air Force Base. They waited on the tarmac as, just after dark, the *Penetrator* landed. Jacob and Maddie, wearing Gustafson's security badge, boarded the ship so Jacob could replace the processor. Within minutes they were headed back across the tarmac to Jacob's car.

The commander of the craft, Captain Green, whistled to himself. "Wow, the way those desk jockeys talk, I assumed Gustafson was an old hag. She is downright hot! Definitely not what I expected."

Jacob sped back into the city to the main SC Intelligence Building. Jacob swiped his card and then held his breath as they swiped Gustafson's card to enter the secure parking garage. Much to his relief, no sirens started blaring and no men with guns rushed from the security building outside his open car window.

Maddie, keeping her head low, left Jacob to deliver his package to SC Evelin's studio; meanwhile, she headed straight toward the administrative wing of the building.

Two hours later, Jacob began to worry as he waited in the car for Maddie to reappear. Reluctantly, he opened the door to go look for her when his phone rang.

On the phone, Maddie whispered, "Mission accomplished. I'm meeting Charlie for dinner. See you at home."

•••

The information Jacob showed Maddie on Gustafson's computer filled in all the missing pieces from her failed mission in South America. It had taken her three days to read through all the files. If not surprised in Bogota and forced to eliminate those she thought were the key players in the conspiracy, Maddie was confident she would have discovered this information on her own. Now, with the pieces presented to her, she wasn't sure how to proceed. Her handler had severed all ties to her.

She finally decided she either had to find a way to contact her handler or cripple the organization on her own. Confident the real mastermind had to be someone highly placed in the intelligence arm of Space Command, she wasn't sure there was much her handler could safely do to help her in any event. If word got out to the wrong people they were on to them, neither she nor her handler would ever escape their grasp. The first thing she needed to figure out was who the mastermind behind all of this was and discern their ultimate goal. The key to finding the traitor had to be the money trail.

She opened the folder containing the financial transcripts and noticed a new file had been added. Someone had sent Gustafson a bill of lading for 125 tons of gold bullion. Quickly doing the math, Maddie shook her head. Over five billion in solid gold. Maddie stared at the computer screen, developing a plan of action. The amount of money she had found in Bogota and transferred to the offshore account had shocked her. By contrast, this amount was insane.

Maddie continued to dig in the file. The Obsidians were shipping the gold on a small craft named the *Peccary* through the Taverius Space Bubble in two weeks, escorted by a half-dozen destroyers. Once the shipment cleared the bubble, the warships would turn back, and the *Peccary* was to leave the cargo on Ceres, the most massive asteroid inside the asteroid belt of Earth's solar system.

Maddie assumed that meant Gustafson was to arrange for transport to take the cargo to its final destination. She studied the file and saw no one else had opened it. Maddie downloaded the file and erased the original. Maddie had seen Gustafson reply to two other flash traffic commands. Each time, she entered "confirm." With haste, Maddie did the same. She watched as her reply disappeared as soon as she sent it.

Maddie walked into the kitchen, grabbed Charlie's cell, and texted Jacob, "Call me. ie."

Chapter Twenty-Four
Present Day, the Strivo Corridor

C harlie and Jacob had been itching to get on the battleship to explore and experiment, but the requirements of the service prevented them at every turn. Only a few hours after their time spent reflecting on their looming legal difficulties with SC, six transport ships appeared out of nowhere. Instead of heading toward the Milky Way galaxy, the Obsidian ships were heading back toward Obsidian space.

The brothers debated whether to just attack and destroy them. Neither wanted more prisoners to guard. Charlie studied their movements and concluded the Obsidians had loaded the ships with cargo. The *Perseus* was well supplied, and they had already overburdened the vessels in the asteroids with every type of supply imaginable, ample ammunition, and a lot of high-explosive charges. Charlie had to wonder if the Obsidians were planning a ground offensive, considering the cargo *Perseus* had been capturing. Charlie decided to capture the latest vessels mostly because he was curious what the Obsidians were backhauling.

The *Perseus*'s crew had mastered the now-familiar attack plan down to the most minute detail. Charlie gave the order to commence the attack. He divided his forces with Peck's SWAL team, attacking from the rear in one of the Obsidian supply ships under Jacob's command. Jacob liked the looks of the small ship and thought it showed a lot of promise as a service vessel for the crew of the *Perseus* to use amongst the asteroids. No sooner had Jacob started his attack run than he discovered at full throttle the vessel handled poorly, tending to gripe to the port side.

Charlie took the *Perseus* and attacked the lead ship head on. News that danger lurked within the walls of the corridor had apparently reached the ears of the captain on the lead ship. The Obsidian ship was already firing in the general direction of the *Perseus* before they had made it up to speed.

Much to the chagrin of the crew, Charlie was in the mood for Fleetwood Mac. With the sound systems on both ships blaring "Tusk," the *Perseus* got into a yardarm-to-yardarm gun battle.

Despite her limited firepower, the Obsidian ship hit back hard. With the music preventing the enemy ship from locking on to the sound of *Perseus*'s engine, the Obsidians could not direct their fire accurately enough to deliver a decisive blow. They got in a lucky shot that disabled all the electronic shields on *Perseus*'s port corner nearest the stern. A second shot following close behind pierced her side and passed dangerously close to the fuel reserves, disabling one of her two main engines. By the narrowest of margins, they decided the battle after Charlie had the crew lock the *Perseus* against the ship and Shealy's SWAL team subdued the Obsidian crew.

Even before the smoke had cleared, Charlie received two urgent messages over the open communication channel from Jacob and Peck. The third ship of the convoy contained 233 prisoners of war.

The prisoners were from SC's Sixth Fleet. Obsidians generally operated on a take-no-prisoners basis, but, for some unknown reason, all the enlisted men were spared and loaded onto the space transport headed back to the Obsidian home planet. The prisoners reported the Obsidian commander had executed anyone suspected of being an officer.

Charlie, Myers, and Jacob put the men to work manning the captured ships hidden inside the asteroid belt. Meanwhile, the crew worked on repairing the damage to the *Perseus*.

Charlie decided it was time to move their base of operations deeper into the Strivo's asteroids. Andrew and Roland found a dwarf planet about one thousand eighty klicks inside the asteroid belt that had a safe passageway leading to it. It also provided several options in case the *Perseus* needed to make an emergency exit. The back side of the small planet was shaped like a concave bowl, which Charlie and Jacob reasoned would make an excellent harbor to hide their prizes. They decided to name the hideaway Aphaea, after the "Invisible Goddess."

On the smallest of their prize ships, which Charlie and Jacob renamed the *Patricia*, a name that held special significance to the brothers, Charlie sent a few members of the crew to mine the passageway leading into the site and the base itself with high explosives. The *Patricia* was roomy considering her size. Her robust frame and turbocharged engines made her ideal for weaving in and out between the asteroids. It was the best hands-on experience the crew of *Perseus* had had for familiarizing themselves with how the Obsidians' sound-detection radar functioned.

Obsidians were universally known for being tone-deaf. With a continuous hum, like the sound of an engine, their sound-detection equipment painted a crystal-clear picture for the operator that was much more accurate than anything Space Command had. When hearing music through the same system, the vibrating sound waves sounded like thousands of whales participating in a mating ritual. The words were discernable, but the accompaniment was overwhelming. The system seemed incapable of determining direction or distance.

If the *Perseus* were to meet a superior force and needed to retreat, Charlie reasoned that by mining the passageway within the asteroids, he could detonate the explosives and the whole thing would collapse inward. That would allow the crew a better chance to escape.

The influx of new men and the help they provided was a welcome relief to the whole crew. Manning the *Perseus*, guarding prisoners, and the time-consuming task of concealing prize ships had left them exhausted. Worse yet, the lack of opportunity for training concerned Charlie. He worried the crew might grow careless if due diligence were not given to at least the occasional drill.

Despite the new airmen's arrival, there was no rest for the weary. For the next sixteen days straight, Obsidian transports traveled the corridor heading toward the Milky Way with supplies for their warships. Many of the ships contained nothing but more explosives. Soon, even with all the extra workforce to help disguise the prizes and guard prisoners, Charlie worried the crew was becoming overwhelmed.

•••

On day seventeen, the flaxen horn awoke Charlie from his berth. On the situation board, Charlie counted ten Obsidian destroyers heading down the pike at full speed. He ordered Myers to spread the alarm to all the prize crews, instructing them to take all necessary precautions to remain hidden.

For the next three days, destroyers screamed up and down the passageway. Myers and many of the prize crews mumbled amongst themselves, asking why Captain Jackson didn't order an attack.

Jacob was glad to see Charlie remaining calm. The thought of the *Perseus* taking on even one destroyer seemed outrageous to Jacob. To attack knowing there were ten in the area sounded more like suicide. Jacob knew Charlie would use … Jacob hesitated. Jacob concluded he could never be sure what Charlie might attempt.

The feeling onboard the *Perseus* was gloomy. Despair seemed to seep from the air ducts anywhere Jacob went. With no clear path forward and crew members sleeping night and day strapped into their battle stations, morale had hit an all-time low. Every time Jacob succumbed to sleep, nightmares would wake him. But then in a change of pace, instead of reliving Hope's car accident, he dreamed about ant lions. For three days and nights, Jacob was repeatedly plagued by the same dream.

In the dream, he was wandering blindly in a desolate desert, striving to fulfill an assignment along the edge of a large, sandy mound. Duty bound, he circled the edge of the mound, searching. Wondering what lay over the knoll to his right, he eased over the lip and immediately his body began to slide down a steep slope. Exerting every ounce of effort he could muster, he managed to turn sideways to stop careening down the embankment.

Methodically, Jacob searched for solid ground to inch his way upward, but each time he began to make progress, something at the bottom of the hill caused a new avalanche of sand to pull him deeper into the chasm. Repeatedly, his efforts were thwarted, and Jacob found himself sinking deeper into a conical pit.

Over his shoulder, he spotted his nemesis. Jacob identified the prehistoric shell of a beast, buried in the aggregate, with large armored scales covering its torso. When the beast moved, Jacob saw long, slender legs protruding from the sides of the body and two short, forward-facing legs directing the beast's movement. Located between these diminutive front legs was the creature's head with its mouth hungrily opening and closing, the small opening pulsing, craving to dine on his flesh.

Huge pincers, garbed with sharp barbs, thrashed the sand every time Jacob found his footing on the loose embankment, causing yet another avalanche. With each thrust, the pincers came closer, threatening to crush him and drag him under to his death.

Jacob gasped when he awoke from the dream. Leaning over his control panel on the bridge, he almost fell from his seat. Through bleary eyes he saw members of the crew manning the bridge. Many studied their monitors, but most slept at their posts. M&M caught his eye, looked at him questionably, then gave him a faint smile of encouragement.

Every time Jacob was startled awake by the nightmare, he found Charlie still in the exact same position. Leaning against the center pedestal, Charlie was studying every movement of the Obsidian destroyers in the corridor, memorizing every detail of each ship and becoming familiar with the personality of each. Jacob knew Charlie's research was not scientific. It was instinctual. The ability to glean the information Jacob knew Charlie was absorbing could not be taught. It was a gift a person could only receive at conception, and it frightened him to think of what insane plan Charlie might formulate. Charlie was born to be a predator, not prey. Jacob realized this idle waiting would last only so long.

For years Jacob had felt guilty, feeling he had hindered Charlie's career. While at SC Evelin, Jacob's team routinely analyzed what made a successful captain. There was no longer any doubt in Jacob's mind Charlie belonged on the bridge of one of SC's few remaining battleships, not shelved away commanding a repair ship. Charlie's predatory instinct was much greater than any captain he had ever studied. Evidence lay in the number of prize ships presently hidden away amongst the asteroids.

To many crew members, the Perseus had executed the same rehearsed attack plan repeatedly. Myers, for example, did not understand or appreciate any of the subtle adjustments or nuances Charlie made to the plan of attack each time they launched an attack. The only crew member who did seem to recognize and appreciate the minute last-second variations was M&M.

Jacob remained apprehensive, waiting with bated breath to learn if Charlie would present a plan to disrupt the Obsidians' search pattern or decide to wait the Obsidians out.

In the end, it didn't matter. Circumstance precluded Charlie making a decision. Space before them became devoid of life. Not a single Obsidian ship dared to travel anywhere within the corridor.

Charlie and Jacob took advantage of the time and spent every waking hour on board the old battleship. Charlie ordered two of the captured Obsidian merchant ships, one under the command of Myers and the other commanded by M&M, to place satellites up and down the corridor to give more advanced warning of future intrusions. It took days, but soon they had eyes from one end of the passage to the other. Charlie also redoubled his efforts to map any navigable parts of the asteroid field. Jacob was convinced he was doing this more to keep the teenagers out of trouble than to find escape routes—because surely, Charlie would not consider drawing the Obsidians into the confines of the floating masses to engage them in battle?

•••

Charlie had sensed the crew's impatience and discontent by the decision to simply go into hiding. Now was the time for patience, not heroics. At present he felt confident he controlled the battlefield. The *Perseus* had basically denied the Obsidians the use of the corridor. They had also forced the Obsidians to remove valuable warships from the true theater of operations in the Milky Way to attempt to end the *Perseus*'s chaotic disruption of Obsidian commerce in the Strivo.

While Charlie sometimes sensed Lt. Meyer's disapproval of how he commanded the *Perseus*, he knew that M&M had always been one of his most ardent supporters. Space Command had assigned M&M to the *Perseus* at the same time Charlie was first given command of the ship. At the time, M&M was the youngest member of the crew. SC had made her an acting ensign and placed her in charge of many people who were almost twice her age. In the beginning, when the ship was being brought back into active service, M&M questioned Charlie's leadership style. But as she continued to serve under Charlie, she formed a deep respect for him.

•••

M&M had been disappointed when she first learned she was being assigned to a reclamation unit. She had wanted nothing more than to travel and see the universe, something not very likely to happen on a low-orbit repair ship. Even more disappointing was her first impression of her new commander at the time. M&M believed Commander Jackson was too familiar and trusting with the crew, yet, while with her, he was always looking over her shoulder, telling her what he expected and ordering her to do things his way.

It wasn't until she learned that the captain had spent much of his career serving under the same seasoned veterans whom he now commanded that she saw him in a different light. M&M's father always told her the village rumor was never wrong. If true, then Commander Jackson would be a great leader. To further emphasize the faith the crew had in the freshly promoted commander, people who had served with him before requested transfers to now serve under him, most of whom left some very impressive postings.

The most shocking transfer, to M&M, was the captain's own brother. Lt. Jackson had given up a position at an SC Engineering think tank, SC Evelin, to serve on the *Perseus*. To M&M, the job he had given up was what she always hoped and dreamed would be the pinnacle of her own career.

The loyalty of so many veteran airmen, many of whom were twice her age, gave M&M pause. She quit finding fault with the commander and decided to be open-minded and give him a chance. Soon, she realized Commander Jackson wasn't trying to criticize her performance; he was coaching and grooming her to fit in his mold. The more time she and the commander spent working together, the more she appreciated how smart he was and what great leadership skills he possessed.

M&M had never respected Myers, on the other hand. Lt. Myers was only worried about one person: himself. M&M had dreams of advancement, promotion, and opportunities to better herself, but the lieutenant was obsessed by such thoughts of his own. In M&M's opinion, he didn't deserve promotion because he lacked the most essential prerequisite: the ability to lead. People followed Captain Jackson because he spoke with authority. M&M had no intention of letting this snake Myers undermine her captain. And much to her relief, she knew Lt. Jackson would stand by her side against Myers if the need arose.

Megan Marie had heard the recent murmuring amongst the crew. She approached Myers about the issue with disarming confidence. Myers knew that while the older crew members might take advantage of her, Megan Marie was not to be trifled with. From that point on, tension between the two remained high. M&M stayed vigilant, concerned Myers could not be trusted.

•••

With every passing day, Jacob grew more and more concerned they had not received a reply to any of the daily deep-space radio communications Charlie sent to SC religiously. Finally, his curiosity got the better of him. He opened the log reports to see what Charlie was choosing to report and, more interestingly, not report. As he was about to cover his tracks so no one would know he had spied, Jacob spotted something curious. Charlie had built a worm into the file he was sending.

Charlie was a smart man, but this, to the best of Jacob's knowledge, was beyond his level of expertise. His first thought was maybe one of the kids tried to piggyback a personal message onto Charlie's official transmission. After Jacob studied the file to learn its purpose, he concluded Charlie most likely recruited one of the teenagers, probably Jake, to help him create the worm.

Jacob reflected on what he had learned about Jake. Jake, his brother Richard, and his sister Olivia had grown up living on the street, having to depend on their wits to survive. Someone had killed their father, an expert computer hacker, in prison while he had been serving a five-year sentence, allegedly for identity theft and financial fraud. Jake's mother left in the middle of the night after his arrest, sending the children to bed and never returning. Social services tried to keep the three of them together, but the social worker was not able to locate a home willing to take all three kids. Olivia was the easiest to place, so social services sent her to a family on the opposite side of Alabama.

Jake learned from an early age everything there was to know about computer programming, malware, hacking, and phishing from his father. Using his talents on the net to find Olivia, he and Richard made their escape from a foster home and retrieved their sister, managing to stay one step ahead of the authorities ever since.

The exceptionally well-created worm, Jacob mused, was designed in such a way that any person who opened the email would then become a transmitter should anyone activate it. If activated, the entire file and all its contents, updated every time Charlie deposited a new entry, would post live on the internet.

"Why would Charlie do that?" Jacob asked himself.

He glanced down and saw Charlie had also sent a private message to Admiral Halsey and another to Maddie. Jacob made a copy on his thumb drive to study the message and the worm closer in the privacy of his room.

Not that Jacob didn't trust Charlie's discretion. From experience, both he and Charlie knew how someone could intercept and use a personal message against you. The admiral had taught them that good communication requires three skills. The most important skill is to listen. Second, make sure any message you send is concise, to the point, and not prone to misunderstanding. The third skill involves recognizing what was omitted. The most critical part of any message is often what *isn't* mentioned.

As Jacob saw it, the problem was none of those rules usually applied when Charlie was talking to Maddie. Jacob questioned whether it was the fact that Maddie had a way of getting people to open up and share things they usually wouldn't, or if Charlie had such a soft spot for her, he threw discretion out the window.

Jacob put his thumb drive in his pocket and queried on the mainframe where he could find Jake. He stopped by the mess hall to grab a sandwich and then headed to the teenagers' living quarters. He needed to learn more about how a computer worm worked.

Chapter Twenty-Five
Present Day, the Strivo Corridor

Jacob made his rounds looking for Charlie, not by pinging him but tracking him down the old-fashioned way: searching room to room, ship to ship. When he finally found him, he was sitting in the command chair on the bridge of the old battleship. Jacob stood in the doorway and studied Charlie. The expression on Charlie's face reminded him of their mom. Not the sweet, loving mom who used to take them to the lake. Nor the fun-loving one who would cook dinner and then watch movies with them on the floor of the living room for hours. Charlie's countenance was that of Lt. Commander Jackson when she was deep in thought, trying to solve a particularly troubling problem.

It was clear to anyone who had known her that Patty Jackson was born to be a mother of boys. It would have been hard to imagine Patty with a little girl, ribbons in her hair and a stroller full of baby dolls in tow. The perception was increased dramatically because she had two healthy boys, obsessed with sports, dirt bikes, hunting, and fishing. They also knew every dirt road and swimming hole between home in the sandhills of South Carolina and Columbia, over twenty miles to the east. They were also intimately acquainted with every horse stable within range of their dirt bikes to the west in the eastern half of Aiken County.

Secretly, Patty always wanted a little girl. Patty had reached the point in life where she realized no more children were in her future. The thing she now looked forward to was the opportunity of having daughters-in-law. She imagined the fun she would someday get to experience, shopping with the wives of her rambunctious boys, sharing stories, and enjoying grandchildren.

With a fondness for history, Patty had fallen in love with the legends of old, the mythological spaceships that once ruled the heavens, and spaceships that were so successful and powerful that over generations, people had begun to see them as more than protectors of their way of life; they considered them. She became so engrossed in these stories, she even did her thesis in college on the subject, concluding they once existed. It was this thesis that alerted Morgan Cotterill to her existence. After she applied to and was accepted by Space Command, he pulled every string at his disposal to have her transferred to his research team. There she had proven to be a priceless asset.

•••

Jacob had cried for days when they learned Patty was missing in action. Charlie was strong and never let Jacob see him break down, but Jacob knew losing her was even more devastating to him than anyone else in the family. From that day forward, Charlie, at the age of thirteen, assumed the role of family protector. After that, if anyone messed with Jacob, they answered to Charlie.

Mom, as the boys called her, was gone much of the time even before her disappearance. But when Mom was home, she was a dedicated mother. Never did the boys have a soccer match, fencing competition, a wrestling match, or even a chess tournament she missed for any reason. Mom enjoyed helping them both do their homework. She made schoolwork fun, something Charlie and Jacob looked forward to. Charlie would even make up assignments to spend more time working with her.

It was Mom who introduced the two boys to the oldies. There had never been a song written Patty Jackson didn't know the words to or didn't know the group's name or the name of the composer. She would allow them to stay up to the wee hours of the night on weekends, teaching them to dance. Charlie was convinced that even after he fell asleep on the couch, Mom would still have the music turned up, dancing with an imaginary partner until the glow of the sun signaled the start of another day.

Patty's love of listening to music, preferably loudly, had more than once forced them to move. Finally, to rectify the problem, Patty bought a small farm in the middle of South Carolina.

Charlie and Jacob grew up in the sandhills located in the middle of the state. A hundred miles inshore, geologists claimed the sandhills were once coastline. The strip of sand, which varied in the width between three to fifteen miles, extended through North Carolina, South Carolina, and Georgia. The sand gnats during late summer could drive a person insane. Jacob swore he felt them fly in his nose, hover behind the cornea of his eye, and fly out his ear.

Mom's first choice had been to move back to the North Georgia Mountains, closer to where she was born. But the vast numbers of people from the Atlanta area had caused property prices to be too far out of reach. Besides, being stationed at the new spaceport east of Columbia, headquartered on the old Fort Jackson army base, made the mountains of north Georgia impractical.

The new base was the home of Earth's largest military space elevator. Camp Victory differed from any other space elevator in service. Anchored in the center of the base was the primary tether woven from a carbon nanothread material produced by Adams Group. The cable extended forty thousand kilometers into space where it was attached to a counterweight, otherwise known as Space Station Victory, Earth's main military space base.

The velocity of the spinning planet kept Space Station Victory in a geostationary orbit, while a second set of cables extending back down were connected to ships in the Atlantic. SS Victory could be repositioned by moving the naval vessels.

What made Space Station Victory so special were the two additional cables anchored between Columbia and Charleston.

Freight elevators ascended and descended using the cables nonstop, carrying supplies to the fleet stationed in low orbit, reducing the cost of ferrying supplies.

•••

Jacob asked Charlie, "Close to figuring out how to operate this thing?"

Charlie never looked up. "I knew you would show up. I think I may have discovered a clue. Rub your palm over this."

Jacob walked over to stand beside his brother.

"Run your hand over the faceplate on the center of the front pedestal," Charlie said. "Right above the royal scepter. What do you feel?"

"Some type of elliptical imprint?" Jacob answered as he bent down to study the spot. "Funny. You can't see anything, but you can definitely feel the impression."

Charlie nodded. "Do you remember in the story how the captain of the *Ares* held out his hand and a jewel appeared?"

Jacob grunted. "Yes, but that is a fable. Jewels do not magically appear in a person's hand."

"No?" Charlie questioned. Charlie reached into his pocket and pulled out the gemstone the prince had given him. "Feel this and tell me it is not an exact match to the impression you felt."

Jacob opened the bag and looked at the stone. He had never studied the jewel up close. Jacob was shocked by the size of it. It reminded him of a large ruby his mother had once pulled from her pocket and shown him. "Okay, I agree. If it isn't the same, then it is a close match. So, now what?"

"I'm not sure," replied Charlie. "Every time I hold the stone close to that spot, I sense something change in the air. Like something is supposed to happen. I am supposed to do something, but I don't understand what."

Jacob wanted to laugh, but he saw the seriousness written all over Charlie's face. So he turned his attention back to the stone. "Charlie, what type of grades did you get in Geology class?"

Charlie glared at Jacob. Jacob knew Charlie had usually made As, his transcript marred by only an occasional B. Jacob never got a B, not once, during his academic career. Charlie assumed Jacob intended to tease him or make him the butt of a joke.

Defensively, Charlie replied, "I don't remember, but I'm sure you are about to remind me."

Jacob laughed. "I was only asking. What was the name of the old jeweler Mom used to love? You know, the one who sold you and me that sapphire to give Mom on her birthday. He said the word sapphire means 'gem of the sun.'"

Still not trusting Jacob didn't intend to make him the butt of a joke, Charlie answered, "So?"

Jacob continued, "He said miners believed a sapphire glowed with its own inner light, even after sunset. Miners would supposedly search for them at night, then go retrieve them the following day."

Charlie reflected for a moment. "What are you suggesting?"

"I have no suggestions. Just studying the situation. I have also been giving thought to what Commander Windsor said about his grandmother calling the stone 'Asteria.' Asteria was a Greek goddess pursued by Zeus. Not sure any of this is relevant."

Charlie took the gem out of Jacob's hand and held it up to the light. With the stone flat in his hand, he pondered for a moment. "*Zeus*, extinguish the lights!"

The lights on the bridge died immediately. Only the pixels emitting from the monitor remained. Charlie continued to stare at the sapphire.

"*Zeus*, I want total darkness. Dim the main monitor."

The monitor dimmed. Charlie and Jacob sat on the bridge in total darkness. Both brothers stared expectantly, sensing something of significance was about to happen but not knowing what.

At first, nothing happened, but then the sapphire glowed faintly. The glow continued to radiate light in the palm of Charlie's hand. The recessed battle lanterns in the ceiling started filling the rest of the room with a soft green glow. Then the scepter on the pedestal glimmered.

Charlie spoke. He sounded much more confident than he felt.

"*Zeus*, I offer you Asteria!"

Immediately, the room flashed with a green light. The ship tremored slightly, and then the gemstone dematerialized. Jacob looked at Charlie in wonder to see what had happened. When he saw Charlie, he panicked. His brother was staring into the palm of his hand. Where the stone was previously perched, there was only a smoldering burn mark.

Jacob tried to help. "Charlie! We need to get you to Doc Laird!"

He reached for Charlie, but Charlie pushed him away. Jacob looked again at Charlie's hand. The wound was healing right before his eyes. Within seconds, Jacob saw only a scar. The smell of smoldering skin hung in the air, burning Jacob's eyes.

Charlie's knees wobbled weakly. "Jacob, help me. I need to sit down."

Jacob grabbed Charlie by the arm and assisted him to the captain's chair. Now things transpired quickly. The whole ship shook, and everything on the bridge transformed, the lights dimming and then coming back on repeatedly. The bridge's general layout changed to the exact design of the bridge on the *Perseus*. Jacob felt he was living in a dream.

Jacob rolled out of the way as the helm shifted position, sliding closer to Charlie's chair, and one by one, joysticks replaced the controls. Everything appeared—minus some obvious minor improvements—identical to the bridge on the *Perseus*.

Jacob remembered how often he had seen Charlie leave his chair to place his hand on his helmsman's shoulder to give him instructions or calm him. The helm's new location was perfect.

Both Charlie's and Jacobs's commlinks lit up at the same time. It was Myers.

"Captain, is everything okay over there? The figurehead on the battleship just lit up, and according to our sensors, all the guns came online!"

Charlie's eyeballs rolled back into his head. Jacob could make out only the faintest trace of his blue irises.

Jacob hit his commlink. "Standby, *Perseus*. We have an unknown situation over here."

He considered ordering Myers to move *Perseus* farther away, just in case, but he could feel in his gut the *Perseus* had never been safer than she was now.

Finally, calm returned to the bridge. Jacob still recognized shaking and vibrations from other parts of the ship, and the dazed look remained on Charlie's face. Jacob keyed his commlink again.

"Myers, get Doc Laird to transfer here from the *Perseus* to examine the captain." At last, the normal day lights replaced the green battle lights, and all the tremors ceased.

Jacob looked at Charlie's hand. There was only a faint trace of the scar in his palm. Jacob tried to take in his new surroundings. Besides the changes to the bridge, Jacob noticed the slight hum of the engines. The engines didn't sound any different, but something had changed. There was now life to the sound. Jacob almost sensed a certain … something. He couldn't put his finger on what. He also couldn't explain what he had just witnessed.

Chapter Twenty-Six

Present Day, the Strivo Corridor

Charlie woke, wide-eyed, and looked around the room. *Wow! What a dream*, he thought to himself. Then he noticed Jacob curled up on the floor with a blanket over his head.

Charlie cleared his throat. "Jacob?"

Jacob woke up and rubbed his eyes. "Boy, you have been out cold. You okay?"

Charlie was puzzled. "Sure, why wouldn't I be okay? Why are you sleeping on my floor?"

The door opened as Charlie was questioning Jacob. Charlie's steward, Thomas, walked in carrying a tray with a bowl of soup.

"He has been sleeping on the floor, in my way, for three days, Captain. Should I have the Sergeant at Arms Wells throw him in the brig?" He smirked.

"Three days?" Charlie asked.

"Maybe not the whole time. He woke up long enough to help us capture two more supply ships," relented Thomas.

Charlie tried to stand, but Jacob stopped him.

"Whoa there. Best to get your space legs back before you try going anywhere too fast!"

Charlie couldn't seem to get rid of the sensation the floor was moving clockwise and the walls to the room were spinning in the opposite direction.

"Take your hands off me, Jacob," Charlie ordered, still disoriented. "Man, I had the craziest dream."

Jacob laughed. "I bet you did. Now you sit there and let me bring you up to date."

•••

Before starting his story, Jacob allowed Doc Laird to give Charlie a full medical rundown on his condition. Laird gave Charlie a glowing report card and finished wryly with, "I believe you will live long enough to be placed in front of a firing squad."

Jacob shot the doctor an evil look. Charlie noticed how rapidly Laird shut up.

From there, Myers picked up the story once they retrieved the captain from the *Zeus* and tucked him in for some much-needed rest.

•••

Myers stopped Laird as soon as he stepped out of the captain's quarters. "How is he? Is he medically fit to be in charge?"

Laird was not fond of Myers. He grumbled a terse reply.

"He will live. Don't worry. As long as he has a pulse, I will not sign anything that leaves you in command."

Laird turned and huffed off, leaving Myers standing there miffed.

Jacob stepped out a little while later, and Myers caught him. "I know this is a bad time. Two nice-sized cargo vessels just entered the corridor on the far end headed this way. What do you believe the captain would have me do? Should I let them pass?"

"I suggest we see how he feels after they get a little closer."

"Do you think he will be up to resuming command?" Myers hesitated, then added, "I think he needs to step aside."

"Why would he do that?" inquired a bristling Jacob.

"I believe the captain is committing a treasonous act by refusing to install the CBC." Myers hesitated again. "I won't lie and say I was happy when I got assigned to the *Perseus*."

"Why?" asked Jacob.

Myers paused, looking at Jacob a moment before saying, "Because serving under a captain only concerned with results, who follows orders only when they suit his fancy, is not a good road to travel if you value advancement within the service. It undermines military discipline. The crew is supposed to follow orders because we, as officers, submit to authority."

Jacob was astounded. "I can see on the surface how it seems the captain is willfully disobeying an order. A captain must sometimes make decisions based on what he believes is in the best interest of the service and to protect his crew."

"As an officer, I will obey the captain's wishes and follow his orders. Hopefully, he doesn't get us all hanged if we ever manage to return home."

"I believe the captain needs a couple days to rest. I doubt Charlie will return before the two cargo vessels get here. You should prepare the ship and crew. If he resumes command before then, we will need to be ready. Should he or the doc decide he needs to take more time off before he returns, then how we deal with our new guests will be your decision."

Jacob intended to request a temporary leave of duty until he was sure Charlie was okay. After hearing Meyer's words, Jacob decided he had best stay close. Myers had never overly impressed Jacob, but for the first time, Jacob did not trust him.

Jacob ran after Myers and caught him as he reached the pneumatic transport. "Myers. Can you promise not to get us killed?"

Myers, with a look of disdain on his face, studied Jacob for a moment, gave a small salute, and stepped into the pneumatic transport.

Jacob watched as Myers disappeared. He did not care much for him, but Jacob felt confident that at least he didn't have a death wish.

Chapter Twenty-Seven
Present Day, the Strivo Corridor

It had taken two days for the large cargo vessels to make it to the kill zone. Charlie, unaware of Myers and Jacob's discussion, decided he should leave Myers in command and remain in his cabin so that his presence would not interfere with Myers's authority.

Jacob walked onto the bridge and strapped himself into Myers's usual seat. He studied Myers sitting there in the captain's chair. Myers had put Stuyck back into his old position at the helm and, only at Stuyck's insistence, placed Andrew in the copilot seat. Myers couldn't stand the fact Captain Jackson was allowing a mere child to sit at the helm of an SC ship. Even he didn't deny the kid was talented, but endangering the entire crew while Rushing received on-the-job training was felonious.

Myers was issuing the same commands Charlie would have given. He even unsnapped his harness and whispered to the helmsman, like Charlie always did, and then took his time strapping himself back in. Myers hesitated as though he had forgotten something. He leaned back in the chair and adjusted the straps so he could move. Despite imitating Charlie to the last detail, Jacob could tell there was something different. When Charlie led the *Perseus* into battle, it seemed he grew more substantial. Not just in physical stature. An aura of authority surrounded Charlie at times like these. Jacob had mentioned this phenomenon to other members of the crew on multiple occasions, and everyone agreed. Doc Laird suggested he measure Charlie at that exact moment to see if he really was larger. Without measurements, he insisted, there was no science.

Myers chose a song from Charlie's playlist and set the attack in motion. The attack was going per the usual script. On their approach, Myers decided to insert both SWAL teams waiting in their balls into the trailing vessel, speed ahead in the *Perseus*, and destroy the lead ship.

It was at this moment the flaxen horn screamed its warning. Four Obsidian destroyers were screaming into position on the *Perseus*'s six. Everyone looked at Myers, but he was wide-eyed and seemed frozen in his seat.

Jacob yelled, "Abort!"

The *Perseus* rolled over onto its port side and performed its awkward but semi-effective version of a barrel roll. Jacob rotated the view to the rear screen in time to see every destroyer open fire in unison. None of the shells came close to striking the *Perseus*, but one of the two Obsidian transport ships they had been pursuing took multiple hits and caught fire.

Jacob watched the destroyers. They were still having problems hitting what they were aiming for, but it appeared they found a solution to their communication issues. As the lead ship rolled to pursue the fleeing *Perseus*, the rest of the destroyers all stayed in a tight formation and followed his lead, much like fighter pilots back on Earth.

Stuyck tried every maneuver he could think of to increase distance between the *Perseus* and the Obsidians. With the gap decreasing exponentially, Stuyck gave control of the helm to Andrew, ignoring protocol by not asking permission from Myers.

Andrew took control of the helm and, like Stuyck, tried every trick he could think of to shake the destroyers off their tail. He managed to add a little distance between them and the warships, but the ships were too quick for poor old *Perseus*. Andrew glanced over his shoulder at his brother Roland and decided he had one more trick to try. He gave Roland a quick nod. Andrew, pushing the yoke slightly forward and hard to the left, turned the *Perseus* as hard as possible to port and shot the gap between the first two ships, straight into the asteroid field.

Jacob grimaced when he saw where the young helmsman was heading. Taken by surprise by the sudden move, two of the destroyers fell out of formation when the *Perseus* unexpectedly shot the gap. The other two reversed direction and were right behind on the *Perseus*'s six, gaining on her; soon they would be so close they couldn't possibly miss.

Myers, finally emerging from shock, screamed at Andrew, "No!"

Andrew tuned out Meyers's voice from his mind. He was tired of the man treating him like a child. Andrew breathed in deeply and held it. Slowly he released his breath, controlling the speed he exhaled, just like his father taught him. Focusing exclusively on the point he knew he must roll the *Perseus* to starboard and placing complete confidence in his brother, Andrew relaxed his shoulders and legs, allowing the tension to dissipate. There was no doubt in his mind the grappling anchor would be exactly where it must be to clubhaul the ship.

Meanwhile, Jacob was holding his breath. He expected Andrew to slow before he hooked around Jaws. Jacob looked up and saw the amber light warning of a probable collision shining. As Andrew neared the hairpin turn, Jacob heard him call Roland's name. Jacob looked and saw Roland eject the starboard bow anchor, pulsing the shields to sling it far from the superstructure. The *Perseus* was moving as fast as she could go, and the anchor hook was being dragged through space on a parallel course. Andrew's move was genius. The *Perseus* lacked enough power to make the turn, so the kid planned to clubhaul the ship around the asteroid. Jacob hastily found the emergency controls used to cut the anchor cable. Andrew shoved the throttle all the way forward past the stops, urging her on. *Perseus* was already giving it all she had, so any increase in speed was negligible. Jacob closed his eyes because he knew everyone on board was about to die.

The g-forces were incredible inside the *Perseus* as the young man barrel-rolled the ship with his joystick and pushed as hard as he could with his foot on the starboard rudder. With his elbow, he ignited the starboard docking thruster to shove the rear of the ship to larboard. Jacob heard M&M to his right puking in her helmet, and two SWALs inside their ball passed out. The *Perseus* skewed sideways as it tried to take the turn. Andrew extended his leg, pushing the larboard rudder pedal, and used his elbow to extinguish the thrust from the larboard and ignite the starboard thruster. The docking thruster provided just enough thrust to prevent the *Perseus* from spiraling into a flat spin. The g-forces dropped when the stern slowly slipped back behind the bow as the *Perseus* exited the corner. Jacob expeditiously pressed the button to release the anchor cable, and the *Perseus* resumed sailing straight.

Milliseconds later, both monitors turned a solid white with crimson lines radiating across the screens. The first destroyer tried to slingshot around Jaws like the *Perseus* but instead skidded sideways into the waiting asteroid. Despite the gargantuan hit, the monstrous rock deviated none from its usual course. The second destroyer, following behind the first, slightly off the lead ship's starboard side, slammed headlong into Jaws and disintegrated. On the situation screen, Jacob watched as the other two bogeys bugged out down the corridor at maximum throttle, not sure what happened. All they knew was the ship their commander sent them to destroy had taken out two of their destroyers.

Myers was taking no chances. He instructed Andrew to pilot the *Perseus* deep into the asteroid belt. Once Myers perceived they were safe, Andrew cut her engines, the music stopped, and the whole universe seemed mysteriously quiet.

Chapter Twenty-Eight
Present Day, the Strivo Corridor

Charlie shook his head in disbelief. "So the kid really did it."

Jacob allowed Charlie to savor the story before he continued. "That is the good news. There is also bad news."

Charlie raised his eyebrows. "What is the bad news?"

Myers interjected before Jacob could answer. "Space Command showed up a few hours ago. They have instructed us to transfer to their vessel, a frigate named *Justice for All*. SC has relieved you of command."

Charlie mumbled, "Yes, that is bad news. How many crew members have already transferred?"

Jacob answered, "No one."

"No one? Why not?" asked Charlie, confusion evident in the expression on his face.

Myers replied, "Every man has refused to accept the order."

"And woman," interrupted M&M.

Jacob, as excited as a kid going to see a parade, wanted to tell Charlie that Myers had ordered everyone to prepare to transfer but refrained.

"What about the sailors we rescued?" asked Charlie.

"Some wanted to transfer until they saw the Obsidian destroyers parked on both ends of the corridor. They decided they had a better chance of surviving on the *Perseus* than they would boarding the *Justice*, for the time being," replied Jacob.

"Has anyone warned the *Justice* about the destroyers?" asked Charlie with genuine concern in his voice.

M&M spoke up. "We hailed them with a warning the second the Obsidian warships appeared on the situation board. They refuse to believe us. They keep demanding we come out of hiding and surrender."

Charlie frowned. "Does the crew realize the *Justice* may be our only ride home?"

Jacob smiled. "I am not sure that is true. It might take longer, but we always have the *Zeus*."

• • •

The standoff with the *Justice* was on day twenty-one. Every day that passed convinced the crew of the *Perseus* they had made the right decision. The *Justice* was sitting in the middle of one of the busiest supply passageways in the universe, and not one Obsidian ship tried to make the journey past her. Meanwhile, Charlie and Jacob were busy transferring crew members to the *Zeus*, deeming their chances better on the small battleship than on the *Perseus*. Charlie drilled the crew relentlessly on the pocket battleship. Slowly, they were finding their way around the new ship and soon had run every plausible scenario Charlie could imagine taking place in the immediate future, from dealing with having to fight against the Justice to coping with the Obsidian destroyers, which seemed more than content to wait for them to come out of hiding.

Even though *Zeus* was longer than the *Perseus*, the crew's quarters were every bit as cramped.

Stidham swore. "At least on the *Perseus* we had the hold to carry cargo. All the captain seems to care about are munitions."

The magazines on the pocket battleship dwarfed the magazines of even the largest SC battleships she had ever been on.

The only amenities the *Zeus* offered that the *Perseus* lacked was the nice-sized mess hall located two floors down from the captain's quarters, adjacent to the brig. It was long enough to accommodate the entire crew.

Benson, helping transfer goods, asked Sergeant at Arms Wells, "Have you seen the new gym? It even has a full-size boxing ring. Now if we only had time to use it!"

Zeus's complement of berths for the crew was 354 beds. Stidham used every berth not assigned to someone as a personal repository of miscellaneous supplies.

Life on the *Zeus* was no different than it had been on the *Perseus*. Most of the sailors had a strict routine to follow. Every day, certain tasks needed to be completed in order to maintain the ship. With the larger ship and greatly increased armament, the amount of maintenance was substantially greater on the *Zeus* than it had been on the *Perseus*. Reveille seemed to come much earlier than the crew was used to due to the increased workload.

With the last of the goods transferred from the *Perseus*, Stidham moved her private stores with help from the only person she trusted, Sergeant at Arms Wells. She took the last of her boxes of precious chocolates and shoved them into the locker above her berth.

She placed her hand on Wells's shoulder and said, "Thank you, Wells. Now if we can only live long enough to run out of supplies so I can sell these chocolates."

"I miss the days where we could at least unwind for an hour or so. I never thought I would miss our games of cards," replied Wells.

Now with all the endless drills on top of the new workload, they remembered the harried pace they had grown used to of hiding ships, moving cargo, and watching prisoners, with longing. Despite the new hardships, the time the crew was spending working so closely together caused them to form even tighter-knit bonds within their divisions.

When neither Charlie nor Jacob could dream up any new scenarios that sounded plausible, the computer aboard the *Zeus* would offer a new possibility. The battle simulation capabilities on the old ship were unbelievably realistic. After some initial disastrous trials with Stuyck, Charlie resorted to training only with Andrew at the helm on the battleship. The explosive power and sensitive controls during maneuvers were giving Andrew fits, but at least he didn't routinely crash and kill everyone on the simulator like Chief Stuyck. Charlie recognized that going from the *Perseus* to the *Zeus* was comparable to leaving a horse on the merry-go-round and instead mounting a wild stallion.

Charlie also recognized how well Andrew was transitioning. Few pilots made the grade to pilot a battleship, let alone anyone as young and with as little experience as Andrew. Charlie had already seen moments of brilliance from Andrew's flying, followed by moments of sheer terror. Neither of these were unusual considering the monumental task of the job.

The captain transferred Stuyck to the *Patricia* along with two of the young teens, Olivia and Richard. Charlie also assigned Shealy and his SWAL team to the *Patricia* to guard the prisoners who were crammed into her hold. Jacob programmed the *Perseus* so the small crew on the *Patricia* could operate her remotely from the maneuverable little craft.

Watching Richard and the SWALs transferring through the access tube to the *Patricia*, Charlie couldn't help but notice how Richard looked every bit a part of Shealy's team. He had often noticed Richard working out with Shealy's squad ever since the unit arrived on board. Richard already had the build of a linebacker but had really muscled up since he started training with Shealy and his men.

Olivia had filled out too, only differently. She was becoming an attractive young lady. Charlie had noticed a couple of the young SWAL team members flirting with her every opportunity they had—particularly young Benson. Charlie made a mental note to speak with Shealy and Peck about keeping their boys in line. Fraternization between personnel was illegal in all military branches but even more important given the rigors of space travel. He also asked M&M to speak to Olivia the first chance she had. The last thing the ship needed was a pregnant shipmate. The young lady adored the ensign, so Charlie was positive M&M's words would be influential.

Charlie later realized he needn't worry too much. Grunby, having given up the bottle, had adopted Olivia as his own. Any young SWAL who got too fresh with Olivia might find themselves needing the care of Doc Laird.

Having the teenagers on board had affected several of the crew members. Their exuberance for life seemed to be contagious. None had been affected more than Grunby. Jacob had only recently commented on the fact that Grunby seemed a changed man. He had not been called to the captain's quarters once since before their jump to subspace. It wasn't that alcohol wasn't readily available. Several of the Obsidian ships carried more liquor than they did water. The defining change seemed to stem from his relationship with the kids, especially Richard and Olivia. Charlie and Jacob watched Richard warmly shake his hand before he departed and observed the hug Olivia and Grunby exchanged before she transferred with her gear to the *Patricia*.

Andrew, while performing above expectations when piloting the ship during simulations, was his own harshest critic. After any dismal performance, he seemed to withdraw. He was growing so peevish, Roland and his cousins tried to avoid him. Every second Andrew was not training at the helm he spent in the simulator. Several crew members noticed he was spending all his time in the training facility. Finally, to squelch any misconception amongst the lower deck that Andrew was avoiding work, Charlie issued an official order for Andrew to spend as much time training in the flight simulator as possible, learning the nuances of flying the old battleship.

M&M, concerned the burden and pressure of Andrew's new post was weighing too heavily on him, asked the captain to speak to him: "I have never seen anyone with so much innate talent. But he is only seventeen. It isn't fair to place so much pressure on him."

Charlie acknowledged M&M's concern and cornered Andrew outside his berth.

"If the simulator is accurate, the ship will be challenging to handle. You feel up to the task?" Charlie asked, trying to sound upbeat.

Embarrassed, Andrew lowered his eyes, shuffled his feet, and hesitated before he quietly replied, "I believe I can handle it, sir. It is taking me time to learn, b-b-but there are things you ought to know that might make you reconsider giving me the opportunity at the position."

With the number of people rushing up and down the hallway, Charlie decided they needed privacy and ushered Andrew into the dining hall. The last of the personnel eating lunch were leaving. Through the serving window on the far end of the room, Charlie saw Sonefeld directing his staff to clean up and begin preparations for the next meal. Dan, seeing Charlie standing with Andrew, reached over and pressed the button that closed the shutters to the hall, giving the captain privacy.

"So what is it I ought to know?" Charlie asked.

Andrew looked at his feet and tried to put his hands into his nonexistent pants pockets. "My father, sir, was an SC helmsman. He was at the helm during the worst defeat of Earth's history. He was the pilot on the *Constrictor*."

"I know who your father is. Ian Rushing was the best pilot I have ever met. I considered him a close personal friend. Is that why you fly so well? Are you trying to compete against a ghost?" Charlie asked, looking Andrew in the eye.

"My father failed when it mattered the most. If the crew ever finds out, it will scare them to death having me at the helm, especially after all the blunders I keep making. It will hurt morale," Andrew replied, a tear forming in the corner of his eye.

He wiped it away and then asked, "How long have you known I was his son?"

Charlie placed his hand on Andrew's shoulder. "I figured it out right after you enlisted. I should have recognized it earlier. You are the spitting image of your father."

Andrew started to speak, but Charlie raised his hand, demanding Andrew listen.

"You should be proud of how well you are doing. It takes years of experience to handle a ship like this. Give me your best, and together we will build from there. You will only get better with time."

"You knew who my father was and still allowed me to take the helm?"

"Son, if you are half the pilot your father was, then I can ask for nothing more. I believe he was the best pilot Space Command ever had. I recognized your talents watching you fly the drones. Son, I was supposed to be on the *Constrictor* that day as her first officer. I was called away on personal business; otherwise, I, too, would have died."

"I know, sir. I found pictures of you with my father."

Charlie reflected on Andrew knowing all this time and saying nothing. He sensed the *Constrictor* was a ghost that would always haunt Andrew. Charlie wished there was something he could say that would wash away his pain. But Charlie had his own ghosts and demons from that fateful battle, and they often troubled him.

"Andrew, no one knows for sure how the Obsidians defeated the *Constrictor*. A lucky shot? A poor decision? No one knows. But I can tell you one thing. It wasn't pilot error. Your father made that ship do unbelievable things. I have faith in you; you, too, have that gift. You are a natural-born pilot, and I am going to trust you will give me your best. That is all I can ask for."

"I will always give you my best, sir," Andrew replied. Still looking at his feet, he wiped more tears from his eyes with his sleeve. "But what if I fail?"

Charlie placed his arm around Andrew's shoulders. "I know you will give me your best. We must learn everything possible about the *Zeus*. When the time comes for *Zeus* to perform the impossible, we must be ready."

Charlie ignored the "what if I fail" question. If Andrew failed, then none of it would matter anyway. They would all be dead.

•••

Training was ongoing everywhere throughout the ship. Despite their youth, the newer members of the crew, rescued from the captured Obsidian transport ship, struggled to keep up with their fast-paced, highly dynamic captain and with the original members from the *Perseus*, who were working hard to bring them up to speed. Not used to the captain or his ways, they were continuously complaining about the excessive time spent training. Lt. Myers, on the other hand, seemed to have developed a loyal following amongst many of them.

The rest of the teenagers had been busy during the few spare moments they had. They tapped live into the internet via the CBC aboard the *Justice*. It appeared the *Perseus* was not the only rogue ship Space Command had to handle. The entire Fifth Fleet under Admiral Halsey had gone rogue and disappeared. This epiphany had the entire crew of the *Perseus* asking what that looked like and what it might mean.

Finally, the *Justice* received orders to abandon its mission and return to Earth. Thanks to the hundreds of small probes lining the passageway, the crew watched as the *Justice* sailed, in plain sight, right past the half-dozen Obsidian destroyers congregated at the end of the corridor nearest the jump point. As soon as the *Justice* left, the Obsidian ships turned and headed slowly down the passageway, systematically searching along the edges of the asteroid belt.

Charlie and Jacob struggled to get a head count on the number of Obsidian ships patrolling the passageway. Their best guess was a half-dozen destroyers were heading toward them from the end nearest the Milky Way. At least three destroyers were guarding the entrance to Obsidian space. The crew of the *Zeus* also determined there were numerous ships at the mouth of the corridor anchored inside Obsidian space. Charlie's best guess was they were cargo vessels waiting for the "all clear" to traverse the passageway.

As soon as the *Justice* passed the last destroyer, Charlie ordered Stuyck to have the now-abandoned *Perseus* leave the safety of the asteroid field and ease up the passage toward the six warships. Once she was in the middle of the passageway, Charlie directed Stuyck to turn on the newly installed CBC. On cue, the Obsidian destroyers formed a line and headed her way.

Jacob had secured all their prisoners on the *Patricia* with Chief Stuyck and his crew. The small ship the *Perseus* captured was loaded to capacity. Chief Stuyck and the two cousins were to pilot the *Perseus* remotely, while Charlie charged Shealy and his SWAL team with containing the prisoners. Charlie now gave the order to release all the prize ships, piloted remotely by Jake and Roland, and start them on their long journey back toward Obsidian space. He had ordered the crew to disperse every ton of their captured explosives amongst the prize ships. Once all the ships were on their way, and Charlie was confident the Obsidian destroyers had time to identify and determine the exact location of each vessel, he hit play on his media player. "Welcome to the Jungle" by Guns N' Roses started echoing up and down the corridor. *Zeus* then discreetly slipped into the line directly behind the menagerie of transport and cargo ships.

The closer the *Zeus* got to Obsidian space, the clearer the picture came into focus. One destroyer guarded the center of the passageway, and her two sisters each protected opposite flanks on the outer edges of the corridor. Behind the three warships was the largest flotilla of transports and cargo vessels Charlie had ever seen. There were hundreds of cargo ships tied nice and tight against each other in three large groupings. Charlie instructed Roland and Jake to have the prize ships divide into three separate groups and direct each group toward one flotilla of anchored vessels.

On the other end of the passageway, the *Perseus* wove back and forth, steadily heading in the general direction of the destroyers. Over the sound of the music, it was apparent the ships were having a hard time locking on to the *Perseus*'s exact location. They slowed but were closing in on the *Perseus*.

As soon as *Perseus*'s prize ships cleared the end of the passageway, the two Obsidian destroyers guarding the flanks converged behind them to protect their stern. The warship in the center of the corridor was doing its best to communicate with the liberated Obsidian transports and cargo vessels. Because of the background noise from the music, the Obsidian captain of the ship assumed they could not hear nor respond.

The Obsidian captain wanted to direct the prize ships to a separate area to be debriefed. The captain was especially curious how they had escaped. Tiring of the fact none of the ships would respond or follow his lead, he ordered a shot fired over the leading ship's bow. It was the crew's best shot all day. With the deafening music messing with their targeting system, the destroyer crew missed their mark. Instead of the projectile going over the bow, the destroyer hit the ship dead amidships.

With smoke rolling out of the lead prize ship, Charlie nodded for the teens to start Operation Fireship.

Charlie directed, "Each of you choose a group of Obsidian transports and fly your ships directly into their mist before setting off your explosives!"

Every transport went to full throttle and spread out to increase the difficulty of targeting for the Obsidians. Flames were now coming out the sides of the prize ship that had been fired upon, but it never wavered off course. It looked like a flaming arrow bolting through space. All the prize ships were headed straight for the three flotillas of moored Obsidian vessels.

The Obsidian merchant ships seemed unaware of the danger headed their way. Much too late, they realized what was happening and panicked. With no way to communicate, each ship captain attempted to disengage from the ships against which they were moored. Rather than retrieve their anchor's cables, crews were simply cutting them. Each executed his or her own idea of how best to escape the blazing ship and her out-of-control compatriots.

The Obsidian destroyers were not having any luck attempting to divert or stop the prize ships. The three were hopelessly spread out, and their weapon control systems were so handicapped that all but two of the improvised fire ships found their mark. One after another, they became entangled amongst the Obsidian vessels anchored together and exploded. Chaos reigned everywhere.

Worse, the three Obsidian destroyers could not provide each other with any overlapping protective fire. Charlie turned up the volume on his player and ordered the crew of the *Zeus* to attack the destroyer on his port side.

The crew of the destroyer never knew what hit them. The salvo from *Zeus* struck the ship like a sledgehammer. Huge gaping holes appeared in the fuselage from the stern to the bow on the ship's starboard side. The lights were immediately extinguished, and the ship glided to a halt. From the undamaged port side, life pods intermittently began ejecting into space.

Zeus made a graceful sweeping arch to starboard and continued firing, now into the crowded merchant ships. Most were burning infernos, but a few were still attempting to make a valiant effort to escape. *Zeus* hit the largest of the merchant ships broadside. The crew of the *Zeus* felt the temperature rise even as far away as they were when the ship exploded. With so many high explosives on the Obsidian ship, many of her neighboring ships simply melted from the heat.

The second Obsidian destroyer was not caught unaware as *Zeus* approached. She was firing wildly in *Zeus*'s general direction. The couple of shells that managed to find their mark bounced harmlessly off the *Zeus*'s shields. *Zeus* ranged alongside the destroyer and opened fire. There was never a pause in the rounds coming from *Zeus*'s port battery. The small warship caught fire near her gun decks, all her lights went out, and it imploded a few seconds later. It was merely a floating hulk as the *Zeus* turned to pursue the third destroyer.

The third destroyer, seeing her sister ships destroyed, first distanced herself, then retreated as fast as her engines would carry her. Rather than give pursuit, Charlie directed Andrew to turn the *Zeus* back toward the merchantmen. One after another, *Zeus* broke the back of the few remaining ships. Life pods were floating everywhere. Many Obsidian crews ejected as soon as they saw the *Zeus* approach. Unlike the Obsidians, who were notorious for plowing over life pods or using them for target practice, *Zeus* did her best to avoid them and allow them free passage.

On the other end of the passageway, the *Perseus* had taken several glancing blows from the destroyers. Tucked away amongst the asteroids, Chief Stuyck received the code word from *Zeus*.

The chief, commanding from the *Patricia* and hoping to lead the destroyers into Charlie's trap, ordered Olivia, "Change the course of the *Perseus* for the gap leading into the asteroid field."

Before the *Perseus* made it, however, the closest Obsidian destroyer hit her square in the engine room, and the *Perseus* glided to a stop. The warships approached cautiously while lobbing shell after shell into her superstructure. The *Perseus*, having succumbed to her many wounds, finally floated off into the asteroids, a lifeless hulk.

The *Patricia*, left with nothing to concentrate on other than survival, stealthily concealed herself amongst the planetesimals.

Chapter Twenty-Nine
Present Day, the Strivo Corridor

As the *Zeus* sped back toward their unannounced rendezvous with the Obsidian destroyers on the other end of the corridor, M&M noticed dark circles under Captain Jackson's eyes. Charlie was wiped out from mental fatigue. The intensity of the conflict and witnessing the death of so many Obsidian sailors had drained him emotionally.

Charlie tried to hail Stuyck on the *Patricia* but received no reply. There were two significant indicator devices that stood prominently in the corners of the bridge for all to see. The one on the left did not function, but Charlie and Jacob determined the one on the right was some type of readiness bar. The readiness bar, as they came to call it, was more of a column. It was one of the few remaining features on the bridge of the *Zeus* that remained from before the ship's revolutionary transformation after Charlie deposited the green star sapphire into the pedestal.

The columns were carved in the Ionic style, which was taller and much thinner than the Doric style. It was also much more decorative than a Doric-style column. The capital on top of the column was decorated with a volute or scroll-like design. At the bottom of the column was a decorative base. The square base started flush to the floor with an ogee, capped by a bullnose on which sat a half-dozen weights, which slid up and down the height of the column.

The columns contrasted against the smooth metallic walls of the ship. They were carved from what looked like a simulated limestone, and the weights were solid gold. The gold bar on top of the stack would rise and fall by its own volition, depending on the conditions on the ship. Judging by the readiness bar, the battle must have severely reduced *Zeus*'s reserves. Charlie contemplated retreating into the asteroid belt to allow *Zeus* time to recoup some of her strength, but he proceeded with his planned attack when he saw the readiness bar rising the closer they got to the destroyers.

Charlie shot another message to Stuyck, warning him the *Patricia* was on her own for a while. Stuyck finally replied, stating he and the crew had to squash a breakout amongst the prisoners. Things were in hand for the present, but he indicated they would appreciate help as early as possible. He closed his message by wishing the crew good luck.

Stuyck, along with the teens, had performed better than Charlie ever dreamed possible using the *Perseus* as a decoy. The software program predicted the *Perseus* might delay the destroyers for up to twelve minutes. Stuyck had played cat and mouse for more than a half hour before the *Perseus* met her demise and almost succeeded in drawing the destroyers into Charlie's trap.

The *Zeus* traveled the passage and then lay in wait behind an oblique hulk of an asteroid for the Obsidian destroyers nearest the Milky Way to make their way back down the corridor. The warships were having a hard time communicating, so they were systematically searching for and destroying all the small drones the *Perseus* had hidden in every conceivable nook and cranny. They were performing their assigned task, unaware of the monumental disaster that had taken place on the other end of the corridor. They were aware, however, that no Obsidian ship could safely navigate the passage until they terminated the awful sound of the music.

Charlie and the crew waited patiently until all the Obsidian warships cleared the bend. From deep inside the asteroids, *Zeus* fired two shells at a time in rapid succession from the rail guns, which ran down the center of her core. Every shot hit home. Two of the destroyers immediately lost power and came to a complete stop. The rest took damage. The one closest to *Zeus* caught fire and exploded in blue flames. The fire spread quickly, and secondary explosions removed large portions of the ship along the gun decks. Soon the inferno reached the magazines. The entire panorama turned bright white when the munitions exploded.

Once the dust settled and the brilliant light from the explosion subsided, Charlie saw that much of the hot molten metal had lodged itself into the second immobile destroyer. Scorching flames were now gushing out of the holes in the vessel's side, but Obsidian sailors were fighting the fire. Charlie suspected they had little hope of saving the warship and prayed the captain would wisely order the crew to abandon ship.

The *Zeus* sprang into action the second the final shot from the rail guns left the muzzle of the weapon. Charlie found *Zeus*'s acceleration exhilarating as she briskly covered the distance between the asteroids and the other four destroyers. To Charlie, *Zeus* felt like she was keeping beat to the music still echoing from every corner of the passageway. Like Jacob predicted, the remaining destroyers speedily formed up. They got into a partial V formation and turned to greet the *Zeus*. Rather than meet the warships head-on, Charlie directed Andrew to take *Zeus* vertical in a hammerhead maneuver. After reaching the pinnacle of her ascent, Andrew stalled *Zeus*'s momentum, flipped over in the opposite direction, and dove through the middle of the destroyers. After a moment's hesitation, the destroyers gave chase.

On the console next to the captain's chair, Charlie saw a pale green light flashing. Charlie looked to see what kind of warning it might indicate. *I have never seen that indicator function during simulations*, Charlie thought to himself. The indicator had an icon showing the large, oversized turbines on each side of the ship had come online. Charlie and Jacob had struggled unsuccessfully for hours to get the two engines that powered the turbines to start and even debated why the ship needed such large turbines. The best they could figure was they must push the *Zeus* sideways into a berth, but the immense size of the turbines puzzled them.

Charlie was curious why the tactical light chose now to suggest he engage the turbines. He heard the engines purr to life the second he toggled the button. It amazed him to see the turbines slide out of the fuselage and swivel to match *Zeus*'s path of travel.

Jacob grinned and winked at Charlie, who was looking over his shoulder at him. "I can't wait to learn what those puppies will do."

Charlie directed his attention back to the situation board. Despite the destroyers being at full throttle, *Zeus* was easily distancing herself from them.

Charlie whispered to Andrew, "We are leaving them. Slow down and let them catch up."

Charlie could see the look of disbelief on the young pilot's face, but dutifully, Andrew eased back on the throttle.

Charlie patted him on the shoulder. "That's more like it. On my mark, I want you to engage full reverse, barrel roll, and flip up and over onto their six."

In a total breach of protocol, the young pilot questioned, "What if they do a split S, fly past us, and roll around behind? They will be on our six at point-blank range. How will I know who to engage if they perform a split Y?"

Under his breath, Andrew added in a whisper, "Worse, what if I miss my landing?"

"Let's hope they don't," replied Charlie, more impressed Andrew possessed the ability to envision a potential problem with his plan than annoyed by the fact he questioned the order. Charlie was also pleased Andrew never vocalized doubt in his ability to perform what even the most seasoned pilots in Space Command would have deemed impossible in a ship the size of the *Zeus*.

Satisfied with the answer, Andrew gripped the throttle, and a determined look spread across his face. The destroyers had almost made up the distance, and twice the lead ship fired, hoping for a lucky shot.

Charlie shouted, "Now!"

Zeus's powerful engines roared like a lion backed into a corner as the throttle was reversed. Then the large side thrusters rolled downwards and the auxiliary engine kicked in. *Zeus* responded, flipping so swiftly that Andrew undershot his mark, landing directly behind the lead ship and in between the three trailing destroyers instead of on their six.

It didn't matter; *Zeus*'s gun crews never missed a beat. Despite the aerobatic maneuver subjecting the crew to immense lateral g-forces, both the port and starboard gun decks opened fire simultaneously. The lead destroyer dove for the nonexistent deck, but the three trailing destroyers took an incredible amount of punishment and went tumbling end over end into space. The crew of *Zeus* did not dawdle. If they had, they would have seen the destroyers come to pieces and evaporate into space dust. Charlie, ignoring the tumbling mess, ordered Andrew to invert the *Zeus* and dive after the final fleeing Obsidian destroyer.

The destroyer captain was desperate to escape. He began ejecting guns from the gun ports and expelling water from the ship's reservoir. The loss of the extra weight helped the ship increase speed, but it wasn't enough. *Zeus* was still easily gaining on her, hand over fist.

Zeus did not have to fire a single shot. The destroyer had already received the mortal wound. During *Zeus*'s initial salvo, a shell buried itself right in front of the port engine intake where the engines inhaled the cold vacuum of space to cool her engines. During the high-speed maneuvers of the chase, the spent shell slogged itself loose and was sucked straight into the engine, disemboweling the port side of the vessel. The ship promptly came to pieces. Several of the ship's life pods ejected, but the spinning and rolling pieces of debris from the destroyer obliterated the pods before they placed enough distance between themselves and the fuselage. Andrew performed an Immelmann loop, flipping the *Zeus* inverted in the opposite direction, then rolled to starboard and turned to orbit the disintegrating craft. The crew on the *Zeus* could only watch and empathize. None of them would have hesitated to rejoice at an enemy spaceship exploding, but seeing the fragile life pods being destroyed made the Obsidian crew's deaths much more personal.

Chapter Thirty

Present Day, the Strivo Corridor

Mop-up duty took longer than the actual battle. After retrieving Chief Stuyck and his detachment, Charlie had the crew search every square inch of the debris fields, under Jacob's instruction. Life pods by the hundreds passed *Zeus*, headed in the general direction of Obsidian space. Myers wanted to run them down, but Charlie ordered they were to be given free passage.

Charlie next ordered all the Obsidian prisoners on the *Patricia* to transfer into life pods and to be released. Soon they fell into an orderly line, and Captain Fernandez, from their first captured prize ship, positioned himself in the middle of the passage, directing all the life pods toward Obsidian space. Charlie almost hated to see Captain Fernandez go, knowing that someday should they meet again they might be forced to kill each other. Over the course of many dinners together, Charlie felt he and Miguel had become friends who happened to serve on opposite sides of an unfortunate conflict.

While the crew set charges on any piece of equipment determined to be salvageable, the *Patricia* was busy ferrying munitions to top off *Zeus*'s magazine. Several of the newer crew members grumbled to the only person who seemed to share their sentiments, Lt. Myers.

"XO, why are we wasting time searching through this mess, and why are we letting the prisoners go? Why not just shoot them?"

Charlie heard none of the grumblings, but Jacob did. He pulled Myers to the side.

"You need to reel your men in, Myers. You said yourself, the men obey because we obey. You must maintain discipline."

The complaints soon abated.

It took two days, but the crew found what Charlie and Jacob were searching for. Jacob slipped the small processor, which was the heart of the CBC on the stern of the *Perseus*, into his pocket and proclaimed the search complete.

All the crew members looked beat. Once they secured the *Patricia* deep inside the asteroids in the cove behind Aphaea, most of them retired straight to their berths without even hitting the showers.

Charlie contemplated spending a few days hidden in the asteroid belt to give his people plenty of time to recuperate. With everything buttoned down, he decided on a course of action. He leaned over Stuyck's shoulder at the helm and placed his hand on his back.

"Let's go home."

Zeus sped up, packing on more speed. It confirmed Charlie's suspicions. *Zeus* was not capable of subspace speed, but she was fast. The engines continued to increase in intensity. Charlie did some mental calculations and deduced that at the present pace, *Zeus* might make it back to Earth in about eighteen months. Finally, Charlie had Stuyck level out at what he deemed to be a comfortable cruising speed for *Zeus*. Not a single member of the crew woke from their dreams.

As the *Zeus*'s speed leveled out, Charlie opened the latest news they had intercepted from back home on Earth. With communications signals taking so long to reach this far into space, the news was, of course, weeks old. Surely their mission to disrupt the Obsidian supply chain had to be having some effect. The absence of the warships, which the Obsidians had been forced to redirect from elsewhere to the corridor, might not have been noticed inside Earth's solar system, but the loss of supplies had to be taking a toll on the Obsidian war effort.

Warships might win battles, but it was logistics that won wars. Without supplies coming through the corridor for the last six months, those warships' ability to wage war had to be diminishing.

Not finding anything to confirm his suspicions in the news, Charlie laid his head back against the top of his command chair and drifted off to sleep.

●●●

The next few weeks were relaxing—nothing but smooth sailing day after day. If it weren't for worrying about Maddie and what awaited with SC when he got back, Charlie would have been perfectly content for the voyage to never end. *Zeus* was making good progress, and everybody aboard was torn between excitement and anxiety of what they might expect once they arrived home.

Having rested, the crew returned to work. Charlie led them in practicing one simulated battle scenario after another. It was a sobering epiphany to many of the crew to see several battle scenarios included potential conflicts against hypothetical SC vessels. The revelation was especially troubling to the young SC sailors who had been rescued from the Obsidian prison ship. One young airman cornered Myers. "Sir, surely we are not going to fight our own when we return to Earth?"

Myers scowled. "I am not sure what to think anymore, airman. We might have to because we sure aren't going to be welcomed back with open arms."

"Then what are we going to do as a crew?" asked the incredulous airman.

Myers looked thoughtful, then replied, "We will have to cross that bridge when we come to it, son."

When the crew members on the *Zeus* weren't honing their skills by practicing, Andrew was spending all his spare time in the simulator. Both Charlie and Jacob were impressed by his work ethic. When duty allowed, both Charlie and Andrew spent time in the simulator training together. Andrew's skill was making serious strides, and the two of them were spending so much time together, they now almost anticipated each other's next move. It was not uncommon to see the captain leaning out of his chair to give the young pilot a fist bump. It had also become commonplace to see the two of them eating lunch together down in the main mess hall.

After a particularly grueling exercise, Charlie paused the simulation midstream. He addressed Andrew. "You are trying too hard to anticipate my thoughts."

"But complex maneuvers require preparation long before you request them."

"I understand that. You and I must anticipate each other's thoughts instinctively. Instinct is key. If you are concentrating on what I might do next, or worse, what I may have overlooked, then you can't focus on what we are doing in the present. You must relax. The purpose for us training together is to develop mutual trust. Reading each other's minds will become reciprocal once we recognize each other's tendencies."

"I apologize, Captain. In your mind you recognize a situation too comprehensively for me to detect any tendency. Where I see a dilemma, you envision opportunity."

"So? You have discovered my tendency. In your mind, search only for opportunity. It is my responsibility to resolve any dilemma we face. Not yours. You must trust me to fulfill my directive, like I must trust you to perform beyond the limits of the ship. Focus on the most obscure opportunity imaginable, and most of the time you will have channeled my thoughts."

Andrew looked thoughtful for a moment. "I can do that."

Both raised their fists and met each other halfway.

No one had seen much of Jacob, who had been spending time down below with young Jake, working on some phantom project. He and Charlie had seen little of each other since the battle in the corridor. Jacob would respond to the call to quarters, perform his duty, and disappear back down below deck as soon as the drill was complete. Charlie made a mental note to invite Jacob to dinner. He would make his attendance mandatory, if needed, to tear him away from his newest project.

Charlie eased back into his chair on the bridge. He glanced to the corner of the room at the readiness bar. It currently read 62 percent, an all-time high. Charlie leaned back farther. From his console, he heard a sound he had not heard since he left the Milky Way: the familiar sound of email. Curious, he reached over and pulled his console in front of him. Sure enough, the familiar flag on his inbox was raised.

Charlie gasped when he tapped the icon to see he had thousands of emails and more were downloading. Then he remembered. Jacob drove the crew hard, looking for every piece of the processor on the CBC that might have survived. Jacob never informed Charlie he found what he was searching for; he didn't have to. Jacob had the family gift of hard-headed persistence. Once Jacob called off the search, Charlie knew Jacob had found what he needed. Somewhere on the ship, Jacob was busy working on a vision he had of being able to open a secure communication channel with Earth.

• • •

Two decks down, Jacob was working. Daily, he dragged Jake out of his bunk, moaning and groaning, and buried him with work on his project.

After a while, Jake forgot he was always tired. Jake lost himself in a world of ones and zeros. Before his father had been sent off to prison for hacking, Jake had spent every waking hour with him. Early on, Jake watched and learned everything his father had had to teach him. Eventually, his father realized it was Jake who was becoming the teacher.

Jake often thought of his father, a man many loathed after the news reported he had stolen people's hard-earned money. That wasn't the man Jake remembered. He remembered his father as someone who spent all his free time playing games with him. A person who was loving. It hadn't been uncommon for them to start a strategy game right after dinner on Friday nights. The two of them would fight it out until either one of them conceded or they became so helplessly deadlocked there was no reason to continue. Many of the games between him and his father would last until the wee hours of Sunday morning. After finally calling the game, Jake would run to take a shower while his dad made a good hearty breakfast with all the fixings: bacon and eggs with hash browns— or even better, grits—plus sliced fruit and French toast. His father would never look at his computer or phone or allow anything to distract him during this meal. It was their bonding time.

It was during those Sunday morning breakfasts his dad would learn everything going on in Jake's life. Not even his darkest secrets did Jake hide from his dad during those meals. When Jake told his dad that boys at school were mean to him, his dad would listen. Rarely would he offer any advice, though; he would just allow Jake a chance to vent. Often, the following week, the problems Jake shared didn't seem so bad anymore—particularly being picked on at school. Middle school was such a horrible experience. What Jake didn't know was his dad had been making mental notes while Jake was sharing his problems. The following morning, his dad would sit in the principal's office, doing something about them.

Many things changed once his mother returned and Richard and Olivia came back home to live with them. Sunday morning breakfasts were no longer as special, having to share his time with his mother and siblings. His dad also seemed much more stressed, probably due to having the extra mouths to feed, children to dress, and homework help to give. Worse was the stress of his mother and father always bickering. There always seemed to be tension between them. Eventually, the weekend games and Sunday morning breakfasts were just a memory. His dad was always on his computer.

At first, Jake assumed he was trying to make enough money to make ends meet and to satisfy his wife's insatiable obsession with money, a fascination Jake could not understand since his father made good money and his mother had a well-paying job with some type of think tank back in Washington. Soon, his father spent even more time trying to cover his tracks to avoid being caught. Jake vividly remembered his mother and father fighting all the time. The arguments at times seemed to have more do with his mother's twin sister, Dianna—Roland's and Andrew's deceased mother—than finances. But it still all seemed to come down to money. Jake and Richard, being close in age, became good friends, and both felt responsible for taking care of Olivia since their parents were no longer there for them.

The evening they came to arrest his dad, his mother had sat despondently at the kitchen table, searching the internet, deep in thought. Shortly after she sent the three of them to bed, Jake heard the car door slam and engine crank. None of them heard from her again. The following morning, the school's resource officer showed up at the house, followed closely by a social worker. Somehow, the authorities knew to come.

Jake remembered Olivia screaming and fighting when the social workers took her away. They promised she would love her new home, but week after week, the emails from Olivia spoke of how miserable and alone she felt. Jake realized, as the oldest, he must do something, anything, to make things right again.

He and Richard got out of their foster mother's car like they always did when she dropped them off at the front entrance to the middle school. They milled around outside the doors to the entryway until the car disappeared. Jake then opened his laptop and forwarded an email from his foster mother's email account, explaining to the headmaster that Jake and Richard would miss school for a few days. He also addressed the same email to Richard's football coach. For the life of him, he no longer remembered what story he concocted to explain why they would be absent. The boys had thrown their books behind the hedgerow in front of the school and wandered down the road to the local rail yard.

Unfortunately, the train they managed to hop wasn't going in the direction Jake expected. Jake reasoned their first mission was to make good on their own escape before going to save Olivia. The train left heading west. Jake remembered sitting with his feet hanging out the open door of the boxcar, watching as the train made its way over mile after mile of swamps and mosquito-infested water. The bridges never seemed to end. When the train finally stopped and he and Richard hopped off, they were on the Mississippi-Louisiana line.

By the time they made it back to Alabama to liberate Olivia, she was gone. That was when Jake used what he learned from his father. Jake carried his laptop with him everywhere he went and usually managed to keep it charged. After several failed attempts, Jake managed to hack into the Alabama Social Services in-house computer system. They had sent Olivia away to a secure group home for children who were particularly hard to handle. Jake wasn't sure what a "secure facility" meant, so he issued transfer papers to have Olivia sent to new foster parents. Two nights after she arrived at her new placement, Richard climbed the trellis on the back side of the two-story house. Richard tied off the rope they had stolen from the local hardware store, following the instructions they had found on the internet.

They decided Richard should be the one to climb the rope because of his superior upper body strength. Olivia managed to climb down the rope safely, but as soon as Richard put the weight of his much larger frame on the line, the knot failed. Richard crashed down, landing in a rose garden planted in the corner of the raised deck against the house.

Jake laughed at how ridiculous they all looked when they climbed in the cab, asking the driver to take them to Red Mountain Park outside Birmingham. He and Richard had slept in one of the old forgotten mines when they had first arrived in the area, searching for Olivia. Now, Richard's arms were bleeding all over his semi-clean football jersey, rose petals all over him. The roses in his hair were especially funny looking.

It mortified Jake when the man announced the price of the cab fare. Not having enough money to pay him, the three of them fled. The driver had no intention of being cheated out of his cab fare, though, so he chased them down. After a lengthy discussion, the driver loaded them back into his cab and allowed them to stay with his parents until the furor over Olivia's disappearance died down. To work off the amount they owed, Richard and Jake raked pine straw for the man, carefully pushing it down tight into a wooden crate and then tying baling twine around it. They then opened the front of the container and added the bale to a massive stack of pine straw in the back of a flat trailer. The driver had attached sides to the trailer, making it look like a huge cage on wheels. Five days and eight loads later, he finally declared them even.

That night they slid into the luggage compartment on a bus. The three of them thought they would freeze to death before the bus finally stopped. Jake prepared them to take off running as soon as the doors opened, but the bus driver didn't seem to notice them hidden beneath the bags. They exited quietly in the general confusion of the passengers unloading and slipped away unnoticed. They discovered they were in the great state of Texas.

The three moved from place to place in Texas for the next few months. They would stay in one area, often sleeping under bridges at night and hanging around behind restaurants and grocery stores until the locals got wise to them and called the police. Sometimes they would discuss turning themselves in so that Olivia could have a chance at a normal life, but Olivia would have none of it. She absolutely refused to be left behind.

After roaming around Texas for almost a year, Jake received word from Roland that Roland and Andrew's father had been killed and that he and Andrew were headed to Texas. They arranged to meet up in Tyler.

Neither Jake nor Richard wanted anything to do with the government or the military. After having lost their father on the battleship *Constrictor*, neither did Andrew or Roland. That included not wanting to have to serve their mandatory time in the armed services. Jake spent days and nights learning to hack into the international registry, by all accounts an impossible feat. Once he was in, Jake set up an account for himself so he could come and go as he pleased.

The five cousins stuck together, moving from place to place in a generally westward direction. They all agreed they would rather take their chances together on the streets than depend on adults in the system.

Olivia complained that she missed going to school, so Richard insisted that Jake find online classes for all of them. Richard was particularly insistent that Olivia and Andrew, as the youngest of the group, were diligent in their studies. He always took them to the libraries in the towns they passed through, and they always took advantage of the free books the libraries displayed in their foyers. The five spent many evenings studying together online when the laptop was charged.

The cousins made their way to Tucson, Arizona, where they discovered a little diner where the owners would give them leftover food at the end of the night and let them eat inside while Jake recharged the laptop and they studied.

Often, the only other late diners were crew members from a reclamation unit, which was working at the airbase nearby. One evening, Commander Jackson approached them and asked if they would be interested in a few days of work.

The crew of the *Perseus* was the first set of adults who ever treated them with respect. Since they had been living on their own, people looked at and treated them as vagrants. Commander Jackson didn't ask too many questions when they first met. He only offered decent wages. Wages, Jake learned much later, he paid out of his own pocket.

When the commander first hired them, he was trying to find someone to help old man Grunby and the chemist CPO Evans. Grunby had a bad back, not to mention some terrible habits. Jake, Richard, and Andrew were supposed to run up and down ladders, taking Grunby tools so he wouldn't strain anything because the commander so desperately needed him to be able to weld.

Roland and Olivia got the much more enviable task of helping Evans. The commander required Evans to move her entire lab from directly below the commander's quarters to the rear of the ship, closer to Engineering. Jake had never learned exactly why. Something about having started a fire and the commander's quarters smelling like burnt acid. CPO Evans was a large woman, and all the physical strain seemed to cause her asthma to flare up. Jake didn't understand how a woman in her condition ever passed the physical exam to enroll in SC.

The fouled anchor on Evan's insignia seemed appropriate on her sleeve, considering all the trials and tribulations life on board the *Perseus* shoved her way daily. Being perpetually short-handed, she was always assigned jobs for which she seemed ill-suited. Currently, she was the lead gunner over the ship's two rotary cannons. She preferred being left alone in her lab performing her unusual experiments. Routinely, she had Roland or Olivia ferry some vial, of God only knew what, to Paschal to try mixing into the ship's energy core. Paschal would always sign for the package, smile, and toss the lethal concoction into the hazardous waste bin.

Jake and his cousins were finishing their initially agreed-upon three days of work. The commander and LT were attempting to load a large piece of equipment they had been working on into the cargo bay of the ship. After several unsuccessful attempts to load the awkward machine using the drones, CPO Stuyck narrowly missed flying his drone into the rear exhaust on the *Perseus*.

Perturbed that the boys were laughing at him, Stuyck tossed his controller at Roland and said, "If you think it's easy, you try it."

Roland jumped at the offer to fly one of the drones they had been watching buzzing around the ship. The rest of the crew, seeing that neither Captain Jackson nor Lt. Jackson objected, offered the three cousins their controllers as well.

Their first two attempts were much more dismal than Stuyck's effort. Stuyck was about to retrieve his controller when Andrew asked to try. Quickly, he explained to his brother and cousins what they were doing wrong. As soon as the machines lifted off the ground, they followed Andrew's lead and slowly rotated the device, continuing to fly the drones in a slow circle until they could set the equipment on the rear deck of the *Perseus*. Andrew complained the drone he was flying didn't have enough power to move at the same rate as the other three. By rotating his machine, he used the torque from his rotors to keep from waffling from side to side with the equipment.

The kids impressed the commander, so he offered to extend their employment for as long as the *Perseus* was working in the area. The commander took a liking to Andrew, while Stuyck in engineering took Roland and Richard under his wing. He seemed particularly impressed with Roland. Olivia decided Ensign Marie was perfect, and she wanted to be just like her. To the boys' horror, she asked Grunby to cut her hair like the ensign's elegant twisted bun, a popular style in the ensign's native India. To their astonishment, the old man did a nice job. Olivia doted on the old man so much he even made her a gold ring and matching earrings. Jake had no doubt he had come by the gold by skimming off thin layers from the gold trim found in the central databank of the ship.

For some unknown reason, it was Lt. Jackson who singled Jake out. It was almost as if he knew Jake had talents and skills he could use. Lt. Jackson treated Jake with respect and didn't act all soldierly. He was smart but didn't act like a know-it-all or like he thought he was better than anyone else. Jake would do almost anything to earn even the smallest word of praise from Jacob.

•••

When the lieutenant first woke him, telling him what he wanted to attempt, Jake was pretty sure he was being led on a fool's errand. He was confident not even his father could defeat the security measures Space Command surely built into their intranet systems. It shocked Jake when Lt. Jackson removed the outside panel and overrode the built-in security protocols. Lt. Jackson seemed to understand exactly what to look for. Somehow the Lieutenant also knew where to locate the system's secret back door. Jake never found the nerve to ask the lieutenant how he knew, but once they were in, it became clear to Jake it wasn't because of the LT's computer programming skills. Once they were past the lockout system, the LT was totally reliant on Jake's talents.

Most of the first week, Jake and Jacob worked to create their own homemade CBC unit using the available hardware. The trick, Jake insisted to Jacob, was not in gaining access to the internet. The trick was in covering their trail once they were in, so no one knew they had access. Once the two of them created a transmitter and installed the chip recovered from the *Perseus*, Jacob left Jake to perform his magic.

Jacob spent his days developing foolproof firewalls. The last thing *Zeus* needed was one of the crew contacting their loved ones and giving away information that would betray the *Zeus*. Once confident his firewalls were secure, Jacob sat back and waited on Jake.

It took several attempts for Jake to wake the Lieutenant. Jacob was deep in a dream and cuddling with a young lady he had dated for a while back when he was in college. For the life of him, he could not remember her name ... Definitely better than his usual dreams.

"Lt. Jackson! Wake up!" Jake kept saying over and over while shaking Jacob. "We did it! We are in!"

Jacob bolted up. "You hacked into Space Command?"

The excitement in Jake's eyes waned, and he replied somewhat sheepishly, "I haven't made it that far yet, sir."

"Oh," replied Jacob. "Sorry, I must have fallen asleep. Now, tell me. What have you done?"

Jake fidgeted. "Like I said, I haven't made it that far yet, but I managed to get a live feed on the net established."

"The net?" asked Jacob.

"Yes, sir. You know, the internet."

"That's a good start. How old is the feed?"

"How old, sir? It's live, sir. Real time." Jake replied, some of his former enthusiasm returning. "The new antenna on *Zeus* is unbelievable. Instead of waiting on the signal to reach the ship, the ship is reaching out and retrieving it."

Jacob pondered this news for a moment and asked, "How is that possible?"

Silently, Jacob wondered how *Zeus* had acquired an advanced capability on the cutting edge of technology. The ability to reach out and draw in a signal was a highly classified secret.

Jake assumed the lieutenant was in over his head. "I'm not sure, sir. There are things on *Zeus* I would not believe possible. Do you mind if I shoot off a few emails to some old friends, sir?"

Jacob's furrowed eyebrows said it all. "That would be a definite 'no.' Deny everyone internet access and keep quiet that we have it working. If someone gets online and gives away our position, it might get us all killed. Do you understand?"

"Yes, sir," Jake said, realizing the foolishness of his request. Besides, he didn't really know who he would have emailed if Jacob had given him permission.

"Good. Now show me what you have done and keep it in layman's terms so I can keep up." Jacob paused. "By the way, you did an outstanding job."

Jake smiled. The praise coming from Lt. Jackson meant more to him than anything.

Chapter Thirty-One

Three Years Ago, Inside Earth's Solar System

After Maddie discovered Gustafson was expecting a gold shipment, she told Charlie she needed to leave for a few weeks to arrange for someone to place a stone on her parents' grave. To her horror, Charlie insisted he should go with her and help. Fortunately, he received orders to report back to the *Atlantis* until the ship was officially decommissioned.

Not having anyone else she trusted, she shared her plan with only two people: Joan and Jacob. Knowing the Obsidians would deliver the load in a discreet, nondescript location and then leave before Gustafson arrived to retrieve it, Maddie planned to swoop in and take the load in the interim.

Jacob almost had a coronary. "There is no way that will work!"

Maddie refused to be deterred, so Jacob went to work improving her idea. Maddie called a former associate she had used many times while working for the agency, Jack Chacon. Chacon, a ladies' man, had always had an eye for Maddie, but he was also a professional. At least as professional as one might expect of a mercenary. He had chased Maddie for years, wanting to pursue a romantic relationship with her, but Maddie never found him desirable. Maddie was confident she could easily persuade him to keep his personal desires in check and be content to make a handsome profit.

His ship, the *Felicity*, and her crew would be perfect for what Maddie had in mind. She intended to retrieve the *Peccary*'s cargo. What she would do with it once she had it she hadn't figured out yet. At the time, she joked to Joan she would find a deserted island and bury it inland of the sandy beaches. Curious, she wondered how big a hole she would have to dig to bury 125 tons of gold.

Jacob was impressed by Chacon. He was knowledgeable, and he seemed to have earned the respect of his crew, although with his thick French accent, Jacob had trouble at times following his orders to his team. The admiral had always emphasized the only effective crew was a happy crew. If that were the case, then the *Felicity* would be up to the task. They were enthusiastic and seemed to adore their captain. Jacob decided, however, he wouldn't trust him any further than he could throw him. Something about Chacon made Jacob uneasy. He seemed to know much more about their mission than Maddie had shared with him.

Jacob and Joan had both taken the week off to go with Maddie on her death wish, as Jacob called it.

The *Felicity* impressed Jacob with her acceleration and maneuverability, and her crew was very well trained. The ship might not stand a chance against a man-of-war, but Jacob felt confident that against any comparable craft the same size as the Obsidian's the *Peccary*, the *Felicity* could easily hold her own. The good news was Maddie's plan did not involve them having to engage the Obsidian ship.

The plan, much to Jacob's surprise, at first seemed to be a complete success. The crew of the *Felicity*, under Chacon's close supervision, easily loaded the massive container into the hold of the ship. It wasn't until they were underway that Jacob grew uneasy. It hadn't taken the crew long to figure out exactly what was in the cargo container.

Chacon, besides shamelessly making advance after advance toward Maddie, had quietly been calculating the weight of the container. He accurately guessed whatever he was hauling was about 1,206 pounds a cube. Jacob knew the three of them were in trouble when he saw Chacon looking up the current price of gold per pound.

Afraid of trouble, Jacob eased out of his seat and slid into the hallway where he had seen the ship's weapons cache stored. He was about to unlock the cabinet when the ship's siren blared. Jacob stuck his head around the corner when he heard Chacon cursing. On *Felicity*'s small situation board, Jacob saw why. Directly on their six was a Space Command corvette rapidly closing the gap between them.

It only took a few moments before the ship's technical officer had the vessel on the primary monitor. Jacob studied the warship and immediately concluded it was approximately a five hundred-ton vessel—too big for the *Felicity* to fight but the smallest corvette SC had ever commissioned. Most SC corvettes were usually four times that size.

Chacon ordered his helmsman to go to full throttle. The *Felicity* and the small corvette began a long, tedious stern chase across space. As fast as the *Felicity* was, it soon became clear the corvette would eventually overtake them.

Jacob crawled into an empty control station near the rear of the bridge. The first thing Jacob did was research, trying to identify the name of the ship chasing them, hoping to learn the capabilities of the craft. By extension, he hoped to find a weakness to exploit. Determining the name of the ship didn't take long. The corvette was the UCSC *Atout*. At the time of its launch, it was considered state of the art, the most powerful of its class. Between its age and the propensity for SC to build bigger and bigger ships, it shortly became obsolete. What the identity of the ship revealed disturbed him.

He motioned for Maddie and Joan to come look. The ship chasing them was decommissioned immediately after the last war with the Obsidians and never put back into service. Joan asked, "If the ship is mothballed, then who is sailing her?"

Maddie replied, "Someone who knows what we are hauling or to whom our cargo belongs."

Jacob zoomed out, searching the surrounding space. Whispering, he said, "I think I have found help."

On Jacob's monitor, Joan and Maddie saw a blip Jacob designated "XD *Penetrator*."

"That is the destroyer our research team has been using to test the new CBC."

Confused, Joan asked, "Is it being sent to hunt us, too?"

Jacob shook his head. "The *Penetrator* is on a space trial. Our team is supposed to be testing some new upgrades over the next month. It has the same skeleton crew you met a few months ago," Jacob said, nodding at Maddie. "The ship is basically being operated like a drone. The crew members are little more than passengers."

Maddie asked, "So how can the *Penetrator* help us?"

"If we can gain control of her, we can use her to intercept our pursuers," explained Jacob.

Joan sounded pessimistic. "Whatcha gonna do? Call them up and ask them to help? Besides, they are twice the distance from us as the *Atout*."

Jacob, tuning out Joan and Maddie, pounded furiously on his keyboard. His first attempt to open the back door to the system he installed on the CBC didn't work. Carefully, he tried entering his password one more time.

Maddie heard him softly exclaim, "Yeah! We are in."

Turning to Maddie, Jacob said, "You need to get Chacon to change course to intercept the *Penetrator*."

"But—" protested Maddie.

"No buts. Do it. Chacon must change course now. I have redirected the *Penetrator* to intercept us. With us heading toward each other, our closure rate should allow it to reach us before the *Atout* overtakes us."

Maddie was in a league of her own when it came to leveraging people, but with all this talk of closure rates and remotely taking control of ships, she was in over her head. She decided she had to trust Jacob. After all, the *Penetrator* just changed course before her eyes.

Firmly, Maddie said, "Jack, I have help on the way. Change course to ..."

Jacob, realizing Maddie didn't understand navigation well enough to tell Chacon what to do, shouted out the desired heading.

Chacon, not happy with the trouble Maddie had gotten him into, fumed. She had promised this would be an easy score. Now, he had an SC warship on his six, and Maddie wanted him to change headings and head straight toward another. Chacon considered his options and, seeing no other way out of the predicament, ordered his helmsman, "Change course and head straight toward the second destroyer."

Before anyone back on Earth could recover control of the *Penetrator*, Jacob speedily severed Space Command's connection and locked them out. On his screen, he received a ping indicating someone on the *Penetrator* was attempting to hail him. Jacob turned the transmitter to audio only. Before the crew could ask any questions, Jacob took control of the conversation.

"*Penetrator*, we have suffered a catastrophic failure and lost control of the CBC. They will force us to initiate self-destruct sequence alpha. You need to eject."

Captain Green of the *Penetrator* protested, "We have no control of the ship, but we detect no immediate danger to justify ejecting, base. It seems like an outside party has taken control of the ship. How is that possible?"

"Captain, time is of the essence. Again, I order you and the crew to eject."

Sounding unsure, Captain Green said, "Sir, I cannot give the order to eject unless I know the ship is doomed. We are not detecting anything wrong other than, apparently, neither of us has control of the helm."

Jacob, trying to sound calm but authoritative, said, "Captain Green, Terrence, we have received orders directly from the Admiralty to destroy the craft after you eject, or with you on it if necessary. Please. Follow orders and eject immediately."

Still wavering, Green asked, "On whose authority am I ordering the crew to eject? I need positive identification."

Jacob hesitated for only a moment. "Gustafson, ID number XT1ST12Y."

Green didn't reply for almost a minute. There was only silence on the radio. Jacob felt confident the captain must be on to him.

Finally, Green said, "Affirmative, Gustafson. *Penetrator* is starting evacuation procedure alpha."

Relieved, Jacob replied, "Affirmative, *Penetrator*."

•••

Maddie and Joan strapped into their chairs and watched the *Penetrator* on the screen moving closer by the second. Maddie also studied the small monitor showing the *Atout* on their six. The ship did not seem to be gaining quickly, but everyone realized her guns could have destroyed the *Felicity* anytime they chose.

Jacob, listening to the headset he was wearing, swore to himself. Maddie looked at him inquisitively. Jacob continued to listen intently to his headset, first glancing at Maddie, then locking eyes with Joan.

"Gustafson is on the *Atout*."

Jacob turned back to his control panel and made adjustments to open another channel with the *Penetrator*.

Joan, wide-eyed, asked, "How can you be sure Gustafson is on the *Atout*?"

Jacob, never looking up from the keyboard he was furiously typing on, said, "One, because I would recognize her gravelly voice anywhere. Two, she is using her authorization string to take control of the *Penetrator*."

Jacob did not mention that, even worse, he intercepted an emergency message from her to the Obsidian destroyers escorting the package into the asteroid belt. She warned them their package had been stolen. The ships replied that unless the *Atout* retrieved the cargo, they had orders to join the chase. They said they would clear the bubble and be inside Earth's solar system in exactly eighty-two minutes. The part that shocked Jacob the most was all the orders seemed to originate from someone inside Space Command's Intelligence service back on Earth.

Jacob was trying to focus on the crisis at hand but also wanted to learn who from SC was orchestrating all of this. He motioned for Joan to sit at the monitor beside him. Reading the communiqué, she immediately recognized what she was seeing. Feverishly, she tried to trace where and from whom the commands ordering all the madness were coming.

Scanning his monitors, Jacob spotted a small fleet of ships. The name of the lead ship he knew well. Quickly, he prepared a priority flash traffic message to the captain of the battleship *Fortuna*, warning of an Obsidian invasion, giving Captain Halsey the exact time and location to expect the Obsidian destroyers. Jacob was careful not to allow anyone to trace the message and then pressed "send."

Concerned, Maddie asked, "Can you stop Gustafson from gaining control of the *Penetrator*?"

Still typing with extreme concentration, Jacob answered, "Probably, but I have another idea. I plan to give her control."

Maddie and Joan both protested simultaneously.

"Why? What are you thinking?" asked Maddie.

From the helm, Chacon looked over his shoulder. "Can you regain control if you relinquish it?" he asked, inquisitively staring at Jacob, hoping he had a plan.

"I won't be able to regain control of the *Penetrator*, but when the time is right, I plan to take control of Gustafson's computer. If we can bring the *Atout* in close, then we might be able to take them by surprise. The *Penetrator* is a lightly armed experimental ship. All her advanced features are about command and control, so the *Atout* easily outguns her," Jacob replied, talking more to himself than to anyone else.

Maddie whispered to Jacob and Joan, "If Gustafson is on that ship, then we must catch her alive. She might be the key to breaking open the whole conspiracy if we can get her to talk."

Joan leaned forward to look around Jacob. With a deadly look in her eyes that left Jacob unnerved, Joan whispered to Maddie, "Oh, we can make her talk. We just have to catch her."

Jacob heard the venom in her voice. He was not familiar with this side of Joan's personality. He turned his attention back to his monitors.

"Chacon, do you have anywhere you can hide most of *Felicity*'s personnel? I want to surrender the *Felicity* to the *Atout*, but I need the *Atout* to board us with as few people as possible. We will need to use the element of surprise to retake the ship once their boarding party is on board."

"Okay. I can manage that. Once we surrender the *Felicity*, then what?" asked Chacon, in his thick French accent, curious of Jacob's plan.

"I need the *Felicity* to go to maximum velocity straight for Ceres as soon as the *Atout*'s boarding party is on board. My suspicion is my colleague from Space Command will be amongst them. I will make sure the *Penetrator* stops the *Atout*, or at least slows her down, but you must make it to Ceres before they catch us."

Chacon glared at Maddie. "Easy score, huh? When this is over, you owe me a large bonus."

Before Maddie could reply, Chacon started preparing the *Felicity*. He had his first officer direct as many of the crew as possible into hidden compartments right under the floor to the hallway directly aft of the bridge.

Jacob was still busy typing as fast as he could on his keyboard. Before he started his plan in motion, he had another idea. He entered the code he had saved the day Maddie was on his computer. Positive he had missed the last few digits, he motioned for Maddie to join him. Looking her in the eye, he asked, "You need to die, right?"

Maddie, confused, studied the screen, and then she understood what Jacob was suggesting. Quickly, she entered the last four missing digits to the code, and Jacob swapped Addison Everett's DNA string in her personnel records with Gustafson's. Once complete, she looked at Jacob and said, "Unless your plan works, then none of it will really matter."

Jacob smiled his dimply smile. "Probably not."

What happened from that point on happened fast. The boarding party made it on deck just as the *Penetrator* arrived, opening fire on the *Atout*. Chacon launched the *Felicity* at maximum velocity, throwing the unsecured boarding party across the bridge into the back wall.

Once the *Felicity* reached full speed, the hidden crew emerged and engaged the injured members of the boarding party. After a brief struggle, the boarding party from the *Atout* was secured.

Gustafson lay on the floor, breathing hard with fury. Joan bent down to secure Gustafson's hands before she saw the gun. Before Joan could react, Gustafson fired into her chest at point-blank range, killing her. Gustafson immediately turned her gun to shoot at Jacob. Maddie fired twice into her chest. Gustafson looked down at the blood coming out of her chest and then stared straight into the depths of Maddie's soul as the light faded from her eyes. Those dying eyes would haunt Maddie for years to come.

The unsuspecting *Atout* never stood a chance. Firing into her yardarm to yardarm, the *Penetrator* continued until the corvette exploded, having never returned a single shot. As soon as it destroyed the *Atout*, Jacob had the *Penetrator* follow the *Felicity*. Things got hairy once the *Felicity* made it to the asteroid field, and once again Jacob was afraid Chacon and his crew were going to turn on them to take the gold. Threatening the *Felicity* with the *Penetrator,* Jacob had Chacon dump the container in space and transfer himself and Maddie, along with Gustafson's and Joan's lifeless bodies, to the *Penetrator*.

After carefully retrieving the gold and hiding it on a nearby asteroid, Jacob had the *Penetrator* retrace its steps to reclaim her crew, who were floating helplessly in space in life pods.

Maddie, who the crew believed was Gustafson, welcomed Captain Green back on to his ship with explicit instructions. He was to deliver her and her colleague, who was down in the morgue cremating two bodies per standard operating procedure, to Earth. She convincingly explained that she needed Green to allow them time to disappear before he reported in. Her explanation was SC had sent her on a covert intelligence mission.

Captain Halsey intercepted the Obsidian destroyers as they exited the bubble. Ships on both sides experienced significant damage. The resulting intergalactic incident had been the catalyst that officially began the present war. The captain was promoted to admiral, and all the decommissioned ships Space Command had been taking out of service were immediately recommissioned.

Later, SC Intelligence's investigators concluded the now-deceased Addison Everett and her friend, Joan Resciniti, had hijacked the crew of the *Penetrator*. Space Intelligence Crime Units confirmed the identity of both bodies, comparing DNA from the ashes against their personnel files. Both Jacob and Maddie were heartbroken that Joan's name had gotten smeared in the process.

On his return to SC Evelin, Jacob learned through the rumor mill that two unnamed SC intelligence officers had hijacked SC Evelin's test ship, *Penetrator*. Rumor was that they had used it to steal a gold shipment. Gustafson was reportedly connected to the theft. She had been missing for three days, and there were all-points bulletins out for her arrest.

Jacob and Maddie assumed the mole in SC would deduce that Gustafson had stolen the gold and run.

•••

While still on the *Felicity*, Jacob held Maddie as she cried, consoling her over the loss of Joan. But the look of shock in Jacob's eyes worried Maddie. It was as though Jacob had consciously shut himself off from his humanity. Maddie had seen only one lone tear fall down his cheek when he had softly closed Joan's eyes. Sweetly, he had kissed her on the forehead and zipped the body bag shut.

Later, Maddie would find out that Jacob had bought the plot next to his mother and buried Joan's ashes there. He had even paid the same stone carver to make her a stone for her grave. And yet to Maddie's or Charlie's knowledge, after that first visit, Jacob never returned.

•••

Jacob soon resigned from the think tank and requested an assignment serving under his newly appointed brother on the lowly *Perseus.*

Maddie had felt horrible for Charlie. She had never been able to decide if SC assigned Charlie to the low-orbit repair craft as a result of Admiral Halsey trying to protect him or if Admiral Cotterill had made it happen out of spite.

Maddie and Jacob had never discussed the events of that day on the *Felicity* once they were back on Earth, but it was obvious from Jacob's melancholy that the tragedy of Joan's loss had affected him deeply. The occasional moments of deep sadness, which Maddie had always recognized in Jacob's otherwise smiling eyes, became much more common.

Unbeknownst to Maddie, the dark clouds that sometimes invaded Jacob's mind and swirled around his head now seemed like a sixth sense, alerting him to things he might otherwise have overlooked. The price of the heightened awareness was a dark reverie that plagued Jacob—a depression for which there was no cure.

Jacob and Maddie were the only two people who knew the exact locus of the treasure trove. Maddie would have given every bit of the Obsidian gold as well as the money from the South American mission back in return for her lost friend Joan.

Chapter Thirty-Two

Present Day, En route to Earth, Intergalactic Space

Charlie handed command of the bridge over to M&M and asked Thomas to bring dinner to his quarters. Once the food was on the table, Charlie locked the door to his cabin and opened his tablet. He paused, nervous to learn what messages he might receive from home. *I hope Maddie has forgiven me for taking the mission*, he thought to himself. He sorted his mail by sender and went straight down the list to read his emails from Maddie.

At first, the emails contained what Charlie anticipated. Maddie was furious with him for accepting the mission and leaving her all alone when she was hoping they might finally live like ordinary people. He was just relieved she never mentioned throwing his stuff in a dumpster somewhere and continuing on without him. This was the pattern for a month. She would fuss but then say she hoped he was safe and ask him to hurry home to her.

Then the emails grew dark. Instead of sounding like she was mad, Maddie sounded concerned. She wanted to know why SC visited her, asking all types of questions. Maddie also sounded paranoid. She claimed someone was watching her.

Charlie felt sick. He pushed his food away and jumped farther down to read some older emails. She sounded livid. To his knowledge, she rarely watched the news anymore, but some reporter had shown up at the door asking about the *Perseus* allegedly turning rogue. The reporter claimed the *Perseus*, or more specifically Captain Jackson, destroyed two other ships with whom they were serving. In all caps, she screamed, "YOU NEED TO DO WHATEVER IT TAKES TO CONTACT ME!" Maddie closed by confirming she was positive she was being followed everywhere she went.

Charlie skipped to the last page of emails. One email had a video, so Charlie opened it. In the message, Charlie saw Maddie crying. Through her tears, Maddie was saying something Charlie had trouble understanding. He determined she was receiving death threats, and without a doubt, she seemed frightened.

Charlie looked at the dates. The next-to-last email was dated two weeks ago. In the email, she explained the admiral called and was coming to take her somewhere safe. She claimed "the Obsidians have placed a sixty-million-dollar reward on your life and ten million dollars to anyone who will deliver me to them. Oh, Charlie. What in God's name have you done this time?"

Tears were in Charlie's eyes. He opened the last email. Maddie had written it a couple of hours after the previous one. It was short and to the point: "Charlie, I love you. Please come home and rescue me from all of this. I need a hero! Love, Maddie."

The message brought back memories that flooded Charlie's mind. Maddie had always made it clear she didn't need a man. She always said, "It would be nice to have one, but I don't need one. I can take care of myself."

Only a couple of days before the war started, Charlie had asked Maddie to have dinner with him downtown at one of the nicer restaurants the city had to offer. That was the only other time she had used the word "hero" in the same breath she was talking about him.

Chapter Thirty-Three

Three Years Ago, Washington, DC, Earth

The meal began splendidly. Maddie and Charlie were enjoying their grilled fish appetizer, but really all Charlie could focus on were how Maddie's dark eyes sparkled. She rarely wore much makeup, but tonight she had applied a navy blue eyeliner, which made her brown eyes stand out. The small amount of mascara she used made her eyelashes flutter like angel wings when she blinked.

The eyeshadow she had chosen matched perfectly with the blue sash that hugged the waistline of her slate blue dress. The sash, accentuating her slim waist, knotted at her side and sashayed to her knees. Long and flowing, just kissing the tops of her feet, the soft folds of the silk-like material of the dress added to her angelic appearance as if she were floating on a cloud. The flattering front came together in a soft knot just under her left clavicle, continuing over her shoulder, leaving her right shoulder exposed. In the soft light of the room, the warm golden glow of her skin eclipsed the beauty of any dew-covered rose.

Charlie knew the most important element to any outfit, in the female mind, was shoes. Distracted by Maddie's gorgeous leg, which seductively showed through the slit up the side of the dress when she walked, Charlie had noticed her silver open-toe pumps.

He also couldn't help but notice her perfect toenails, freshly painted to match her deep mauve fingernails.

Charlie was positive Maddie was the most beautiful woman he had ever seen.

With no explanation, Charlie rose and went to the stage. Maddie watched, puzzled, as he talked to the singer and lead guitarist. The guitar player unstrapped his Feder guitar and retrieved his acoustic while Charlie grabbed a microphone. The musicians started playing and Charlie sang:

"I'm looking for the last girl I'll ever kiss
She'll be the girl that is first on my list
She'll be the one that will love me back
When I am good, or when I am slack
She'll be the one with the key to my heart
I think I'll know her from the very start
I'm looking for the last girl I'll ever kiss
For the rest of my life ..."

Maddie sat transfixed. She had no idea Charlie could sing. She listened carefully to his words.

Finally, Charlie reached the final verse. He stared lovingly at Maddie as he sang:

"I have found the last girl I'll ever kiss
She is the girl that is first on my list
She is the one that loves me back
When I am good, or I am slack
She is the one with the key to my heart
I really loved her from the very start
I have found the last girl I'll ever kiss
For the rest of my life."

Maddie rose to give Charlie a big hug as he reached the table while the other diners clapped and whistled.

"That was really good! I never dreamed you could sing. Whose song was that?"

Embarrassed, Charlie said, "That song is yours. I wrote it for you."

Maddie didn't know what to say. She gave Charlie another hug and a tender kiss on the cheek.

The light conversation they usually enjoyed did not seem to come after that. Maddie was nonplussed and looked down at her food, and Charlie became uneasy, afraid he had embarrassed both himself and Maddie. Charlie did his best to change the topic, and he explained to Maddie that he worried about his future with SC, talking hesitantly about his fear that his career might be over. He quietly explained how he felt confident he would have no problem finding a well-paying job in the private sector. Maddie readily agreed that he would, assuring Charlie she believed he could do anything he put his mind to. She had never seen Charlie this nervous and unsure of himself. She had never known him to seem vulnerable.

Charlie took a deep breath and steeled himself. Exhaling, he blurted, "I will find happiness doing anything if I can do it with you."

Maddie felt heat rise to her cheeks and butterflies flutter in her stomach. "Charlie Jackson, you'd better be careful. That was dangerously close to a proposal."

Charlie lost himself in Maddie's eyes. He was captivated by the profundity of feelings and emotion he sensed within their depths.

"Maddie, I know I sound like a blubbering idiot." Charlie took another deep breath. "If you will marry me, I would like nothing better than to spend my life with you."

Maddie's heart skipped a beat. The butterflies in her stomach took flight and began to dance. She barely knew this man. She'd had more than her fair share of men who had suggested they tie the knot. But she knew Charlie was not just flippantly throwing the idea out. He brought her here tonight with a purpose. She was ready to say yes when from the corner of her eye she spotted Admiral Cotterill.

Charlie watched the color fade from Maddie's face, and he deflated, thinking he had made a terrible mistake. He felt his heart thud at his feet.

Suddenly, she leaned across the table and whispered, "Charlie, quick, save me. Behind you, to your right, is an admiral I cannot let see me under any circumstance. We must go! Now!"

Charlie started to look over his shoulder, but Maddie hastily grabbed his hand and said, "No, don't look. I must slip out the back. Can you distract him and meet me in the car?"

Charlie, his heart hurting, his pride deflated, expressionlessly answered, "Sure. Absolutely."

As he rose to stand, Maddie grabbed his hand one more time and stared into his eyes. With a quick smile, she answered, "Yes." Even though she knew that if the admiral saw her, her life would be in peril, she didn't care. For the first time, she was confident someone truly loved her.

Confused, Charlie asked, "Yes?"

Tears glistened in the corners of Maddie's eyes. She always dreamed an amazing man would someday sweep her off her feet and then ask her to marry him. Never in her dream did he also need to help her escape harm immediately after popping the question.

"Yes, I will marry you. If you will have me." She prayed he wouldn't bail when he learned who she really was. "But first you have to rescue me!"

Charlie's heart almost leaped from his chest with joy. But her urgency kept his elation in check. He wondered why on earth it was so important that Maddie escape unseen. He glanced over his shoulder and grimaced. Of all the admirals, Admiral Cotterill was his least favorite. Calm descended on him as he took charge of the situation.

Maddie immediately sensed a change in his demeanor, wondering if Charlie hadn't just increased in both size and stature. Charlie's usual confidence, which Maddie found so attractive, returned to his voice, and she could sense he was now in command of the entire room. Admiral Cotterill's presence no longer intimidated her.

"I will cause a scene. Be ready to escape out the back door."

Before Maddie could say anything, Charlie stood up, briskly turned with his water in his hand, and ran headlong into the admiral, violently knocking him completely off his feet onto the floor. Around him, the whole restaurant turned to watch as Charlie quickly bent over, theatrically wiping the water off the admiral with his napkin, preventing him from regaining his feet.

Once Charlie felt certain Maddie had had enough time to make her exit, he stood and extended his hand down to help the admiral up. The admiral, cursing, refused his hand and almost pulled the tablecloth off along with the dinnerware and drinks from the table he was attempting to use to pull himself up.

Oblivious to the people staring at him, the admiral roared, "Jackson? What the hell is wrong with you?"

Feigning innocence, Charlie replied, "I am so sorry, Admiral. I didn't see you."

Never had anyone dressed Charlie down so thoroughly as with the admiral's tongue-lashing that followed. Charlie didn't care. He was the happiest man in the whole world tonight. Besides, as he told Maddie, his career was likely over anyway. Charlie couldn't help but smile as the admiral raged on.

When Charlie made it to the car, he found Maddie standing there waiting for him. As soon as she saw him, she leaped into his arms, almost knocking him off his feet, exclaiming, "You. You are my hero! I love you."

Charlie laughed as she wrapped her arms around his neck. "I love you too," he said, and he pulled her in close.

Chapter Thirty-Four

Present Day, Intergalactic Space

Charlie marched onto the bridge and handed M&M a new course heading. She studied the coordinates for a moment.

"Captain, these coordinates have us heading back to the corridor."

"I know where they have us heading, Ensign. Turn this bird around," Charlie answered curtly. He turned and stormed from the bridge.

Myers looked over at M&M and Jacob. "What was that all about?"

M&M shook her head. "I don't know, but I do know if this bird isn't facing the other direction when he comes back, things will get ugly."

"I am not sure what has happened, but I recognize his mood," Jacob added. "Better pass the word around to expect squalls. You two might also want to figure out what is wrong with the readiness indicator. It seems to think we have serious problems."

Sure enough, the indicator was just above the flat line. Unbeknownst to the three of them, besides Charlie's nasty mood, there was also trouble off the stern of the ship. Close behind, in the wake of the pocket battleship, was an equally lethal predator.

Chapter Thirty-Five

Present Day, Intergalactic Space

It had worried the *Whisperer*'s captain, Captain Scanlin, that the *Zeus* might run off and leave them—at least until she changed course and headed back the way she had come. Ever since she turned to her new heading, her huge engines did not seem to produce as much thrust.

Captain Scanlin almost panicked and ordered his crew to flee the area when *Zeus* unexpectedly changed course. He could not imagine someone had detected them, but he preferred to err on the side of caution. He knew the odds of his being discovered were almost nonexistent. Only one time in the history of his race had a cloaked Royal Kesmit ship ever been successfully captured by an Earth vessel. The history books recorded the event and documented the name of the vessel that had achieved the unspeakable feat. Still, other vessels had been accidentally detected, and the captain did not cherish the thought of what being caught might mean for him and his crew.

The *Whisperer* did not have enough firepower to fight off a red skiff, let alone any ship as powerful as the *Zeus*. Stealth, not armament, was the reason the *Whisperer* was formidable. Information was all she was after. Ever since the epic feat the

Whisperer had seen *Zeus* achieve in the corridor, *Zeus* had become the exclusive center of all her attention.

So far, the battleship's firewalls had not given up any secrets. Captain Scanlin and the crew of the *Whisperer*, like all their race, were patient. Gleaning the databanks on the *Zeus* for the information the *Whisperer* needed might take weeks, maybe months, but the *Whisperer* would learn what they needed to know. Time, unfortunately, was of the essence now. The Recondite Kingdom needed to know whether the *Zeus* might change the balance of power and the course of the war between Earth and the kingdom's most dangerous nemesis.

Even without hacking into the onboard computers on the *Zeus*, the *Whisperer* had already learned much. The captain of the *Whisperer* knew the name of each crew member on the battleship. He knew from where they hailed and that people on both sides of the conflict wished them dead. His sister and the king had briefed Captain Scanlin on many of those facts long before he and his crew left port to find the mysterious crew in the Strivo who were reportedly wreaking such havoc on Obsidian supply lines. At that time, he never dreamed he would discover the *Zeus*. He expected to find the *Perseus*, who was causing such a stir across the universe.

He learned much more information from the *Perseus*. The second she activated her CBC, every byte of data on her mainframe came flooding into the *Whisperer*'s control room. The plethora of data was still being analyzed by his diligent crew even now. The captain found it mysterious that none of the crew members had any family to speak of other than the ship's captain, who was reportedly married. Captain Scanlin also found it interesting when he discovered that only two of the crew had been assigned to serve by Space Command itself. The best he could tell, almost every member had either volunteered or, he suspected, been recruited by the ship's captain. Whether these clues meant something or were just coincidental, he had not yet decided.

If either Space Command or the Obsidians had placed a mole on board, then it was probably the first officer, Lt. Dillon Myers, or

Ensign Megan Marie, the only two crew members assigned by SC. The more the captain studied the situation, the more convinced he was that neither side in the conflict had ever considered the *Perseus* a plausible threat and therefore would not have bothered with a shipboard mole. They had obviously underestimated the captain and crew they sent to the Strivo.

Curiously, not one byte of information about the *Zeus* was ever mentioned in any of the logbooks on the *Perseus*. Even in the reports Captain Jackson sent back to SC, never once did he mention the *Zeus*.

Still, the *Zeus* she was. The captain did not require logbooks to identify the ship in front of him. History books provided him with all the confirmation he needed. The *Zeus* and her sister ships were legendary. They knew of her existence for as far back as his race had sailed the heavens.

Legend or not, the captain did not see how the *Zeus* could change the inevitable outcome of the war between the Earthlings and Obsidians. He would love to imagine a different result since the outcome of the war had such dangerous implications for his own race. The captain knew the CBC units on the SC ships were hopelessly compromised. Who was responsible for compromising the system was one bit of information the *Whisperer* needed to learn.

If the *Zeus* could somehow convince the rest of the human fleet the Obsidians had compromised the CBC, then Earth might have a chance to survive as a race. However, the probability of survival would be small, given the might of the B Class battleships the Obsidians had in their possession. The B Class warships were, without a doubt, the most devastating weapons ever designed and built by any race. They were the real deal breaker, which, at this point, sealed the fate of Earth in the captain's opinion. Earth had nothing that could feasibly engage even one, let alone a small fleet.

The warning bell sounded and broke the captain from his thoughts. He watched *Zeus* cautiously in case she turned to attack.

No, just more drills. The captain could not believe it. He had never known any captain who drilled his crew so incessantly.

Captain Scanlin had also never encountered any captain who regularly performed live fire-training exercises. Normally a training exercise was performed using only simulators. The captain of the *Zeus* clearly wanted his men and women to experience everything they would encounter in real battle. G-force and lateral g-force could not be adequately simulated any other way than performing actual maneuvers.

Most impressively, Scanlin had never witnessed anyone who could pilot as well as whoever was at *Zeus*'s helm. Already he had witnessed acrobatics that denied physics. Even his own helmsman on the *Whisperer*, Venery Elliott, paled in comparison to the caliber of flying they had seen to date. Any adversary facing the *Zeus* would have their work cut out for them.

Chapter Thirty-Six
Present Day, Headed Back to the Strivo, Intergalactic Space

The latest drill was the final straw for Jacob. Charlie initiated a pointless scenario where the crew had to battle an Obsidian B Class battleship. As the exercise had proven, to engage a B Class would be suicide. The key to Charlie's attack plan was to use the rotary cannon to knock out the shield emitter on the large B Class ship so *Zeus*'s heavy caliber cannons could do their job.

Grossly undermanned, the only person available to man any of the rotary cannons full-time was the chemist, CPO Evans. Even if all six gun posts were manned, the task of hitting a shield emitter with the *Zeus* traveling at maximum velocity was nigh impossible.

Evans's assigned post was the most isolated position on the entire ship. To access the rotary cannon action station, poor Evans had to crawl through an extended access tube. With her larger frame, this proved difficult and quite strenuous. Once she reached the action station, she was all alone. Jacob watched her during previous exercises and knew the stress of reaching her post caused her to break into a serious sweat. Worse, being so far from the centerline of the ship, the g-forces were greater at her post than any other station. Jacob was surprised Evans had never passed out from the physical exertion.

•••

Everyone on the ship had called Evans by her last name since she had first joined the crew—at least until the SWALs signed on. The team members called her by her first name, Lydia.

Self-conscious of her weight since she was a teenager, Lydia felt uncomfortable when Peck insisted she join his team on their daily run. She worried the team's encouraging words were spoken in jest. But Peck was relentless and never allowed her to miss a workout. Now, after months of working out with Peck's team, she found she was having difficulty with the G-suit in her uniform. It was too loose to function correctly.

For the fifth time in less than ten hours, the siren wailed its ear-splitting call to quarters. To Evans's dismay, she found Lt. Jackson had chosen to join her for the drill. Jacob carefully explained why her role in the present scenario was so important. The captain hypothesized that if the rotary cannon could eliminate the shield emitter on the B Class in the simulation, the *Zeus* might stand a fighting chance.

Before the lieutenant released his harness from the seat next to Evans, he praised her performance but suggested she continue to practice. As he lowered himself into the tube to leave the station, he cocked his head and studied her. "Evans, you have lost serious weight. Go have Stidham issue you a new uniform and replace your battle gear. This part of the ship and the insertion balls experience the greatest g-forces on the ship. We can't have you passing out." Before she could reply, the LT disappeared. She turned back to restore her workstation. She startled as his head popped back out of the tube. "The weight loss looks good on you, Evans."

Lt. Jackson's head vanished as soon as the words left his mouth. Evans smiled. She had noticed earlier after a shower her midsection was thinner than her hips. She had a waistline. Then she frowned. The reason the crew had failed during the simulation was she hadn't done her part well enough. Silently, Evans mouthed to herself, "That won't happen again." She looked longingly at the exit to her firing station, buckled her harness, and flipped the control to activate the rotary cannon's combat simulator.

•••

After the simulation, Jacob did not stay to oversee Evans put her battle station back together. Instead, he stormed the bridge to confront Charlie. The bridge, under M&M's direction, was slowly regaining its usual state of readiness as he entered, but Charlie was already gone. Jacob turned and disappeared back into the pneumatic transport. He almost knocked Thomas over the table as he barged into the captain's quarters. Soup sailed all over the place, the empty bowl spiraling around on the floor with the remainder of its contents on the table and in Charlie's lap.

The steward cursed under his breath, but when he saw the look on Jacob's face, he wisely made his exit. Jacob glared at Charlie.

Charlie sat there and glared back at Jacob. At long last, he spoke, "Maddie is in trouble."

Jacob looked puzzled. "What do you mean? What type of trouble?"

Not a muscle on Charlie moved. He continued to sit there with a blank expression on his face. He said, "Even as fast as the *Zeus* can travel, we are still over eighteen months away from home. Not that it matters. If we were there, I doubt I could protect her."

Charlie stood up, kicked the empty bowl across the room, and then looked out the rear-facing windows. "What matters is *Zeus* is probably in immediate danger too."

Jacob stepped closer to Charlie. "That seems to be situation normal."

Charlie shook his head. "No, the danger we face now differs from anything we have faced before."

Charlie wiped the soup off the table and then leaned against the clean edge, continuing to use his napkin to remove spots of soup.

"I have always loved history. Every problem we tackle has been faced before. It is all recorded for infamy," Charlie said, continuing to clean. "If only we understood which ensuing script applied to us next, we could peruse the history books and foresee our present and future challenges."

Charlie hesitated and grew misty-eyed. "When I learned Maddie was in jeopardy, my knee-jerk reaction was to get there as fast as possible."

Jacob said nothing. He only listened.

Charlie continued. "I also decided we need to drill the ship for every plausible scenario. I am obligated to imagine any and every threat we may face. So, getting a fresh perspective, I thumbed through the ship's logbook."

Jacob pulled out a chair and sat down. "That couldn't have taken too long. *Zeus*'s logbook isn't substantial."

Charlie shook his head. "No, I mean the entire logbook. It goes back farther than time itself."

"Are you researching history or mythology?" Jacob asked.

"I can't explain it. I cannot even pretend to understand. With the *Zeus*, they are the same. They are interchangeable," Charlie answered defensively.

"Even if they are the same thing, you cannot see the future by looking in the rearview mirror."

Charlie looked at Jacob with a solemn expression on his face. "I believe you can. History has an extreme tendency to repeat itself over and over, like an echo. Besides, we have no other resource."

Jacob conceded. "Okay. I misspoke. History repeats itself and should be heeded. It might possibly make a great resource on the macro scale. But on a micro level, it might not prove useful."

"True. Very true. However, reading the ship's history made me aware of a serious problem."

"Which is?"

"The *Zeus* has a ship directly on her six."

Jacob looked perplexed. "So if there is a ship back there stalking us, why haven't we confronted her?"

"Because I know who she is. Not by name, but I have an idea of her capabilities and from where she originates. Come here and look out the window."

Jacob stepped over to the window. "Okay. Where is this mystery ship?"

Charlie pulled out a piece of paper. The paper had a hole punched into the center. Charlie held it up and told Jacob to look through the hole and find the star that was directly astern of *Zeus*. "Okay, what do you see?"

Jacob was very curious what Charlie was trying to prove, so he kept focusing on the pinprick of a star that shone through the hole. Jacob joked, "Twinkle, twinkle, little star, how I wonder—"

"Stop," Charlie ordered, holding up his hand. "On Earth stars twinkle because of the atmosphere. There is nothing in space to disrupt the light rays. Keep watching."

Jacob looked back through the hole and tried to steady himself against the windowsill. He stared at the star until his eye was watering. Then he saw it. It looked like a small box shape passing ever so slightly in front of the star before disappearing again. "Okay, you have piqued my curiosity. What is it? Why doesn't it show up on our situation board?"

Charlie grinned and opened his tablet, scrolling through the pages of the ship's log. Decisively, he stopped and pointed. "Start reading right here. Read the next thirty-one pages, and you tell me if I am just paranoid and should be relieved of command."

Chapter Thirty-Seven

Present Day, Dahlonega, Georgia

Maddie closed the door to the small cabin with her foot and dumped the wood onto the hearth. Wood. Who the hell still heated with wood? Before, when she and Charlie had visited, she had found the fireplace romantic. Now she only wished to go home because she was tired, dirty, and cold. Maybe she had made a mistake coming here. When Admiral Halsey told her people were looking for her and she needed to hide out, Maddie was furious but also relieved to at least know: her worst dreams were now coming true. Her only question was: Were they searching for the wife of Captain Jackson or for Addison Everett? Did they understand the two were one and the same?

After they had loaded her bags into the admiral's SUV at her and Charlie's house, Maddie went back to lock the front door ... Every time she thought about that night, she cried.

As she turned to go back to the SUV, she spotted the dark sedan that she had been seeing tailing her barreling down the road and slamming into the middle of the admiral's large SUV, barely missing the admiral standing near the back of the vehicle. The marine the admiral had brought to help provide security leaped over the vehicle with his gun in his hand. His feet never made it to the ground. The admiral's personal guard shot him in the back, and then he turned the gun on the admiral. A fight between the guard and the shocked admiral ensued.

Maddie dropped to the deck and crawled back into the house. Once she was inside, Maddie regained her feet and ran to the small safe under the bed where she and Charlie kept essential documents. Frantically, she searched for the clip to her 9 mm handgun.

Not being able to find it, she ran to the hallway closet. In one fluid motion, she shoved all the hangers and clothes onto the floor. Maddie slid open a small concealed door and pulled the 12-gauge Remington shotgun off the shelf. Grabbing a box of shells, she started out the door before she realized her mistake. She dropped the box of bird shot on the floor and retrieved the much smaller box of triple-aught buckshot.

Maddie was still sliding the three-inch shells into the magazine as she carefully slipped out the side door onto the patio. The shooting out front had stopped. Instead of running from the gunfire, her training kicked in and she searched for the source. Carefully, trying not to make any noise, she slipped between the hedge and the house.

Once she reached the edge of the driveway, she carefully peered around the corner. The admiral was face down, and a huge man had zip-tied his wrists. The man she had seen driving the sedan started toward the open door of her house.

Her heart racing, she released the safety on the shotgun and spun around the corner of the house. The triple-aught buckshot greeted the man at point-blank range. With no hesitation, she ratcheted the gun and fired again.

From the corner of her eye, she saw the admiral's rogue bodyguard scrambling for his weapon. Maddie hastily grabbed the bloody 9 mm Beretta from the hand of the shot-riddled body in front of her and ran for the front door, leaping in time to throw her body through the open door of her house. The door frame shattered as multiple shots rang out from the driveway.

Inside the house, Maddie jumped to her feet and ran toward the back of the house. Thinking quickly, she opened the breaker box and killed all the power to the house and partially opened the back door. Then she backed herself carefully into the dark corner where she and Charlie left shoes.

She heard two shots ring out as the man entered the front door and heard him knocking over furniture. Her heart stopped when she heard him open the bedroom door. If he went that way and circled through the bathroom, she would be fully exposed. Her mind was racing, trying to decide what to do. Then she heard feet on the kitchen floor. When the man saw the back door partially open, he broke into a run. Reaching it, he cautiously looked around the backyard before he stuck his head out the door. He kept the door handle in his right hand and his firearm in his left as he carefully looked around the yard, then turned to circle back through the house.

Maddie made out his massive frame silhouetted by the lights from behind the house. She had hoped he would run out of the house in pursuit of her so she could escape out the front door, but it wasn't to be. This was the moment of truth. Much to her surprise, she realized she was no longer trembling. A surreal calm had descended upon her.

With a determined resolve, she stepped out of her hiding spot to face her adversary. Maddie locked the Beretta firmly in both of her hands in front of her. The second the man saw her, he froze, and Maddie squeezed the trigger. *Click.* The weapon misfired. Maddie could not believe it, and, obviously, neither could her assailant. Momentarily, he stood there, having seen his life flash before his eyes. Then, realizing what the sound meant, he laughed while slowly raising his weapon and carefully aimed at the shadow in front of him.

All of Maddie's firearms training kicked in at once. She had so much adrenaline pumping that she didn't have time to feel panic. In one fluid motion, her muscle memory took over. *Tap, rack, bang!*

The man shuddered as the round slammed into the center of his chest. Maddie squeezed twice more, releasing two more rounds center mass. After the third round hit the man, she heard his weapon crash to the floor, but still he stood there. She squeezed again, and another round pounded the man in the chest. Maddie felt the weight of the gun change as the rack flew back into the open position. The gun was empty, and she didn't have another magazine, so she threw the weapon at the man. At first, the man studied his chest and stood there in shock. Then he reached up and grabbed the door frame to help steady himself and methodically stepped toward Maddie.

Maddie slowly stepped back one step, then another step until her foot bumped into the all-too-familiar antique butter churn that used to belong to Charlie's great-grandmother. She realized she had one more weapon close at hand.

Gracefully she turned, and with her left hand, she grabbed the ball bat, which Charlie kept in the churn. Charlie had two antique ball bats that had been handed down to him by his mother. Maddie didn't know how old they were or exactly where Charlie's mother had acquired them, but she remembered they were both autographed by a ballplayer named Fred McGriff. One ball bat Charlie left in the butter churn, while the other he had on board the *Perseus*.

Continuing her spin, Maddie's right hand locked on to the handle of the bat, and with all her weight now on her rear leg, the bat contacted the man's head. The sound was sickening, like the sound a watermelon rolling off a picnic table. The man's head flew back, and his body staggered. Now all the rage inside Maddie exploded. She swung the bat again, and he staggered back farther, stepping out the back door. With every swing of the bat, he staggered farther across the patio. Each time, Maddie recognized the sound of breaking bone, but each time he recovered his balance he continued to reach for Maddie. With one last swing, he sailed backward over the side of the patio wall and disappeared.

Maddie did not search for the body. She scurried to pick up the weapon the man had dropped, and she sprinted out the front door. The admiral's hands were still zip-tied behind his back, but he had made it to his feet and was limping across the drive toward the house. Maddie saw cuts and bruises on his face, and his clothes were tattered. Far in the distance, she heard the wail of sirens.

As soon as she had managed to cut the zip ties, the admiral said, "There isn't a moment to lose. We must leave."

In the exposed driveway next to her vehicle, Maddie and the admiral agreed it would be best if even he was ignorant to her location. After a change of plans, they hastily unloaded her bags from the admiral's destroyed SUV and placed them into her own car. While shuffling bags, the admiral brought Maddie up to speed on what was happening with Charlie in the Strivo and what he knew of the new development of people searching for Maddie. He stopped short of saying they were looking for Addison Everett. He only suggested many of the people looking for her were interested in more than just her connection to the captain of the *Perseus*. They decided on a system by which they might communicate by posting on an anonymous blog site. Maddie assured him she could take care of herself. Before they parted company, Halsey gave her a fatherly kiss on the forehead and wished her Godspeed.

•••

In his heart, Halsey wanted to protect Maddie, if not for her, then for Charlie, but as she had proven, she was much more qualified to take care of herself than he was. Halsey cursed himself for allowing all of this to happen. He wished he had never seen the jewel or studied the prophecy.

He had been so close to retiring and putting it all behind him when the war started. If only he hadn't received that anonymous email. At the time, he assumed Jacob had sent it to warn him about what was about to happen. It hadn't taken him long to figure out it was more likely Maddie who had emailed him. Or should he say Ms. Addison Everett? Yes, he had known her true identity for years, but that wasn't important to him. What was important was that one of his two adopted sons loved her. He always worried about what might happen if her enemies discovered who she reinvented herself into. In the beginning, it had concerned him for Charlie's sake, but as he got to know her and love her as a daughter-in-law, he feared for her sake as well.

The anonymous email he received warned him of the exact time and location of an Obsidian invasion. If only SC hadn't overridden the controls of the *Fortuna* when they did, he would have stopped them instead of just slowing them down, and possibly this war could have been stopped before it started. The battle, while not a victory, finally won him his promotion to admiral, but with his hands tied so severely since by Space Command and the CBC, he sometimes wondered if he shouldn't have retired as he had planned.

●●●

The way the admiral had come to get her but then had sent her away on her own confirmed to Maddie what she had always suspected: Admiral Halsey knew about her background in intelligence. Still, it hurt. The admiral who raised her husband was pushing her away to fend for herself. Once again, she was all alone with no one to protect her. None of her former assets from Space Intelligence were available to her. The admiral had been unable to provide assistance, and Charlie was on the other side of the universe. As always, anyone she thought would be there for her had left her.

Now, throwing another log on the fire and rubbing her hands together to get warm, Maddie thought about the fact that she had not communicated with or heard from the admiral since that awful moving day. She had managed to keep up with him somewhat via news reports whenever she ventured into town to find an internet connection. But Maddie knew it would be foolhardy to mine SC for intelligence. To mine Space Command's servers was asking to be caught. Other than concentrating on food, and now that the cool autumn air had given way to winter, trying to stay warm, all she had to occupy her time with was worrying about Charlie and praying he would come home to her.

Chapter Thirty-Eight

Present Day, Headed Back to
the Strivo, Intergalactic Space

C harlie and Jacob spent the rest of the day pondering what to
do about the ship they were sure was somewhere off their
stern. Meanwhile, the crew learned Jacob had stormed into the
captain's quarters to set him straight and proclaimed him as their
champion, since they had not been called to quarters since.

After twelve hours of brainstorming, Charlie and Jacob decided
they were at an impasse. If their hunch was correct about who
might be trailing them, Charlie determined, he must do something
about it. They decided on a course of action to verify whether
their suspicions were correct. The brothers mapped out a series
of high-speed maneuvers that would catch all but the most alert
SC or Obsidian ship by surprise. Possibly, if they got lucky and
their suspicions were correct, they might net an even greater prize:
a ship which only existed in a book of mythology. The ruse they
intended to execute depended entirely on being able to perform
the high-speed maneuver flawlessly and on their uninvited guest
believing the crew of *Zeus* was just performing another training
session. Hopefully, they would catch their tail napping.

As soon as the plan was prepared, Charlie sent word for Andrew
to replace Stuyck at the helm and sent the maneuver he planned to

execute to the bridge for Andrew to familiarize himself with. Soon the entire ship was abuzz with rumors of another training exercise, and men and women began lurking near their duty stations.

Charlie had already decided that if the exercise turned out to be fruitless, they would continue heading back to the corridor. Something dawned on Charlie that he should have picked up on much earlier: the corvettes the crew encountered in the Strivo passageway had not belonged there. Generally, corvettes protected the space near a home planet or space station where they might easily resupply. Charlie could not determine any location in a close-enough proximity to the corridor for the corvettes to use as a base of operation. The brothers debated this subject for so long, they missed the appointed time to start the drill.

"Captain on deck" sounded out on the bridge as Charlie stepped out of the pneumatic transport. Charlie looked over at the preparedness indicator bar and was pleased to see it had recovered. Myers removed himself from the captain's chair, and Charlie sat down to strap in.

Charlie asked, "Myers, has the crew finished eating?"

Myers looked dumbfounded. He knew the captain always liked to feed the crew before going into battle, but never had he fed them before a training simulation.

"No, sir ..."

He then faltered as though he wanted to say more, but the words escaped him.

The answer seemed to take Charlie by surprise, but then he realized where the error originated. Any strategy involving the first officer on a warship should have been discussed with him present. Charlie felt terrible; he had been remiss far too often with Myers.

"Very well, lieutenant. Perhaps some further delay is in order. Sound to quarters and then have the crew fed at their duty stations."

The jarring sound of the flaxen horn immediately started its wailing cry throughout the ship. The few groggy men and women who had not been lurking near their assigned post rolled out of their bunks and scrambled to their appointed stations. At length, the indicator light came on to let Charlie know everyone was in position. Charlie looked dismayed. The response time was lethargic.

Charlie pressed the button on the ship-wide intercom to address the crew. "All hands. This is the captain. Discipline is not a means to punish. Discipline is a tool to prepare us for the expected and the unexpected. Training tires everyone on the ship, but we must remain vigilant because the enemy might strike any time, not only when we are fresh and alert. As a crew, we will fight only as well as we train. You must always assume every time you strap into your cockpits we are about to have to fight for our lives."

After his words had enough time to sink in, Charlie continued, "I am ordering rations be handed out. Eat and then prepare yourself for action. Presently, we have an unidentified ship trailing us somewhere directly off our stern. We are about to execute a series of high-speed maneuvers to attempt to catch them off guard. Our primary mission is to identify and capture this vessel. If that fails, then we will try to either destroy or lose her.

"This is not a drill," Charlie added, and with that, he turned off the commlink.

The mood around the ship grew somber.

Charlie keyed the commlink to speak privately to Jacob, who was at his post on the bridge. "I know why you stormed into my quarters. Never hesitate to let me know when I need a head check.

Jacob did not reply. He merely acknowledged Charlie's apology with two clicks on his commlink.

Charlie received his acknowledgment with a smile and then spoke to Jacob again. "You know even the best crew can become complacent and lulled to sleep. We have been drilling nonstop for days. Now, we should use that to our advantage. Let's be a little more aggressive than we discussed. Maybe they have grown bored watching us drill and have become complacent too. As soon as we start the third tight turn to our starboard side, let's find out how large an electrical charge those probes on the side of *Zeus* can produce."

At first, Charlie worried Jacob may not have heard him because he did not respond. As Charlie keyed the mic again, Jacob answered, "It took me a moment to understand. We intend to create a directional EMP?"

Charlie clicked the commlink twice as Jacob had done earlier.

Jacob didn't have time to notice. He was scrambling to improve on Charlie's idea. In the early 2000s, while the public fixated on terrorism, the military planners of the time knew the real threat was the use of an EMP, or electromagnetic pulse. The fear was someone might launch a nuclear warhead into low orbit and detonate it. The EMP would have disabled anything and everything electrical. On Earth the weapon was obsolete. Whatever ship was on *Zeus*'s tail had possibly never heard of the device.

●●●

Captain Scanlin of the *Whisperer* had just crawled into his berth to get some much-needed rest when the bridge hailed him.

"They are at it again, sir. They started another training exercise."

The captain acknowledged the update and mumbled under his breath, "If that crew ever finds someone to actually fire at, they will be too tired to fight."

He took a couple of moments longer than usual to step from his cabin onto the bridge because he could not find one of his boots.

As he stepped onto the bridge, he took a moment to study the tracking board, which showed the path of travel the *Zeus* made in her imaginary fight. As he turned from the board to watch the main viewing monitor, the *Zeus* followed its nose vertical, then the forward momentum stalled and the *Zeus* belly flopped back into its original path of travel. Elliott pulled back on his yoke to follow the second *Zeus*'s nose rose, reacting too slowly to compensate for the ship to fall back into its original path of travel. The *Zeus* immediately performed a ninety-degree flat spin to port in a maneuver the captain would have never believed possible and illuminated every square inch of space with a short burst of electromagnetic energy. The light emitted by the burst was as bright as a star being consumed by a black hole. The flash coming through the monitor was so intense, it temporarily blinded and disoriented everyone on the small ship's bridge. Then everything went dark and shut down. Even the ship's life-support system died.

Meanwhile, on board the *Zeus*, things happened quickly. As soon as Jacob set off their homemade EMP, a small ship magically appeared on the situation board. The vessel was straight off the port bow of *Zeus*. Charlie's astonishment was evident. The ship was much closer abaft the *Zeus* than either Charlie or Jacob had imagined. It was so close, in fact, the pulse almost missed and dissipated directly off her stern.

From the keel of the *Zeus*, two devices resembling eagle claws descended. *Zeus* banked hard to port and the giant claws snatched the *Whisperer* and pulled her up against the hull. Within seconds of the blast, both SWAL teams came through the breach made by the claws and efficiently subdued the crew of the small ship.

•••

It surprised Charlie how small the ship was. He couldn't believe the *Zeus* had found enough room to grab hold. Myers quickly informed him that the only weapons found on the ship were two ancient ceremonial swords discovered in the captain's quarters. The SWAL team had caught the captain desperately trying to retrieve them.

Soon, the prisoners were safely transferred, questioned, and locked in the brig on board the *Zeus*. When Charlie and Jacob were satisfied the small ship was safely secured to the docking port, Charlie ordered M&M to continue traveling back to the corridor. He stopped briefly by the brig to welcome the captain of the *Whisperer* aboard. Other than being disheartened and sullen about their capture, the captain appeared to be a perfect gentleman.

Charlie was proud of the skill and poise Andrew had demonstrated during the skirmish. Andrew had vanished immediately after he was relieved from the bridge, disappearing back to the room housing the simulator, despite having just been at the conn for hours waiting for the exercise to begin. Charlie went to congratulate him and encourage him to get some sleep. He was surprised to find Andrew studying for a chemistry exam with Evans. In the corner of the room, Charlie spotted Olivia and Richard napping, their calculus curriculum still on the monitor the two were studying together. Charlie suspected Olivia was doing the tutoring. The girl was extremely sharp. Each of the kids possessed certain talents, but she was the most well rounded of them.

Exhausted, Charlie and Jacob bade each other goodnight and retired to their respective berths to get some much-needed sleep. Charlie adjusted his pillow and reached for his picture of Maddie. He knew he was lucky to have married such a smart and beautiful woman. Charlie said a small prayer for her as he wondered where she was and if she was okay.

Despite being in a deep sleep, both Charlie and Jacob were aware when the ship watch changed four hours later. Jacob rolled over and buried his head deeper under his pillow. Charlie opened one eye long enough to look at his clock and then drifted back off to sleep.

Chapter Thirty-Nine

Present Day, Dahlonega, Georgia, Earth

C harlie knew he was in a dream, but it was so vivid. Ever since Charlie had given Asteria to *Zeus,* he found he had been having more and more dreams that seemed startlingly real. He looked around the room. Charlie somehow recognized the place. He stood up and laid the blue blanket he had over him on the back of the couch he had been sleeping on.

It was the smell that triggered the recollection of where he was. He was at the cabin where he and Maddie stayed during the previous autumn while he was on leave a little over a year ago. He picked the blanket back up to smell it. It smelled like Maddie. Maddie rarely wore perfume. She would occasionally use a lavender-scented skin lotion, but none of that was what Charlie smelled. He could not describe the scent; he just knew it was Maddie.

He tried to awaken himself. He knew this dream would not improve his anxiety. A captain of a warship must not let himself become too excited or depressed. This dream seemed way too substantive, and he already sensed the blues creeping into his mind, threatening to take hold of him.

Charlie sensed something move on the opposite side of the room, so he eased around the couch to investigate. He glanced up the stairwell and then turned to his left and walked behind the couch toward the kitchen. Charlie shivered from the cold. His breath hung in the air despite the friendly fire burning in the fireplace on the other side of the room. Outside the windows, on both sides of the fireplace, Charlie saw the moon reflecting on the bright white snow. Over the fire, the small mantle clock struck midnight.

In the kitchen he saw the flicker of a candle, so he walked that way. Halfway there, he walked past a waist-high curio cabinet, which had a mirror on the wall behind it. He glanced in the mirror. There, staring back at him in the mirror, holding a candle with the fireplace behind her, was an apparition of Maddie.

Their eyes met and Maddie lifted her hand to the mirror to place her open palm flat against it. Charlie raised his hand and put his palm against hers.

Back at the cabin, Maddie's heart stopped beating when she saw Charlie standing there. She, too, knew she was dreaming, but it seemed so real. When Charlie lifted his hand to the mirror, she thought how unfair it was to only be able to spend time with him in a dream.

Charlie broke the silence. "Fancy meeting you here."

Hearing his voice after so many months made her wish she could stay in this dream forever. She wrinkled her brow and said, "You took long enough to show up."

"I am stranded a little far from home," Charlie replied. "I promise I am working on a plan to make it back."

Maddie scowled. "You had better hurry. I desperately need my hero."

Charlie laughed, "Thanks. Well, this is definitely just a dream. My Maddie always says she doesn't need a hero."

Maddie protested, "I have never said that. I said I'm not looking for somebody with some superhuman gifts."

Both laughed. Charlie's subconscious told him the ship was in the middle of changing the watch again. He knew two decks below him, young Andrew was trying to shorten the straps on the harness in the helmsman chair because he would take Stuyck's place for the next four hours. Charlie wanted desperately to reach through the mirror and kiss Maddie goodbye.

"I believe I hear duty calling. I will send you an email and ask about the color of my blanket on the couch. If you get my email, reply with the answer."

They both smiled, and Maddie replied, "I will reply to that email, buster. The very next time I sneak into town and find the internet."

Somehow, Charlie was aware the shift change was complete. Before he added a final "I love you," Maddie vanished.

Charlie stretched and threw back the covers. He crawled out of his berth, made up the bed, and folded the bunk away. He sensed the blues gnawing at his insides while he slid on his pants and secured his boots. "The best way to rescue her is to complete the mission and go home."

Charlie started for the door but stopped himself. He reached overhead and pulled down his tablet and opened his email. No new messages. He hurriedly composed a letter to Maddie. "I saw you in my dreams last night. The dream seemed real. What color was my blanket? I love you."

Charlie hit send. He glanced over at his alarm. To clear his mind, he did a mental exercise to calculate the time back home in the North Georgia Mountains. It was a little after midnight there. He smiled and headed for the bridge.

Chapter Forty

Present Day, Headed Back to the Strivo,
Intergalactic Space

"Captain on deck," belted the sentry.

Charlie headed straight to the situation board. He couldn't believe it. He had correctly calculated *Zeus*'s exact speed, course, and location in his head, even before he saw the board. Charlie glanced over at the preparedness indicator. He knew the answer without looking.

"Lt. Myers," Charlie asked, "where might I find Lt. Jackson?"

Without waiting for a reply, he stepped into the pneumatic transport and headed for the vault where the mainframe was housed.

Jacob saw Charlie enter the room and rang out, "Quite an improvement in here, wouldn't you say?"

Charlie glanced around and noticed someone had installed several new towers housing the data banks.

"Did you sleep at all? How did you manage to install all this new hardware?"

Jacob smiled. "It wasn't me. Paschal from Engineering paged me right after the first shift change. He said the hard drives appeared sometime after we connected to the *Whisperer*. He claims they materialized out of the walls. It didn't take Jake any time to break into the database. We must have taken the crew of the *Whisperer* by surprise. They never had time to log out. Jake changed the access codes, so we can come and go as we please. I have also concluded *Zeus* has a mind of her own."

Charlie shook his head. "Sounds like what happened after we installed the jewel. *Zeus* reinvented herself again."

Jacob nodded. "Sounds about right. Have you been by the brig to visit our guests? Do you have any idea on how you plan to interrogate them?"

Charlie had to think for a moment. "That will depend on you. I need you to study the *Whisperer* and tell me what they were attempting to do. Before I make any rash decisions, I need proof they had hostile intentions. How long do you need to discover sufficient evidence to reach a conclusion?"

Jacob looked dumbfounded. "Hostile intent? They were tailing us. Besides, have you read their logbook?"

Charlie nodded. "Yes, I read their logbook. But I need a threat assessment on which to base my decisions, and that assessment consists of more than their logbook."

Jacob relented. "I understand. I might be able to provide a clearer picture in a few hours, depending on what I find. Then again, given how much data is on their mainframe, I might need a lifetime."

"Okay. In two hours, I want an update," Charlie ordered.

Chapter Forty-One

Present Day, Headed Back to the Strivo, Intergalactic Space

Charlie entered the brig with one of the ceremonial swords in his hand. The captain of the *Whisperer* stood up and faced his captor. Charlie studied the man for a second, noticing his pale complexion and freckles, and then spoke.

"I apologize for my tardiness in providing you with an appropriate welcome aboard the *Zeus*. I am afraid at the time of your capture, I would not have made a fit host. I hope you have been treated satisfactorily and will accept my apology. My name is Captain Charlie Jackson from the planet Earth."

The captain greedily eyed the sword, then most graciously answered, "Our stay on board the *Zeus* has been most satisfactory, however unjust. I am Captain Bradford Scanlin of the planet Kesmit. You may call me Brady."

"My SWAL team leader found this on board your craft. Its counterpart is currently locked away safely in our armory. I wish I could return it to you as a gesture of our goodwill; unfortunately, our fleet policy does not allow guests on our vessels to carry weapons. I assure you I will return it, along with the other one, as soon as we part company."

Charlie placed the sword next to the sentry by the door before he continued, "I have come to invite you to dine with me in my personal quarters. Should you choose to join me, how long might you need to prepare?"

Charlie had surprised the captain; an invitation to dinner was not what he had expected. He was hoping to negotiate parole, but soberly he was expecting to be interrogated until they forced him to take decisive action—not be invited to dinner.

"I accept your gracious invitation. I am at your command at the time of your choosing."

Charlie waved his hand toward the door. "Then by all means, let's go. I have not eaten since our encounter yesterday and I am famished."

•••

Captain Scanlin fell in step behind the sentry leading the way. He lustily eyed the sword as he passed by, the purple amethyst on the pommel glowing dimly as he neared it. When he got to the pneumatic transports, he hesitated. Charlie noticed his hesitation and instructed the sentries to go first so the captain could see how the tubes worked. Once Captain Scanlin was confident he understood how the pneumatic transport functioned, he stepped forward and disappeared.

When Charlie stepped out of the pneumatic transport, he found the *Whisperer*'s captain rubbing his hand over the door frame and admiring the low-relief carving of an oak tree that spanned the two hardwood sliding doors to Charlie's cabin. The doors were the only wooden structural element on the *Zeus*, and they gave the entry into the cabin a sense of wonder and antiquity.

When he stepped into Captain Jackson's quarters, Captain Scanlin was shocked to see how much room the captain had. In his fifteen years of service on the *Whisperer* and other Silence-class vessels, he had never enjoyed any personal space so large as this. Charlie didn't seem to realize the favorable impression the cabin had made, so he apologized, "A battleship of any size does not allow much room for her officers or crew. Welcome to my small personal corner of the universe."

"Amazed. I am quite amazed. Apparently, you have not toured my ship, the *Whisperer*. If you had, you would know our ship designers only found a place for the crew to live as an afterthought," Captain Scanlin replied.

Charlie was embarrassed to admit he had not yet seen the *Whisperer*. "I have not had the opportunity, although Lt. Jackson looked around and told me your craft is very remarkable. It would honor me if at the appropriate time you might guide me on tour yourself, Captain Scanlin."

The captain accepted the compliment with a smile and said, "Please, call me Brady."

"I am pleased to have you join me for dinner, Brady. As our dinner will be an informal affair, I hope you will call me Charlie."

"Thank you. I apologize if this is not the appropriate time, but first, I need to ask your intentions."

Confused, Charlie asked, "My intentions?"

Captain Scanlin stood erect and pulled back his shoulders. "Yes, Captain. I would like to inquire if there can be any discussion of you allowing myself and my crew parole."

Now Charlie understood. "Captain Scanlin, I have not considered giving you or any of your crew parole. To my knowledge, our people haven't declared war on each other. Am I mistaken?"

"According to our history books, I find our two races may have had minor altercations in the past. Perhaps *Zeus* has failed to inform you of our history," Captain Scanlin answered, confused.

Charlie laughed. "Of course, I can request my people do some further research. How long ago might this altercation have occurred between our people? What was the nature of the dispute?"

Captain Scanlin did not smile. "The altercation happened over ten millennia ago. Please do not trifle with me, Captain. I am aware the captain of any ship of this class is ... how best to say ... is in complete unison with their vessel."

Charlie was no longer amused. Worse yet, he was hungry and growing short of patience. "Captain, I am not sure what you mean by 'in unison with my ship.' Perhaps you would like to clarify?"

It offended Captain Scanlin that the captain of the *Zeus* would try to play coy with him. His annoyance was evident on his face. "If you do not know, then how did you detect us trailing you?"

"If I do not know what, Captain?"

Now Scanlin was confused. He sensed no evasiveness from Captain Jackson. Surely this captain could not have devised such an effective means of capturing them on his own.

"Captain, I may have spoken too hastily. Perhaps I should ask my first question differently. If you are not willing to discuss our parole, then what are your intentions for my crew and me?"

Charlie reflected before answering.

"Captain, I can assure you any difference our people might have had over ten thousand years ago is not a justification for me to detain you any further. Unless you plan to take hostile action against my ship or our nation of people."

"So, are you suggesting we are free to go?" inquired Captain Scanlin.

"I would be shirking my duty if first I do not read you the riot act, expressing my displeasure for trailing our ship so closely. Unless Lt. Jackson finds a legal claim under which we need to detain you further, then I will have the privilege of seeing you off to continue your journey. In the meantime, I hope you will stay and enjoy a meal with me."

"My crew and I will be most grateful, Captain Jackson," said Captain Scanlin as he gave a small bow. "That unfortunate business behind us, it would be an honor to dine with you, Charlie."

Charlie smiled, but he was obviously still musing over what the captain meant by his being in unison with his ship. "Then, by all means, have a seat and let's eat."

Charlie turned around and motioned to Thomas and Dan, who were standing outside the open door.

"This is Thomas Lapillus, my steward, and Dan Sonefeld, our culinary specialist. Sonefeld can do just about anything with what we call a chicken. Lapillus and Sonefeld will be serving us this evening. I'd like to offer you one of my favorite meals. It is a casserole my wife and I call 'Mexican chicken.' If it has a more common name, I am not aware of it."

Scanlin could smell the aroma of the garlic and chili powder as Thomas and Sonefeld entered the room. His stomach growled in eager anticipation.

"I look forward to trying your Mexican chicken, and I hope to be afforded the opportunity to repay your kindness aboard the *Whisperer*. Our chef, Mike Hennigan, is also famous for what he can do with the meat from a humble chicken."

• • •

It was Charlie who finished his second helping first. He leaned way back in his chair and stretched. He spotted Thomas standing just outside the door to the cabin, gesturing for him to not forgot his manners and unbuckle his belt to unbutton his trousers like he so often did.

"This is one meal I like reheated better than straight out of the oven. I believe it is because the garlic and chili peppers have more time to absorb into the rest of the ingredients," Charlie said.

With his mouth still full, Scanlin enthusiastically replied, "This is the best dish I have ever eaten cooked by anybody other than my own chef."

Charlie laughed. "If word were ever to get back to your wife that you praised your ship's cook and forgot to mention her cooking, then it might not be safe for you to go home."

Scanlin laughed so hard, he egregiously snorted. "My wife's cooking is the only reason I serve on a ship in a galaxy far from home! A man has to eat."

Both captains were laughing. Soon, the two captains were sharing stories and were so jovial Thomas and Dan commented they sounded like long-lost friends. Thomas could be seen cocking his head at the two, who had grown comfortable talking on a first-name basis.

After enough time had passed, Thomas slipped in and asked if either captain would care for dessert. Both Charlie and Brady waved him away, saying neither of them had room for another bite.

As Thomas backed out the door with the service tray, Jacob slipped by him with a concerned look on his face, wearing a sidearm. When Jacob spotted the sword leaning in the room's corner where the sentry had placed it, he froze. He put his hand on his weapon and stared at Captain Scanlin.

Brady noticed how intently Jacob stared at the weapon. He continued to stare into Jacob's eyes but addressed Charlie. "So, Charlie, you really aren't in unison with your ship?"

Charlie looked at Jacob, a bewildered look on his face. "Jacob? What's wrong?"

Jacob never took his eyes off Captain Scanlin. "If you move toward that sword, Captain, I will have to shoot you."

Brady, still looking Jacob in the eye, stated in a matter-of-fact tone, "I do not blame you."

Brady turned his gaze toward Charlie. "The sword, Captain Jackson, is our most powerful weapon."

The luminosity of the amethyst on the pommel increased exponentially.

Charlie chuckled. "In that case, you are braver than I thought. It would be foolhardy to take on any size vessel armed only with a sword."

"No, Charlie," Brady answered. "It is foolish to allow anyone to bear that sword on or near your ship. The sword cannot be defeated."

Jacob interjected, "I believe I should remove this and place it somewhere safe." Carefully, he lifted the sword and cautiously backed out the door. As Jacob stepped out the door, the intrinsic brightness of the amethyst diminished.

Charlie was perplexed. He looked at Captain Scanlin. "May I ask you to explain Lt. Jackson's reaction?"

Captain Scanlin's demeanor changed back to that of a professional captain. "I am afraid, Captain Jackson, you and your crew have committed an act of war by infiltrating our databases. If you are truly not in unison with *Zeus*, then that means your Lt. Jackson has committed an egregious crime against our people."

Charlie looked astonished but contained himself. "Captain, if accessing your computer is an act of war, then you fired the first shot. Do you deny that the contents of all of *Perseus*'s database are on your computer?"

It was Scanlin's turn to look astonished. "Probing your potential adversary is not the same thing as boarding someone else's ship and taking what you want. I admit we probed the wreckage of your previous ship. If we found copies of your database, then that is salvage, which is fair game."

Charlie stopped, apparently to consider the gray area and study the legal consequences of Captain Scanlin's argument. Charlie had to have known the *Whisperer* had gotten the *Perseus*'s database by means other than salvaging it from the wreck. The crew on the *Zeus* had combed every square inch of that site. To their knowledge, there was nothing for the *Whisperer* to find, much less recover. The problem was that knowing the truth and being able to prove it were two very different things. Charlie wished he could consult with SC for guidance in this instance.

Charlie appeared to finally decide what to do with his captured prize. "I believe you to be a man of your word. Are you allied with the Obsidian Empire, or are your people considering hostile action against the people of Earth?"

"First, the Obsidians are my people's second most despised enemy, close behind the Spright Realm. Second, we have neither any desire nor means by which to threaten your kind."

Charlie asked, "Then why are you spying on us? Espionage is a capital offense. If I were to find proof you are guilty, then I would be forced to have you lined up in front of a firing squad and executed."

Scanlin lowered his head submissively. "Our intentions are not hostile. My mission was to discover your capabilities and relay an opinion to our king as to whether or not you are capable of influencing the outcome of the war between your people and the Obsidians."

"Why would anyone choose to send you to evaluate our capability to make war in some obscure asteroid belt? If what you say is true, then you would need to study our fleet's capabilities in the Milky Way."

"They did not send me to study your fleet's capabilities. We already know the status of your planet's space forces. They sent me to learn about you and the *Zeus.*"

"What do we have to do with determining the Earth's defensive capabilities?"

"Trust me when I say if the Earth has any chance at all, it lies with you and the *Zeus.* If I determined your connection with *Zeus* was strong enough that the two of you might swing the pendulum, then I could extend help to you. Not give you a complete copy of every piece of knowledge our race possesses, mind you. But I have free rein to use my judgment on how best to promote your cause against the Obsidians."

Charlie didn't seem to know where to start. "Surely you don't expect me to believe every important byte of information your race possesses is on the database we retrieved from the *Whisperer.*"

"I can assure you it is. That is why I cannot allow you to take it. You would have in your possession the ability to end our existence."

"Why would any one person possess that much information? Stored, no doubt, on a ship prone to fall into enemy hands at any time?"

Scanlin was indignant. "In the entire recorded history of our existence, I can tell you only once has any ship captured one of our royal ships and stolen our database. That was over ten thousand years ago. Not once since have any of our ships been forcibly detained and the captors survived to tell about it."

"Dead men tell no tales. How many of those detained crews were hung as spies?" asked Charlie.

Captain Scanlin explained, "In most cases, if a ship captures one of us, they usually release us, not recognizing us as a threat. Should someone capture and execute a captain on one of our royal ships, or if an unauthorized party tries to access our database, then our ships are designed to self-destruct, destroying our database and any nearby ship."

"That is interesting. I assumed you would tell me about the sword that can't be beaten. How do you explain the fact that Lt. Jackson copied your database onto our mainframe?"

Before Scanlin could reply, Jacob returned to the cabin and answered, "Because *Zeus* already knew the password and downloaded it."

Charlie looked at Jacob in disbelief, then back at Scanlin. "What was the name of the ship who captured your ship and stole the database?"

Scanlin looked Charlie in the eye and answered, "It was the *Zeus*."

Chapter Forty-Two

Present Day, Dahlonega, Georgia

Since the day of the attack at her home, Maddie had avoided any and all electronic devices. She had also given up sending Charlie any post and was sure whoever had orchestrated the attack on her was still out there searching for her. Maddie felt confident whoever was looking for her would expect her to communicate with her husband. If capable of gaining access to and intercepting her email, then they were also capable of determining from where she sent and received it.

Maddie couldn't understand why she was so agitated by a dream. At least it was a change from the nightmares, which made her so afraid to sleep. When she would succumb and fall asleep, she would only rest for a few hours before she would wake up trembling, drenched in sweat.

Maddie looked through the barren tree branches at the sun. She still had enough time to make it to town to get supplies and find an internet connection if she left soon; she would have to walk, in case law enforcement was looking for her car. She also wanted to get back early to feed wood to the fire and warm the house before dark. She learned once the sun dipped below the horizon, the temperature would drop at least another thirty degrees. Still, she had to admit to herself the comment Charlie made about sending her an email had been bothering her all day.

Maddie put on her heavy coat and looked everywhere she could think of for her mittens. Restless and impatient, she gave up and put on the leather gloves she wore to carry wood into the house from the small woodshed out back by the creek. Painfully aware she had used much of the firewood, she made a mental note to look for signs on the bulletin board at the grocery store for the phone number of anyone who might cut wood and deliver. She had not asked permission to use the house because she did not want to endanger her friend who owned it. She knew her friend wouldn't mind her using the firewood, but still, she wanted to leave the house as close to the way she found it as possible.

The gloves were hard and stiff from the thin layer of snow that had fallen on them the night before. They had been misshapen so severely Maddie barely got her fingers into the holes.

Maddie rummaged through her duffel bag and found an extra pair of socks, which had been worn so many times the toes had holes. She pulled them on over the ones she was already wearing. After her boots were laced up, Maddie headed out the door. She stopped by the car to retrieve her other handgun and put it in her backpack. She checked the time and realized she would not be able to both get supplies and access the internet before dark, but she had her heart set on sending Charlie an email.

Maddie locked the front door and leaned a piece of firewood against it so she could tell if anyone had entered the house. Turning, she trudged up the steep driveway. It was unbelievable anyone ever considered building a house at the bottom of this hill.

The walk was much worse than usual. The roads were slick. At least there wasn't any traffic. Like most southern towns, just the mention of snow was enough to send people to the store to buy milk and bread and then hide in their houses until all the mess melted.

When Maddie finally made it to the store at the end of the road, right before the intersection where she usually turned to walk into the town center, it relieved her to see the little yellow convenience store was open. Desperate to warm her hands, she stepped inside and looked around. Outside at the fuel pumps was a sizeable four-wheel-drive pickup. Maddie saw no one in it or pumping gas. It was just sitting there, idling.

Behind the counter was a young girl in tight jeans and a modest but close-fitting blouse. She had her hair pulled up in a ponytail, and it looked as though she had been wearing a stocking hat. Cheerfully, she asked, "May I help you?"

Maddie smiled at her. "No, thank you. Honestly, I just stepped inside on my way to the internet cafe to warm up for a second. My car wouldn't start, and the house I am renting doesn't have internet, so I am walking into town to check my email."

The girl looked at Maddie like she was an imbecile. "Oh my. What on earth were you thinking? You haven't heard about the snowstorm about to hit? The internet cafe and about everything else in town closed early today. We would be closed too if my cash drawer would balance."

"I haven't heard. As I said, I haven't had internet. How bad are they saying it will be?"

"My boyfriend says we might get a foot or more in the mountains. It's supposed to get bad starting about midnight. He's around here somewhere waiting to take me home. Where are you staying?"

"A friend of mine owns a cabin on this side of Black Mountain. It might be five miles if I had to guess."

The clerk whistled. "Wow. That is quite a walk. My boyfriend lives off Black Mountain Road. Maybe he can give you a lift after he takes me home."

Maddie sounded relieved. "Thank you. It sounds like that would be wise."

The clerk held out her hand. "My name is Anita. You said you needed to check your email? We don't have free Wi-Fi, but you are welcome to check your email on the computer in the office if you like. Hopefully, I won't be much longer."

"Aw, you are too sweet. I am Elizabeth," Maddie replied, remembering to use her middle name just in case. "That would be awesome."

Talking about the storm had momentarily preoccupied her mind for a moment. Now she felt a wave of silly nervousness. *It was just a dream*, she thought to herself. Still, while she had access to the internet, she should check her email and look at the website where Halsey said he would leave a message in case of an emergency. She reminded herself to make sure she erased her browsing history before she logged off.

Anita pointed Maddie to the office and went back to work. The best Maddie could tell from her mumbling, she was looking for a $113 difference in her cash drawer. Maddie wasn't sure if Anita's cash drawer was over or under.

Anita sang out, "I found it! I forgot to put the receipt in for the fuel Alton bought. Ten minutes, Elizabeth, and we are out of here."

It took Maddie a minute to find the web browser. It looked like the owner only used the old desktop to run an accounting program and play games. Maddie clicked the web browser, and the first thing that popped up was the news, the huge storm headed her way dominating the headlines. She cursed herself for not having already bought supplies.

Maddie scrolled down a little and then entered the web address for her webmail service. Before the news page disappeared, Maddie saw her own picture in a news article near the bottom of the screen and promptly hit the back button. They had published a picture of her from her old military identification card. The article stated they wanted her for the murder of three federal agents. It also said she was the wife of Captain Charlie Jackson of the *Perseus,* who recently went rogue and destroyed two SC warships. It closed by adding she should be considered armed and dangerous and that "anyone with any information on the whereabouts of Mrs. Jackson should notify the authorities immediately."

From the other room, Anita called out, "Two more minutes! I'm almost done."

Maddie entered the web address for her mail server. She held her breath. *What on earth am I thinking? It was only a dream.*

Quickly she scrolled through her email, and then her heart stopped. She opened Charlie's email and hit reply. She wrote: "Cerulean is the color. To save you the trouble of having to look it up, that is a shade of blue. Love, ie." When Charlie and Maddie had first met, she introduced herself as "Maddie with an 'ie.'" So many people tried to spell it with a "y."

Her heart took a minute to beat again. Once it did, she immediately went to the settings on the computer and deleted her web history. She rolled back from the desk and studied the mirror behind her. Carefully, she pulled her stocking cap farther down over her forehead and blew the stray hairs hanging down over her eyes to the side. Anita was turning off the gas station lights and called to her, "Turn off the computer for me if you don't mind. Let's go!"

Maddie obliged. When she rounded the corner, Anita had her arms around a huge man, hugging him. When he turned to look at Maddie, she almost fainted. Anita's boyfriend had on dark brown pants with a khaki shirt, covered by a thick, dark brown bomber jacket with the Lumpkin County Sheriff's Office patch on the arms. On his right side, Maddie made out the faint outline of the deputy's service weapon.

Maddie's first instinct was to run out the door. Instead, she made herself stop and concentrate on breathing. Then she stepped over to the deputy and held out her hand. "Hello, I am Elizabeth."

The deputy took her hand and shook it. "Anita says you walked into town from Black Mountain Road. Are you the one staying at the Pence place?"

Maddie wasn't sure of the best answer. She couldn't tell the officer she knew where her friend always hid her house key. "Yes. A mutual friend of ours made the arrangements for me to visit for a while. I have always loved it up here in the mountains."

The deputy replied, "I'm Alton. I saw smoke coming up and over the hill the other week, so I knew someone was visiting. I've been meaning to stop by and introduce myself. The Pences are snowbirds. They always head to Florida once the temperature starts to drop."

Anita was fussing with her coat. "Alton knows everyone up here. Someday he will run for sheriff. I must warn you if he drops in to check on you and you feed him, he is like a stray dog. You'll never get rid of him."

She laughed and reached up to give him a sloppy kiss on the mouth.

Alton laughed at her joke, accepting her kiss greedily, and Maddie watched as he reached around and squeezed Anita's butt. "That only happens when I come to your house. I can't help it your momma likes me and tries to feed me every time I pass near your place."

Maddie could tell as she stepped out the door it was already getting colder; the falling snowflakes were so cold, they caused a burning sensation whenever they landed on her cheeks. She jumped up into the truck after Anita and buckled her seatbelt.

"I appreciate the ride." she said, smiling slightly and trying to stay calm.

It only took two minutes to get to Anita's house, but it seemed like it took an eternity for them to say their goodbyes, standing on the frigid front porch.

Finally, the deputy ran back out to the truck. Before he closed the door, the front porch lights of the house came on. "They have invited me back to dinner. I told them it wouldn't take long to drop you off," he offered with a friendly smile.

Alton obviously knew the roads well. As soon as they passed the city limits sign, any trace of the highway vanished.

"You obviously have plenty of practice driving on snow. Your driving hasn't frightened me once," Maddie lied as she gripped the door handle.

Alton had evidently never considered the possibility of slowing down. As they approached her stop, Maddie said, "The driveway is really steep. Just drop me off at the church on top the hill."

"Yep. That thing goes straight down," Alton agreed. "It's gotta be at least a nineteen percent grade."

Finally, they pulled up to the church, and Alton reached across the truck to help Maddie open the door.

"Myself or another deputy will drop in on you in a couple of days to make sure you are okay," he said.

Maddie pushed open the door and slid out of the truck, but she turned back and gave him a thumbs up. "Sounds good. Thanks again."

"It is getting dark. You'd better take this." He handed her a small flashlight. "I can get it back when I drop in."

The last thing Maddie wanted was him or anyone dropping in, but he was right. It would be dark sliding down the hill to the house. "Thank you. If I'm not home when you come by, I'll leave it on the woodpile on the front porch."

"Sounds good." Alton asked, "Do you need help walking down the hill?"

"No, I'm good. I climb that hill every day."

Alton waved as he pulled the truck door closed, and the big pickup turned around and disappeared into the darkness.

Maddie turned on the flashlight and scanned the area around her before heading down the hill. She stopped, her heart immediately racing—there were fresh wheel tracks on the driveway. She scrutinized them quickly and turned off the flashlight, steadying her breathing and trying to move through the snow now as quietly as possible. She had seen just one set of tracks, which meant that whoever had driven down the drive was still around.

She couldn't decide if she was trembling because of the bitter cold or because of the revelation she had company. She considered walking back to town, but if she didn't freeze to death on the way, what would she do once she got there? Once she neared the bottom she reached into her bag and replaced the flashlight in her hand with her Beretta. Carefully, she made sure the cartridge was chambered, and she flipped off the safety.

It was too dark to see what kind of vehicle was parked farther down the road, but nonetheless she could make out its general shape, some type of SUV. Her only consolation was that if it were too dark for her to see the car, then whoever else was here would, hopefully, find it equally hard to spot her—unless they had thermal imaging night goggles. She approached the car carefully, then lowered her body against it to use it for cover.

As far as Maddie could tell, no one was in the car. But from here, she could smell smoke from the fireplace. She also detected a faint hint of grilled chicken. Whoever was here had helped themselves to some of her chicken and had cooked it on the grill on the back porch.

Maddie studied the vehicle to determine who her guest might be. Law enforcement, federal agents, bounty hunters ... or maybe simply friends of the Pences who had stopped in to check on the property and had found her car and belongings?

If she could see the license plate, it might provide a clue. Maddie eased behind the vehicle and ran into the trailer hitch. She held her breath, hoping no one had heard the awful noise of her shin hitting the hitch.

If the visitors were indeed friends of the Pences (her preferred choice), they would have left and called the cops. Unfortunately, the fact that Alton had not heard over his radio that someone had called in a home invasion helped her rule out local law enforcement. The fact the SUV had a trailer hitch seemed to rule out federal agents. They would not have a trailer hitch on their automobile, Maddie knew, because federal regulations prohibited federal employees from pulling a trailer. That left Maddie with the most likely possibility: a bounty hunter.

Maddie eased back behind the vehicle and waited, scanning the house. Sure enough, she saw the silhouette of an individual appear in front of the double windows of the living room. Her toes were starting to go numb inside her boots. She slipped around the front of the car and worked her way to the back porch. As she reached the grill, she could still feel the heat coming off the stainless steel sides. She paused long enough to warm her fingers, crammed into the stiff leather gloves. As soon as the feeling returned to them, she stowed the gloves in her backpack so she could more confidently work her gun.

Chapter Forty-Three

Present Day, Headed Back
to the Strivo, Intergalactic Space

The talks to decide the fate of the *Whisperer*'s database, and under what terms the *Zeus* and the *Whisperer* might part company, resumed early the next morning. Charlie and Brady debated throughout the day. Brady shared the history of the *Zeus* capturing his people's craft in as much detail as he could remember. Then Brady again pleaded his case for Charlie to destroy the database now under the protection of Peck and SWAL Team Two. Charlie ordered that no one was to explore the copy any further until he gave more instructions.

At times, the discussion grew heated. Jacob posted SWAL Team One outside the door to the captain's quarters with instructions to intercede if things got out of hand. Twice the SWAL team leader, CPO Shealy, considered interjecting, but Thomas convinced Shealy to give the captain time. Thomas had grown fond of his captain and had an unshakable belief in him.

It was getting close to midnight by the time they adjourned, so the two captains agreed it would probably be best if they took a recess and continued the conversation after dinner. The second they finished shaking hands, Thomas strolled in with the food cart. Charlie was pleased. The arrival of the food was timed perfectly.

When the cover to the meal was raised, Brady snorted. "So, our database has been sealed? It appears even your cook has been researching it."

"Members of your crew said this is your favorite," Thomas interjected. Our cook, Dan Sonefeld, was doing his best, but your own cook, sir, had to jump in and help."

Brady's expression softened. "Well, if our cooks can cooperate, there is hope for us all."

Charlie nodded his head. "I wholeheartedly agree."

Even though Charlie could not make his tongue correctly pronounce the name of the dish, he took one bite and declared it to be extraordinary.

Hennigan served a fish roe dip called taramasalata, which he made with olive oil, lemon juice, and grated onions, and served it with pita bread. Brady said the dish was a staple of almost any meal on his home planet. Along with the creamy, smooth dip, which Charlie noted had the consistency and a taste similar to mayonnaise, the *Whisperer*'s cook had made a savory charbroiled asparagus.

Charlie hardly touched the asparagus but declared the taramasalata excellent. The asparagus didn't go to waste. Jacob gulped it down straight from his brother's plate.

Brady seemed pleased at Charlie's enthusiasm for the dish. "The crew is correct. This is my all-time favorite. I am surprised our cook shared the recipe. I tried to get him to teach my wife, but he refused."

"To have a cook refuse the request of a captain is tantamount to insubordination in our service," Jacob said, laughing, as Myers and Captain Scanlin's First Officer Venery Elliott walked in to join them for the meal.

Brady grinned. "To refuse to follow an order is tantamount to treason on our ship. My cook defended himself by saying it was for my own good. He has eaten my wife's cooking and does not have much faith in her ability, even with his recipe!"

Brady laughed so hard his pale skin turned pink. The men sat down and began to eat, murmuring their appreciation.

Charlie was also laughing. "I hope someday we find ourselves as allies and friends. I would love to introduce our wives and truly get to know each other."

"I would like that too," Brady replied. "Tomorrow we will take the first step toward building mutual understanding and trust. Those are the first steps toward making our hopes a reality."

Charlie clasped Brady's hand. "I agree."

After the meal, Jacob stood and said to Brady, "The SWALs will escort you to your cabin, sir. Might you be up for some company?"

Jacob turned to look at Charlie. "Of course, if that is acceptable, sir? The crew from the *Whisperer* has suggested Captain Scanlin is the most esteemed chess player in the universe, and I would love to try my hand against him."

Charlie nodded his approval.

Brady had been watching for Charlie's reply. With permission given, Brady rose, nodded his goodbye to Charlie, and proclaimed, "By all means. Please join me."

Chapter Forty-Four

Present Day, Dahlonega, Georgia

Maddie inched her way under the kitchen windows over to the back door. As she reached toward her pocket to pull out the keys, she hesitated and instead gently turned the knob far enough to realize it was unlocked. She peered around the corner and investigated the kitchen. It was too dark for Maddie to see anything, though she noticed the flickering fire in the living room fireplace. She was concerned the draft from opening the door might alert whoever was in the house, but she couldn't think of anything to mitigate the risk. She turned the handle to ensure the deadbolt was also unlocked, then opened the door and slipped into the kitchen.

From the living room, she heard someone stir, but it sounded like the restless stir of someone napping on the couch. Satisfied no one had heard her enter, she stepped across the kitchen and pushed her torso against the kitchen cabinets, sliding to the entryway into the living room. Around the corner, she saw the mirror where she had seen Charlie the night before. She used the mirror to survey the room. Maddie made out the fireplace. Silhouetted against the fire in the fireplace, she recognized the hand of a man hanging off the love seat.

Satisfied there was only one person in the room, she confidently stepped around the corner and placed her gun against the head of the man reclined on the love seat. Maddie heard the faint sound of him snoring. She sidestepped around the couch and cleared her throat loud enough for the man to hear her. The man startled from his sleep and looked at Maddie, almost knocking his half-finished beer from the table with his elbow. He was lying under the blanket Charlie had placed on the back of the couch. Under the blanket, Maddie made out the distinct profile of a handgun. She waved her pistol back and forth at the man and shook her head. "Don't move."

The man had obviously been drinking since his arrival. Through bloodshot eyes and with a mist of foam from his beer still on his stubbly face, the man studied the firearm Maddie was holding and glanced down at his lap. Maddie firmly said, "If you try to reach for that gun, I will shoot you between the eyes. Now, slowly with your left hand, I want you to reach down and pick up the blanket and the gun at the same time and push them both off your lap onto the floor at my feet."

The man continued to stare at the firearm in Maddie's hand. Maddie did not repeat her order. She squeezed the trigger and shot the man in his left leg. He leaped forward in pain, and the blanket and handgun tumbled off his lap onto the floor at Maddie's feet.

The man yelled at Maddie, "Arrrgh, you will pay for that!"

Maddie raised the gun a little higher. "Who will make me pay?"

The man snorted. "With the size of the bounty on your head, you are already dead. You just don't know it yet."

"So how did you locate me?" asked Maddie.

"I was coming to check here anyway. You and your husband have stayed here before." The man laughed. "Then earlier today your car showed up on a satellite. You aren't smart enough to get away by yourself. If you put the gun down, in return, I will help you."

Maddie fired again. The round slammed into the other leg, causing the man to scream again. "I might not be smart enough to run forever, but at least I can run. Who is offering a reward for me?"

"The question is: who *isn't* offering a reward for you," the man spat through clenched teeth. "There is a bidding war for your head, and most bidders don't care if you are dead or alive. The Obsidians also want your husband dead. Rumor has it the price on your head has risen as high as the price on his. Are you and your husband competing? You two have pissed off half the universe."

Maddie fired again. This time between his legs. The bullet hole was visible on the couch.

"In case you are wondering, I hit exactly where I was aiming. I will not fail to hit six inches higher if you don't answer my questions. Foreign empires don't run ads on the local news offering bounties. I want specifics!"

The man hissed at Maddie, "I will not tell you anything, you stupid—"

"I am not in the mood to drag information out of you." Maddie fired again, twice.

The man's body slumped over and fell onto the floor. The man had already told her everything she needed to know.

Maddie stepped over the man's body and walked into the bedroom. She shoved a few items into her bug-out bag and walked back over to the man. Maddie rolled him over and retrieved his wallet and cell phone. She pressed the button on the cell phone and was relieved to see he did not have password protection.

First, she scrolled through his recent calls list. He had received a call from a number earlier this afternoon, about an hour after she left to walk to town. She thought back but did not recall passing an SUV on her way to the gas station in Dahlonega. Next, she opened his text messages. There were a few obvious personal messages. The most recent message was part of an ongoing chain. The man's final outgoing message stated, "I found where she has been hiding, but she is not here. She must have abandoned the car. It is outside in the driveway."

Whoever the man was texting with had replied, "Wait there. We will join you as soon as the weather breaks. Don't forget, people will pay more for her alive than dead."

Maddie turned the phone over and removed the back cover. She took the battery out of the phone and slipped both into her coat pocket.

She was going to roll the man over to look for his keys but spotted the dongle to his car on the coffee table. Maddie slipped it into her coat pocket along with his handgun and extra clips, then turned and picked up one of the five-gallon buckets of kerosene she had been using to start fires in the fireplace. She doused the man's body, and carefully she soaked the rest of the room, then placed the small bucket of kerosene on the mantle beside the clock. Satisfied, she left the front door open as she walked out.

Once she got the SUV to the top of the driveway, she stopped and walked back down the hill until she had a clear view inside the house. She fired one shot and hit the kerosene bucket over the fireplace. The kerosene spewed down onto the floor, and the whole house went up in flames. By the time she made it back to the car, she already saw flames towering over the trees behind her from the bottom of the hill.

Maddie was in shock at how fast the house went up in flames. She had hoped it would take a while before anyone was alerted to the fire. She knew whoever was looking for her would assume she was in the house and send someone to verify the identity of her burned remains. Hopefully, it would take a while before they realized she had not perished in the fire. Meanwhile, she intended to be hundreds of miles away.

She put the SUV in drive and slowly started toward town. Before she made it to the city limits sign, two fire trucks passed her with their lights and sirens blaring, headed toward Black Mountain. Close behind was the large four-wheel-drive pickup belonging to Alton, and two sheriff cars. She pulled off to the edge of the road so they could pass. Before they were out of sight, she turned on her right blinker and headed into town to hit the bypass headed south.

As soon as she made it to Gainesville, she used the man's credit card to top off the fuel, then headed west toward Atlanta. She drove a couple hundred miles before she found a truck stop on the outskirts of Birmingham where she parked the SUV in between two tractor-trailers near the back row facing the store.

As she reclined her seat to get some rest, the tears came, her mind racing. She felt confident her enemies from her past had discovered her when she first found the man watching the house. Now it was confirmed. She so longed for her and Charlie to just disappear. Now she knew her dream would never happen. Even with all the funds she had at her disposal, there was nothing she could do to change her fate.

To encourage Charlie to not reenlist in the service, she had told him her parents had passed away and left her a small fortune. He had never asked—and she had never told him—how much money she had locked away in her offshore accounts. She left him a note on her third-party server telling him how to access it in her will shortly after they married. She had entrusted access to the only other person alive she trusted implicitly: Jacob.

Her third-party database contained everything she had learned from her connections through SCOPE. She was so close to solving everything. If only she had more time ... but her time had now run out.

Maddie, her mind swirling, exhausted, and with no more tears to cry, fell asleep.

Chapter Forty-Five

Present Day, Headed Back
to the Strivo, Intergalactic Space

Charlie stopped on the bridge to check on the status of the ship. Then he headed to his cabin to sleep. He crawled up into his bunk, grabbed his tablet, and opened his email. There were several official-looking emails from SC, but then he saw an email from Maddie.

"Cerulean is the color ..." he read. "To save you the trouble of having to look it up, that is a shade of blue. Love, ie." His heart stopped short. He could not believe it. It had been more than just a dream.

He considered replying but thought better of it. No doubt someone somewhere was reading their posts. He pulled the sheets up over his head, but as hard as he tried, he could not fall asleep. Between the email and all the unforeseen drama with the *Whisperer*, he couldn't stop the thoughts swirling inside his head. In the end, tiredness won out, and he drifted off to sleep.

At first, Charlie was mortified. The first vision he had in his dream was of firemen slipping and sliding in the snow, trying to put out a house fire. The heat from the fire was unbelievable. The house by this point was only a smoldering ruin, but he knew it was the cabin from his dream. The brick fireplace was the only thing standing. On the left of the smoldering house was the burning hulk of their car. The remains of the vehicle were unrecognizable, but Charlie knew without a doubt it was his and Maddie's.

He almost woke up, but the pile of ruins vanished, and Charlie found himself standing in a truck stop parking lot. He had to sidestep rapidly to keep from being hit by a red Freightliner truck pulling out from between the fuel pumps. His surroundings confused Charlie, so he walked toward the convenience store to get out of the cold. He almost made it to the door when, from the corner of his eye, he spotted a vehicle in the back of the small parking lot flashing its headlights. The headlights were lodged between two semi tractor-trailers.

Charlie thought the flashing lights were unusual, so he walked back to investigate. As he got closer to the vehicle, he saw someone waving at him from behind the steering wheel. Charlie took off in a run when he realized it was Maddie. The windows on the driver's side had snowflakes frozen to them, so it took a moment to scrape them off so he could see her better. He pressed his hand against the window. When Maddie saw his hand, she raised her palm and placed it against the window to match Charlie's.

Charlie and Maddie exchanged tired smiles. Maddie leaned against the window with her face so she could see better, and her elbow unlocked the doors. Charlie, hearing the doors unlock, grabbed the handle and pulled. The door opened, and Maddie jumped out of the car and into Charlie's arms, kissing him all over. Charlie embraced her, then pushed her out of the cold, following her back into the car.

He stopped kissing her and looked her in the face. "About time you let me in."

For the next hour, they held each other in the cold car and talked.

"What is your plan?" Charlie asked, concerned.

Maddie confessed she did not have a clue. Charlie thought for a moment.

"Ditch the SUV and the man's phone. Come with me."

He opened the door and pulled her out of the car by her hand. Maddie wondered what Charlie was thinking. It wasn't like she could return to his ship with him. Or could she? Charlie headed straight to the door of the truck stop. As they passed the fuel pumps, the smell of diesel fuel greeted them. Trucks were lined up three-deep on the influent side of the pumps, waiting to get fuel. Most of the truck drivers needed fuel along with a place to weather the storm.

Once they were in the store, Charlie led Maddie around by the hand, browsing. Maddie thought how conspicuous Charlie looked wearing his lightweight flight uniform. They stopped at the magazine rack. Charlie handed Maddie a magazine, and he inched closer to the end of the aisle to listen to the men talking in the line at the counter. Two of the drivers were hoping to make it to I-85 and head north ahead of the worst of the storm. The older gentleman was planning on continuing west to I-20. He needed to drop his load in Jackson, Mississippi, and then head south to his home in Bunkie, Louisiana.

The two cashiers motioned for the drivers to approach, so the two younger truck drivers stepped forward to pay their bills. Charlie stepped around the corner and spoke to the older man. "Excuse me. Did you say you are heading to Jackson, Mississippi?"

"I have to drop a load tomorrow. Hopefully, I can drive far enough west to get out of this storm," answered the old man.

"I am trying to get my wife back to Shreveport. I must report for duty tomorrow afternoon, and this storm is messing up our plans. Is there any chance she can catch a ride as far as Jackson?" Charlie asked.

"The way the war is going, I recommend you both head west and never return. I was in SC years ago. Which fleet are you with?"

Charlie thought quickly. Not being current on events, he did not want to throw up any red flags. "I was teaching at the academy. I am headed to Mobile to be reassigned when I get there."

"Well, I guess I can help and give the little lady a ride. It's against company policy, but it's the least I can do to show how much I appreciate you being willing to serve."

"Thank you. I will sleep better knowing my wife is in the hands of a former airman," Charlie said.

Charlie placed his hand on the small of Maddie's back and pulled her beside him. "My name is Scott, and this is my wife, Elizabeth."

The old truck driver held out his calloused hand and shook Charlie's. Charlie noticed how gently he took Maddie's hand when he offered to shake hers.

"My last name is Melancon. My friends and family call me Greg. Everyone else calls me Bear."

Maddie stepped a little closer. "It's nice to meet you, Greg."

The cashier motioned for him to come to the counter, and the driver grunted.

"Mine is the old red Pete in front of line eighteen. If you are there when I get done paying for my fuel, then I'm sure I can make room for you. I can't be waiting for you, though. You better go pee before we leave. I can't be stopping every two hours."

Maddie smiled and said, "I promise I won't delay you. I will grab my bag and meet you at the truck."

"Don't forget to pee," said Greg.

Charlie took Maddie by the hand and headed toward the door. Charlie had noticed the clerk at the far register was eyeing them, so he stopped in front of the inquisitive girl's register and kissed Maddie.

"I will see you in Boston next week," he told her.

Before Maddie replied, he led her out the door.

The couple headed back across the parking lot to the SUV. Charlie grabbed Maddie's bug-out bag while Maddie squatted behind the SUV to empty her bladder. When she came back around the corner, he told her to give him the cell phone and battery.

Charlie walked across the lot with her, gave her a big hug, and watched Maddie climb up into the old red Peterbilt. As she reached back to pull her door shut, she gave Charlie one last pining glance.

The smoke belched from the stacks as Greg cranked the big rig, then pulled off.

Charlie saw the two drivers who were heading north. The closest one was climbing up into his truck. Charlie eased between his tractor and the pumps, carefully stepping over the fuel hoses while reinstalling the battery into the phone. Charlie turned the phone on, and when he reached the rear of the truck, he secured it under the tarp covering the truck's load before the driver drove away.

In the distance, Charlie heard his alarm clock buzzing. It was time to negotiate with the captain of the *Whisperer* and resolve their dispute.

Chapter Forty-Six

Present Day, Headed Back
to the Strivo, Intergalactic Space

Charlie woke up shivering. As he reached across to turn off his alarm, he noticed snowflakes on his arm. Under his breath, he whispered, "Good luck, ie. Be safe."

"Captain on deck," rang out as soon as Charlie stepped out of the pneumatic transport onto the bridge. He walked straight across the bridge to the situation board and examined it.

"Status of ship readiness?" he asked no one in particular.

Around the room, the crew reported on their areas of responsibility.

Satisfied, Charlie turned and walked back to the pneumatic transport and disappeared. Charlie's next stop was the brig.

He looked at the sentry and inquired, "Is our guest up?"

"Yes, sir," answered the young sailor. With that, Charlie stepped forward, entering the room where he immediately stopped short. In front of him sat Jacob and Brady immersed in a game of chess.

Brady grinned at Charlie and laughed. "Your brother is good. But I am better."

With that, Brady moved his knight and proclaimed "checkmate." Jacob did not look happy. He turned to address Charlie. "Good morning, Captain."

With disbelief in his voice, Charlie asked, "Did you two play all night?"

"It appears we did!" Brady cried out, proudly, "Eight games to six. My favor."

Brady beamed, then added, "And I believe the lieutenant and I have found the solution to our dilemma."

"We have?" asked an incredulous Jacob.

Wryly, Charlie said, with a questioning glance at Jacob, "I hope you haven't traded away the keys to the *Zeus*. First, let's eat breakfast and then you can update me on the status of the negotiations."

Charlie walked back out the door. "Please escort Lt. Jackson and our guest to the conference room."

Charlie's humor seemed to improve after his second plate of eggs. Meanwhile, Jacob and Brady never quit talking. Move by move, they recapped their victories and losses on the chess board.

To include Charlie in the conversation, Brady told Charlie, "Every time he made a move, he shared with me the move you would most likely have made given the circumstance. I can see why Jacob is the better chess player and you make the better ship's captain."

Charlie replied defensively, "I win my fair share of matches against Jacob."

Both Brady and Jacob burst into laughter.

Not amused, Charlie bit into his last piece of bacon. "Ha-ha, I am glad it amuses you two."

Brady, still laughing, said, "Don't be annoyed with either of us. Are we eating breakfast as men of rank or as friends?"

Charlie conceded. "Meals are better when served in the company of friends."

With that, Brady winked at Jacob and then addressed Charlie. "If it pleases you, may we resume our prior discussion, Captain Jackson?"

Charlie, still sour, said, "By all means. I thought you two already ironed out an agreement."

"Yes," replied Brady. "Lt. Jackson has uncovered a way you and I can move forward."

Charlie tried to give a retort, but Brady held up his hand.

"After you forbade Lt. Jackson from doing any more exploring of our database, he continued to research our culture by other means."

Charlie glared at Jacob. "If he violated my order, then there will be consequences for Lt. Jackson."

"No, I believe Lt. Jackson followed your orders to the letter," Brady answered quickly.

Confused, Charlie asked, "So, will one of you enlighten me and bring me up to speed?"

Brady and Jacob looked at each other, and Brady nodded for Jacob to answer.

"Captain Scanlin's family rules the Kingdom of Kesmit. They practice what we would call socialism, only with a twist. The people of Kesmit are governed by a benevolent socialist monarchy."

"Isn't that a contradiction in terms?" asked Charlie.

"You must emphasize 'benevolent,'" Brady urged.

Jacob continued, "They permit no one outside the immediate royal family to possess a copy of that database."

"Wouldn't its presence on the *Whisperer* contradict that statement?"

Brady jumped in to clarify. "Besides serving as the captain of the *Whisperer*, I am also known as Prince Bradford Scanlin. I am second in line, behind my sister, for succession to the throne of the Kesmit Kingdom in the Recondite Galaxy."

Jacob jumped back in. "The Kingdom of Kesmit is constitutionally required to use every resource the kingdom has to destroy us and our copy of the database unless Prince Bradford enters into a legally binding relationship, which permits us to possess it. The prince may not grant access to anyone who is not a member of the royal family."

Brady picked up the discussion. "The Scanlin family has ruled our small kingdom for many millennia. Our greatest strength is our ability to judge one's character. Not only do I deem you to be a man of an exceptionally true character, but I also believe you will prudently use our knowledge and wisdom."

Charlie, not wanting to offend Brady but feeling inclined to point out the absurdity of the conversation, said, "It's a shame we aren't long-lost distant cousins."

Brady ignored the sarcasm. "There are only a few ways you can become a member of our royal family. For instance, I suggested Jacob take the hand of my sister in marriage; however, for his sake, I do not recommend the match."

Jacob laughed. "The captain showed me a picture of her. I would rather take our chances against their assassins."

Both Brady and Jacob laughed so hard they had to stop to catch their breath.

Charlie, growing impatient, tried to move things along. "I do not see how any of this helps solve our current crisis."

Brady took the hint and proceeded. "There is a rite of passage where you and I can become blood brothers. That would, in fact, make you a member of our royal family. To be a member of our family is a privilege, which comes with responsibility. The responsibilities associated with protecting our people means you are a servant to the people. While your obligations to your people must always be honored, you must also pledge the same loyalty to my people."

Charlie's head was spinning.

"As the Captain of the *Zeus*," he said, "my responsibility is to my crew and our own people."

"Our people consider themselves the protectors of all races. The accumulation of knowledge to assure the survival of humanity is our most important aspiration," said Brady. "You should take time to consider my offer. Your life will serve a greater purpose."

"I hate to point this out," Jacob interjected, "but SC has condemned you as a traitor, Captain. You can never go back. I don't know if any of us can."

Charlie considered Jacob's point and the ramifications of what Brady proposed.

"I will have to give your offer consideration," he said, frowning.

Charlie pondered: *Would becoming blood brothers with Scanlin actually make me guilty of treason? What other options are available to me?* Then, and perhaps most importantly, he asked himself, *What would Maddie think?*

Chapter Forty-Seven

Present Day, Headed Back
to the Strivo, Intergalactic Space

T he Obsidian cruiser had spotted the pocket battleship that wreaked so much havoc in the corridor several hours before the Recondite vessel suddenly appeared and was captured. No longer was the captain of the Obsidian cruiser interested in the battleship. His concentration was on being able to catch and possess the most fabulous prize in the entire universe. This obsession now possessed his every thought. His name would be legendary.

Tracking the battleship was not possible while it had been engaged in battle. The reports he received stated the strange sounds emanating from the ship made the vessel impossible to track or pinpoint in the usual manner. So far, the white noise was not an issue. Not once had the ship showed the ability to mask its signature. At this range, he could only track the vessel using a scope anyway.

His orders were to use his ship's sensitive sound array to track down the elusive ship. He was then to notify his admiral so dozens of destroyers, perhaps even a battleship, might come to destroy it. The captain had been on the cusp of sending the notification when he witnessed the appearance and the impossible capture of the Recondite vessel.

The admiral would show gratitude for reporting his find, but the captain did not want crumbs. The captain wanted to possess the Recondite ship himself. How to do so was the question. Then, as if fate had deemed him worthy, the battleship reversed course and headed straight to him.

It had taken a couple of days for the battleship to make it back to where the Obsidian cruiser was lying in wait. The captain had used this time wisely to camouflage his ship and to eliminate its electronic signature as much as possible.

Fear engulfed the heart of the battle cruiser's captain when he saw the Recondite vessel undock from the battleship. But instead of disappearing, the small ship had only fallen into position to fly in formation, and the two vessels continued straight into his ambush.

•••

Charlie had decided he could not serve two masters, so he allowed Brady to oversee erasing the Kesmit database. The *Whisperer* undocked from the *Zeus*, but most of the crew stayed on board to celebrate the new friendship between the two ships.

Prince Bradford gave Charlie his duplicate invincible ceremonial sword as a token of their friendship. The long silver blade felt heavy in Charlie's hand compared to the slim, lightweight weapons he sparred with at the academy. The blade shined so brightly, Charlie could see his reflection. On the pommel inside a girth was a dark blue sapphire. It seemed to lighten when Brady placed it in Charlie's hand, and Jacob noticed the color changed to a perfect match of the color of Charlie's eyes. Between the hilt and the two arms of the guard was an oval medallion. The medallion looked conspicuously unfinished against the ornate leatherwork on the hilt.

The Royal Order of the Sword Ceremony complete, members from both crews gathered in the seldom-used conference room behind the bridge for refreshments. Unexpectantly, the flaxen horn sounded its eerie cry just as the first salvo hit the *Zeus* broadside. Jacob ordered *Zeus* to accelerate to full speed. The huge engines roared to life as the second salvo from the Obsidian cruiser fire struck *Zeus* amidships.

The *Zeus* stopped accelerating and glided to a full stop, and a third salvo pounded the two port-side docking bay doors into one. Gun crews on the *Zeus* were finally making it to their stations, and slowly one gun after another returned fire. Soon the port side of the *Zeus* was answering the Obsidian cruiser blow for blow.

An Obsidian cruiser easily carried as much firepower as a battleship, but they built cruisers with economy in mind. In return for massive amounts of firepower, the designers had traded away armor. The return fire from the *Zeus* was brutal. Many of her shells entered one side of the ship and exited the other.

The Obsidian captain saw the small Recondite vessel momentarily dock with the battleship on her starboard side. He was about to order his cruiser to retreat to a safer distance to pepper the ship from afar when he saw the Recondite vessel uncloak and start fleeing back in the direction the two had arrived from. He abandoned the fight with the battleship and ordered the helm to pursue his real quarry.

There was chaos on the bridge when Charlie arrived. Myers reported, "We have lost all propulsion, and the port-side docking bay is a shambles, sir."

The good news was neither of the gun decks had taken much damage, but the aft rotary cannon and the docking bay were all but destroyed.

Charlie commanded, "Get the auxiliary motors online so we can raise the shields. Use the directional engines to lay the guns so they bare. Let's give them a reason to back off!"

Just as he gave the order, the entire ship shuddered as another round pierced the armor belts amidships.

Leaving Myers and M&M to their tasks, Charlie and Jacob left the bridge and scrambled from post to post, helping the gun crews who were coming online target the cruiser on the main screen off their port side.

As soon as a steady rate of return fire was established, Jacob disappeared into a pneumatic transport headed back to help in Engineering, and Charlie headed back to the bridge.

Brady prayed the XO on his ship would expect his return as he climbed through debris to the docking port. Sure enough, he saw the *Whisperer* bravely sliding into position to dock. Venery performed a fast barrel roll and slid the *Whisperer* into the starboard docking bay with such incredible skill that even Brady would have not believed it possible. Brady dived into his ship the second the doors opened and ordered Lt. Elliott to take off. The XO asked if he should go to stealth mode.

Brady strapped into his harness. "No, make certain they see us leave. We need to draw them away from the *Zeus*."

Captain Scanlin was almost sure the *Whisperer* was the cruiser's primary target; the *Zeus*, its secondary.

Elliott interpreted Captain Scanlin's intent. He slingshot the *Whisperer* around the forward bow of the *Zeus*, did a barrel roll, and sailed his ship right between the gun mounts on the top of the Obsidian cruiser. The Obsidian gunners momentarily ceased firing as they ducked for cover, positive the small craft was about to plow right into their position.

The captain on the Obsidian cruiser was furious.

"Stop shooting! Stop shooting! We mustn't damage the small ship."

All the guns stopped firing. Relieved, the captain ordered the crew of the cruiser to abandon the fight with the pocket battleship and pursue the *Whisperer*. He gave the command for the assault team to prepare to board. Finally, after a long, stern chase, they closed the distance, and the captain instructed the helm to move in close and lock on.

It had taken time to get the *Zeus* back online. Jacob got one of the four large engines operational, and Charlie immediately ordered the *Zeus* to give chase. Unfortunately, the *Zeus* was not responding to her rudder and had to return to a full stop.

At last, Charlie had a green light, and the *Zeus* slowly gathered speed to chase down the cruiser. Charlie worried about *Zeus* because he had only once before seen the readiness bar so low. By the time the Obsidian warship showed up on the situation screen, *Zeus* was slowly recovering.

Charlie ordered Jacob to the bridge as they approached their foe. He pointed to the main screen and asked, "What do you make of that?"

Every light was shining on the cruiser. None of the damage to the cruiser looked severe, but the Obsidian ship wasn't moving. She was sitting there with a slight counterclockwise roll. Once the vessel rolled enough for *Zeus* to see the underside, Charlie spotted the *Whisperer* perilously hanging underneath. He saw the cruiser had latched boarding tubes on to every port on the *Whisperer* so the Obsidians could board her.

The *Zeus*'s approach to the cruiser took an hour. *Zeus*'s gun crews were prepared, already locked into their battle positions. Charlie ordered the helm to approach cautiously and keep *Zeus*'s undamaged starboard side facing the guns on the cruiser. Charlie ordered Myers to hail her. After getting no reply, Charlie ordered the SWAL teams into their insertion balls.

The SWAL teams were already strapped into the insertion balls when Charlie and Jacob stepped out of pneumatic transports from different ends of the ship at the same time. Both strapped on armor and grabbed a weapon. Jacob noticed Charlie was carrying the sword draped over his shoulder in its sheath. Once they strapped into the insertion balls, Charlie gave the order for the teams to board the Obsidian vessel.

Everywhere they stepped on the Obsidian cruiser, there was nothing but blood and bodies. They found Brady and his XO, Venery Elliott, in the mess hall. Brady was eating a sandwich and drinking a beer. Elliott looked as though he had been there a while. He was passed out with his forehead on the table and beer bottles littered all around him.

Charlie looked at Brady, questioning, "The sword?" He nodded at the sword lying haphazardly on the table in front of him.

Brady shrugged. "I tried to tell you. It cannot be defeated."

It took several days to patch up the worst of the damage to the *Zeus* and the *Whisperer*. Satisfied for the time being, Charlie proclaimed an evening of celebration. Instead of working on the *Zeus*, the whole crew of both the *Zeus* and the *Whisperer* prepared for a feast. Rumors spread between the decks on the *Zeus* about what transpired on the bridge of the *Whisperer* that evening during the festivities. Prince Bradford spoke eloquently about the ties between their two ships and said he was proud of the bond he felt existed between the *Whisperer* and the *Zeus*.

Charlie stood back, taking it all in. The seasoned veterans from the *Perseus* welcomed their new comrade in arms. He was especially touched seeing the young SWAL, Benson, embracing Prince Scanlin. *This new alliance might be a greater achievement than all we accomplished in the Strivo*, thought Charlie.

Chapter Forty-Eight

Present Day, Headed Back
to the Strivo, Intergalactic Space

Since the celebration, things had become bad. Night after night, Charlie searched his dreams for Maddie with no luck. It had only taken a few weeks to travel from the corridor to where *Zeus* captured the *Whisperer*. Twenty-two days after the run-in with the cruiser, neither the *Zeus*, the *Whisperer*, nor the Obsidian warship was anywhere close to having all the needed repairs complete. The crews of both the *Zeus* and the *Whisperer* had been working double shifts to make all the necessary repairs, particularly on the captured cruiser.

Finally, repairs on the *Zeus* and the *Whisperer* were declared complete. *Zeus*'s engines sounded better than when they had discovered her. The cruiser wasn't close to being declared space-worthy. Once the *Zeus* was declared space-worthy, Jacob dedicated most of his time to work on the cruiser. Brady was busy making improvements to the *Whisperer*. He claimed he had a list of repairs and disappeared. Charlie observed Elliott and Hennigan both stayed on the *Zeus* to help them instead of helping their captain on the *Whisperer*.

Even with all the people coming and going and all the activity, Charlie felt all alone. He never realized how beneficial it was to have

Jacob as a member of the crew; captains usually lived somewhat solitary lives. To make matters worse, he woke up tired every time he fell asleep. He assumed the endless searches for Maddie in his dreams caused his exhaustion. Aware she was running for her life and knowing there was nothing he could do to help was taking a toll on him.

Charlie finally found Maddie in his dream, but this time she seemed extremely tired. The visit they had was mostly an update on where she was and what she hoped to do next. She discussed the possibility of trying to stay in the bungalow they had rented for a weekend while Charlie was working in Tucson. Seeing Maddie did not help revive Charlie's spirits as much as he hoped it would.

Brady arrived the following morning, having declared the *Whisperer* fit for service. Charlie promptly asked Thomas to prepare an extra-special dinner for the two of them. For the first time since running into the cruiser, Charlie got to hear the story of how Brady allowed the Obsidians to lock on. Once the Obsidians breached the hull to the *Whisperer*, Brady fought his way onto the Obsidian ship and, using his sword, killed everyone on board.

Charlie felt guilty. He had thought Brady was staying aboard the *Whisperer* to avoid having to help with repairs. After hearing the tale and seeing Brady's disheartened countenance while recounting the events, he realized how emotionally drained Brady must have been from so much death.

But it was Brady who eyeballed Charlie. "You are still not in unison with your ship."

Charlie shook his head. "*Zeus* is in great shape. But I am worried about the readings on the readiness bar on the bridge. For some reason, *Zeus* still isn't full strength."

Brady lowered his voice. He knew Thomas loved to eavesdrop. How else did Thomas always know when they needed something?

"Charlie, the *Zeus* has unlimited energy and is always as ready as her captain. The bar on the bridge is not an indicator of *Zeus*'s condition. It is a scale. It is the measure of her captain."

The blow hit Charlie hard. He wanted to protest, but deep inside he realized Brady was right. Charlie leaned forward. "Brady, can you teach me how to become in unison with my ship?"

"It is simple. Do less talking and do more listening. *Zeus* is trying to speak to you, but you can't hear her. Have you ever wished something on the ship was built differently and come back to find it modified to your wishes?"

Charlie thought back to *Zeus*'s transformation of the bridge. He watched as the one fault he had found in the *Perseus* resolved itself when *Zeus* moved the helmsman closer to his chair.

Brady continued, "My people know a lot about Poseidon-class warships. Part of the deal with *Zeus*'s former captain was an exchange of database. *Zeus* is the youngest of her class ever built, but she dominated over all the others. Even the *Athena*, considered the Goddess of War, and the *Ares*, the God of War, grew shy when they were around the *Zeus*."

Charlie shook his head. "There are hundreds, maybe thousands, of battleships in the universe stronger or faster than *Zeus*. By today's standards, she is little more than a pocket battleship. The days of other ships cowering or shying away from her are history."

Brady disagreed. "To my knowledge, there is only one ship in the universe that is both faster and stronger than the *Zeus*, and you will not find this ship bearing an Obsidian flag. Someday you and the *Zeus* must face this ship together, and her captain's readiness will ultimately determine *Zeus*'s fate, not her own."

"Assuming I can carry my weight, how will I know if *Zeus* and I are in unison?"

"You will know. The *Whisperer* is a Silence-class ship. I became in unison with her slowly over many years. Like Silence-class ships, a Poseidon-class ship has many mystical properties. Many gifts she will share. For instance, my sister is in total unison with her ship, the *Hushed Tone*. She has visited the opposite side of Kesmit in her dreams. I am not as talented as her, but I can receive and share short messages with people who I know well in my sleep. You face many challenges, but there are countless opportunities through your connection with *Zeus*."

The epiphany that others could also visit places in their dreams startled Charlie. The mystical powers he had associated with the jewel he had given *Zeus* were becoming more of a part of how he perceived himself. *Maybe I am not as crazy as I believed?*

"What is this mogul ship's name?"

Brady shook his head. "That is a question for another day. You have many challenges to overcome first. For now, you need to become in unison with your ship. She has never been stronger than the person who commands her. The connection is like being so in love with someone you feel as though you are one."

Charlie sat quietly, deep in thought, and Brady went back to eating his food.

Once the plates were gone, Charlie asked, "How much do you know about what lies past the Obsidian entrance to the corridor?"

Brady laughed. "Well, the last time I visited, it was full of space junk. Someone left shattered hulks everywhere!"

Charlie joined in his laughter. "That isn't what I am asking. When I was in command of the *Perseus*, we destroyed a few small corvettes. It didn't dawn on me at the time, but a corvette can't operate far from a base. Do you know of any bases near the corridor SC might not be aware of?"

Brady thought for a moment. "It has been decades since Kesmit has sent a ship near that part of the galaxy. I know there is a natural space bubble several hundred-thousand klicks from there that the Obsidian military uses for their capital ships to hyperjump into the Milky Way galaxy. There are also a lot of archaeological sites located between the asteroid belt and the Wilhelm galaxy. It was the site of an ancient empire that existed long before the discovery of the Recondite Galaxy."

"I am aware of the bubble. The primary mission given me by SC was to disrupt commerce. If the Obsidians have a base anywhere in the general proximity of the corridor, then all our accomplishments can quickly be reversed in rather short order. New supply ships could have easily passed through the passageway and replenished their ships in the Milky Way by now if that is the case. Minus any theoretical base, the *Perseus* likely set their timetables back by at least six months."

Brady reflected. "That makes sense. Surely you are not suggesting attempting to destroy it if there is one?"

Charlie smiled. "That is exactly what I am suggesting."

"But what about returning to Earth? That will take months."

"Not if we use the space bubble."

•••

Maddie, far away on Earth, was lying on her back, staring at the stars and wondering where Charlie was in the heavenly bodies she was seeing. She so longed for just a normal life—one where she had a husband who came home at night and where she did not have to live in fear.

Maddie thought back on all the decisions she had made that led her to her present predicament. She remembered all that she had lost and she still couldn't believe that capturing the Obsidian gold shipment had not resulted in her and Jacob's death. Well, technically, she supposed, it had. Remembering how close they had come to dying dampened her already-low spirits even further. Of all the friends she had lost, she missed Joan the most.

Chapter Forty-Nine

Present Day, Headed Back to the Strivo, Intergalactic Space

The following evening, Brady suggested Charlie dine with him on the *Whisperer*, but Charlie declined as politely as he could. What he needed was time with Jacob.

Charlie entered his cabin to find Jacob already on his second plate of food. "Sorry, Captain. I was starving."

"No problem. Knock yourself out."

While Jacob continued to eat, Charlie came close to telling Jacob about visiting Maddie in his dreams but decided to hold back. But he did share he had received emails from her and told him about the bounty placed on their heads.

Jacob whistled. "They must want leverage to force you to surrender. What are you going to do?"

"Step one is to hope she can stay one step ahead of them and not get caught."

"You and her sending each other emails is only going to help whoever is looking for her locate her. What's step two?"

"I agree emails might cause problems. I am working on the rest of the plan and will let you know when I figure it out."

•••

At first, Charlie could not fall asleep after he crawled under the covers. Once he drifted off, he found himself in a dark and musty room. Quietly, he whispered, "Maddie, are you here?"

In a groggy voice, she whispered, "Where are you?"

"The better question is, where are you? What is that smell?"

"I had to leave the bungalow. There were men in the neighborhood asking questions, searching for me." She yawned, then added, "I'm in the basement of an old church north of Phoenix. They were having a covered dish dinner. No one noticed when I crashed it, and then I disappeared into the sanctuary until everyone left. I washed my clothes, took a shower in their gym, and was just about to get some sleep on this couch."

Charlie sighed and lay down beside her, burrowing his face into her neck and hair. He breathed her in deeply, his whole body aching with how badly he missed her. "At least it is warmer here than the cabin in the mountains."

Maddie agreed and turned to face Charlie. Touching his cheek, she whispered, "Tomorrow night I plan to find somewhere with proper heat and better air and a nice, firm bed."

She seductively moved her hand along Charlie's chest. "You had better come find me tomorrow night, Charlie."

Softly, she bit his ear.

They both laughed, but then Charlie kissed her deeply. "Tomorrow night, Maddie. Hang on to that thought."

She curled into him, interlocking her fingers with his. "Okay, it's a date. Don't be late."

Charlie faded away, but Maddie could still smell the slight scent of him in the air. "Good night, sweetheart," she whispered.

When she awoke hours later, she realized she felt at peace. She had come to love these moments she and Charlie spent together even though they were light-years apart. *Intimate*, she thought. She had never experienced anything more intimate.

•••

Charlie opened one eye and looked at his alarm clock. *Grrrr.* He desperately wanted to go back to sleep and return to Maddie. Instead, he closed his eyes and thought about what Brady had said about being in better unison with the *Zeus*. Maybe he needed to apply that idea to Maddie too. He started repeating to himself, "Talk less, listen more, talk less, listen more—"

The world suddenly became unlike anything in Charlie's experience. He was breezing through the gears, bearings, and slides on the *Zeus*. He blazed along fiber-optic cables and occasionally stopped to look at a circuit or transmitter. Charlie noticed two minor shorts in the wiring and made a mental note to make sure someone repaired them. Then he left the ship. He was sailing through the stars. Occasionally, Charlie would see a planet he recognized from books he had read, but many were unlike anything he had ever seen or heard of.

At long last, the scenery slowed, and before him was a massive battleship. Silently, he asked, "Is that for real?"

In his mind, he heard a faint reply: "Yes, and we must destroy it."

"How?"

In the dark recesses of his mind he heard, "When the time comes, you tell me. That is our future. Now, let me share a little of my past."

Charlie couldn't explain it, but he knew the *Zeus* was talking to him. Now, he was hovering over the bridge of the *Zeus*. He saw a previous captain caressing the royal scepter on the center pedestal and felt *Zeus*'s heartache. The captain stepped back and demanded *Zeus* give him the jewel. The pain was unbearable as he felt *Zeus*'s soul being ripped from her superstructure.

Charlie shouted, "*Zeus*, enough!"

The drama ended, and in his mind, Charlie faintly heard, "You and I must never experience that."

Charlie's eyes popped open, and he looked at the alarm. He sprang out of bed. He felt so alive and full of energy. In his mind he envisioned the situation board. Any question he imagined, he immediately found the answer to in his mind. Charlie understood better now what it meant to be in unison with his ship. Charlie was also aware the readiness bar on the bridge just spiked at 80 percent. He was painfully aware he still did not measure up to 100 percent.

Charlie quickly got dressed, and right on cue, Thomas entered his quarters. Thomas looked confused. "Something told me you are ready for your breakfast, sir?"

Charlie smiled. Being in unison with his ship would be convenient.

The simulation drill started as Charlie stepped out of the pneumatic transport. Myers looked confused because he knew he had not started a training exercise. Across the ship, people arrived at their duty stations in record time.

The drill, though somewhat unorthodox, showed weaknesses the crew needed to overcome. The team cringed, waiting to hear the rebuke they knew was coming. Charlie keyed the ship-wide intercom.

"We lost to a superior opponent just now. Next time we will not. We did record our best response time to date. Keep up the good work. Think of anything that will help you respond even faster. This simulation is over. Secure your stations and then proceed as you were."

Charlie turned off the intercom. "Myers, invite Captain Scanlin to breakfast with me in the conference room. Tell him I have something I would like to discuss with him."

With that, Charlie left the bridge. He wanted to visit with Jacob before Brady arrived to explore the possibilities of making improvements to the *Zeus*.

Jacob's response to Charlie's ideas was incredulous.

"I would have thought we would be working to make *Zeus* stealthier," he said.

Charlie replied, "True, there are times we would like our approach to remain unobserved, so I want you to continue with your improvements. Though, if an enemy does survive an encounter with us, I do not want them to ever forget meeting us. I want the fear of God to enter their hearts when they see *Zeus* coming. My hope is our mere presence will create chaos and the enemies' first response will be panic and to retreat."

Jacob laughed. "I can guarantee that after I make your improvements, no one will forget meeting us. The whole fear of God thing I will leave up to you and *Zeus*."

Charlie nodded his head, accepting Jacob's challenge, and added, "Now, I would like you and Myers to meet with Captain Scanlin, Lt. Elliott, and me in the conference room."

Brady and his XO, Elliott, had made themselves comfortable when Charlie and Jacob entered the room. Myers nervously stuck his head in the door. "You needed to see me, sir?"

"Yes, Myers. Please, come join us," Charlie said as he motioned Myers toward a chair.

Charlie, aware he had a bad habit of excluding Myers when he was discussing strategy, wanted to correct the error. He felt much more comfortable brainstorming with Jacob. That did not change the fact that Myers was the ship's XO, and Charlie understood he had been remiss in the past by not including him.

Charlie sat down. "Gentlemen, soon we will be within the range of any Obsidian ship's sound detection equipment that might be in the corridor. We need a plan."

"First," Brady started, "the *Whisperer* should explore and discover what opposition exists."

Charlie agreed. "Yes, I would like you to take the *Whisperer* and warn us if, for example, God forbid, there are any battleships. Assuming there aren't, I need you to deploy a few small probes to replace those the enemy destroyed since we were last there."

Jacob spoke up. "If we replace the probes, then link them together like before, we will know what we must face and where. We will also be able to blind them and deny them the ability to organize a defense."

Releasing the probes concerned Brady. "The stealth technology on the *Whisperer* will make our journey through the corridor predictably safe. However, every time we release a probe, we risk detection."

"I plan to keep any Obsidian craft adequately preoccupied," Charlie interjected. "We will provide a distraction so they will not notice you."

Charlie turned to his XO. "Lt. Myers, I am granting you a battlefield promotion to the rank of Commander and giving you full command of the Obsidian cruiser. I hope someday Admiral Halsey will recognize your merit and SC will confirm the promotion if we ever make it home. I would also like to propose we rename the cruiser the *Persephone*."

The promotion surprised Myers. "Captain, though honored, I must be honest and say Lt. Jackson is much more qualified to take command of the *Persephone*."

"I disagree, Commander Myers. I believe Lt. Jackson is the better-qualified officer to serve as the XO on the *Zeus*. But, without a doubt, I believe you are the perfect choice to command the *Persephone*," Charlie replied.

Myers blushed. "Thank you, sir. I will not let you down."

Charlie accepted Meyer's hand and congratulated him on his first command.

"Of course, she will need a crew." Charlie turned to Jacob. "Issue a request amongst the crew for volunteers to man the *Persephone* and serve under Commander Myers."

Jacob stood and saluted Charlie and then turned to offer his hand to Myers. "I would like to be the first to congratulate you on your promotion, Commander."

Jacob stepped out of the conference room and onto the bridge momentarily to post the news and create a sign-up sheet for volunteers to serve on the *Persephone*.

Myers seemed moved by the sincerity of Jacob's gesture. He also accepted congratulations from Captain Scanlin, who stated his faith in Myers's ability to lead.

"I have routinely observed that men will follow your lead. Make sure you are wise where you lead them," Brady said, though Charlie noticed that Brady didn't seem as enthusiastic as he had hoped he would be.

Once Jacob returned and regained his seat, Charlie continued: "While the *Whisperer* surveys the corridor, I want Commander Myers in the *Persephone* to tow *Zeus* into the passageway."

Everyone's eyes lit up at the brilliance of the plan.

"Jacob, I need you to recreate garbled messages using old logs from the *Persephone*. We will use them to convince any ships we meet that we have damaged transmitters on the *Persephone*. Hopefully, this will allow us to move closer before we spring our trap."

Myers interjected, "Captain, I can handle the garbled messages if Lt. Jackson's time can be utilized better elsewhere—like simulating battle damage to the *Zeus*?"

Everyone at the table agreed this was a good idea.

"Our objective is to secure this end of the corridor and work our way toward Obsidian space," Charlie added. "Once we have secured the whole corridor, we should reconvene. From there I plan to search for an Obsidian supply base. There must be one. I cannot imagine any other explanation for the corvettes we met in the passage in the past."

Myers asked, "What are our intentions if we find a base?"

"That we will decide once we know what we face," answered Brady.

"I believe this gives us a good baseline from which to build our strategy. We can build on these plans as soon as the *Whisperer*'s data starts to come in."

Brady stood. "Gentlemen, if we are all in agreement, then I propose the *Whisperer* should depart company immediately."

Charlie agreed, and each person at the table bade their farewells. The volunteers who offered to serve under Commander Myers seemed to segregate between the original members of *Perseus* and the rescues from the Obsidian cargo ship. At first, it concerned Charlie that such a division might leave the *Zeus* shorthanded, but after talking to Jacob, he decided the *Zeus* was more comfortable with the leaner crew.

In the end, the SWAL teams were of the most significant concern. Both teams unanimously preferred to stay on the *Zeus* where they believed they might see the most action. Though neither team leader would say so, Charlie detected a certain hesitation, or lack of desire, by each team leader to serve under Myers. Charlie relented and informed Commander Myers he planned on retaining both teams on the *Zeus*. Much to Charlie's surprise, Myers seemed relieved.

Chapter Fifty

Present Day, Headed Back to
the Strivo, Intergalactic Space

L ate that evening, Charlie got into bed. He tried listening instead of talking, but he heard nothing from the *Zeus* other than a chuckle and "Best wishes." The silence felt strange to Charlie. All day, the *Zeus* had been communicating inside his head. Finally, deep sleep took over and Charlie sank into the abyss.

Charlie could smell the sweet fragrance of Maddie long before he saw her.

Obviously, fancy undergarments had not been a priority for Maddie when she packed her bug-out bag. But she had decided she was reasonably sure Charlie's favorite was au naturel anyway. She caught the lustful look in his eye as soon as he materialized. She smiled and let the book she had been reading fall off the bed onto the floor. Maddie had taken a thin silk scarf with a rose print on it and draped it over the top of the lamp. The diffused light cast a warm, rosy hue on the walls and ceiling of the room.

Maddie cocked her head slightly to the side and smiled. "About time you got here."

Neither of them was sure how many times they made love that night. Charlie only knew when he peeked at the clock with one eye, he panicked and leaped straight out of bed. He jumped up so fast he hit his head on the ceiling above his berth.

He chastised *Zeus*, "How could you allow me to sleep this long?"

It seemed to him that *Zeus* laughed. In his mind, he heard, "Some things are more important than work."

Charlie was still putting on his shirt when Thomas walked into his cabin with Jacob right behind him. It startled them that Charlie had slept so long, but his appearance was even more of a shock. Thomas set down Charlie's breakfast, and he and Jacob hastily retreated out the door.

Charlie finished buttoning his shirt and rushed over to the mirror. All over his face was red lipstick. Even worse, Charlie made out the soft purplish hint of a love bite above the collar of his shirt.

Charlie washed his face and downed the bacon and fruit, leaving the eggs on the plate, then headed for the door. Before he opened it, *Zeus* tacitly warned him that Jacob, Thomas, and Lt. Paschal were all standing outside the door waiting on him.

Never before had Charlie wished for a back door to his quarters, but he was careful not to wish too hard for one now lest he return and discover *Zeus* had found a way to add one. Charlie needed a plan and quickly formed one in his mind.

The flaxen horn gave its low, mournful cry throughout the ship. The entire crew was strapped in before Charlie made it to the bridge. Charlie sat down, strapped in, and then turned to look at Lt. Jackson. "Response time?"

The new XO, Lt. Jackson, gave Charlie an evil look. "Only one person prevented us from beating our best time ever."

Charlie was truly curious, even more so by the fact that *Zeus* had not already whispered the answer in his ear.

Lt. Jackson answered, "I would like the ship's record to reflect that the only party who prevented us from setting a record response time was the captain of the ship."

The only members of the crew not able to contain themselves were poor Andrew and Roland, who happened to be manning the helm. Charlie ignored the stifled laughter.

"Lt. Jackson and Commander Myers, I would like to meet with the two of you in the conference room," Charlie ordered.

"Aye aye, Captain," Jacob replied with a rather obvious, annoyed smirk; the tone of his voice conveyed his disappointment.

Jacob pulled Charlie to the side as he left his post, headed for the conference room. He leaned in close to Charlie and looked him in the eye to chastise him.

"I haven't a clue who you are seeing." Charlie tried to stop Jacob, but Jacob raised his hand and continued. "Besides it being wrong, it's dangerous. Maddie is sweet, but I would not cross her. You stand a better chance against an Obsidian B Class."

Charlie tried again to stop Jacob so that he could explain, but Jacob turned and walked away. Charlie thought to himself, *Just as well. He would never believe me anyway.*

As Jacob and Myers stepped into the conference room, Charlie shook his head and returned to his silent rebuke of *Zeus.* "Now, maybe you can explain to me why you let me oversleep?"

In his head, Charlie heard *Zeus* reply, "The best captain I ever had was Captain Pat Ballentine. She, too, was an Earthling. She wasn't as aggressive as I would have liked, but like all women, her mind worked differently than the male captains I have served."

"Different?" asked a curious Charlie.

"Men have boxes in their minds. They seldom use more than one box at a time. Women's brains have many little boxes, and all their boxes connect. For instance, the fact the starboard rail gun needs greasing is relevant to the fact that the crew servicing it will have to wait while Chief Stuyck makes his usual trip by the galley to see what leftovers are available. The fact Sonefeld is having his teeth cleaned will further delay him. Stuyck will then have to spend extra time there consoling Marybeth over the fact Davis has left to join the *Persephone.* She is distraught he did not choose to stay on the *Zeus* with her. He—"

"Woah, whoa, whoa! More information than I want. Let's only focus on the part that dictates I cannot be allowed to oversleep."

Zeus chuckled. "I did not believe you would have appreciated me interrupting you and Maddie."

Charlie chose to ignore the smart comment. "You said Ballentine was an Earthling. I didn't realize you have served other races before."

"Captain Ballentine was from the planet Mars inside the Milky Way. But even though all my captains have been from your galaxy, I aspire to serve the greater good of the universe, not one particular planet or race of people. Life will force you to make decisions based on the greater good. I have tremendous faith in the wisdom of your choices, Captain Jackson."

"I think I need to concentrate on being punctual for now, but I am glad you have so much confidence and faith in me. Unfortunately, now my brother thinks I am a cheat."

Chapter Fifty-One

Present Day, the Strivo Corridor

With the readiness bar hovering at the 90 percent mark, it had taken much less time than predicted to make it back to the corridor. The cruiser had no trouble keeping up with the *Zeus*. Charlie suspected, if given the opportunity, the *Persephone* might outrun them.

Captain Scanlin's data mining exceeded all expectations. The amount of information and detail on the situation board was almost too comprehensive for Charlie to absorb.

Charlie gave the SWAL teams the responsibility of untethering *Zeus* from the tow cables connecting her to the *Persephone*. Team leaders Peck and Shealy relentlessly practiced their men releasing the *Zeus* from her bonds. Charlie's concern was the teams would not have enough time to make it back to their duty station inside the insertion balls before the *Zeus* had to perform high-speed maneuvers, which might cause the team members harm. The speed with which the two teams untethered the ship increased exponentially as they competed for the fastest time.

Despite how fast the teams were, the two SWAL leaders decided it would be best instead to use explosive rope. Charlie hesitantly approved their plan, despite his concern the lines might get sucked into a motor on the *Persephone* or the *Zeus*. But the team leaders showed how effectively they could eliminate the entire line by placing small charges inside the rope.

As the *Persephone* and the *Zeus* entered the corridor with the *Zeus* tethered behind, Myers played his part perfectly. The *Persephone* flew the Obsidian banner, and on the *Zeus* was the Obsidian flag right above the SC banner.

Dr. Laird protested, "Our ships are sailing under false colors! Isn't that a breach of the rules of war?"

Jacob never looked up from his console as he replied, "The ruse is perfectly acceptable. I can assure you the banners will be replaced promptly before the first shot is fired."

Obsidian ships all around the mouth of the corridor began firing their guns in celebration as they spotted the captured prize. Two Obsidian destroyers sailed alongside the *Persephone*, proud to be part of the procession. Once the two warships were positioned alongside, Myers gave the signal to attack. The banners on both ships were rapidly pulled down and replaced with the blue and white SC banner.

No sooner than both banners were secure, the *Persephone* opened fire from both her port and starboard batteries. The tethers holding *Zeus* evaporated into dust as the explosive charges ignited and her large engines sprang to life. Andrew rolled the *Zeus*, dropping below the *Persephone*, and then throttled up.

By the time the third salvo from the *Persephone* had been discharged, both destroyers were listing. The fourth salvo ignited fires upon one of the warships. By the time the *Zeus* made it up to speed, Myers had annihilated both destroyers, and he was maneuvering the *Persephone* to attack the shell-shocked support ships in the area.

Charlie and *Zeus* ignored the plethora of ancillary ships, leaving them for Myers to destroy. As the *Zeus* sped away, Charlie hailed Myers on the *Persephone*.

"Remember, avoid hitting any life pods if possible. Allow them to pass unmolested. We are here to destroy Obsidian ships. Not take any unnecessary life."

With Myers's acknowledgement, the *Zeus* sped down the center of the passageway; the *Zeus*'s quarry lay at the other end of the corridor. The *Zeus* barely covered half the length of the passage when the situation map showed four destroyers and six corvettes falling into formation and heading up the passageway to greet them.

Charlie nodded to Jacob. "Light her up."

Small bolts of lightning began arching away from the sides of *Zeus*'s hull. The sculpted bow seemingly came to life as Jacob illuminated it. The *Zeus* looked savage as she soared toward her prey. Casually, Charlie thumbed through his playlist, and the sound of "Whatever It Takes" by Imagine Dragons flooded the corridor. Aboard the Obsidian warships, they could no longer pin the exact location of the monster that was heading their way. A couple of the captains seemed to consider turning to run, but the lead destroyer fired a shot over the bows of two of his compatriots and they returned to their proper positions.

At that moment Charlie gave the signal. Dozens of mirror images of the *Zeus* appeared all around her. The lead Obsidian captain roared for his men to aim at the one in the middle.

The *Zeus* rolled, and all the mirror images turned with her. It was like watching dice being shaken inside a cup. Panic set in amongst the Obsidian crews. All but one of the corvettes broke ranks and began to flee the area. The four destroyers and one lone corvette stayed in formation and anticipated their head-on collision with the *Zeus*. Jacob gave the signal to his weapons officer, and hundreds of small explosive charges started tumbling in the *Zeus*'s wake. The umbrella of area being mined with the explosive charges increased exponentially with each passing second.

The *Zeus* and her mirror images flew straight through the small Obsidian flotilla at breakneck speed. The *Zeus* passed between the two closest destroyers, so close M&M later shouted out that they might have thrown a stone and hit one of them. The small warheads following astern of the *Zeus* began detonating as the lead destroyer turned to starboard to cross her wake. The destroyer and the corvette were destroyed immediately as the explosions lit up the passageway.

Their tight formation disrupted, each of the remaining Obsidian destroyers took the initiative to pursue one of the spectral images of the *Zeus*. The whole flotilla of mirages was still screaming down the center of the corridor toward Obsidian space.

As soon as the lead Obsidian ship started to bank, the real *Zeus* went utterly dark and circled behind the pursuing destroyers. The music continued to fill the void between the walls of asteroids. The only other sound was the sound of roaring engines and the distinct sound of destroyers exploding. Occasionally, the sounds of secondary explosions were heard, then felt, when a burning inferno reached a dying ship's magazines. One by one, every destroyer met her end as the long-range rail guns on the *Zeus* used them for target practice.

As the battle ended, the last of the probes emitting the replicated images of the *Zeus* exited the corridor still in pursuit of the fleeing corvettes.

Charlie ordered the *Zeus* to turn back up the corridor to the rendezvous with Myers and the *Persephone*. Each time they encountered a retreating support ship fleeing back toward Obsidian space, the crew on the *Zeus* patiently waited until the escape pods were clear and headed home before the *Zeus* destroyed their vessel.

The Obsidians recognized and appreciated the mercy. Several of the merchant and support craft dipped their flags in salute before ejecting in their escape pods. On the opposite end of the corridor, however, the *Persephone* showed no mercy. After destroying the Obsidian ships, the *Persephone* ran alongside the desperate airmen and used the escape pods for target practice. Silently, *Zeus* interpreted for Charlie what the long-range sensors showed on the monitor.

Charlie immediately turned the *Zeus* and headed straight up the corridor at maximum velocity. Myers ignored Charlie's desperate hails and continued breaking open the fragile escape pods. As soon as the crew of the *Zeus* closed the distance between them and the

Persephone, Charlie placed the *Zeus* between the *Persephone* and the small pods to protect as many of them as possible. Charlie ordered a warning shot fired across the *Persephone*'s bow. At first, the shocked sailors on the *Zeus* thought the *Persephone* was going to return fire. After a couple more random shots at the escape pods, the *Persephone* ceased fire.

Charlie was furious and sent orders for Myers to report aboard the *Zeus* immediately. The pain caused by all the unnecessary loss of life could be seen in Charlie's crestfallen shoulders. Incredulously, Myers refused. The *Persephone* drifted astern of the *Zeus*, and Charlie could not believe his eyes. Between the engines on the ship was the spare CBC unit.

Once again Charlie hailed Myers and asked for an explanation. But Myers said he was only following the orders he received from Space Command.

Myers continued, "Captain Jackson, SC has ordered me to escort the *Zeus* home and to take you into custody to stand trial for high treason."

"Treason?"

"Yes, treason. I explained to SC that the crew and I were innocent parties to your refusal to obey orders." Myers then lowered his voice. "There was no other way, Charlie. It's the only way they will ever allow us to return home."

Charlie was furious. "And if I refuse?"

Without expression, Myers replied, "They have ordered us to eradicate you and the *Zeus* if you do not comply."

Charlie refused to allow the *Persephone* to destroy the *Zeus*. He also understood he couldn't bring himself to mandate his crew to fire upon their fellow sailors. Before he could decide how best to respond, Jacob alerted Charlie that the *Whisperer* was landing on the back of the *Persephone*.

Charlie screamed over the radio, "Brady, no! Don't do it!"

Chapter Fifty-Two
Present Day, the Strivo Corridor

Charlie and Brady sat alone in his cabin and ate in silence. Brady had only spared sixty-three members of the crew on the *Persephone*. They had begged for mercy when the doors to the brig flew open, and Brady stood silently in the doorway with his sword quivering indignantly in hand. Brady never said a word as they poured out their hearts and told how they had protested the order to fire on the life pods and tried to stop Myers by force when he installed the CBC.

In the silence of the cabin, Charlie listened as Brady shared every morbid detail of the horrid story. Brady somberly finished by saying, "I may never lift my sword again."

Charlie consoled Brady as best as he could, but he, too, was heartbroken. His grief felt so great, it caused physical pain throughout his body.

Finally, after a lengthy silence, Brady concluded, "I have to return to my home. I am no longer fit to serve my people."

"You should go home, but you did what duty demanded. The lenience you showed my men and women locked in the brig on the *Persephone* proves you are exactly the person who should serve your people. Our people."

Brady looked up at Charlie. "Yes, our people. You and I are truly the same, but I need time to reflect. We are now in unison like you have become with *Zeus*. When you need me, seek me out, and I will respond."

Charlie led Brady to the bridge on the *Zeus* and nodded at Jacob. Together, Charlie, Brady, Jacob, and the whole crew watched on the main viewing screen, with tears flowing down their faces, as the *Persephone* drifted into the asteroids where Jacob had chosen to entomb her along with their former shipmates.

Having seen Brady's love of humanity, witnessed his capacity for self-sacrifice, and shared the core experience of combat had a profound effect on Charlie. He felt he and Brady now shared a commitment to safeguard each other's lives that was nonnegotiable. The privation of their shared emotions had created a bond, a love that could only compare to the feelings Charlie had for Maddie, Jacob, or Admiral Halsey. He was positive the bond with Brady would only grow stronger.

With great humility, Charlie told Brady, "I would like to accept the honor of embracing you as a true brother."

Brady's eyes glistened as he responded, "The honor will be mine."

The following evening, the crews of the two ships crammed into the *Zeus*'s long mess hall. Prince Bradford carefully cut his arm, and then the captain used the same sword to slice his. Then the two joined their arms together. First Officer Venery Elliott from the *Whisperer* and Lt. Jacob Jackson wrapped the captains' right arms in a silk bandage, and both captains repeated an oath of allegiance.

Chapter Fifty-Three

Present Day, Outside the Wilhelm Galaxy

Before the *Whisperer* disappeared beneath her stealthy facade, she saluted the *Zeus*. *Zeus* continued to return her salute long after she had vanished. Before Brady departed, he left two gifts. For Charlie, he restored the entire database of the Recondite Galaxy and Kesmit Kingdom on the databanks he had previously destroyed. For Charlie and the whole crew, he left a highly detailed map of everything that awaited the *Zeus* beyond the other end of the corridor.

Charlie gave Brady the only gift he had to offer: his prized antique autographed baseball bat, which once belonged to Atlanta Braves first baseman Fred McGriff. Brady gave the bat a place of honor inside the door to his quarters.

The *Zeus* made her way down the corridor into Obsidian space. Every ship she encountered saluted her as she sailed past. Even the two corvettes the *Zeus* startled at the gates of the corridor gave her a wide berth. Even before the *Zeus* was out of sight, the two corvettes returned to their task of rescuing men from the continuous stream of life pods emerging from the passageway.

Zeus whispered to Charlie, "It's time to let them go. The time for mourning fellow soldiers is intense, but it must be brief. Our enemy awaits us."

Charlie knew *Zeus* was right. The readiness bar had spiked. Charlie realized *Zeus* was sharing her strength and power with him. Charlie was close to being in complete unison with his ship. Brady had told him it usually took all but the strongest of captains years to become entirely in unison with their vessels. He sensed power, strength, and fortitude from the mighty ship flowing in his blood, and *Zeus* was even sharing strength with the members of the crew.

Every Obsidian post Brady warned him about was vacant as the *Zeus* sailed across Obsidian space. The main Obsidian base, a lone medium-sized asteroid, was visible on the situation board. It looked like a beehive with ships leaving the port and fleeing. Charlie failed to grasp what he was seeing.

Jacob studied the board for hours and interpreted what was happening. "The ships are not fleeing back to the Obsidian home planet. They are fleeing to the Wilhelm Galaxy."

"Why would they do that? Isn't that the galaxy that rebelled against Obsidian rule and formed their own state?" asked Charlie.

Jacob answered Charlie like a professor instructing a student. "I would not say they have their own state. The Wilhelm Galaxy is a hideout for rebels. All those ships are joining the rebellion."

"Why?" asked Charlie.

"The Obsidian Empire is built on lies. I believe the mercy we have shown to their sailors has exposed this lie. We are not the barbarians some have led them to believe."

Charlie sat back in his chair. "We will not show any mercy to that base."

Charlie formed a plan of attack and considered ordering the *Zeus* to close with the base at full speed. *Zeus* whispered, "Patience is a virtue. Give those with the desire to flee time to retreat."

With the same stately stride the *Zeus* had been maintaining, she finally arrived at the mouth of the Obsidian space harbor. Several ships made a last-minute frantic dash to make it into open space before her arrival. All of them headed in the direction of the Wilhelm Galaxy.

Carefully, Charlie had the crew align the *Zeus* with the mouth of the harbor. Charlie studied the base carefully. It looked surreal. There was absolutely no sign of life.

"Lt. Jackson, load the rail guns with kinetic warheads. We must make this place uninhabitable."

Charlie knew his response before Jacob replied. "Loaded and ready, sir."

"Commence firing."

The thump of the two large guns reverberated the ship as the crew fired round after round. The impacts looked even more devastating than an asteroid strike. Soon, even the ingress to the harbor was unrecognizable.

Charlie gave the order, "Cease firing."

•••

That night, Charlie reflected on how many lives had been saved thanks to the forfeiture of the *Persephone*. First, the crew on the *Zeus* showed the Obsidians mercy, allowing them to escape in life pods; then, they had demonstrated that the crew of the *Zeus* was even willing to fight her own people to preserve their honor.

As his hand reached up to fluff his pillow, he found a package and pulled it out. Brady had written, "To Prince Charlie Jackson from Prince Bradford Scanlin."

Charlie had not seen a piece of parchment like this anywhere outside of a museum. It was a handwritten letter on old-fashioned paper. Under the package was a data strip, which Charlie laid aside. He was thankful his mother had insisted he learn to read and write cursive. In an eloquent hand, Brady parceled out secrets too sacred to share on a hard drive.

Charlie's eyes almost popped out of his head when he got to the third page where Brady shared the inconceivable. There was a known group of traitors in Space Command. Brady shared who they were and provided proof of their treachery.

Brady ended the letter, "My sister gleaned this data from a third-party server on Earth. The server in question belongs to

Addison Everett! She had all the pieces. She just hadn't put the puzzle together yet. I am sure you will know best how to use the information. Your most loyal servant, your brother, Brady."

Charlie wondered about the significance of the name Addison Everett. He did not recognize it. The most important thing was that Brady could speak to the authenticity of the information on the disk.

Charlie wanted to share the letter with Jacob, but first, he needed to see Maddie. Yet as desperate as Charlie longed for her, he was too agitated to fall asleep. Instead, he sat on the side of his bed with his tablet and read all the damning evidence the data strip contained. Finally, he could no longer stay awake. With the tablet precariously perched on his nightstand, he fell asleep.

As he emerged from his dream-like trance into Maddie's world, he saw Maddie lying on the floor in the back of a van, unresponsive. Charlie was on the opposite side of the moving vehicle. He made several attempts to reach her, but there seemed to be an invisible barrier between them. Not able to reach her, Charlie worked his way toward the front. He saw several police cruisers through the front windshield escorting the van. Their blue lights were revolving and casting eerie shadows on the banks bordering the sides of the road. The man in the passenger seat swore. "That heifer bit me."

The driver laughed coarsely. "You should have been happy with the reward instead of trying to get in her pants."

The man riding shotgun swore again. "They only said they wanted her alive. They never said we couldn't have a little fun."

Charlie went into a fit of rage. He reached through the opening, grabbed the man's head, and twisted. The sound of his neck breaking filled the silence in the dark van.

The driver swerved. "What the—"

He turned to look over his shoulder, and Charlie's palm crushed the man's nose upwards, the bone penetrating his brain and killing him instantly. The van started swerving back and forth and skidded to a stop after it slammed against the safety rail along the road.

The sudden stop knocked Charlie to his knees. He tried to crawl back to check on Maddie. He stood, and a rifle butt struck the side of his head. Charlie had not seen the man guarding Maddie reclined against the wall in the dark recesses of the van. Charlie almost blacked out, but then he felt himself starting to wake up on the *Zeus*. He slowed his breathing and concentrated on staying in the dream. A foot connected with his ribs and Charlie fell back down. The man lifted his rifle to strike Charlie again, but Maddie's foot flew up and kicked him in the groin.

Charlie roared, "You are in my dream!"

Charlie's open hand flew into the man's thorax. The man looked down in terror.

Maddie tried to stand up and screamed, "Charlie!"

Charlie leaped up in his bed, his tablet crashing onto the floor. Sweat covered his forehead, and he looked down at his hand. Locked tight in his grip was a still-beating heart.

Chapter Fifty-Four

Present Day, Headed for the Tavarius
Space Bubble, Outside the Wilhelm Galaxy

The whole ship was abuzz. Captain Jackson had showed up on the bridge covered in blood and only wearing his boxers. The sentry outside his door swore the captain handed him a human heart as he exited his cabin and stepped into the pneumatic transport.

Charlie ordered the helm to change course and go to full speed. M&M paged Thomas, who quickly showed up with clothes for the captain. Meanwhile, Jacob was trying his best to get Charlie to calm down and tell him what was going on. Jacob could not fathom the amount of blood that was all over Charlie. Finally, he forced Charlie to stop hyperventilating and allow Dr. Laird to examine him. They left for the sick ward only after they had assured Charlie M&M would maintain course and speed.

Laird reported the captain had a contusion on the side of his head and a bruised rib. He could offer no explanation, and Charlie would not provide any details of what had happened. Secretly, Jacob and Laird ordered a complete head count of the crew to make sure no one was missing.

After Charlie cleaned up, he returned to the bridge with his damaged tablet and the data strip. He signaled Jacob to come speak with him. Handing him the tablet and data strip, he asked, "Jacob, can you repair my tablet? I need to make sure the contents of this data strip are still intact."

Leaning in closer, he added, "Do not let anyone other than you or me see any of the files on the strip."

Charlie, satisfied Jacob understood his orders, leaned back in his command chair and watched the primary monitor, willing the *Zeus* forward. Finally, Charlie's body gave out, and he fell asleep in his seat. Jacob felt relieved to see him calm. One by one, each staff officer on the bridge hushed their neighbor while pointing their finger at the captain.

Charlie began searching frantically for Maddie as soon as he fell asleep. He found her on the floor of a jail cell a little too soundly asleep. Gently at first, and then not so gently, Charlie shook Maddie, trying to wake her. It appeared someone had drugged her.

She looked up at Charlie, but at first, her body didn't move. At long last, from the drugged stupor, she awoke enough to wrap her arms around his neck and pull his head to her chest. They both lay there while she cried. Charlie never said a word; he held her close and let her tears wash away her pain.

Finally, she lifted Charlie's head to eye level. "They are using me to get to you."

Charlie sighed. "I know."

Desperately she cried, "Don't let them. Promise me you will not let them. You must run and never return."

Charlie softly ran his fingers through her hair. "Don't worry. I promise, I am coming to save you."

Maddie shoved Charlie away. "Don't you dare! I don't need a hero. I need for you to run!"

Charlie tried to hold Maddie's hand to calm her, but she pushed him away again.

"You were going to quit and come home to me. But instead, you run off ... Now, this ..." Maddie was crying hard. "Leave. I never want to see you again."

Before Charlie could say another word, he woke up, and Maddie was gone.

Chapter Fifty-Five

Present Day, En route to the Tavarius
Space Bubble, Near the Obsidian Galaxy

When Charlie opened his eyes, he realized someone had placed him into his berth. He rolled over to look at his clock. Quickly, Charlie did the math and realized he had been asleep for almost ten hours. Still, he continued to lie in his bed. Charlie felt strangely in tune with his ship and had clarity of purpose. He knew what he must do. He was allowing outside forces to control his destiny. It was time for him to assume command of the situation.

From where he lay, he could tell the throttle on the *Zeus* was at full, but he also was aware that the *Zeus* was only cruising half speed. Silently, he whispered, "Thank you for protecting me from myself, *Zeus*."

In his head, he heard the soft reply, "You are welcome."

With his head still on his pillow, he examined the situation board with his mind. Satisfied, he reached over for his commlink and paged Jacob.

"Yes, sir," replied Jacob.

"Do we still have internet access available?"

Jacob hesitated before he answered. "Yes, sir."

"Excellent. Please change the filters to allow me full access."

Jacob inquired, "Are you still concerned SC might use it to locate us?"

Charlie replied, "I am counting on it."

"Aye aye, Captain," answered a bemused Jacob.

Charlie reached for his tablet, which Jacob had repaired and placed next to his bed. He addressed a post to Admiral Halsey. He then sent another message to every person in the upper echelon of Space Command, copying every ship captain in the fleet. Finally, Charlie addressed his final email to the one person in SC he wanted to meet face-to-face. It was the only email he sent that he was confident would be delivered without being reviewed by anyone else at SC.

After he had sent the posts, Charlie closed his eyes, laid his head back on his pillow, and tried not to think, only listen. He could feel his thoughts traveling through space. After several minutes, he got a response from the person he was looking for.

"Charlie? Are you okay?" inquired Brady through his mind.

"I am, Brady, but I need your help."

"Okay," answered Brady. Charlie updated Brady on what was happening and his intentions.

With no hesitation or questions, Brady responded, "That sounds like a well-thought-out plan. I will meet you there."

Neither of the blood brothers bothered saying farewell. There wasn't any time. They both needed to prepare for the cataclysm that was coming.

The cabin door to Charlie's quarters opened slowly, and Lappilus stuck his head inside the door. "Good morning, Captain. You wanted bacon and eggs?"

"Yes, I do. It will be a long day."

Charlie took his time eating his breakfast. He then showered, dressed, and headed to the bridge. Charlie exited the pneumatic transport, and before the sentry could announce, "Captain, on deck," Charlie gave the order to reduce to two-thirds throttle.

At the helm, Chief Stuyck had a bewildered look on his face when he throttled back but felt the *Zeus* accelerate instead of slowing down.

Charlie looked at Jacob. "Good morning."

"Good morning, sir."

The original plan was for the *Zeus* to attack the Obsidian relay station before making a run for the space bubble. That would delay Obsidian reinforcements from being able to follow the *Zeus* through the bubble. Instead, Charlie ordered, "Lt. Jackson, feed the crew. We are going straight to the bubble. It is best we do so with full stomachs."

Suspicious, Jacob inquired, "Yes, sir. We no longer intend to attack the relay station first to prevent reinforcements from following us?"

"Let them come," Charlie answered and then winked at Jacob.

A wave of relief swept through Jacob. He sensed Charlie was back to normal and had a new plan.

Halfway through the crew's breakfast, Jacob warned, "The *Zeus* is almost within detection range by Obsidian forces."

Charlie did not respond or reach for his music player. Instead, he silently thumbed through his playlist in his mind and chose an old song from the twentieth century, which immediately started playing.

Jacob nodded and commented to Charlie, "There isn't a more appropriate song for right now than 'Highway to Hell.' Mom used to love it. Wasn't it by AC/DC?"

Charlie gave Jacob a small smile and said, "Helm, full throttle. We will have to race to enter the bubble. Hopefully, we can do so without having to engage the enemy. Otherwise, I am not sure we will make it."

The *Zeus* us leaped forward like a racehorse that had had spurs dug into its side. Soon there were over a dozen Obsidian bandits in pursuit of the *Zeus*, and more bogeys appearing in the distance every second. True to form, the few random shots fired at the stern of the *Zeus* were far off their mark.

Up ahead, off the starboard bow, one of the massive Obsidian B Class battleships appeared on the situation board. Andrew and Chief Stuyck were both pulling to port on the joysticks, trying to keep the *Zeus* on course. Charlie sensed *Zeus*'s eagerness to engage the battleship. Silently he whispered to *Zeus*, "Not now. One thing at a time."

He could feel *Zeus*'s disappointment as well as the crew's as *Zeus* veered slightly to port to avoid an engagement. He was proud of the courage and faith his crew members had in their abilities, willing to attempt fighting the B Class battleship.

The *Zeus* continued to barrel toward the bubble. Jacob motioned Charlie to look at the situation screen, sharing his anxiety at how close the narrowing window was for the *Zeus* to make it without having to engage an Obsidian warship.

Just then, the battleship fired a massive round at the stern of the *Zeus*. The huge projectile was as large as a small box truck back on Earth and came dangerously close to making contact before the *Zeus* entered the dead center of the bubble. Then there was total silence.

The first experience in a space bubble was always surreal. The light was bending around the hull into the wake of the *Zeus* as the ship first exceeded the speed the light particles were traveling, and then the crew could sense time itself stretching and contracting. No one on the *Zeus* had ever made such a jump, and Charlie detected in the recesses of his mind the silent whispering of the crew between the decks of the ship. The jump only lasted a total of sixteen minutes before they were back in the Earth's solar system.

The crew had been practicing for this moment ever since Charlie announced his intention to return through the space bubble. No SC ship had dared venture anywhere close to the section of space they were in since the Obsidians first invaded the Earth's solar system years earlier. Everyone called the strip between the bubble and Jupiter the "Highway to Hell."

The music of AC/DC repeated from the beginning for the sixth time in a row, still booming out of the large exterior speakers mounted on the hull of *Zeus*. Rotating vents designed to redirect the sound slowly turned, continuously changing the proximity from which the music originated. The *Zeus* traveled the entire passage at full throttle and emerged from the bubble going so fast the Obsidian ships guarding the passage were taken entirely by surprise. It seemed the plan was working and the *Zeus* would leave any potential threats far behind, unable to catch up with her.

Suddenly, a second B Class battleship appeared on the situation board. Once again Charlie sensed *Zeus* pulling against her controls, wanting to engage the mammoth ship. Charlie whispered once again, sternly this time, "No, *Zeus*. Not yet."

The battleship never even came close enough to bridging the gap to bother firing a shot at them before the *Zeus* coasted into the inner ring of the sun's planets unscathed and managed to vanish. Charlie ordered the throttles back to one-quarter and pulled his monitor over in front of him. As he hoped, he had a multitude of replies to his emails.

Charlie had the crew set a course that kept them as far away as possible from any known shipping lanes either side in the war might use. Jacob set to work making the old battleship as stealthy as possible given her size. Charlie suggested to Jacob that while the crew should remain vigilant, he should allow as many of the crew members as possible to get some rest. Not a single crew member left their post. They merely curled up and went to sleep right where they were in case of a conflict. The only person who left their position was Charlie. He retired to his personal quarters and locked the door.

After several hours, Jacob began to grow concerned. No one had seen or heard from Charlie since he had retreated to his cabin. Jacob was about to go check on him when Charlie emerged from the pneumatic transport. He walked slowly to his seat and sat down. In a low monotone voice, he ordered, "Lt. Jackson, *Zeus* knows the coordinates to our destination. Please proceed at one-third throttle."

Jacob issued the command, worried. Something felt wrong. His heart leaped up into his throat when he glanced at the readiness bar and saw it had dropped to less than 5 percent. He started to alert Charlie but realized there was no need. Charlie already knew.

It took just over another hour for the *Zeus* to reach its destination. The crew spotted the SC cruiser *Justice for All* headed on an intercept course for them, but no one uttered a word. Charlie sat in his chair and despondently watched the monitor. As the *Justice* approached, Charlie ordered the crew to moor the *Zeus* alongside on her port side. The crew was speechless when Charlie ordered a transfer tube installed to allow a connection between the two ships. Jacob could even hear murmuring on the bridge, within earshot of Charlie.

Chapter Fifty-Six

Present Day, Inside Earth's Solar System

Charlie stood when Captain Hildreth of the *Justice* entered the *Zeus*'s bridge. He walked around to where Charlie stood, with six military police officers directly behind him.

"Captain Jackson, I hereby relieve you of duty, and you are under arrest for sedition and high treason."

Several members of the *Zeus*'s crew reached for their weapons, but Charlie stopped them. Then Captain Hildreth turned to Jacob.

"Lt. Jackson, you, too, are relieved of duty and are under arrest to appear before a board of inquiry."

Once again members of the crew started to lean toward their weapons, but this time it was Jacob who stopped them. With disbelief in his eyes, he stared at Charlie.

The *Justice*'s captain turned to address the crew. "I am Captain Donald Hildreth. By the power vested in me by Space Command, I am now the captain of the ... this ship."

They could hear more murmuring, and the uncomfortable MPs behind Hildreth tightened their grip on their weapons.

Captain Hildreth walked over to Charlie. The crew heard Charlie protesting, "Arresting Lt. Jackson was not part of the agreement."

Hildreth replied, "I am sorry, Captain. Those are my orders."

Charlie glared at him. "And the rest of our agreement?"

Hildreth replied, "I am pleased to say there have been no further modifications to the negotiations between you and SC officials. I would like to extend you the courtesy of allowing you ten minutes to visit with your wife in your personal quarters, and then she will be transferred into the custody of Admiral Halsey."

"Thank you," Charlie whispered.

"Charlie," cried Maddie as they escorted her onto the bridge. Charlie turned his back on her and started leaving the bridge. The MPs quickly fell in behind him, grabbing him by the arms.

"Charlie?" Maddie cried out again.

Charlie stopped but did not turn around. "*Zeus*, see to it Mrs. Jackson makes it safely into the hands of Admiral Halsey."

"Charlie!" Maddie screamed one final time, but it was too late.

Charlie entered the pneumatic transport, ushered by the MPs. Maddie looked at Jacob, but before she could speak to him, they also guided him from the bridge. She looked inquiringly at Megan Marie. Seeing the tears in M&M's eyes, Maddie broke down and started crying.

Every member of the crew now comprehended the situation. The captain had traded his life in return for the safety of his wife and the crew of the *Zeus*. More MPs entered the bridge and took up positions along the walls of the room. Down below, the SWALs were being quarantined in their quarters, and all nonessential personnel were ordered to stand down.

Captain Hildreth gave the order for the *Zeus* to undock from the SC ship and ordered young Andrew to have the *Zeus* fall in line directly astern of the *Justice*. Soon they were steaming toward Space Station Victory directly behind the *Justice* with two SC destroyers, one on both the port and the starboard sides of the *Zeus*. The arduous trip was far from the rendezvous point, but soon the crew on the *Zeus* made out the faint outline of the space base on the primary monitor.

As they neared the entrance to the spaceport, Hildreth leaned over Andrew's shoulder. "The wake of this ship had better not rock a single vessel in this harbor, or you will find yourself in a cell with Lt. Jackson."

The PA system voluntarily crepitated, and Elton John began singing a primeval version of the song "Sacrifice." Captain Hildreth ordered the melody terminated, but none of the *Zeus*'s crew members offered to oblige.

The music touched the crew members deeply. They could feel how deeply moved the soul of the old ship was by the sacrifice Charlie was willing to make for each of them. His strongest motivation was his love for Maddie, but his love for every crew member was made evident by the terms he had obviously negotiated on their behalf. Every team member knew that the price Space Command would demand of Charlie was death. No doubt they would be the ones chosen to man the firing squad that would end his life. That would be the price Space Command would require for their redemption.

Evans was sitting on her bunk openly weeping. Old man Ballentine pined for the wife he lost and wished he had been given the same opportunity as Charlie to give his life, instead of God calling her home so many years ago. Even the battle-hardened SWAL team members' emotions were beginning to show as they watched the door to their quarters seal like a tomb meant to separate their souls from the world of the living. They snapped out of their reverie, though, when Peck and Shealy started dismantling the divider that separated their living quarters from Stidham's repository for their equipment.

Across the ship, men and women's despair turned to resolve. This injustice would not be tolerated.

Zeus had been closely monitoring the craft ferrying Maddie to the safety of Admiral Halsey's flagship. M&M concentrated on remaining inconspicuous, scrupulously watching her controls and keeping one finger on the lever that would activate the worm Charlie had been sending out via email. Captain Jackson's secret orders stressed she must make sure Maddie made it to the admiral before all else.

The MPs carefully combed both Charlie and Jacob for weapons before depositing them in the *Zeus*'s brig. Once the MPs closed the door to the brig, Charlie browsed around, casually covering the lens on the security cameras, then carefully reaching under the mattress and pulling out the ceremonial sword Brady had given him.

Jacob looked over at his brother and grinned. "It can't be defeated, can it?"

Slowly, Charlie pulled it from its sheath. "No, it can't."

The sword felt different in his hand. Before when he had held it, it had felt bulky. Now it seemed to move of its own accord. Charlie could sense power traveling through its core. He studied the sword. It had transformed since he had concealed it under the mattress. Thunderbolts, emblazoned down the length of the sword, had materialized. In the intersection of the leather-bound hilt and guard, an aegis had appeared. The phosphorescent dark blue sapphire on the pommel glimmered.

Meanwhile, Andrew, still seething at the rebuke from Hildreth about the wake zone, discreetly flipped on the warning light, bypassing the alarm, warning the crew of a possible collision. Around the ship, crew members, seeing the light, silently buckled in and tightened their harnesses. None of the MPs or Hildreth paid the light any attention.

Suddenly, Charlie perceived something had gone wrong. *Zeus* whispered in his ear, "They have transferred Mrs. Jackson to a small Obsidian transport, and it is headed back to the Obsidian fleet."

Charlie, noticing the pale-yellow collision light on the overhead status board, braced himself and turned to face the door of the brig. The treble in his voice turned to a deep bass. "*Zeus*, change of plans."

At that exact moment, the readiness bar on the bridge spiked as the entire crew of the *Zeus* seemingly achieved unison with the ship. The engines slammed into reverse and the ship rapidly slowed, throwing everyone not buckled-in forward. The door to the brig flew open, and Charlie pulled the sword back over his shoulder, ready to strike.

Instead of facing the MPs from the *Justice*, there was Thomas, who asked, "I suspect you are heading to the bridge, Captain?"

As Charlie stepped through the doors, he saw SWAL team members zip-tying the MPs' hands behind their backs and dragging them to escape pods, unceremoniously dumping them inside and sealing the doors.

Charlie did not reply to Thomas's remark, but Jacob answered as he walked past Charlie's faithful steward. "You would be correct, Thomas."

As Charlie stepped onto the bridge, he found the crew of the *Zeus* wrestling and overwhelming the MPs. Charlie walked over to Captain Hildreth, lying on the floor against the front pedestal, and said, "Captain, you and your men have outstayed your welcome on my ship."

SWAL team members rounded up the unwelcome guests and loaded them into life pods.

Andrew addressed the Captain. "Sir! They are almost ready to dock us up against the pier."

Charlie knew once they connected the considerable anchor cables to the bow and stern of *Zeus*, there would be no escape. From the corner of his eye, Charlie noticed a CBC unit sitting on the pier ready for installation.

"Andrew, spin the *Zeus* around. It is time for us to leave."

"We are in the no-wake zone, sir."

Charlie grinned at Andrew. "We can observe and pay homage to the no-wake zone next time we visit."

Charlie turned to look at his brother. "Jacob, plot a course. It is time to go retrieve my wife."

"Aye aye, sir," Jacob replied enthusiastically.

The entire crew cheered. The SWAL teams ejected the life pods, and Andrew reversed the engines and started to turn. Once *Zeus* was facing the mouth of the harbor, Charlie gave the order: "One-tenth power."

The men and women on the pier looked startled as the big engines on the battleship came to life. They made a mad scramble for shelter inside the nearest buildings to avoid the *Zeus*'s exhaust.

All over the ship, gun crews strapped into their battle positions while Jacob issued orders on how to disable the *Justice* and the two destroyers escorting the *Zeus*. A soft voice whispered in Jacob's ear, telling him his preparations were not going to be necessary. He glanced up at the situation board, and sure enough, the *Justice* had already slid into her berth and the two destroyers were making room for the *Zeus* to exit.

All over the harbor, warships were moving to the side, giving *Zeus* a clear path. M&M had activated the worm the second she witnessed the treacherous exchange commence. Captains everywhere were viewing and listening to the story of the crew of the *Zeus*. They had also been alerted that someone in SC had turned Charlie's wife over to the Obsidians.

The *Zeus*'s wake rocked ships as she went by, and Charlie looked at his young helmsman. He no longer looked like the gangly young boy Charlie had first met at the diner in the desert. Andrew was now a confident young man. He also looked eerily like his father.

He gave Andrew the order to go to 20 percent throttle. The blast from the *Zeus*'s giant engines rocked several more ships hard against their berths as she accelerated.

Admiral Mitchell of the Seventh Fleet was drinking coffee and trying to absorb the shocking developments that had all of SC reeling. The news was there were traitors within SC, and the names of the guilty parties did not surprise him in the least. He swiftly scanned all the proof documenting their high treason and was about to go back and read all the pages of data more thoroughly when he heard cursing and swearing amongst his crew. He turned and yelled, "Belay there. What the—"

His XO interrupted him, "Admiral, you have to see this. Read the latest post from the pocket battleship they brought in and watch the video."

Admiral Mitchell, on the *Tyche,* was watching the video of Captain Jackson's wife being transferred onto a small Obsidian transport. Precisely at that moment, the *Zeus* roared past the *Tyche.* The shock wave caused the admiral's coffee to shoot into the air and come down all over his uniform.

Instead of cursing at the ship, the admiral stood up, looked at his main monitor, and with his Scottish burr yelled, "Damn right! Go get yer girl, son!"

Looking back over his shoulder, he yelled, "XO, get yer butt to Engineering. I have a job for ye!"

His order was almost indiscernible due to the staccato of his Highlander dialect.

Still surrounded by dozens of SC warships, Charlie passed the order to go to one-third throttle. Long after *Zeus* cleared the mouth of the spaceport harbor, ships were still bouncing and rubbing against their berths.

More so to let Maddie know he was coming to save her than to cover the sound of the engines, Charlie started Bonnie Tyler's "I Need a Hero" on his music player. Every vessel in the area heard an ear-shattering concinnity of sound.

"Bum, bum de bum bum. Bum, bum de bum bum. Bum, bum de bum bum, bumm, bumm."

Charlie keyed the mic to Jacob. "Light her up. I want the captain of that Obsidian ship to know exactly who is coming."

Chapter Fifty-Seven

Present Day, Inside Earth's Solar System

On board the small Obsidian transport outside the space harbor, the captain was trying to plot a course for their rendezvous with his admiral. He had almost locked in his heading when his sound man lost contact because of the insufferable sounds their commander had warned them about. The captain grabbed his light scope and located the ship he had orders to meet. He ordered his helmsman to point the vessel toward that general locale. The captain also spotted two Obsidian destroyers form up, headed in his general direction at what he guessed must be close to full throttle. Curious where they were going in such a hurry, he turned his scope back toward the general bearing from which he had come.

He felt a wave of nausea. It was now clear what the destroyers were en route to intercept. The craft he saw behind him lit up the space around its frame like a rising star. It looked like the space monsters in the stories his grandparents told him as a child. Those stories were myths, but mythology or not, he recognized the beast in his scope. Without a sound reading, he could not be sure, but it looked like it was heading straight for him.

Through the hull of his ship, the beat of music was rattling dust from the ceiling plates over the flight deck. The monster was far away, but the sound was crisp and clear. Listening carefully, he could just make out the words.

Even being from Obsidia, the captain recognized the ultimate rock anthem. In every galaxy, movies had used Bonnie Tyler's "I Need a Hero." He could picture the desperate heroine wondering: What had happened to all the good men, and had the gods all disappeared? Where was the illustrious Hercules, the demigod who could win against all odds? He pictured the damsel lying in her bed, trembling, seeing in her dreams, the man—that hero—she so desperately needed.

It was cold inside the ship, but sweat began forming on the captain's brow. He turned and looked accusingly at his female prisoner. Her previously panic-stricken eyes were now beaming with joy.

"Who is this god they seek?" asked the captain.

The staccato of a horse's pursuing hoofs hung in the air, and she replied with defiance in her voice, "You have pissed off the angel of death, and now, the daughters of Nyx are coming for you! You are about to meet the man who is the lightning before the thunder."

The captain knew Keres, the daughters of Nyx, were death-spirits, specifically the goddesses who personified violent death.

Angrily, the captain ordered, "Secure the prisoner. If we are boarded, I will shoot her myself!"

In a huff, he turned to watch the monitor, gripping the back of his command chair with his hands. The remaining color in his face vanished, his skin now a pasty white.

Aboard the *Zeus*, Charlie gave the command, "One-half throttle," and the ship leaped forward even faster.

The white lights Jacob installed to illuminate the bow were now being overpowered by the aura of *Zeus* herself. The illuminated eyes on the bow first glowed bloodred by their own volition, and small electrical discharges began sparkling on the edges of her hull; then the eyes turned a deep, insightful, radiant blue. Maddie, watching the screen with bated breath, immediately recognized on the small monitor the determined eyes of her own husband. She remembered how on the first night she met Charlie, his eyes had radiated with confidence even though she had just pointed a gun between them.

The distinctive husky voice of Bonnie Tyler hung in the air once again. Maddie recognized the message Charlie was sending, and she knew she must hold out. She knew he was strong, his ship was fast, and there was no doubt he was ready for a fight.

On the Obsidian transport ship, the captain yelled at his helmsman, "Faster, faster, faster! We must go faster!"

The music was growing louder by the second, and the captain could see the ship was growing more substantial in his scope.

On the *Zeus*, Charlie ordered Andrew to increase to 60 percent throttle.

The Obsidian captain had been watching the battleship and was surprised when the two Obsidian destroyers he had seen only moments before streaked by at full throttle, heading straight toward the approaching ship. The Obsidian crew members cheered, and the captain sneered at Maddie.

"That will slow down your angel of death." He started laughing, pushing his eye hard against the scope to get a better view of the battle about to take place.

On the *Zeus*, Jacob sounded the alarm. "Captain, two bandits on an intercept course. Obsidian destroyers, the best I can tell."

Charlie responded, "I see them. Helm, sixty-five percent throttle."

Sonar rang out, "Destroyers one thousand and eighty-two klicks and closing, sir."

Still the song echoed through the heavens, crescendoing, and the music was taking on a desperate tone. Maddie prayed Charlie would be in time.

Charlie ordered, "Seventy percent throttle. Helm, you have enough room to go in between the hostiles."

Silently, Andrew started doing the math, calculating his margin for error. With determination engraved into the lines on his forehead, he focused his full attention on the small gap between the two destroyers, blocking out everything else going on around him.

The music grew louder, and the electrical discharges around the *Zeus*'s hull grew larger and brighter. The *Zeus*'s eyes now looked like the eyes of a demon, and anger permeated the surrounding space. The music was becoming unbearable on board the Obsidian transport. There were no words, just a growing intensity as the sound came from *Zeus*'s speakers, her engines sounding like a rapidly approaching storm.

As the distance between the three warships closed, activity on the *Zeus* started to happen in quick succession. The months of continuous training were evident as each person performed their assigned task without a single command being issued. Detonation bombs were rolling into the rear chutes on the *Zeus*'s stern. Gun crews tightly gripped their controls, and everyone braced for impact.

As the music climaxed, sonar sounded out: "The destroyers are one hundred and ten klicks out, sir."

The bombs rolled out the back of the *Zeus*, and at the same time, Charlie shouted, "Seventy-five percent throttle."

Zeus barreled toward the void between the two ships as the bombs tumbled in her wake. Andrew inhaled a large breath of air, held it, and then slowly began releasing it.

Far astern of the *Zeus*, outside the mouth of the spaceport, three dozen SC warships watched the *Zeus* with amazement on their long-range scanners. They were sure the engagement would be the end of the pocket battleship and her crew.

With a silent rescript from Charlie, the *Zeus* sped up even more. Small bolts of lightning were now rippling down the sides of her hull, and then in a blur, she shot the gap between the destroyers.

The displacement of space in the *Zeus*'s wake caused the sterns of the two destroyers to start skating outward, and it pulled their bows inward, threatening to put the ships into a flat spin. Then the trailing detonation bombs hit the warships on their bows and partially exposed sides. Both ships exploded and rapidly disintegrated.

The *Zeus* never slowed down. The deafening noise coming from the amplifiers on the sides of her hull and the ferocious roar of her engines covered the sound of the dying craft.

Maddie watched all the color drain from the Obsidian captain's face again. She could not stop herself. At the top of her lungs, she yelled, "Hell, yeah!"

Now Maddie could make out the thundering roar of the engines on the *Zeus* herself. The heat from the Obsidian ship was sweltering, and Maddie could feel the sweat causing her blouse to stick to her back.

Andrew started reversing the engines to slow the *Zeus*, and the huge claws descended beneath her. SWALs were already releasing the safeties on their weapons when Charlie jumped into the forward insertion ball with his unsheathed sword radiating angrily in his hand. The *Zeus* snatched the small Obsidian craft in mid-flight and banked lazily to starboard while continuing to decelerate. The sudden surge of energy threw the Obsidian captain across the bridge.

Holes appeared in the Obsidian ship's ceiling forward of where the crew had secured Maddie. The SWAL team dropped into the ship along with Charlie, who was swinging with purpose at Maddie's wardens. The Obsidian captain scrambled to his feet and raised his weapon to execute his prisoner. Charlie's sword stopped in mid-swing, and a large force field pulsed from the long, slender shaft of the blade. The bullet fell to the floor at Charlie's feet.

The last of the words to "I Need a Hero" hung in the air like a ghost, echoing amongst the stars.

After the last Obsidian fell to the floor, Charlie turned and yanked off his helmet. He grabbed Maddie and pulled her close in a big hug. She wrapped her arms around him and buried her face in his neck, tears of joy streaming down her face.

As fast as the team materialized, they started vanishing one by one back into the pneumatic transports inside the insertion ball. SWAL team leader Shealy placed his hand on Charlie's shoulder and looked at Maddie. He said, "We have to go, sir."

Charlie picked Maddie up by the waist, lifted her into the ball, and she found herself on the bridge of the *Zeus*.

Chapter Fifty-Eight

Present Day, Inside Earth's Solar System

Charlie stepped out of the pneumatic transport right behind Maddie. A few decks below him, he heard the claws unclasp their grip on the Obsidian vessel. Charlie studied the monitor displaying the port side of the *Zeus* and saw the small boat drifting away from the superstructure. The *Zeus* continued her slow forward motion, and within seconds, Charlie no longer saw the Obsidian transport. Instead of turning to look at the aft screen to follow the ship, he changed his focus to the situation board. Everyone on the bridge, except Maddie, was giving the board their undivided attention. Charlie quickly understood why the enthusiasm had waned over their successful rescue and why everyone was now so studious.

Jacob turned and gave Maddie a loving embrace and kissed her on both cheeks. He finally broke the silence.

"I am glad you are safe." Then he pointed at the situation board and, nodding at Charlie, said, "Now, we are between a rock and a hard place."

Maddie was confused. "I don't understand what we are seeing. What's wrong?"

Charlie motioned to the situation board. "The first of our problems are those red dots. It appears they have scrambled half of Space Command to track us down."

Jacob took over. "Worse yet, those two contacts represented by black dots are Obsidian B Class battleships. They dropped out of subspace right on our six moments ago. It's only a matter of who gets here first and who wants us more."

To everyone's amazement, Charlie laughed. "It looks like we have all of our enemies conveniently located."

The crew looked at Charlie as though he had lost his mind. Then M&M started laughing, too. Soon everyone on the bridge joined in.

Charlie walked over to sit in his chair and keyed the ship-wide intercom.

"Crew. Everyone who wants a piece of us is now within striking distance. It appears we can take our pick who we wish to fight. We must address these challenges individually. I sensed on our journey through the 'Highway to Hell' that many, including *Zeus* herself, wanted a crack at those two B Class battleships. Now we are being given that chance. Before we take on either of them, we must first put more distance between ourselves and our friends from Space Command. Everyone report to their battle stations and let's find out how fast those battleships really are."

The sound of the flaxen horn started its mournful wail. Over the sound of the cry to battle, Charlie heard the crew cheering.

Charlie turned and gave Maddie a hug. She pulled him close and said, "If this is the end, then I am glad we get to finish it together."

Charlie stepped back and gave her a kiss.

Jacob stepped over and said, "Are we going to put distance between us and Space Command or stand here and share a romantic moment?"

Maddie smiled and quickly gave Charlie another kiss on the lips. She released him and said, "It's time for you to go be a hero."

Jacob took Maddie by the hand. "We had best find a place to strap you in."

Jacob guided her to the empty battle station located directly behind Charlie's command chair. Giving her a compression suit along with a helmet, Jacob tried to help her strap in, but she shooed him off. "I have served my time on ships bigger than this one. I know how to strap in."

Two floors up, CPO Evans reached for the ladder to crawl back up into her isolated gun position. A gloved hand gently grabbed her shoulder from behind. Evans didn't have to turn around to recognize to whom it belonged. The combat gloves of the SWAL teams were different from any of the rest of the crews, but only one of the SWAL team members had gloves with red-colored palms. She glanced over her shoulder inquiringly at Peck. Through her visor, she saw him wink at her.

"We sure as hell won't take those battleships by boarding them, so I figured I might keep you company. Who knows, you might even make me useful."

A wave of relief swept over Evans. All the SWAL team members knew how much it frightened her being so isolated. They were always her biggest supporters and cheerleaders, even while on the *Perseus*. Behind Peck was Shealy and three more team members. The tube leading to her isolated post didn't seem so long this time. Resisting the urge to give Peck a hug as he crawled into the seat next to her, Evans smiled and instead studied the steadily approaching targets on her monitor. Her rotary cannons would not leave a dent in either warship. Evans had learned during their endless drills if she could destroy the shield emitter on either ship, her guns would take down the Obsidian's impenetrable electronic shields. That would allow the *Zeus*'s heavy firepower to make its presence known.

Charlie turned his attention back to the bridge and sat down in his chair. Carefully, he strapped himself into his seat and then checked each shoulder strap to make sure they were comfortable. "M&M, plot a course that will have the *Zeus* cross those battleships' bows. Keep us beyond the range of those huge guns."

He looked over at Andrew manning the helm. "Helm, twenty percent throttle."

In a quieter voice, Charlie touched Andrew's shoulder and whispered, "Those two ships are the Suidae and the Sus Scrofa. Those are the two ships that destroyed the UCSC *Constrictor.* It is time we repay a debt, with the interest due for the loss of your father and my friends."

No expression showed on Andrew's face, only a steeled determination. He responded simply with two clicks on his commlink.

Directly astern the bridge, Charlie heard the seldom-used auxiliary motors as they coughed a couple of times and then roared to life, propelling the *Zeus* forward. In the corner of the bridge, Charlie saw the bar, which judged the *Zeus's* captain was at an all-time high: 100 percent.

The *Zeus* was getting faster as she made a broad, sweeping arch, packing on more and more speed, slowly turning away from the SC warships. Charlie ordered, "Helm, go to thirty percent throttle."

The *Zeus* continued to pick up speed at a spectacular rate. Already, a small discharge of electricity was forming around the edges of her hull. "Helm, go to forty percent throttle."

The *Zeus* leaped forward again and continued increasing in speed.

For the first time, the large, cogged gears that anchored the circular gun decks started creaking and groaning until the enormous bolts that locked the deadly gun decks in place released their hold. The sound of the bolts locking in the open position reverberated throughout the ship. The cylinders housing the gun decks liberated, they slowly started revolving around the core of the ship. The background of the sculpted bow was beginning to take on hues of Prussian blue and gamboge. With its titanium base and gilded copper and gold veneer, the escutcheon was blazing like a green flame from the atomic excitation of the copper alloy absorbing energy. Blue and yellow flames were now burning in the whites of the *Zeus's* eyes, on the top curve of her bow, producing a wicked shade of green.

In the far distance, crews on the SC ships had watched the entire rescue with amazement. The commanding officers expressed concern that the *Zeus* had possibly ignited her engines to head back to engage them. They were scrambling their gun crews to defend themselves. The admiral kept trying to hail the small battleship but to no avail. Finally, a wave of relief passed through him as it became clear the *Zeus* was shying away from them. Relief was replaced with awe when the admiral realized the ship was pivoting in the opposite direction to engage the two B Class battleships instead, ships that were only a blip on their long-range sensors.

Charlie gave his command directly to Andrew. "Helm, fifty percent throttle."

The *Zeus*'s engines were begging to go. The increased acceleration pushed everyone back into their seats. Diaphragms inside their flight suits squeezed in and out to maintain an even blood flow, the suits forcing blood from the legs and other extremities to the heart.

Zeus had almost completed her large arch and was now facing the two battleships head-on. The electrical discharges around the extremities of her hull continued to spread and were about to cover the entire fuselage.

Charlie ordered, "Helm, never mind maneuvers. Head straight at them and then lead them away from the fleet. Proceed to seventy percent throttle."

The *Zeus* now leaped forward with a vengeance. As she continued to pack on speed, everyone within range heard massive eruptions of energy and felt the rumble of the sound wave, battering their vessels like a wall of snow during an avalanche. Lightning bolts collected in her wake, impersonating the tail of a comet. Bolts of lightning enveloped the rear half of the fuselage as an explosion of energy providing electric shielding covered the ship's stern, and the *Zeus* leaped forward even faster.

The *Zeus* straightened out in a linear path toward the behemoth ships. Charlie instructed *Zeus* to play some music. The song "The Final Countdown" by the group Europe filled the heavens. As soon as the sound reached maximum magnitude, the electrical discharges around the ship's hull exploded again, and this time they were so brilliant that the blinding light encompassed all the surrounding vacuum of space. Every ship within the line of sight felt the delayed effects of the deep, low rumble of the explosion when the sound waves reached them.

On the fastest Space Command vessel, the XO announced the pocket battleship had exceeded their own vessel's maximum velocity. Then the electrical shields exploded around the hull of the *Zeus*. The vessel's captain, Rickenbaker, swore under his breath when the *Zeus* sped up so fast that it zoomed off the monitor he was using to track her.

All of the *Zeus*'s crew were again pushed firmly back into their seats. Charlie gave the order, "Helm, eighty-five percent throttle."

Zeus and Andrew were now in their element. The *Zeus* streaked through space like a bat out of hell. The inferno in the *Zeus*'s eyes was no longer comprised of individual blazes. They were a solid conflagration. The electrical discharges on the sides of her hull were steadily creeping their way around the bow of the ship.

"Helm, ninety percent throttle and bank to starboard. Add more distance between us and SC."

The *Zeus* had never come anywhere near achieving these speeds before. As she accelerated even faster, she turned to starboard and then straightened back out. Charlie noted to himself that the *Zeus* had surpassed the maximum speed of any SC ship ever built and was rapidly approaching—and about to exceed—the rumored top speed of their immediate adversary.

The two Obsidian battleships maintained formation and slowly banked to match the *Zeus*'s course, straining to keep pace. Guns on the port-side battleship fired, and two boxcar-sized hulks of red-hot metal streaked off her starboard bow.

Charlie, realizing he had misjudged the range of the enemy craft's guns, ordered Andrew, "Go to ninety-five percent throttle and get us out of the range of those guns."

The *Zeus* sprinted to add distance, but Charlie was confident she had even more power in reserve. The next shots fell short, and

Charlie ordered Andrew, "Discreetly drop back down to ninety percent throttle. We don't want to dishearten them."

The *Zeus* slowly decelerated enough to match the speed of the two battleships. The second battleship fired two shells. They were much farther off their mark than the first battleship, but the munition still had a lot of velocity as it streaked by.

"Andrew, the helm is yours to maneuver. Avoid colliding with their ordnance."

The discharges of electricity surrounding the hull of the *Zeus* were solid and no longer recognizable as individual lightning bolts. The aura of the *Zeus*'s electrical shielding surrounded her like a cocoon. It extended like the tail of a dragon behind her and encapsulated her bow. The first battleship tried another ranging shot. The shell grazed the edge of the thunderbolts. It was promptly shoved away as bolts of lightning engaged the shell.

Andrew, maneuvering the *Zeus*, did a barrel roll and altered course hard to port. The battleships chasing her started a slow parallel turn and leveled back out in the *Zeus*'s wake. As soon as the warships settled on a new course, Andrew rolled the *Zeus* back in the other direction. The *Zeus* and the battleships repeated this ballet with each refrain. The two battleships were attempting to coordinate but soon gave up, unable to discern each other over the music.

The ships discharged another round, and Charlie realized that, somehow, they were once again putting too much distance between the *Zeus* and the battleships. Charlie also sensed *Zeus* was tired of retreating and growing agitated. She was ready to turn and fight.

"Andrew, bank hard to port and slant back toward them at forty-five degrees."

The *Zeus* leaned hard into the turn and headed back at the ships. The two ships also turned, but the *Zeus* overpowered them to the point their two paths should have intersected.

"Andrew, on my mark, bank hard to port again and let's cross their bows. Gun crews, assemble to fire from the starboard battery." Charlie ordered, "Jacob, leave them a present in our wake."

"Andrew, mark!" The plan seemed to unfold in slow motion. A millisecond after the *Zeus* banked hard to port, the two battleships started their long, slow parallel roll in the opposite direction to intercept the *Zeus* where they expected her to be. The *Zeus* barrel-rolled counterclockwise and crossed her own wake, and every gun commenced firing on the forward bows of the two beasts as bombs rolled lazily out the back of the *Zeus*.

The gun crews operating the large weapons on the Obsidian battleships were caught by surprise and could not react swiftly enough to return fire. The damage, however, was minimal. Even the exploding proximity bombs did not leave discernible marks on the large battleships' bows, all exploding harmlessly against their invisible electronic shields. Charlie greedily eyed the shield emitter on the top of the nearest battleship. He highlighted it on his monitor and flashed the target to CPO Evans, operating the rotary cannon. His unspoken message was clear. Her only mission was to eliminate that emitter.

Charlie gave another series of quick orders, and Andrew theatrically faked to his port side as though he were going to attempt to escape, but he instead looped back into a hard, unyielding turn to starboard. He faked so well that for a split second, Charlie thought Andrew had misunderstood his order. The months of training and discipline on the *Zeus* showed.

The two battleships took the bait Andrew gave them and momentarily turned to their starboard sides, giving Andrew the perfect opening. Before they could compensate for their error, the *Zeus* rolled into their paths of travel and crossed their vulnerable sterns. Every shot fired from the *Zeus* hammered home as the crew unleashed months of frustration and anger. Their projectiles flew deep into the bowels of the starboard battleship, causing havoc and destruction. The Obsidian gun crews never knew what hit them. One of the colossal engines on the ship flamed out, and both battleships had to reduce speed to remain in formation.

As Andrew turned the *Zeus* farther starboard to circle the ship on her starboard side, the Obsidian battleships' gun decks opened fire. The leading edge of *Zeus*'s shields took multiple hits, but the shots were deflected by bolts of lightning that either sent the projectiles flying off innocuously into space or merely dissolved the shell. Charlie directed Jacob to cautiously drop the *Zeus* deeper into the halo of the comet-like aura of their shield to deter any other close calls. The two battleships, deprived of any form of targeting other than line of sight, failed to detect the deception and continued to fire ahead of the *Zeus*.

The Obsidian captain, with a shocked expression on his face, turned to his XO in disbelief. "Only one man who has ever lived can fly like that, and I killed him. But now it appears I must kill him again."

Charlie keyed his microphone. "Jacob, convince them they winged us."

Jacob only replied with two clicks, and a red haze rolled out the back of the *Zeus*'s stern. Andrew turned back to port, and soon the *Zeus* was once again leaving her quarry behind.

Charlie leaned forward and placed his hand on Andrew's shoulder. He spoke softly and slowly, wanting Andrew to remain calm and focused. "Son, you are putting too much distance between us. I need you to bring them in closer. I want them to think we have taken damage. Slow down. Once we draw them in close enough, on my order, feign a dive, then immediately do a barrel roll and go vertical. I want you to place us directly between them."

Andrew didn't question the order. He had matured and grown into his own skin. He was calm, well-collected, and confident in his ability. Andrew only acknowledged the captain with a simple nod and two clicks on his commlink as he continued to face forward in deep concentration. Part of his mind focused on the *Zeus*'s position in relation to the battleships, the rest concentrating only on breathing. He drew air deep into his lungs and slowly exhaled. In his mind he heard his father's voice, reminding him to relax. The gap started narrowing precipitously, and the Obsidian ships' gun crews began firing in earnest. Andrew weaved, rolled, and bobbed to keep the *Zeus* from being hit. Still, Andrew could hear his father's voice, calmly talking him through each maneuver, step by step, which would place the *Zeus* where Andrew wanted her to go.

On board the bridge of the lead Obsidian ship, the captain was barking orders and celebrating.

"They have been hit! Cease fire and prepare to fire all weapons simultaneously. They will dive to loop under us," he proclaimed with complete confidence. "On my command, fire everything we have when the nose of their ship starts to dip. They are ours!"

Charlie leaned forward again, carefully studying the monitor. No emotion showed on his face. His voice was calm and passionless, speaking softly in Andrew's ear as though not wanting to interrupt Andrew's father whispering in the other. "Draw them in closer. That's it. Even closer."

Charlie sensed the self-assurance and resolve amongst his crew. He felt the *Zeus* pulling hard at her bit. The massive gun decks on the *Zeus* revolved even more swiftly. They were going so fast the individual guns could no longer be distinguished. Still, Charlie willed Andrew to draw the behemoths in closer.

Back on the SC flagship, the admiral and crew were mesmerized by the engagement. One of the technicians surmised to the admiral, "The Obsidians are overtaking her, sir. The *Zeus* is wounded and losing speed!"

In a remorseful voice, he added, "It is only a matter of time, sir."

Countering, the admiral said in astonished disbelief, "Son, those battleships aren't overtaking the *Zeus*. The *Zeus*'s captain is reeling the Obsidians in, like a mongoose toying with the cobra."

His awe of the tactical masterpiece he was viewing was evident in his voice. Silently, the admiral whispered to himself, "Charlie, what are you doing? Now is not the time for heroics. It is the time to run."

A moment later, he whispered again, even softer, "Run, son, run!" With pleading in his voice and tears forming in his eyes, his hands clutched his armrests so tightly, his knuckles were turning white.

The range was now perilously close. The battleships prepared to fire their gargantuan guns. His arm in the air, the Obsidian captain was growling with anger in his voice, "Ready … Aim …"

As the Obsidian captain dropped his hand and ordered, "Fire!" Charlie, with passion, yelled, "Now!"

Andrew feigned a dive, and the battleships' bows followed. Simultaneously, both Obsidian ships fired every weapon. Instead of diving, the two lateral side motors near the *Zeus*'s bow flipped downwards, thrust-vectoring the nose of the *Zeus* up. The two aft propulsion units flipped up, shoving down on the stern and as they rotated, pushing the stern under the *Zeus*'s bow, causing her to tumble abaft her beam. All four of the rotating directional motors were roaring at full power and pivoting, impelling the *Zeus* to go where Andrew commanded. Simultaneously, Andrew throttled the large stern engines to maximum. The extra propulsion caused the *Zeus* to flip up, up, and then over; Andrew eased his yoke to his left, and *Zeus* spun into a barrel roll.

Zeus was in a spin to starboard and rolling backward, end over end. The massive Obsidian barrage whistled right through the space where the *Zeus* milliseconds before had been. Andrew landed the *Zeus* directly between the dyad of warships, flying parallel to their direction of travel. The back end of the *Zeus* skewed back and forth, up and down, as Andrew struggled to maintain control.

The *Zeus*'s gun crews, despite being thrown around and subjected to enormous g-forces, immediately poured massive amounts of fire into the sides of both ships. The *Zeus*'s guns were firing so hard and so fast that the heat from the casings were beginning to turn the guns shades of red and blue. Two floors up on the rotary gun deck, Peck was yelling in disbelief at how close Evans came to knocking out the shield emitter. The maneuver happened so rapidly, neither Obsidian ship returned fire. Frozen in their seats, Obsidian gun crews were paralyzed by the fear of hitting their sister ship.

The *Zeus*'s momentum momentarily carried her underneath the Obsidians' keels and slightly astern. Andrew was still struggling to steady the *Zeus* after her quick roll. Still, the *Zeus*'s guns never slowed down, and the large rail guns fired in rhythm into the stern of the larboard craft as the *Zeus* momentarily fell behind.

Andrew pulled back on the yoke and pushed the throttle forward. The *Zeus* was immediately propelled forward and floated back up, overtaking her prey, and continued to pour fire straight into both Obsidians' sides. Bolts of lightning extended their wicked venom like fingers reaching across the void, disrupting shields and causing even more destruction. Before the *Zeus* pulled ahead, the steady torrent of blistering fire from Evan's rotary cannon tore into the side of the shield emitter on the starboard ship. The emitter exploded and shattered into shrapnel. Evans's hands were sweating as she continued to fire at the second emitter. Then, it too exploded.

Peck shouted across his microphone, "Evans got them! The Obsidians' shields are down! She destroyed the shield emitters!"

Both Obsidian ships slowed because of inflicted damages, and the *Zeus* sped away, banking hard to starboard. Luminous reddish-orange flashes imitated high-atmosphere sprites, like the ones in the atmosphere back on Earth, flickering like fluorescent tubes in the *Zeus*'s wake, showing her path of travel as she sped away.

As the *Zeus* sped up and pulled away, the shaken captain on the lead Obsidian battleship cried out, "Pursue them; they are escaping!"

The terrified Obsidian helmsman, watching his screen, exclaimed, "But, sir. They are chasing us!"

The stunned captain looked at his monitor. A look of horror spread across his face, and he screamed, "Run! We must run!"

The *Zeus* rolled from her hard turn directly on the battleships' sterns, ignoring the now intermittent stream of fire coming from the two warships' aft weapons, and proceeded to glide straight back into the void between the battleships. Every gun on the *Zeus* began a blistering stream of fire, mercilessly pounding away at the Obsidians, the large gun decks accelerating even faster, the shots coming from her weapons now rolling in a continuous torrent on both sides. The sides of the two Obsidian warships were shredding, metal exploding like popcorn as the walls methodically disintegrated. Behind both battleships was a cloud-like debris field of magnesium and beryllium alloy metals, the cloud formed from the missing pieces of the warships.

The entire SC fleet watched the whole battle utterly dumbfounded. Captain Rickenbaker on the flagship, his voice raspy, turned to his admiral. "Can you believe it, sir? They are going yardarm to yardarm against two of them!"

The admiral was speechless. He couldn't say a word as he continued to watch in astonishment, tears freely flowing down his cheeks.

Charlie, Jacob, and Andrew heard the *Zeus*'s warning simultaneously. Before Charlie could give instruction, Andrew pulled back on his yoke and put the *Zeus* into a barrel roll to his port side, coming perilously close to hitting the port-side battleship. The stern of the starboard Obsidian battleship detonated, and secondary explosions ignited all over the rest of the ship. The center of the fiery inferno was a bright purplish flash surrounded by a blinding blue flame. Andrew punched the throttle all the way forward, and the *Zeus* leaped ahead as though she were running for her life. In her wake, explosions lit the heavens as the engines on the second Obsidian battleship started exploding. The *Zeus* barely cleared the bow of the port-side battleship before it, too, erupted into an atomized mist of heat and molten metal.

Aboard the SC flagship, the primary monitor went solid white from the flash of the second explosion. It looked as though they were watching the birth of a star. On every ship, radar and sonar men were scrambling, trying their best to detect and locate the *Zeus*. There was total silence, and despair descended on the armada as they stared at the catastrophe. The admiral openly wept, still gripping the armrest to his chair.

Then a solitary sonar man wailed out, "There she is, sir! There she is!"

Sure enough, out of the blazing inferno, the *Zeus* materialized.

Chapter Fifty-Nine
Present Day, Inside Earth's Solar System

The sound of the explosions was deafening. Charlie's ears were still ringing, as were everyone else's on the *Zeus*. Even the protective padding in their fully enclosed helmets did not damper the sound of the blast.

When the noise subsided slightly, Charlie called out, "Lt. Jackson, damage reports."

Jacob was at his post, feverishly working. "I have requested every station chief to report in, sir. None of our sensors show any significant structural damage. The blast knocked most of our sonar and radar equipment offline, but they are coming back online now."

Charlie looked over his shoulder at Maddie. He winked at her, and she gave him a big smile. Her hands were still locked on to the hand rests on the sides of her seat. Charlie observed there would be lasting impressions where her fingernails dug into the leather.

Simultaneously, both sonar stations started frantically chattering. Charlie didn't need to be told the cause of the crew's animated chattering. Visible on the situation board, bearing down on the *Zeus*'s bow, were at least three full squadrons of SC warships. More showed up as the sonar and radar equipment came back online.

Farther away but right on his six, Charlie identified the distinctive signature of dozens of Obsidian destroyers. Charlie checked the straps holding him tightly in his seat and then ordered Andrew to divert their course to intercept the SC fleet head on.

"Lt. Jackson, hail their flagship."

Jacob was immersed in his work. M&M chimed in, "No need, Captain. They are hailing us."

"Put them on screen," Charlie replied in a flat, monotone voice.

On the monitor directly to the left of Charlie appeared the scowling face of Admiral Halsey. His gravelly voice barked through the sound system, "Captain Jackson, would you please ask your crew not to shoot at my ship?"

Charlie could not believe it was Halsey.

"First, sir, I must request you tell your ships to stand down and redirect their course away from the *Zeus*."

Halsey roared, "Son, if you will look in your rearview mirror, you will see half of the Obsidian fleet bearing down on your six. I need you to step aside. We are on our way to kick their asses."

Charlie let out a sigh of relief. "Aye aye, Admiral."

The crew watched and waited as the Fifth Fleet approached, then saw nothing more than a blur as the ships roared past them. The *Fortuna* was leading the way, the admiral's fleet in a nice tight formation.

Only moments after the Fifth passed, Admiral Mitchell and the Seventh Fleet screamed past. The *Tyche*, traveling at maximum velocity, was slowly gaining on the Fifth. Directly in the wake of the Seventh was an eclectic mix of ships from a plethora of miscellaneous fleets.

Charlie turned to watch as they sped away. He could make out the remains of CBC equipment dangling precariously from the sterns of many of the ships. Far to their starboard side, Jacob pointed out the three Royal British Guard Units—the *Clarkson*, *Hammond*, and *Mays*—just in time for the *Zeus*'s crew to see the *Hammond*'s CBC unit come loose and go skipping erratically through space in the vessel's wake, causing the *Hammond* to almost collide into the other two.

Jacob said, "Captain, the *Fortuna* is hailing us again."

Charlie continued to watch as more craft sped past the *Zeus*, struggling to catch the admiral and his fleet. "Put the *Fortuna* on the screen."

The admiral's voice was crackling over the airwaves. "Captain Jackson, I need you to return to Earth and join the Eighth Fleet. The traitors are fleeing and taking the entire First Fleet with them."

Charlie faced the admiral. "Sir, we will be glad to pursue the First Fleet, but I am no longer a member of Space Command. If you check your posts, you will find my resignation, which is effective immediately."

Charlie muted his microphone. "Besides, SC arrested me and has relieved me of command," he mumbled under his breath.

"Son, I don't have time to argue. SC and the Eighth need you."

Jacob stepped into view on the monitor. "Admiral, I do not believe the crew of the *Zeus* would be as effective as you would like with too much guidance from Space Command."

The admiral's eyes grew wide, and then his gaze softened and he laughed.

Charlie interrupted before the admiral could speak. "Sir, the *Zeus* desperately needs supplies before we can be of much help to anyone."

The admiral looked thoughtful for a moment. "Perhaps it may not be safe for you to return to Earth at this point, anyway. There is no clear verdict on either of our futures. I will have my XO send you coordinates so you can rendezvous with a resupply ship from the Fifth."

"Thank you, sir," Charlie replied.

"Jackson, one more thing," the admiral growled. "I refuse to accept your resignation. We can discuss it over dinner when I return."

"Thank you, sir," Charlie replied. "Admiral?"

"Yes, Jackson?"

"Good luck, sir."

Charlie signaled for M&M to sever the connection.

The entire crew on the *Zeus*, except for Charlie and Maddie, watched the whole battle. As the leading SC warships made first contact with the enemy, Charlie reached over to his music player and chose a song from his playlist. True to form, it was an oldie. Charlie took Maddie into his arms, and they held each other close as Charlie Puth's song "Patient" flooded the interior of the *Zeus*.

•••

As the *Zeus* set easy sail toward her new coordinates where she would take on supplies, Jacob reflected on the last year. He and his fellow crewmates had performed mission after mission that no oddsmaker would have ever placed money on them being able to accomplish. None of the team members had ever stopped, to Jacob's knowledge, to consider their odds. They kept fighting, facing one problem at a time until they had persevered. He knew he had had the privilege of serving with the greatest heroes ever to sail, members of the legends of old.

They were the crew of the *Zeus*!

Epilogue
Present Day, Location Unknown

Patty sprang from her sleep, sweating. She was positive something significant had just taken place. Sliding her finger into the inner liner inside her waistline, she slid the ruby out of the secret pocket she had sewn. The ruby seemed to be glowing and putting off heat. It was hard to describe. Passion. Patty could think of no other description to accurately describe the gem in her palm. The stone seemed to emanate passion.

Power undoubtedly encompassed the stone. Silently, she whispered, "What has happened? What are you trying to tell me?"

www.ingramcontent.com/pod-product-compliance
Lightning Source LLC
Chambersburg PA
CBHW030356030726
47497CB00002B/365